D0531042

'With the establishment of the People's Republic of China in 1949 came a redistribution of land – the "land reform." To millions of Chinese peasants who had labored for centuries in direst poverty, with neither land nor hope, the agrarian revolution meant at last a means for them to support themselves – and hope. It brought to some as well a new revolutionary ardor to sustain them on the further slow and difficult journey that they faced.

In 1950 I was eighteen years old. I had just gotten my first real job, at the Central Film Bureau in Peking. The following year, I joined many other urban workers – artists, writers, and office workers in the countryside with the peasants, carrying out the land reform. Over the next twenty years we lived and worked for months at a time in villages scattered across the vastness of China.

This novel is based on my experience during those years. Like Ling-ling, I went first to Gansu Province, in the Northwest, an area as foreign to me – young and city-bred – as the moon. This is the source of most of the incidents and events described; the characters are people I met, knew, or just glimpsed in passing. They are real people. This story is fiction, but it is true.'

陈元珍

Yuan-tsung Chen

About The Dragon's Village
'With fascinating detail, Chen describes Ling-ling's journey to a remote, poverty-stricken village where she sets about organizing the peasants, forms a group to discuss "women's questions", and demands retribution from the anxious landlords. She confronts violence, cold and famine, superstition and fear among the peasants and treachery among the landlords who desperately try to buy off their peasants with false land deeds. Ling-ling's fellow activists, her own motives and self doubts, the peasants and their way of life are all drawn with remarkable candor and sympathy.'   *Publishers Weekly*

Yuan-tsung Chen
THE DRAGON'S VILLAGE

An autobiographical novel of Revolutionary China

The Women's Press

To my husband and son

For valuable encouragement and support, I would like
to thank Harrison Salisbury and Jay Leyda; for incisive
questioning and advice, Wendy Wolf.

First published in Great Britain by The Women's Press Limited 1981
A member of the Namara Group
124 Shoreditch High Street, London E1 6JE

Published in the USA by Pantheon Books, Inc, 1980

A complete list of books published by The Women's Press
is available from us at the above address. Please send postage
with your enquiries.

British Library Cataloguing in Publication Data

Chen, Yuan-tsung
  The dragon's village.
  I. Title
  813[F]

ISBN 0-7043-3865-3

1 ★

To the Sound of Guns

As I look back at it now, the cool unconcern of my family and friends—and I do not exclude myself—was astounding. We were in the middle of a bloody civil war that had paused, but only briefly, to "discuss peace" while each side prepared for the final, furious round. A thin line of Guomindang government troops was dug in on the southern bank of the Yangzi River, braced for the expected onslaught of the Communist-led insurgent army massing on the northern bank. A million men were getting ready to slaughter each other just a few hours' drive from Shanghai where my aunt and I sat at our well-laid breakfast table waiting to hear my uncle declaim his latest poem.

My uncle was handsome, well built, and worldly wise. He had married my aunt for her dowry; after twenty years, in spite of—or perhaps because of—civil wars, invasion, and revolution, he had more than tripled our fortunes. Now the problems of meeting the right people and making money were no longer pressing. We lived in a comfortable villa in Shanghai's old French Concession and he had taken to cultivating his poetic talent.

He was proud of his lyrics and liked to read them to us after dinner, particularly if we had guests. "I have a new poem," he would announce at a pause in the conversation, and without waiting for an invitation he would recite it. If it was on the subject of love or beauty he would dedicate it with an Italianate gesture of his outstretched arms to the most attractive lady in the room. If the guests were more numerous than his inspirations, sometimes the same poem would have to suffice for several women in turn.

As the old Chinese saying has it, "You listen to the man who feeds you." So my aunt and I—they had adopted me as a child when my parents died—listened and, when we had guests, led the applause.

My uncle's muse usually arrived on Sunday mornings before breakfast. My aunt and I would wait in the breakfast room, scanning the newspaper while he took his time muttering and humming to himself in bed. When he joined us he would have his poem jotted down on his scratch pad. But this Sunday morning, in February 1949, he came to the table empty-handed. Inspiration struck only in the middle of breakfast. He halted his chopsticks in midair, the little jade oval of a pigeon's egg delicately held. Then he gulped the mouthful down, pushed away his bowl, and with a faraway look in his eyes began to tap rhythmically on the table. My aunt motioned me with her hand to continue eating and not disturb him, and soon we were rewarded. With a cry of triumph and satisfaction, he thumped the table with his clenched fist. The poem was born. I can't remember the beginning, but it ended with the lines:

We may waver, we may falter, yet we march against the foe
Glory to the people armed with pick and hoe!

The poem so delighted my aunt that she decided then and there to give a special dinner party to introduce it to our friends and acquaintances. "It hits just the right note of democracy," she said.

For the next week she was so occupied with preparations for the hastily summoned party that I hardly saw her at all. I ran errands for her but I had no idea what was really in her mind until just before the party when she called me into the sanctum of her dressing room. The air was heavy with the scent of perfumes, and the subdued light hinted at the exchange of intimate confidences, but she asked me abruptly, "Ling-ling, have you read today's newspaper?"

I was standing by her side, and the big, three-leaved mirror reflected the two of us in multiple images. My mind had floated off, daydreaming: "My long, arching eyebrows are my pride." I bent over and kissed her cheek before answering, "Yes. But what is special in it?"

"This may be the last dinner party we'll ever give here."

"But the Guomindang and Communist Parties are talking peace now!"

"That's just another way of making war. Both are trying to win people over to their side. Several of our friends have been approached by . . . uh . . . certain persons. Quite a few are talking to both sides while they make their plans. But today's newspapers report that everything may come to a head in the next few days."

"And Uncle?"

"He has consulted Mr. Li."

"Uncle trusts Mr. Li. He can do what Mr. Li does."

"That's not so simple. Mr. Li has a large family. He doesn't have to put all his eggs into one basket. It seems that he himself will stay on in the mainland. His younger brother will go to Taiwan to open a branch store. And Third Brother will set up a factory in Hong Kong. But we're in a different position—there're only the three of us in the family, and two are helpless women."

"Auntie, would you be happier if I were a boy?"

"You still can't forget the servants' gossip, can you? When you were little, they used to tease you: 'Your auntie would be happier if you were a boy. A son can bring glory to his parents.' So you wanted to show you were as good as any boy. You fought them. When you came home after school, you boasted about how you had jumped higher and run faster or even eaten more than the boys. That's a child's world." She fell silent. "Now, this is a grownup's world for you, and it's a man's world."

She stretched out her fingers and for a moment silently contemplated the glittering pink nails.

"How do you like this nail polish?" she asked, looking at my reflection in the mirror.

"Perhaps it's a bit extreme."

My aunt considered this for a moment and then silently nodded her head. Then she stoppered the small, pink bottle and put it carefully aside in a drawer filled with other little bottles of various shades of red and pink. Slowly closing the drawer, she thrust another question at me.

"Young Bob Lu and you are suited to each other. Isn't that so? If we combine forces with the Lu family we'll have more bargaining power with both sides. A Communist intermediary has talked to your uncle and tried to persuade him to stay on in Shanghai and carry on the milling business here. But for the moment we don't say yes and we don't say no. We are friendly to everyone. Who knows? They may still form a coalition government. However, I would like you to pay special attention tonight to Madame Lu and her son."

"Auntie, may I wear my new earrings?"

"At your age you have no need of artificial embellishments," she replied with sudden sharpness, standing up and beginning to take off her dressing gown. I knew I was dismissed.

But just as I was leaving, she called me back. Sitting down again in front of the vanity's mirrors, she cupped her chin in her hands and looked at me thoughtfully.

"Auntie, there's something more you wish to tell me?" I coaxed.

"You don't think much of your uncle's poems, do you? I don't either."

She knew her question puzzled me, as we had always avoided discussing Uncle's talents. "But it's his way of relaxing. You know, we've gone through hell to establish ourselves in our present position."

"Auntie, I'll do whatever I can to help," I said, putting my arms around her neck.

"Sit down."

I took a seat on a low hassock.

Resting her hands on the arms of her chair and looking down at me, she continued: "When you were about six or seven, we nearly lost our business and were on the verge of bankruptcy. I still remember that awful day. Our creditors had set a deadline for us to repay our debts. Your uncle went out to try to raise another loan on a mortgage to save us. I waited and waited, but he didn't come home. I grew more and more anxious. I wanted desperately to get away from everything. I took you and got on a train for Jiading, half an hour from Shanghai. There was a beautiful old park there, not far from the station. I sat on the grass and you took your shoes off and waded in the shallow water of the pond. You knew nothing of our trouble. You were so happy. You were 'adventuring.' You splashed through the water and then climbed up the bank and followed a crooked little path. I got up to follow you to tell you to be careful. But I let you go on adventuring. At the top of the slope was a ruin, the corner of an old fort, overgrown with gnarled old trees, just stumps, their roots exposed among the rocks and rubble. You called me and showed me new shoots of green leaves sprouting from those stumps. I thought it was a happy omen, and I was right.

"We were lucky. Your uncle got the loan we needed. That was the turning point. But your uncle and I still worked day and night to pay off our debts."

"Auntie, you have a good memory."

"Not about everything."

"But that's all in the past."

"The past? If the Communists take over, they may take everything away from us. They promise not to, but you know what government promises are. They are for the poor, and we are rich. They are polite to us, but behind our backs they still call us 'bourgeois parasites.' Parasites!" Auntie smiled disparagingly at the epithet. But soon her dimples disappeared, and heavy lines that I had not seen before on her face appeared. "We must show no fear and we must take necessary precautions. Do you understand me?"

"Yes, Auntie." But in truth I didn't quite.

Say what you will, my aunt knew how to arrange a party. The best cooks from the Xin-Ya Restaurant were hired and our drawing room was redecorated. Aunt's special chairs, Ming dynasty copies in red-brown teakwood, were brought out; two genuine Song dynasty paintings were hung on the wall. Large lanterns decorated with paintings of classical beauties were hung in the hallway. Uncle's jade carvings were displayed in cabinets, and brocade covers from Suzhou were put on the cushions.

The guests were also dressed to honor their hosts. Madame Lu, my prospective mother-in-law, whose husband had made his money as senior Chinese comprador for the British Kailuan Mining Corporation, came in all her glory. Her thin, once beautiful face was meticulously made up, and, as on all gala occasions, she had covered her neck, arms, and fingers with emeralds, pearls, and diamonds. Standing tall and statuesque in the center of the room beneath the chandelier, clad in some dark green patterned brocade that befitted her age, she looked like a Christmas tree decorated with small, glittering lights. The party swirled around her.

After dinner, we returned to the drawing room. Young Bob Lu, lanky and pale-faced, tagged along at my side with his customary air of world-weariness. Even the wine he had drunk had not made him any merrier.

"Won't you have some liqueur?" my aunt asked him as she raised her glass to some guest on the other side of the room and silently formed her lips to convey the word "Cheers!" in English.

"Why yes, thank you," Bob Lu replied and turned to ask me, "How about you, Ling-ling?" As I nodded yes he moved to the bar cart with the liqueurs.

"Ling-ling"—my aunt seized this opportunity to prompt me—"you've chatted with him too long. Don't make yourself an easy conquest."

Bob Lu returned with two glasses.

As my aunt sipped her drink she signaled me almost imperceptibly with a glance towards Madame Lu and two other guests who were with her, a lady and a gentleman all in animated conversation. The lady was short, plump and vivacious. She alternately whispered some confidence to Madame Lu and then chuckled at her own witticism

Her husband, lean and withdrawn, stood by her side and now and then added a word which, judging from Madame Lu's demeanor, evidently carried considerable weight. Gossip was that he had just returned from Peking where he had represented a powerful anti-Chiang Kai-shek faction of the Guomindang in peace talks with the Communists. His wife gaily denied this and insisted that he had just taken a rest cure at a northern resort.

My aunt had left us, so I asked young Bob to excuse me. "Where and when can we meet alone?" he asked me timidly, tracing circles on the carpet with the toe of his patent leather shoe.

I hesitated, then replied, "In the small study, in an hour."

I crossed the room to reach Madame Lu, squeezing through groups of guests and apologizing as I went. Mr. Chang, a banker, was about to take a glass of vermouth from a servant's tray when a petite beauty put her folded fan over the top of the glass. We went to the same school; she was two years older and was called by the English name Lily. "Enough," she said imperiously. "You have more important things to do."

"Like entertaining you or doing what all the others are doing: deciding their futures? But I have already decided mine," he said, looking at her intently. He bowed his head obediently and withdrew his outstretched hand. "I would stay on the mainland if I could be certain that the new government will allow people to dress properly. Did you see that latest picture in the newspapers? All their officials are dressed like tramps, and women are dressed up exactly like men."

"Are you serious?"

"I am," he said as he ran his hand over his mane of jet black hair. "I simply cannot imagine myself in those baggy trousers. To dress properly is a way of life."

The latest political gossip was on everyone's lips, and I moved through a parliament of opinions as I passed each cluster of people. I caught the words of a longtime friend of my uncle's, a portly textile manufacturer, the smart Mr. Li. He nodded with quick movements of his head to emphasize his points. "Sure, sure enough. You're right. The Communists are wooing me now, but they'll kick me around as soon as they've consolidated their power. Sure. No doubt about it. But no matter what I do, I'll be kicked around by someone. Here at least I'll be kicked around by Chinese who are my fellow countrymen, even though they are Communists."

The gentle old man he spoke to agreed: "For my part I intend to live and die here and be buried on my native soil."

"I am old, too," said Mr. Li. "I tell my sons and daughters that if they want to leave China they can take their share of our property and go ahead. They don't need to worry about me. I'll keep my share here. If the Communists nationalize my factories, that's all right. I have plenty of know-how. I went into industry because I thought China could find salvation through industrialization. I'll help run things for them." Mr. Li crossed his arms over his stomach, which curved gently beneath his long grey silk Chinese gown. He was a modern textile manufacturer but he still liked to wear a Chinese-style gown over his Western trousers and leather shoes. This symbolic stand against complete westernization expressed his patriotism.

"That's all very well," his companion concurred, then looked a little skeptical as he continued in a slightly lowered voice, "Are you keeping all your share of the property here?"

Mr. Li smiled an ambiguous smile but made no answer.

Among his listeners, one man seemed completely out of place. Humming and grinning at the sense and nonsense he heard around him, the genuine concern and wry regrets, he shifted his feet rhythmically back and forth. His eccentricities were well known and tolerated. He was the best highway engineer in the country.

"I am either above politics or beyond . . . or perhaps they are beyond me," he complained, buttonholing the stout man before him, a lethargic Guomindang minister. "My job is to build roads, and every country needs roads. I don't see any reason why I can't go on building roads here."

The minister had mastered the art of speaking in nothing but platitudes.

"The people need your talents. Communism will reduce the country to chaos."

"But the Japanese have already done a pretty good job of roadbuilding in Taiwan."

"There is always room for improvement."

Finally, I stood beside Madame Lu. The lady with her had noticed me first. She looked me over as if I were some commodity at a sale, and, concluding that I was indeed marketable, she gave her appraisal: "You are a pretty girl."

Madame Lu thereupon gave me a rapturous embrace and having displayed her affection, turned back to Madame Gui who completed the sentence I had interrupted.

". . . and everybody says that if the Communists win, we will have to give away our wealth. Well, I don't know how that will work. Would a peasant appreciate all this?" and she gestured all around the room at the fine rugs, the chandelier, the paintings, the bejeweled guests. "After all, it takes quite a while to cultivate taste."

Having done my duty, I wandered off to where our highway engineer was now engaged in earnest conversation with a dapper, youthful-looking officer, General Xu, and the banker Mr. Chang. I didn't interrupt them, but listened intently.

After greeting me with an amiable squeeze of my shoulder, Mr. Chang went on rolling a Cuban cigar gently between his palms. This was a habit he had learned on his foreign travels. It made the cigars draw better, he explained.

"General, will the Communist army attack Shanghai soon?" the engineer asked.

"Not much of a chance. They haven't got the modern landing craft to cross the Yangzi River."

The general was handsome and he liked the ladies. He was also rich. Back in the thirties when Generalissimo Chiang Kai-shek still admired Hitler, he had invited Nazi military advisers to help him in his campaign against the Communist Red Army, and he had sent a number of young officers, General Xu among them, to study military science in Germany. General Xu had returned every inch the Prussian officer. After the German debacle in the Second World War, however, Hitler and his military theories were no longer fashionable, and—so I was told—our general's style underwent a subtle change. He still clicked his heels together when he bowed, but the click was not as resonant as before. In fact, it was almost inaudible. And now the bow had just a hint of a Viennese gallantry, especially when he wanted to flatter the fair sex, which he accomplished with considerable success.

During the war against the Japanese invaders, our hero was one of those "running generals" who always managed to keep two steps ahead of the advancing enemy. He had never fired a shot in anger at the invaders, but he was never idle. When the battle lines became stabilized, he shifted his attention to the quartermaster's office. He ran a black market route through the area of his command and also made a name for himself as a commander of dead souls: He drew rations and wages for thousands of nonexistent men in his army, dead or missing peasant lads who still remained on the army's payroll.

Mr. Chang was not impressed. I think he had better sources of information than the general, and, irritated by the general's response, which he thought too crudely deceptive, he answered him with some acerbity.

"Don't be so optimistic. The Yangzi River won't save us. Your soldiers are all peasants. In one way or another they have learned that their families in the Communist areas have been given land after the land reform there. If they fight hard and the Guomindang wins, they know the landlords will take back that land and cut off their relatives' heads to boot. On the other hand, the Communist soldiers will fight to the death to defend the land their families have just gotten. You've lost more than half your armies to the Communists already."

"Don't believe Communist propaganda!" retorted the general. "The peasants don't want to steal land from the

propertied classes. They want property themselves.
Twenty years ago the Communists in South China instigated the peasants to take over the land, and the result
was chaos and anarchy. They miscalculated and they
failed, just as they will fail now. The peasants know their
place and they respect the traditions which have held China together for over two thousand years. If you give them
the freedom to choose, they will choose to support the
system of private property. They don't want Communism."

"If you are so certain of that, General, then why don't
you give them the vote?" Mr. Chang chuckled. The smoke
from his cigar went down the wrong way and he coughed.
Pretending not to hear Mr. Chang's last remark, General
Xu turned to smile at my aunt, who now approached us.

Following my aunt's whispered instructions, Mr. Chang,
talented man of money that he was, seated himself at the
piano and, with a series of running chords and a glissando,
brought everyone to attention. Lily, myself, and some
other chosen ones arranged ourselves around the piano
and my aunt announced that we would sing my uncle's
latest poem, entitled the "New Marseillaise," set to music
by Mr. Chang. We sang with spirit right down to the rousing finale:

We may waver, we may falter, yet we march against the foe.
Glory to the people armed with pick and hoe!

We were given a round of applause, and when Mr. Chang
cleverly shifted the music into a cheerful dance rhythm
everyone began to dance. I found myself in the arms of the
general until the highway engineer cut in.

I had completely forgotten my tryst with young Mr. Lu
until my aunt asked me why I wasn't dancing with him. I
ran to the small study. He was there pacing anxiously.

"I'm sorry."

"Ling-ling, I want to tell you something." These words
came out automatically. He must have rehearsed them
again and again.

"Yes?"

He knelt down on one knee.

"Are you going to propose to me?" I asked him, sitting down with my hands demurely folded in my lap.

"Yes," he stammered, somewhat put out.

"Then kneel down properly on both knees." I could see my aunt's face beaming with joy when she listened to my report about my conquest.

Towards eleven, when the party was at its height, I saw my aunt get a whispered word from a servant. She drew herself up, her eyes sparkling, the mistress of the house. She sought out my uncle, and with an air of great importance and suppressed urgency the two of them went out into the hall. Soon they reappeared ushering in the mayor and his wife. Suddenly there was a great flurry and to-do in the drawing room as everyone tried to show that he or she was well acquainted with the great man and his lady.

In the midst of this decorous confusion, the mayor smiled owlishly through his tortoiseshell glasses. A genial man, he had acted this role of the social lion so many times that it was now second nature to him. My uncle told me that the mayor was considered a sort of liberal. Generalissimo Chiang Kai-shek couldn't possibly trust a man like the mayor, but neither could he dispense with him. With the regime crumbling all around him, it was good public relations to maintain some semblance of democracy and freedom before the foreigners and foreign correspondents in cities like Shanghai. This was the cosmetic role assigned to the complaisant mayor. That was why in Shanghai, on the one hand, you could hear all sorts of opinions voiced by vociferous pseudo-liberals, while on the other hand real revolutionaries or people the secret service did not like disappeared without a trace.

Timed by the mayor's efficient secretary, the ceremonial visit lasted exactly fifteen minutes. Yet brief though it was, the mayor's appearance ensured the success of my aunt's party.

After midnight, the departing guests tipsily complimented my aunt as they left. "A charming evening. Such fun."

My aunt answered modestly, "Thank you. It was so nice to have you. We must do it again." She reserved a particularly friendly good-bye for a tall man with a charming manner and a spring in his step. Later I learned from my aunt that he was a Communist go-between. She hoped he had been suitably impressed with the "New Marseillaise" and the presence of the mayor.

2

A Glimpse of the Other Side

"Marseillaise" or no "Marseillaise," my uncle was a practical man. He soon put aside lyric poetry—or even revolutionary poetry, for that matter—and made ready to move
the family out of Shanghai and down to the British colony
of Hong Kong where a house by the sea awaited us. He
had already transferred funds there and most of his milling interests. In the meantime the truce talks broke down.
The Communist army poured across the Yangzi and
within days had occupied Nanking, the capital of the
Guomindang government. While others carried on the
government from Canton, the city in the South an hour or
so by train from Hong Kong, Chiang Kai-shek himself disappeared. We heard that he was going to make a last
stand with his picked troops on Taiwan island, a hundred
miles off the southern coast.

The Guomindang generals left in charge of Shanghai declared that they would defend the city to the death. Their
army dug itself into trenches before the city. Inside the
city, police and army patrols kept order and a curfew was
imposed from dark to early dawn.

Some of our family friends had already left Shanghai for
various refuges abroad, Taiwan, Hong Kong, or even further afield in Singapore or America, but quite a number
were doing the same as my uncle: getting ready to flee but

still waiting to see if it would be at all possible to remain in the different China that would emerge when the Communist Party took over.

Even as the fighting continued, peace talks and negotiations went on. We watched to see who went over to the Communist side and what official positions they took. If a sufficient number of "responsible leaders" joined the coalition government being put together by the Communists, my uncle would stay. Otherwise we would leave for Hong Kong.

While my uncle made the big decision my aunt and I simply waited to be told what to do. Auntie had perfect confidence in his good sense and ability to fix things up, and I had no say in such matters one way or the other. It never occurred to me to question my uncle's decisions.

I found myself on holiday when the nuns who ran my high school, St. Ursula's, closed down that fashionable missionary establishment because they did not want to be responsible for the fate of the students at such a time. At first it was like a relaxing vacation. I got up late and spent hours in my bathroom and before my mirror admiring myself. I went window shopping, picking up small bargains at knockdown prices from merchants anxious to sell out. I read interminably, whiling away the time as we waited to leave or rearrange things and stay.

After a few days, this idleness palled. Outings, parties, dances were infrequent now and not many new movies were being shown. I grew bored. Evenings were the worst. In bed, I lay tense and still, scared of the darkness engulfing me. I associated death with darkness. I often imagined that my dead parents were out there somewhere in the dark. I thought of death as a physical transformation that would separate me from my loved ones. It would keep me silent in eternal darkness. Yet somehow I would know what was going on in the world and, like other spirits, sometimes take a hand in it too until I would utterly fade away.

Then one evening an unexpected telephone call roused me out of myself. Ma Li, my old school friend whom I had not seen for more than a year, asked me to meet her in half an hour at the Plum Blossom Cafe on the Avenue Joffre.

I softly closed the front door, hurried through our little garden into the street, and with a few more steps was lost to view among the budding elms. It was mid-spring, but the evening air was dank and cold. Dark clouds hung low and, drifting slowly, hid the rising moon. I hurried to reach the main avenue where the lights were brighter.

At the crossroads by the Cathay Cinema, a Guomindang soldier struggled desultorily to shore up one side of the nest of sandbags that was his makeshift defense post. I could see a pair of feet in worn khaki sneakers comfortably crossed atop the other side of the sandbag "fort." Beyond this post the bright lights of the French Circle Sportif sparkled amid its lawns and garden trees. A huge cutout of Lana Turner sprawled voluptuously above the marquee of the Cathay Cinema. Two policemen stood together on the corner. The French Concession had been ceded to France about a hundred years ago, but it had been returned to China after World War Two. It was a favorite residential area for many affluent Chinese families and had retained something of a French character. It was always well patrolled and I felt sure it was safe to go on. The curfew recently imposed for the emergency did not start for another hour or so.

When I turned into the broader avenue on the main thoroughfare, the Avenue Joffre, the air curled cold around my neck and I snuggled into the collar of my jacket. It was only half past seven, but some apprehensive shop owners were closing and shuttering their places early. Others carried on business as usual, and their show windows were brightly lit as if defying the misty twilight outside. But there was no doubt that unease was in the air. Few people were on the usually busy avenue. I quickened my pace, hurried past the row of small boutiques, and two blocks down I entered the Plum Blossom Cafe.

The sweet aroma of coffee filled the snug room. The lights were dim beneath pink shades. There were a few customers, mostly teenagers like myself, and they sat in the little side cubicles in couples with their heads close together. I glanced around quickly. Ma Li was sitting alone. The last time I had seen her she was fresh-faced and without makeup. Now she wore rouge and lipstick, but her face, framed in a bob of glossy black hair, seemed unusually pale. She wore a well-cut black velvet dress.

"Hi," I greeted her quietly and, as she had instructed me over the phone, without using her name. "How have you been?"

"I've no complaints."

"It's been such a long time—are you enjoying your new life?"

"My theater troupe has been on tour and I've been to a lot of places. You know I love to travel."

"How I envy you," I exclaimed, and then I caught the half-humorous look in her eyes and the quizzical tone in her voice.

"What will you have? Coffee?" she asked as the waitress approached.

"No. Cocoa, please," I said. "I haven't learned to drink coffee yet."

"How have you been?"

"As usual," I replied with a shrug. I faced the French windows which opened onto a small garden. Plum blossoms gleamed misty white on a background of dark pine trees. A miniature red-roofed pavilion stood by a wooden bridge over an artificial stream. "Perhaps that's not quite so. My uncle had a poetic plan for us all to go down to Hangzhou this spring and drink Dragon Well tea. That exotic tea would be made with fresh-picked leaves brewed in snow water melted from off the plum blossoms. But that plan fell through."

"You sound cynical," Ma Li commented, looking at me with a steady gaze.

"Do I? My aunt has been bemoaning the thwarting of our Hangzhou plan for the last three days. So that is naturally what I thought of first when you asked me what we've been doing."

Ma Li drank her coffee in silence for a minute. "Don't you want to ask me something?"

"Why did you suddenly call me up?"

"Because I need a favor. Can you put me up for the night?"

"Of course." I said this without thinking. It was so natural, but then I asked a bit tentatively, "What's the trouble?"

Ma Li was what my uncle in his most scathing tone dismissed as "radical." He usually ended his tirades against such people with a warning that they caused young people "to lose their bearings." Ma Li, in fact, was always in the middle of some patriotic campaign or other. First it had been "Let's have peace," then "Yanks get out." Once I had stood on a street corner and seen her go by with a crowd of students demonstrating against the government's corruption. Afterwards I had heard that two of them had been shot and a lot of them injured. As for her theater, most of their plays were about social problems and other controversial subjects that embarrassed the Guomindang government.

She noticed my hesitation and said, "You don't have to if it's not convenient."

I glimpsed a strange man looking at me over the top of his glasses. To cover my confusion I motioned with my hand to a phonograph on a little table. "I'll put some music on."

As I picked up a record, I raised my eyes and looked out through the glass door. Three men were walking towards a parked car, but the man in the middle seemed to be supported by the other two. He walked with bent head and bowed shoulders as if a heavy weight were hung around his neck. He made a sudden movement and almost immediately one of his companions brought an arm crashing onto the back of his neck and he went limp. They dragged him to the waiting car. It had all happened so quickly that it was almost unnoticeable. I had not uttered a sound, but I stood paralyzed beside the phonograph. Ma Li's soft voice beside me brought me back to action. "Don't worry what the record is. It doesn't matter. Put it on."

We returned to our seats. Soft, inane music filled the room and I wondered if what I had just seen had really happened.

"I don't dare go home," Ma Li whispered. "They're on the watch for me there. You can still change your mind if you like."

I shook my head. "Let's finish our drinks and then we'll go home together." I spoke firmly. Inside, doubts might grow, but I was determined to be a faithful friend.

I opened the front door of our house, paused, and listened. From the living room came a hum of conversation. In the hallway, safe amid familiar things, I heaved a sigh of relief.

"Ma Li, sneak upstairs. Remember, my bedroom's the last one on the left." I gestured to the door of the living room. "Go to bed, and I'll tell my aunt. She won't drive you out."

Ma Li nodded her thanks.

When I told my aunt that a girlfriend was staying overnight with me because of the curfew, she asked no questions. It was a natural thing.

Next morning when Ma Li was preparing to leave and picked up her large, bulging handbag from a chair, I teased her and inquired, "Forbidden books?"

"Not exactly that." She shook her head after a pause. "It's instructions that we want to print and distribute to factory and office workers calling on them to prevent the Guomindang from destroying anything before they flee."

"Ma Li, you were carrying these with you last night—the secret police could have stopped you! They might be searching for you now. If . . . they . . ." I stammered nervously. "For God's sake don't go out. Stay here."

"No. I have to go. We're holding an important meeting today. But there are some papers I certainly wouldn't want them to find on me. Oh . . . no, I can't impose this on you." She fidgeted with the straps of her handbag.

My heart sank, but weighing things up I thought that it would be better to keep such papers here in my room than have them found on Ma Li when she went out of our gate. I said, "Better leave them here than take them with you."

"If you could keep them for me today, I'll send someone to pick them up this evening before the curfew." She sounded relieved. "Will you really do this for us?"

"Do you think I'm a coward?" I asked, half joking, half defiant.

"All right, then. Be sure to be home about seven this evening. I don't know who will be able to come, but we'll use a code. He will say, 'Ma Li wants her book back.' Now let me see, what book? Maybe a book only you know that I love or hate."

"How about *The Bible of Filial Piety for Daughters*."

"Good! There's no book I hate more than that one." Laughing, she handed me a popular movie magazine. Scattered among its smirking starlets were thin slivers of paper covered with tiny script. Quickly I thrust the whole thing under my mattress and made up my bed.

"There are names there," Ma Li warned.

"It will be all right."

"Ling-ling, why don't you try to talk some sense into your uncle? Ask him not to take everything out of his mill. It's the workers' livelihood, you know, not just his." Her face was grave.

"He's leaving some things here," I began to defend him.

She could see that I was beginning to panic. Concerned that she was asking too much of me all at once, she added, "Do what you can."

Around six that evening, Ma Li telephoned again. She spoke hurriedly, without introduction. "I'm speaking from a phone booth. This place is surrounded by insects and I think quite a few of us will be bitten. They may come to you next. Do whatever you think necessary. That medicine I gave you is no good at all. Perhaps it's best to pour it down the drain and get rid of it. Unless, of course, the doctor comes soon. Well, take care." She hung up.

I felt as if all the blood were draining out of my body. Someone in Ma Li's group might know of her friendship with me and betray it. I had heard about the police agents and their methods of breaking a victim. I sat on the chair by the telephone until one of the maids helped me to my bed, where I fell into an uneasy doze.

I woke in a panic and looked at my watch: seven o'clock. Quickly I grabbed the magazine from under the mattress, hid it under my sweater, and opened the door; its creaking sounded like a screech in the quiet house. I moved swiftly but as silently as I could down the stairs. From outside in the roadway came the sound of a truck with a loudspeaker warning that the curfew would soon go into force. The small front garden with its many trees was empty and silent. I hid between the wall and a lilac bush so I couldn't be seen from the house, and watched the wrought-iron gateway leading to the street. Before I had time to catch my breath I heard someone rattling the gate.

"What do you want?" I asked.

"I want to see Guan Ling-ling," said a voice. I approached the gate and saw a young man on the other side. He seemed rather well dressed. I began to realize that it was safer to be out dressed that way than like a student.

The young man looked me squarely in the eye and continued, "Ma Li wants her book back, *The Bible of Filial Piety for Daughters*."

I took the magazine out from under my sweater and pushed it through the grill of the gate. He gave a quick glance through it and was gone.

I spent the night sleepless and troubled. I was appalled at what I might have done to my aunt and uncle. The next morning I came down late to breakfast to find them already at the table.

"You look nervous." My uncle peered around the side of his newspaper. "What are you thinking about?"

The question found me in a daze, and I mumbled, "Nothing, Uncle."

Uncle and Aunt exchanged glances.

"Why did you ask me that?" I asked him, collecting my thoughts.

"You held up your spoon but you paused and never put your rice gruel in your mouth," said my uncle's voice from behind the newspaper.

I breathed hard. Perhaps I had already gotten them into

trouble. It was impossible not to tell them about it. I couldn't leave them unprepared for whatever might happen.

"Last night . . ." I began my confession. Uncle slowly lowered his newspaper, glowering. My aunt could not have looked more astounded if she had seen the legendary bird with nine heads flying by.

I left my bowl of rice unfinished and rushed to my room, where I hid myself for the whole day. Even by the evening I couldn't muster enough courage to face the family. Soon after suppertime they sent the maid to ask me to join them with some friends in the drawing room.

A burst of light and animated chatter flooded out into the hallway as I opened the door of the room. Several of our intimate friends had gathered at the urgent call of my uncle and aunt, and I found them sitting in a semicircle around the fireplace. From the way they turned to smile at me as I entered, the kind of smile that was meant to reassure a wayward child of its parents' love, I knew this was a tribunal organized for my benefit. I groaned inwardly. My uncle looked solemn although he tried to appear as if nothing unusual was happening. It was my aunt who formally opened the proceedings.

"Ling-ling, tonight I invited our very dear, old friends in to give us some helpful advice. They knew your parents before you were born. And they know your uncle and I brought you up as one of our own." My aunt's nose became red. "I took on a terrible responsibility when I promised your mother I would always treat you and love you as if you were my own child. I am thankful that our friends have kindly agreed to share my responsibility."

Looking around at the gathering, I remembered once when my aunt had taken me along to help the black sheep of a friend's family to "see the light." I had sat on her lap happily munching sweets, wondering what that black sheep had done to make his family so bitter. Afterwards I asked my aunt, but she replied, "You are too young to understand. You see, it's not only his fault, but his parents' as well. Family upbringing is very important. They spoiled him and now it's difficult to change him." Kissing my forehead, my aunt's face had lit up with affection as if to say, "But you are a good child; you will always be my joy and comfort." Poor Auntie.

Mr. Li, because of his age and position, spoke next. "Ling-ling, I know you won't like what I'm going to tell you. You may think we are interfering in your private affairs. But has it occurred to you that you've done something which could very well bring disaster to your family? The secret police are on the lookout for subversives and Communists and it's clear that the papers your friend gave you were of a most compromising nature. It's possible nothing may come of this; on the other hand, the danger of your being implicated is great, and that would bring in the whole family."

"But Ling-ling didn't know what those papers were." Madame Lu was already devising my defense. "If she knew they were bad business, I'm sure she would not have been a willing accomplice. She's a good girl." Madame Lu seemed to wear fewer jewels nowadays, with the fighting so close, and she was dressed for this solemn occasion with elegant simplicity. Only three rings encircled her fingers; each was a treasure: a tiny museum there on her hands. "I don't think we should worry. If the secret police come to bother you, we'll all write letters attesting to your good character."

My aunt looked at me anxiously: "Ling-ling, have you done anything else, you know, anything else illegal apart from what you told us this morning?"

"No." I squeezed the word out.

"I'm sure you are telling the truth."

"It's the truth." I tried to conceal my rising agitation beneath a toneless voice, but I couldn't fool my aunt.

"Don't be impatient," she admonished. "You are young and impractical. I know you believe all this nonsense about fighting for a better future, lifting up the people and so on and so forth. But you must forget about all that. Believe me when I tell you that just now the most important thing for you is to survive."

"Your idealistic notions may cost us a lot of money. If the secret police got hold of you, we would have to buy them off," my uncle grumbled. "And just at this moment I am hard up for ready cash."

"We will pool together what we have. No problem," the banker Mr. Chang reassured him.

To everybody's surprise, I stood up, turned to my uncle, and said in a cold voice, "Uncle, you can use the money that my mother left me to bribe the police." I had never spoken to my uncle and aunt like that before. I spoke with a brutality I hadn't seen in myself before, and it hurt them deeply.

"You are overreacting," interposed Lily, that gracious little beauty. She gently pressed my forearm in a sisterly way, and looked questioningly at my aunt.

My aunt motioned us away. She thought that she could not have found a more suitable person than Lily to put me in the right frame of mind, and in a way she was right. It was hard for me to be angry with Lily with her face like a Chinese Botticelli beauty come to life. I also just liked her. Two years older than I but a poor student, she was in my class and we had struck up a friendship. At times she seemed to be my affectionate, frivolous twin, but another side of me was often critical of her.

Like many of my schoolmates at St. Ursula's she was a quintessential product of cosmopolitan Shanghai—even to preferring an English name. She was a dull student but a bright young lady with great expectations. Our parents hired tutors to give us all the social graces considered necessary at that time for a well-brought-up young lady. We learned to tinkle tunes on the piano, to dance and paint. We could read the classics and write neat characters on rice-paper greeting cards from the famous Yung Bao Tsai Studio. We learned to serve tea, dress well, and chatter politely; to smile, walk, and act in a pleasant and graceful way. We were trained to be manhunters, and were being groomed for success in this avocation. Our ordained role was to flirt subtly and tastefully and then move in for the kill. We were successful if we "made a good marriage" and consolidated our positions by bearing heirs and bringing up our daughters the way we had been brought up. We failed if we "got into trouble" or otherwise made fools of ourselves, frittering away our chances by marrying some struggling writer or impecunious student. Lily, perhaps in her own way the smartest of us all, was sure to be a success. It was natural that my aunt should look to her to help me see the light.

Lily took me to the other side of the room. We sat side by side on the long piano bench.

"Ling-ling, how on earth did you come to get mixed up with the Communists? They are horrible people. Did you see the latest pictures in the *Morning Post*? The terrible things they are doing! Everybody is organized—men, women, and children. Endless meetings and demonstrations. My father says that when the Communists come in, that will be the end of polite society. I don't want to see that day. I can't wait to leave."

I suddenly hated to see her diamond earrings glittering and splintering iridescent light into my eyes. I wanted to do something she would never dare, to really outdo her. The words came tumbling out, as they too often did with me, before I had really thought out what I wanted to say.

"Suppose I wanted to find out if they are really as awful as you think?"

"How?" she asked, intrigued, but still with a dazzling smile, hardly understanding what I meant.

"I may stay on for a while—how about that? You know, to see what happens."

"You must be out of your mind," she exclaimed in genuine astonishment. I got some satisfaction from shocking her out of her complacency. I had found a game in which she couldn't compete with me. She and the other girls would run away like rabbits from the revolution, but not me.

Lily pouted silently for a while. When she had drunk up her wine, she rose and said to me, "It's time to go. I hope that whatever you do, you'll take your aunt and uncle into consideration. They love you. And who knows, you may change your mind." We crossed the room to join the others.

"Ah, yes, it's time to go home. My son Bob will be getting worried," said Madame Lu, getting up from her seat.

"Tonight it's a little too quiet here. Is something going to happen?"

"Don't worry. They won't fight here," said Mr. Li. "It's just a show. Our handsome general is already shipping his soldiers off to Taiwan. They're throwing in the sponge."

"What are your plans now?" Madame Lu asked him.

"We have a month or so left to decide. No good leaving a decision till the last minute," he answered matter-of-factly.

"It seems that most of us are doing the same thing," added my aunt. "It's hard to decide to move away for good. It's a tragedy."

"Yes, a tragedy. But thank God this fighting is coming to an end. This endless fighting and killing! Civil war has been going on for nearly twenty years!" said the banker.

When we opened the front door to the quiet spring evening outside we could hear muffled thuds that sounded like distant thunder. It was the first time we had heard distinct and systematic gunfire. The chattering of farewells ceased as we strained to listen. For a moment we were all silent. Finally the banker threw up his arms as if to say, "It's all in the lap of the Gods." Then he seized Lily by the arm and rushed her off saying, "I'll drive you home. It's not safe."

Her diamond earrings caught the light of a street lamp and flashed. She giggled at something he said as he bundled her into his big black car.

3

I Choose My Future

Events moved with lightning speed in the next few weeks. The fall of Hangzhou on May 3 cut the railway to the South, leaving only a hazardous roadway link by land. Airplanes and ships leaving the city were packed as the well-to-do rushed to evacuate. The poor and bewildered piled their few belongings onto carts and rickshaws and pedicabs and scattered into the surrounding countryside to await the end of the crisis. The really poor, with nothing to lose, simply closed their doors and sat inside their hovels. The foreigners who had dominated the city for a century sold what they could and left the rest in a mass exit. At one point gunfire drew near enough to rattle the windows in our living room.

In ones and twos and small groups, Guomindang soldiers straggled into the city where they threw away their guns and uniforms and merged back into the populace. Then, abruptly, the cannon fire ceased.

Rumor followed rumor in true Shanghai style. My uncle was informed by "reliable sources" that the main Guomindang army had been ordered to retreat due south to avoid being trapped in Shanghai. On May 26, red flags appeared as if by magic over the buildings and factories taken over by the underground revolutionaries. Ma Li's proclamations had evidently had their effect. When I saw one pasted on the door of the local post office I felt a small thrill of excitement.

Shanghai that day seemed quieter than I had ever remembered. A few heavy plumes of smoke rose lazily into the air. The only raucous sound was the occasional clang of fire engines racing to put out a fire. We heard that there had been a few street skirmishes in the suburbs, but we ourselves never heard a single rifle shot. Still, my aunt would not take a chance. She bolted the front door and gate and stationed one of the huskier male servants there as a guard. None of us were permitted to go out.

The dining room clock was striking twelve and we were just beginning our lunch when the maid came in. She bent over Auntie and spoke in a low voice. For a moment my aunt looked startled, then knit her brows and considered something carefully. Finally she said, "Ling-ling, your friend Ma Li is here."

I stood up. "Auntie, if it's not convenient to let her in, I will take her somewhere else."

"Where?"

"To some friend's home." I was not sure how to answer. "I have to find a place for her. We still don't know who really controls the city."

My aunt leaned back in her chair and stared hard into her cup for a long moment.

"I won't invite her in, but I won't throw her out," she said.

I went up to her, wanting to kiss her cheek, but she turned her face away with a trace of petulance.

Ma Li sat subdued like an unwelcome guest on the bench in the hall. I rushed to her, overjoyed to see her. I hugged her, then held her at arm's length. "You haven't changed your clothes since I saw you two weeks ago."

"No, there were too many prisoners and not enough uniforms for us all." Her eyes flashed with a smile from under her disheveled hair.

"So they got you." I made a bitter grimace. "You must be tired and famished. Let's go to my room."

"It happened right after I sent that young student to you. We had just finished our meeting when we were raided. Several of us got away but quite a number were caught." Ma Li took off her coat and sat on the edge of the bed.

"But how did you get out?" I asked. I gently brushed back her hair. Powdery dust fell from it. She breathed with difficulty. The taut muscles of her throat moved spasmodically.

"We made a deal with our jailers. If they saved us now, we would save them later." Her voice dropped to a low murmur. She was worn out with the tension of her ordeal. Her face suddenly looked pinched and lifeless like some faded old photograph. She closed her eyes and slumped down deathly pale on the satin quilt. For a second I thought she was dead.

"Ma Li," I wailed. "What did they do to you?"

She opened her eyes in embarrassment, as if she had done something wrong, slightly astonished to find herself looking up at the ceiling. At my cry my aunt had hurried in; now she took charge of the situation, putting Ma Li to bed, sponging her face, doing all the things that she would have done if I myself had been lying there helpless on the bed.

All was quiet the next day, a fine May morning. The sky was misty blue, and birds sang and twittered in the trees. We had scarcely noticed them for days. When we turned on the radio, triumphant music blared and the announcer told us that the People's Liberation Army had taken over Shanghai; the Guomindang was in headlong retreat everywhere, though Chiang still hoped to make a stand in the South, in Canton, the last major city and port in his hands.

Ma Li looked her old self again when she woke, and I offered to see her home. Along the Avenue Joffre, a whole army of Communist soldiers were resting, lying, or sitting in rows on the pavements. Most of them were young peasants hardly older than myself. They wore much-washed khaki uniforms with sneakers or straw sandals on their feet. They looked back at us with as much curiosity as we looked at them. When their commanders gave the order, they jumped to their feet, the onlookers forgotten. Falling into line, they straightened ranks and marched off.

Cars, buses, and trolleys were not yet operating, so Ma Li and I shared a pedicab. The bolder merchants were already opening their shops, and the streets were coming alive. We soon left the old French Concession behind and entered the former British Concession, the financial and commercial hub of Shanghai. Many patrols of armed workers' militia and the Liberation Army men kept order, and here too the life of the city was returning. Only the big department stores remained closed.

As we drove, Ma Li told me how she had left her parents' home because of their objection to her political activities. Now she shared a room with a factory girl in the cheaper part of the former Japanese Concession beyond Suzhou Creek where the boat people lived in their overcrowded sampan homes. I knew the Garden Bridge over Suzhou Creek, but beyond was unknown territory to me. My uncle and aunt had never allowed me to go across the Garden Bridge by myself, and certainly not by pedicab. Close by the bridge was the towering and expensive Broadway Mansions, but just beyond it was the port area nearer the sea—a warren of gambling, drinking, and drug dens, cabarets, brothels, and massage parlors frequented by seamen, gangsters, and other tough characters. If Shanghai was a Paradise of Adventurers, this was a Paradise of Vice. I turned to Ma Li in astonishment as we entered this area. "Why in the world do you live here?"

"Not quite here, but not too far from it. I live where the factory hands, laborers, and other poor people live. That's why I dress the way I do. When I went to meet you at that cafe, I changed my shabby clothes in the dressing room of the theater. The police themselves are scared of coming in here and our people have a deal with the locals. We're working for them, so they are glad to protect us. You see, this is an industrial area. It has textile mills and metal foundries. The girl I share my room with works in a cotton mill—that one on the left."

Our pedicab driver turned sharply left along the tall wall of the mill. We were in a slum area of low, rickety wooden

houses with grey tiled roofs. They were packed tightly together, and the narrow alleys between them formed a
maze. There was no room even for the pedicab to turn, so
we left it and continued on foot. The walls seemed never to
have been painted. There were no drains, and pools of
stagnant water, black and oily, mired the middle of the
lanes. We took a shortcut to her back door. Nearby was a
large, evil smelling garbage can filled with ashes, decayed
bits of vegetables, old crocks, and rotten wood. There was
nothing so useful in it as a single scrap of paper or a tin
can.

The place was deserted; everyone was out watching the
city change hands. Inside, a grimy kitchen with its clutter
of small stoves served several tenants. What had once
been a junk closet was now occupied by a family of four
glad to have even this airless space for their home. The
stairwell was a black hole. I stumbled up the steps and at
Ma Li's warning held my head low. The space above the
stairs had been filled in to form a bunk for a single person;
a small bundle of indistinguishable rags, the occupant's
total household goods, marked the home. Ma Li said she
had never figured out how many people lived in these tiny
spaces. Some doubled up, using the same bed, one on the
day shift and the other on the night shift, each twelve
hours long.

In Ma Li's room a double bunk, one over the other, and a
wooden crate were the only furniture. There was no room
for anything more. Worn pieces of cotton held up with
string screened the bunks. That was all the privacy they
had.

"Where is she?" I pointed to the upper bunk.

"Maybe still in jail. She'll be out soon. We have sent
people to open the jails and get all the political prisoners
out." Ma Li sat on her bunk and gave me the wooden crate
to sit on.

"The room I had in the British Concession was much
better. For a time that was fairly safe and the theater
troupe had funds to pay us wages. But later on, as the
Guomindang tried to trap as many radicals as it could, our
money ran out. Anyway it was safer to live here."

Ma Li looked round at the rattrap she had been living in. "Fortunately my mother never saw this place. She would have had a fit. A year ago, when my father threatened to disown me, she came to see me and begged me to go home. 'Why do you want to make your life so difficult?' she said. And I told her, 'Mama, I think your life is harder to endure.' She understood what I meant. She had been active when she was young, but her dreams and plans had all faded away. Vanished. And she ended up just like the women she despised when she was young. She grew old and fat. She was always trying on some new kind of perfume or skin freshener. All the trouble she took with her dresses just made her look more ridiculous. Did you ever see a fat dummy in a department store show window? They are all skinny; yet she used to buy those same dresses and have them remade to fit her bulky figure."

"There's no air in this room." I reached out and pushed open the small window. A thick board had been nailed between the window and the sill of the window in the house opposite.

"That's our outdoor kitchen. We put our little stove up there when it's not raining."

"I could never have followed your example two years ago," I admitted, "but now it's different."

"Now you have a good chance to strike out on your own. Listen to this: The new cultural department that's to be set up in Shanghai has a plan to combine a number of small theatrical troupes like mine into one large theater with several touring companies. We'll need many new people."

I shook my head. "My uncle has arranged for my aunt and me to leave for Hong Kong while he stays on here to see how matters work out. I'll wait in Hong Kong while Bob Lu finishes his last year of college here. Then we'll get married and go to the United States. He'll work there for his Ph.D."

"And what are you expected to do?"

"Just be his wife. Did you know Lily is going to marry the banker Mr. Chang? They plan to go to the Philippines. My aunt thinks that Lily is doing the right thing."

"What do you think?"

"It's probably the right thing for her."

Ma Li tossed her head contemptuously. Out of curiosity I stood on the box to peep into the upper bunk.

"Why don't you strike a bargain with your aunt and uncle? Take a job and wait for Bob Lu here, then join them later in Hong Kong. That way you'll be able to see for yourself how things work out. You can make up your own mind what you want to do. How about that?"

"That's a great idea!" I gestured too emphatically and tumbled backwards off the rickety box. When I looked up there was no bunk, no books, no Ma Li. I was in another tiny room. Ma Li's hand stretched out to me through the door I had unwittingly fallen through and she pulled me to my feet.

My uncle and aunt were not happy about the prospect of a long separation, but they knew my proposal was not unreasonable, and they didn't oppose it too vigorously. They were apprehensive of provoking me to revolt at a time when more and more young people were boldly going their own way. Tired of school and home with their constraints, with adolescent, half-baked convictions but ready to try out our own wings, we were eager to join the revolution that now surrounded us. However, my family insisted on one condition that I, in turn, could only agree was reasonable: I had to complete my last term of high school. So, as normal life returned to Shanghai, I went back to St. Ursula's.

The week before my aunt left for our new house in Hong Kong, I spent all my free time with her. Despite our growing differences we still had a deep affection for each other and tried our utmost to avoid thoughts of parting. Only once did she let go. She had come into my room to tell me something, but as she walked back to the door, she suddenly spun around and spread her arms against the opening as if to stop me from running out of it.

"Ling-ling, come with me!" she pleaded. Her face, once plump and commanding, now sagged like a dried, slightly squashed pumpkin. I felt a surge of pity for her, but I knew that what she asked was already impossible. I could not share the life she wanted to lead in Hong Kong any more than she could live her old life in the new Shanghai. The Western world was boycotting the new China. Foreign ships no longer called at the ports. The cinemas were running out of their store of American movies and eventually would cease showing them altogether. Nearly all the foreigners had either left or were leaving. The party-going and hobnobbing among the wealthy and influential had ended. Austerity was the watchword. Shanghai, resilient and adaptable, was learning new ways, but for people like my aunt and uncle it was hard, almost impossible, to change.

"Auntie, I'll come to you as we agreed, when young Bob Lu leaves."

"I hope so," was all she said with a deep sigh.

My aunt left Shanghai in the autumn of 1949. When the train started moving I ran along beside it on the platform waving frantically, hardly seeing for the tears in my eyes. For a second I had the urge to jump on it and go with her.

On October 1, 1949, the People's Republic of China was formally established at a great meeting in Peking. By the end of the year, the Guomindang had withdrawn from the mainland completely. I left St. Ursula's at Christmastime, armed with my high school diploma, and Ma Li immediately made an appointment for me to see one of the leading officials of her theater. His name was Wang Sha; he was a playwright who now devoted most of his time to theatrical administrative work and helping younger playwrights.

Ma Li met me at the theater entrance and led me to a corridor of offices backstage. She knocked on a door, put her head in, and without ceremony said to the person inside, "Comrade Wang Sha, here is Guan Ling-ling whom I told you about." I was surprised at the familiar way she addressed him, but she whispered, "He hates formality."

"Please come in."

"I hope I'm not interrupting your work." I looked

around as I entered to see a workroom more than an office, with well-stocked bookshelves around the walls, an old, greyish-white, cloth-covered table piled with papers and magazines, his desk, and a few plain wooden chairs. That was all.

"No, I was expecting you. Come in." He stood up to greet me. He was lightly but strongly built with slightly bowed shoulders and a shock of black hair topping a high-browed, thin face. He seemed quite pleasant-looking. "Please sit down," he said, indicating a chair next to his desk. "So what work would you like to do?"

"This will be my first job," I apologized.

But he put me at ease: "We have quite a few young people doing work for the first time."

"I have no college training. I just finished high school at St. Ursula's."

"Not many of us here have had any sort of college education. Some have only completed junior high or elementary school. You are well educated compared to most. I imagine you can read classical Chinese as well as English?"

Feeling more confident, I admitted that I could. "I love to read. I read a lot."

"That's fine. How about starting work in the library? There's a great deal to do there. We're going to hold a series of discussions about the role of art and the artist in society. We'll be inviting well-known artists, writers, actors, and others to join us. You can take notes at the meetings and then help to write up the final report. How's that?"

I couldn't have wished for anything better. I thanked him and rushed off to find Ma Li and tell her of my good fortune.

That's how I became a cadre. White-collar employees of all kinds—ministers, department heads, industrial managers, clerks, typists, doctors, artists—working in state institutions or organizations, did not like to be called officials, for that smacked too much of the old society, so a new word had been coined for them—*ganbu*, "doers" or "cadres."

． ． ．

The work in the library was not demanding—simply cata-
loging and stacking the books and magazines as they
came in. I put my name down for a playwrighting course
to start shortly. Combing the library shelves, I read vora-
ciously, growing more and more involved in the craft of
writing and its problems. And I looked forward to meeting
some of the writers whose work was beginning to affect
me.

The day of the first discussion meeting I came early.
From my place at the note-taker's table in front of the
platform I had a close-up view of all the speakers. All
those we invited promised to attend and the list was like a
Who's Who of the modern literary world—Ba Jin, whose
novel *Family* had led countless young readers to rebel
against the feudal family system and its arranged marriages; Lao She, who wrote *Rickshaw Boy* and, influenced
by Dickens, created a whole gallery of portraits of the un-
derprivileged, the common people of China; Cao Yu,
whose play *Thunderstorm* brought modern Chinese drama
to maturity. Mao Dun's *Midnight* gave such a truthful and
biting picture of my uncle's business world that I felt sure
he knew many of our friends. He was the newly appointed
Minister of Culture and was preparing to go to Peking, but
he said he would come if he could.

Wang Sha, it seemed, knew everybody. He had a nod
and greeting for us humble note takers even as he settled
the most eminent of authors in their places. I liked his way
of dealing with people.

"In this open forum," Wang Sha proclaimed, beginning
his remarks, "everybody should be heard. We are here to
help the Party Committee of the theater hammer out its
guidelines. To decide, for example, what kind of new plays
we should write and what old plays we should stage."

"I think the theater should take the *Yanan Talks* as its
guideline," a man in his mid-thirties with a ruggedly handsome face interposed from the back of the hall.

I was glad that I had done my homework before the
meeting. The talks he cited took place in 1942 in the then
Communist headquarters in Yanan. The Party's Chairman,

Mao Ze-dong, had spoken at this forum, and his two addresses were regarded as the key exposition of the Party's cultural policy.

Wang Sha responded immediately: "The *Yanan Talks* call on writers to write from the Communist point of view. The writers in Yanan then were either Communists or intended to accept this philosophy. But the situation has changed. Most of us here tonight are not Communists and therefore probably do not wish to subordinate ourselves to Party discipline. Does that mean that we will not be allowed to write until we have agreed to write as instructed by the Party? Does that mean that we should not stage any plays written from a non-Communist standpoint? For example, Mr. Cao Yu's plays?"

"That would definitely rule out my *Metamorphosis*," Cao Yu added with a self-deprecatory smile.

"Why should it?" inquired Feng Xue-feng, a well-known Communist critic, jerking his white-haired head. He spoke with a nervous intensity that dated from the imprisonment in a Guomindang jail which had wrecked his health. "Why shouldn't your play be staged? Because its hero is a Guomindang commissioner? Because no one who has worked for the Guomindang government should be depicted as a hero? Now look here, I was locked up in one of the worst Guomindang concentration camps. Shang-rao Concentration Camp. Yes, that's right." He thrust his body violently forward as if he were about to get at some invisible opponent. "I hope that nobody will accuse me of apologizing for the Guomindang if I say there are good, decent people working in that government. We should write about real individuals, not stereotypes."

Cao Yu, whose penchant for dramatic tricks was a feature of his playwriting, suddenly gave an unexpected twist to the drama of the moment. "I wrote the *Metamorphosis* during the Second World War; the drama school I taught in evacuated to a small backwoods town, far away from Japanese air raids, and the stifling atmosphere there reminded me of the settings in Chekhov's plays. I had always been an admirer of Chekhov, but it was only then that I began to feel deeply for his characters, people who are constantly chasing after rainbows—not even real ones, but just imagined ones. I realized that some people need dreams to chase or they would find life unbearable. That was when the hero of *Metamorphosis* took shape in my mind. The hero happens to work in the Guomindang government, nothing more—this way he can fit into the story. He is a Chekhov character of my invention. Instead of simply daydreaming he takes it upon himself to turn a dream into a reality. When I finished that play I felt free of that stage in my past. It was a good feeling."

That was when Ai Qing, acclaimed as one of the best of the contemporary poets, woke up, or at least seemed to wake up. He had been sitting for quite a while with his eyes closed; now he opened them wide as if perplexed to find himself in such company. We had not known he was in town so we had not invited him, but hearing of the session from theater friends, he came anyway. He spoke in his soft, sleepy voice.

"To regiment and impose restrictions on writers, Communists or not, is to kill their creative urge. I have been writing for years. But many of my poems—and some I consider the best—have never been published and never will be if some people have their way. The reason is simple: I was told first in Yanan and then in Peking, 'They are not revolutionary. Why do you waste your time describing a cloud lit by the morning sun?'

"Sometimes when I take these poems out and recite them to myself I feel like an actor playing in an empty theater. Without lights. Without an audience. With neither applause nor hisses; surrounded by emptiness that responds to nothing I say or think. When people are constantly telling me to write this or that I feel my brain drying up. If this goes on, one fine day it will be as dried up as the orange peel that old wives use to make herb medicine." This quiet outburst caused a considerable stir; he was a Communist and had spent the war years in Yanan.

He was just about to resume his seat when on the spur of the moment he pulled out a sheet of paper and began to read aloud a poem, the very one describing the cloud in the morning sky. When he finished, the audience applauded noisily while he himself bowed ostentatiously to all the prettiest actresses.

As he replaced the poem in his pocket he reminisced, "I wrote that on the first day I returned to Shanghai from Paris. It was in 1932. Or was it '31? Anyway, on the third day the French Concession police arrested me. In those days I hadn't a thought in my head but poetry, but they said that my poem about the cloud was obviously revolutionary because the sun tinted the cloud red and furthermore nobody but a Communist would go all the way to Paris just to study poetry. It took years to convince them that I had gone to Paris to study painting and the information they had got from their Guomindang spies was wrong. It was shameful. The Guomindang government handed over their own innocent people to the foreigners who occupied our land, and treated not only them, but their top boss, Generalissimo Chiang Kai-shek, like dirt. However, they had put ideas into my head. What they didn't like, I liked, and I became a Communist."

When he finally sat down, he leaned his tall frame over to speak to a neighbor and his movement revealed a short, middle-aged man in the seat behind him.

"Who's that?" I asked Dai Shi, another note taker sitting beside me.

"Chen Bo-da," she whispered. "He is one of Chairman Mao's chief secretaries. Now be quiet. I think he is going to speak."

"Did we invite him? When did he come in?" I turned to ask Ma Li, who was sitting behind Dai Shi.

"No, we didn't. But he likes to play the inspector-general incognito."

"Comrades, I find the meeting most interesting. Everybody speaks out what is on his mind. May I do the same?" The newcomer spoke modestly, but I couldn't help thinking it was a bit forced. He must have known that most people in the room knew who he was. "I personally believe that if a writer takes a firm Party or pro-Party stand, he will produce a better book or play." Then he praised Mao Dun's *Midnight* as the most effective satire in modern Chinese literature directed against the bourgeoisie. "Comrade Mao Dun, will you tell us how you wrote that novel?" It was a shrewd move. Mao Dun was a formidable figure among Chinese intellectuals. It would be quite useful to set him up as a revolutionary proletarian writer.

Mao Dun rose slowly and stood for a moment as if debating with himself. With a smile on his elfish face, he declined the role assigned him and said, "I must be frank. I was hard up at the time. I borrowed money from a friend and tried my luck on the Shanghai stock exchange. I lost every cent I had and was worse off than before. When a publisher suggested I do a book about the business world and pay off my debts that way, that's exactly what I did!"

The hall erupted in laughter and cheers. Mao Dun held his hand up for silence and added, "Don't follow in anyone's footsteps. Write as you think best."

Chen Bo-da's face flushed red, but when I glanced around I saw many faces looking up with glowing eyes.

I too put down my pen and began to clap. Dai Shi restrained my arm and whispered fiercely, "You're just supposed to be taking notes!"

"Comrade Minister," a soft voice from the back of the hall addressed Mao Dun respectfully. "Please advise us how we can come to grips with contemporary life?"

"Go among the people; go among the peasants." He paused for a moment to look around at the walls as if considering whether he ought to say more. "I don't think I am letting out a secret when I tell you that the land reform movement will soon start in all the newly liberated areas."

"Will volunteers be called for?"

"Naturally," Mao Dun answered. "Scores of thousands of educated young people will be needed to help the peasants carry it through."

To "go among the peasants" was a movement that had started in the mid-twenties when revolutionaries first realized that no revolution could succeed in China without the support of the ninety percent of the people who were peasants. In those days, in reality or in fiction, it was the man-hero who made the choice between revolution, love, and family. Women were almost condescendingly awarded the role of helpmate, or were condemned to pine at home and wait for their men to come back and share their glory. Maybe now it was the woman's turn. I smiled involuntarily.

"Why are you smiling when everyone else is wrapped up in a heated discussion? We are in a meeting, you know," Ma Li whispered to me.

"Hush," someone hissed at us.

". . . I am glad that question has been raised," Wang Sha was saying. "After talk comes action. We must not neglect plays that deal with the past, but we would be delinquent if we didn't write about the present. China is charting new paths and you young people will confront a new world and experiences which will often seem baffling. You young writers face the challenge of creating a literature that will truly reflect reality and by its truth invigorate the struggle for the new.

"Our veteran writers here—Mao Dun, Pa Chin, Ai Ching, and all the others, have taken over the inheritance of the traditional Chinese literature—the beautiful short stories and poetry of the Tang dynasty, thirteen hundred years ago, the wonderful novels and plays of the Ming and Qing dynasties. But they found there an almost total lack of psychological portraiture of individual characters. Those characters are vivid. They come alive through action and dialogue. But their creators did not delve deeply into their minds and thoughts as the great writers of modern Western literature do. Our modern writers have made a breakthrough, but much still remains to be done to create a literature worthy of our times. Where is the full-blooded portrayal of our modern heroes that we are all waiting for?"

At this, Ding Ling, the firebrand feminist, jumped to her feet and cried: "Heroes! Heroes! I have been waiting in vain for someone to say even one word about our heroines. About our women. It's as though half the population doesn't exist. What about looking deep into their minds!"

The women in the audience got to their feet and gave

her a standing ovation. Wang Sha, to show his contrite-
ness, leaned over to shake her hand.

But time had run out. The meeting was over. The partici-
pants dispersed, continuing the discussion in noisy groups
as they left. I busied myself putting my notes in order and
then tidying up the hall, which doubled as our reading
room. A magazine lay on the speakers' table near where
Wang Sha was chatting with the director of the theater.
As I stretched out my hand to pick it up, Wang Sha
glanced at me, and I drew back.

"No, I don't want it," he said politely, interrupting his
conversation. He added, speaking to his companion, "This
is our future playwright."

"How did you know I want to write?" I asked.

"Just a guess," he replied, laughing.

"If you find playwriting too much of a headache, switch
to acting. We need actresses too," the director joked, sizing me up as he spoke. "Anyway, if you want to try writing first, you won't find a better tutor than Wang Sha." At
which he left.

"Well, I do want to write," I confided to Wang Sha.

"So? Then you must have found tonight's discussion interesting."

"I certainly did. Will the report of what was said be read
in Peking? Will it get to the real authorities there?"

"Certainly, they will get it and I hope they pay attention
to it. The fact that Mao Dun has been appointed Minister
of Culture may mean business. You see, he's not a Communist and has often disagreed with the Party's cultural
policy. That's why he didn't accept the Party's invitation
to stay in Yanan during the war years."

"If he had, he might have been purged like the others
who opposed the *Yanan Talks*," I said.

"The 1942 Yanan purge was a disgraceful episode!" The
vehemence in his voice was more eloquent than his words.
"On the other hand, he and many others were persecuted
in the Guomindang-ruled areas. By defending their social
and artistic ideas, they'd gotten their heads into a noose

and at any minute the Guomindang might have drawn it
tight around their necks."

The theater was more than a place of work for us; it was
our school and university and club as well. Although I still
lived in our villa in the old French Concession, I spent less
and less time there. I was up early and at work by eight,
and I came home just in time to catch supper before rushing out again to a play or film or to attend a study meeting.

I joined a writers' workshop, and the plays we wrote
were terrible. I can't remember one that didn't preach
some message or spout slogans before its pat ending.
However, in helping to write them I got to explore parts of
Shanghai life that were utterly unknown to me. Taking our
cue from Zola, when we wrote playlets about ending pros-
titution, wiping out organized crime, cleaning up the
slums, or about a model worker we went to visit former
brothels and streetwalkers, prisons and gangsters, slum
dwellers and factories. Our efforts to describe their lives
so intrigued the girls of a former brothel that they took
over the whole project and wrote, staged, and acted the
play themselves. It took Shanghai by storm and played to
full houses for weeks. Actors and audiences were all in
tears in the climactic scenes and shouted with joy at the
end. It only ended its run when the energy and freshness
of the amateur actresses flagged and, tired of living
through their old life again and again on the stage, they
began to act as badly as our professional actors acted
when they tackled characters they knew nothing about.

My history books had taught me to be proud of China,
and I wanted to express that pride and wonder at what her
people had done; but a book or a play needs a hero, and I
found that I did not know the hero of my future play, that
enormous character who was a composite of China's people, because I did not know those people. Everything and
everybody was changing right in front of my eyes. A drama was being acted out in Shanghai, but it was so diverse,
so vast with its cast of six million characters that I could

not take it in. If I did not know Shanghai, how could I know China?

Two events determined what I should learn next. War broke out between North and South Korea in June 1950, and the Americans joined in.

This was too much for my uncle. War again! He was certain that the new government would now accelerate its radical policies and tighten control over the business community. He decided to leave as soon as possible for Hong Kong.

October 1950 was a month for decisions. The American army was advancing in North Korea and had neared the Chinese border. Its planes dropped bombs in Northeast China, just over the border from North Korea, and Chinese troops were ordered into action to back up the North Korean army in a counteroffensive across the Yalu River. Young people like myself who felt that we had missed the historic fight for the establishment of the new China did not want to miss this new battle to preserve it. Many of us, myself included, volunteered, but only two young people in our theater were accepted. The armed forces, we were told, would handle that situation with some special volunteers. Civilian cadres would have another task: The government issued a call for volunteers to help carry out the recently passed land reform law. The lands of the feudal landlords would be confiscated and shared out among the landless and landpoor farmers. The reform had already been carried out among the hundred million peasants in the area that had formed the Communist Party's base at the start of the final civil war. Now it would be carried out in the areas taken over from Guomindang rule in the final offensive. Three hundred million peasants would be involved, the great bulk of the population in Central-South, South, Southwest, and Northwest China. About twenty-eight million landlords and their families would be affected.

Like every other able-bodied cadre in the theater I volunteered to go. This time I was accepted.

The day the decision to carry through the land reform was announced, my uncle greeted me with a gloomy face. "I told you so," he said. "Things are heating up. We can't delay any longer. No one knows what this war will lead to. We'll leave the house to the servants and be off as soon as we can pack."

"Uncle, what has the land reform got to do with us personally? We don't own farmland." I tried to prepare him a little before dropping my bombshell. "And . . . well, you see, I've just volunteered to go out and help with the land reform." There.

My uncle was stunned. Words failed him, until finally he stuttered, "My God! Madame Lu still owns land near Shanghai and collects rent from the farmers there! What will happen if you're sent to the place where her estates are? What will happen to her and Bob? What will happen to our marriage plans?" His world was collapsing.

Uncle prepared to turn the house over to an old, loyal servant and began to pack in earnest. I too began to pack: first the things for the rest of my stay in Shanghai, in the theater's dormitory for single cadres; then, another trunk to send with my uncle to Hong Kong. We still held on to the plan that I would join them there later.

When the war began in Korea, it had already been decided that Bob Lu should leave China rather than run the risk of being caught up in the fighting. The day after the decision on land reform was announced, Madame Lu sent word that they were leaving immediately for Hong Kong, and they were sure that we would understand. We would all meet there soon, the note ended. I never saw Madame Lu or Bob again. I wasn't heartbroken and I didn't grieve. It had just been one of those typical Shanghai family arrangements, I suppose. A matter of putting two people and their money together.

4 ★

Journey to the Northwest

Lana Turner had disappeared. A huge painting, the size of a billboard, had been hoisted up to take her place over the marquee of the Cathay Cinema. Center left was a determined-looking worker in blue overalls carrying an oversized hammer. He clasped the hands of a smiling peasant holding a sickle. Behind the worker were smaller figures of white-collar workers, men and women, professionals and intellectuals, carrying red banners, a whole forest of them. Factory chimneys spouted smoke in the background. Behind the peasant were serried ranks of other peasants marching against a background of neatly ordered fields being ploughed with tractors. A morning sun rose red in the cloudless blue sky. Over all floated the words "Land to the Tillers."

All over Shanghai, billboards that had once extolled Camel cigarettes and other goods now sang the praises of worker-peasant unity and land reform. Every day the press carried articles and editorials instructing and exhorting the cadres selected to go to the villages. We volunteers were given a crash course in the theory of agrarian revolution. Each of us was presented with a folder of documents to study. Meetings, lectures, and study groups were organized for us. Wang Sha and other veteran cadres who had already taken part in the land reform in North and Northeast China tried to pass on as much of their experiences to us as possible, but it became even clearer to me that without firsthand experience of working and living with the peasants in their villages it would be hard for us tyros to understand exactly what we had to do or how to do it. The landpoor peasants, sharecroppers, tenant farmers, and farm laborers were a vast mass of faceless strangers, separated from me by a wide gap of incomprehension. And yet it was precisely for them that I would be going to help carry through the land reform.

And then there was that other, so much smaller group of faceless strangers—the feudal landlords. The men now termed feudal landlords had been chosen by the former Guomindang government, just as they had been by the emperors for centuries past, to run the show in the rural areas. They were the gentry, the literates, lording it over the vast mass of the illiterate. They rented out land at exorbitant rents, charged high interest rates on loans, and in especially backward areas were real rural despots, using their power to amass wealth by every means. Now they and their families would have to atone for these sins.

And yet, although there were indeed some very large landowners, the material difference between the good poor and the bad rich was often no more than 180 *mu* or about thirty acres a family. Some tyrannous landlords abused their power and position and deserved punishment, but it seemed harsh to me that because of some small difference in wealth, a small landlord family should be assailed and its children stigmatized as members of an "exploiting class." It seemed unfair too that the really big landlords had been able to flee the country, leaving behind their puppets, these millions of little landlords, to deal with the consequences. Then I thought of Madame Lu. But it was hard to picture my erstwhile proposed mother-in-law as a "feudal landlord," or, as I now learned to categorize her, "part feudal landlord, part capitalist," who would be slated to lose her land but not her bourgeois capital.

Between these clearly "good" and "evil" classes were two more groups, and here it wasn't always easy to draw distinct lines. The largest group between the two extremes—and our greatest hope for allies—were the "middle peasants." Where the poor peasant was always on the verge of sliding down into the abyss because of drought or flood or unpayable debts, the middle peasant could just about make do. Then came the much smaller group of "rich peasants." These relatively well-to-do farmers had more land than they could till themselves so they hired laborers or rented out a portion to tenants or sharecroppers. They were closer in spirit and interests to landlords, though not as established in wealth and power. We were warned in our preparatory classes to keep a wary eye on them while avoiding action that would force them over to the side of the landlords.

At the bottom of the social scale were millions of rural dispossessed—beggars and bandits.

I might have been able to grasp everything more clearly at that time if I'd had more time to study all the documents we were given and listened more attentively to the lectures. But because of the Korean War there was a special urgency about the land reform. Unless the peasants were able to begin tilling their own land by the time the spring sowing started in February or March, there would be a national disaster. That left only about four months in which to accomplish the task for the year. What remained to be done would have to be completed in the next winter lull in farming. The leaders were therefore anxious to have us on the road as soon as possible. But after the lectures we still had to shop and make the warm clothes needed in the remoteness of Gansu Province where the weather was much colder than in temperate Shanghai. All this barely left time for even basic orientation courses.

When I met Wang Sha to discuss my application he joked with me. "I thought you would choose Gansu, where the Silk Road goes and the Great Wall ends. You have romantic ideas. Well, I'll approve your application, but don't blame me if you find it too tough." Despite his words, there was a hint of tenderness in his teasing. I didn't answer, but just watched the way he ran his fingers through his tousled hair as he left the room.

. . .

Two weeks later, we gathered in the early morning at the theater to start our journey to the Northwest. Two buses and a truck were soon filled with the seventy of us and our belongings, and we were off to the railroad station. The lead driver took us by way of the Bund, the riverside embankment road, to give us a last look at the Huangpu and its shipping. "You won't see a river like that for a long time," he told us. "The place you're going to is a real desert."

Even at that early hour the river was alive with activity. Big ships swung at anchor from the buoys in midstream. Scurrying launches set junks and sampans bobbing in their wakes. On the far side Pudong was shrouded in morning mist that made its smoking factory chimneys seem like silent, stiff sea wraiths with gently waving hair. We passed the skyscraper banks and hotels and then turned away from the river up teeming Nanking Road with its many-floored offices and department stores with their glittering window displays. It would be five months at least before we saw such sights again. The part of Gansu Province we had been assigned to was more than one thousand miles away, three hundred miles beyond the railhead west of Xian. There was little chance of returning from there on leave. I turned my head back for a last look at the broad river before it was lost to sight amid the traffic and the throng of pedestrians in the morning rush to work.

Shanghai people, like no others in China, know how to make an "occasion" of an event. The station was filled with a hurrying, jostling throng of cadres and their relatives and friends come to see them off. As more and more buses rolled up with groups from other organizations and districts, the noise and commotion reached a peak. To avoid being separated we formed a tight phalanx and pushed our way through to our train. Wang Sha had been appointed to lead our group of seventy going to the Northwest, and we found him waiting for us on the platform, holding up a card on a tall stick with the name of our destination—Gansu—written on it. A score of posters with other names cataloged the many other destinations of land reform workers that day. Writers, musicians, film workers, dancers, singers, artists, producers, scholars, and a sprinkling of office workers and veteran cadres like Wang Sha moved along the platforms to their trains. The director of our theater and the heads of many departments and organizations of Shanghai were there to wish us well. There was even a band of our orchestral musicians tuning up for a farewell song.

Wang Sha called the roll—still a few missing—and then in a moment of immense confusion we piled into the train with our belongings, trying to find our compartments and places. Like soldiers we had little baggage. We had been told, "Only essentials; no luxuries, please." Like most, I carried a backpack of a bedding roll and a change of clothes, wrapped in a piece of oilcloth or raincoat, with an enamel basin tied to the outside and an extra pair of cotton shoes or sneakers. In practical fashion, we girls all wore cadres' uniforms: trousers and soldier-style jackets of blue, grey, or khaki. We tied our enamel drinking mugs or bowls to our leather belts. A couple of notebooks, a pen, an extra sweater, little bags and baskets of goodies for the journey, and that was all. It was autumn and we could travel light. Our bundles of warm cotton or floss-padded coats and jackets and trousers and winter underwear had been sent to the baggage wagons. Everything else we possessed we had left with our families or stored with our organizations.

Ma Li wore a floppy soldier's cap pushed back on her head, the cardboard peak forming a halo over her thick bobbed hair. Now she was a girl soldier like those we had seen in the propaganda pictures. I had changed my long pageboy hairdo to a straight bob cut just below my ears. It seemed more appropriate to life in a farming village.

A bell clanged a warning to us all to take our seats. For one awkward moment, all the good-byes said, there was nothing more to say. Anyway, I had no one special to say good-bye to except office friends. My uncle had already left Shanghai. Impatient to leave, we kept eyeing the station clock. Two minutes. One minute. The first whistle. There was a wave of movement across the platform as a late arrival pushed his way through the crowd. Of course it was our amateur archaeologist, Hu, late as usual. We shouted and beckoned him to hurry, but with packets and bags big and small under both arms threatening to slip down at any moment he could only jog along, body swaying like a duckling waddling to a pond. The guard bundled Hu aboard and slammed the carriage door shut just as the final whistle blew. People took out pocket handkerchiefs, shouted last messages. Mothers wept and waved. A bedlam of good-byes. With the loudspeakers playing a sprightly folk song, we were off.

The train moved slowly at first through the railway yards and past the factories that crowded down the railroad tracks, picking up speed beyond the sheds and hovels of the suburban slum, and finally racing as we got out into the countryside.

As the morning wore on, and the excitement of leaving wore off, conversation in our compartment flagged. I watched the lush landscape pass by. Here in the "Land of Rice and Fish," south of the Yangzi River, every inch of rich black soil was neatly cultivated up to the very verge of the narrow footpath. The square sails of a junk moved above the tops of the mulberry trees and seemed to be sailing on land.

Ma Li, curled up in one corner, dozed. The troupe's soprano, in the seat opposite me, gazed silently out of the window. Chu Hua, a pretty ballerina, dexterously knitted a winter sweater.

Someone peered into our compartment.

"Is this seat occupied?"

It was Cheng, the comedian. We had recently seen him playing the steward Malvolio in Shakespeare's *Twelfth Night*. His performance was superb. He gave a sensitive and convincing portrayal of the buffoon in love with his high-born mistress. When he spoke about his unrequited love with anguished tears in his eyes, the audience was moved in spite of the fact that he was clowning. Even I had found myself wishing that Olivia would return his love, although she, fine lady, would never even dream of being loved by such a clownish inferior. After that performance the nickname "Malvolio" had stuck permanently.

"There's plenty of room. Sit here," Ma Li answered, inviting him to take the empty seat between us.

He rubbed the top of his head and sat down obediently. His head was oddly shaped: a narrow forehead but broad in the chin. He dressed untidily no matter what he wore. Even his best clothes seemed wasted on him. It was the way he wore them on his ungainly body. He was always playacting. Now he looked like a farmer with his sturdy neck and broad back dressed in an old peasant jacket, a perfect picture of a country bumpkin traveling by train for the first time, sitting straight up on the edge of his seat, a bamboo basket covered with a piece of white cloth balanced on his knees.

The train attendant, making his rounds with a huge tin kettle, filled our mugs and bowls with tea. I took one sip, frowned, and put my mug down. It was strong red tea such as northern Chinese like; we southern Chinese, especially Shanghai people, love our delicate green teas. Malvolio Cheng, after swallowing down a mouthful, held his mug as embarrassed as though it were he who had poured out the wrong tea and now did not know what to do. At last he put down his mug as I had done.

"Pfui," exclaimed Chu Hua, the young ballet dancer, making a comic grimace. "That red tea is so bitter!"

"Yes, it's too bad," commiserated Malvolio Cheng. "I'll get you something better." Without waiting for a reply, he left the compartment and soon returned with a thermos bottle of hot chocolate which he shared out among us. It was an unexpected treat.

Encouraged by our response, he diffidently held out his bamboo basket to us, looking from one to another. Ma Li lifted the square of white cloth and exposed a basketful of delicious food: pieces of smoked chicken, preserved duck, fancy sweets. We could not restrain our cries of surprise and delight as we sampled his delicacies and came back for more. His eyes moved merrily from one mouth to another.

Liao, a dancer from Chu Hua's troupe, looked in to find us all munching away at Malvolio Cheng's food. "What a feast!" he exclaimed.

"I'm afraid you've come too late," I apologized.

"There's one chicken wing left," Cheng said, peering into the basket and fishing it out.

Ma Li passed it to Liao, inviting him in. When he had picked the bones clean, he wiped his fingers, stretched his long legs out under the opposite seat, crossed his arms over his chest, and closed his eyes in an exaggerated expression of bliss. Ma Li was wiping her hands on a towel. Suddenly she turned to Malvolio Cheng with a look of dismay on her face:

"But you haven't eaten anything!"

Chu Hua threw her head back and laughed. "We completely forgot about him!" Malvolio Cheng himself seemed delighted and laughed with us.

I noticed the admiring glance that Liao gave Chu Hua before he shyly turned away. With Liao sitting beside her, Chu Hua grew light-headed and giggled all the time like the teenager she was. Her gaiety was contagious. Liao hummed a lively tune and our soprano joined in.

In sight of the huge grim battlements surrounding Nanking, the "southern capital," our train was ferried across the mile-wide Yangzi River. The rice fields of the South were left behind, as we rattled north across the central wheat and millet plains. The harvests were in, and the dry, brown, stubbled fields were bare. The only spots of color were the orange-yellow corncobs drying on the roofs of the cottages. At the big junction of Xuzhou we turned due west, making for the ancient heartland of China in the valley of the Yellow River. Here and there through gaps in the hills we caught sight of the river's turbid, cocoa-brown waters, heavy with the silt which it carried to the estuary far to the east, into the Yellow Sea.

The day passed quickly. From time to time Wang Sha dropped in to see us. The long train ride gave him a chance to relax a bit after the hectic organizing to get together the work teams in Shanghai. He was in a genial mood. As he sat by the window, a beam of afternoon sunlight lit up his face. The color of his eyes changed from dark brown to lighter brown, giving them a milder look.

Malvolio Cheng too was a welcome visitor, and when we were all together we joked and fooled around. Our jokes drew disapproving frowns from one of our companions, Dai Shi, the girl who had tried to stop me from applauding Mao Dun at the first discussion meeting in our theater. Dissatisfied with the people in her own compartment, she had taken to visiting ours. She was young and not bad-looking, and when in a good mood she even looked pretty. She chased after men indomitably, but her sharp tongue and mischievous gossip frightened them away. Now, unable to reach the grapes, she decided that they were sour. Unhappy, she poked her nose into other girls' affairs. Offering caustic comments, with the air of a moralist, she criticized "loose behavior," and now, to cap it all, she assumed an unbearable air of superior revolutionary fervor. I once heard her proclaim in a strident voice: "The best way to deal with these liberal dissidents is to give them a good blow to sober them up."

Dai Shi would have depressed me less had she been a Jezebel full of venom. But she was not. She was just an ordinary person but with a narrow mind, caricaturing the revolution while believing that she was helping it. Bit by bit, she dampened spirits all around her. When I saw that catty, disapproving look come over her face, I grew self-conscious and could no longer enjoy myself. I averted my eyes from her and looked out the window.

The scenery was absorbing. Because of the years of war, many of us, and all of us younger ones, were seeing these northlands for the first time. As we chugged westward, another visitor, our archaeologist, Hu, grew more and more excited, and finally persuaded me to give him my place by the window.

Hu had been the cashier at our theater. It was difficult to

find a job in the field of archaeology during the war years in the Guomindang regime, and so he had gone into the more practical business of counting money. But his first love was history, and he would spend all his spare time reading about the past and going to museums and antique shops. Periodically, at our discussions about work and discipline, he would upbraid himself for thinking too much about history and not enough about money. Now, money forgotten, he sat with his eyes glued to the window. The dusty old cities of Kaifeng and Luoyang, every mountain, mound, and river brought forth his "ohs" and "ahs" as he picked them out on his map. "This area was the cradle of Chinese civilization," he explained his absorbed interest almost apologetically.

Ma Li was in a carping mood. "I suspect you joined the land reform work with your eyes on the past," she chided. "You shouldn't think of this as a free trip to visit historical sites."

Hu shrugged his shoulders and pursed his lips. With his small, kind eyes, fat, round nose, and chubby cheeks, he seemed to be a man who preferred to be at peace with the world.

Chu Hua gazed up at the ceiling light. Her smiling eyes, perpetually amused, peeped out from under a fringe of black, luxuriant hair that fell out from under her khaki cadre's cap. "I plan to see as many ancient sculptures and paintings as possible. They'll help me to create new dance movements. What's wrong with that?"

But Ma Li would not retreat from her dogmatic stand. "You know we've been told again and again that we should keep our minds on our task," she insisted, "and that's the land reform."

Chu Hua tipped her head to one side and turned her round, doll-like eyes to Ma Li. She was obviously not satisfied with Ma Li's answer, but she did not rebut it. She too would rather shun than provoke an argument, partly out of good nature, but also out of a coquettish urge to please.

Yet her words had emboldened Hu. "In my opinion, one of the purposes of the land reform is to put new life into our dying culture. To do that we must also rediscover it."

Ma Li opened her mouth to speak but then thought better of it. It promised to be a complicated argument and she doubted if she could wage it single-handedly. Besides, she had also noticed that Dai Shi, listening from the inside corner, was girding herself for battle, and she had no wish to have Dai Shi as an ally.

As the train completed a wide curve, the landscape suddenly changed as if someone had shaken a kaleidoscope into a completely different pattern. At the foot of a mountain we saw a cluster of white-walled cottages with black-tiled roofs, a creek with a rushing stream, and a stone bridge. It was as beautiful a scene as any in the rich South and doubly entrancing after those miles and miles of dun-colored plains. Reminders of our gentle southland rushed through my brain, and I took a deep breath of happiness.

"The Hua Mountains!" someone cried in great excitement.

"It's our southern scenery right up here in the North," exclaimed Liao. He started humming some nostalgic southern tune and then said abruptly, "Let's sing its praises!" It was a cry from the heart. He was a southerner in the North, already homesick for the South.

"Good, let's sing," we all cried.

Liao gave the key and beat the rhythm. The carriage resounded with our voices. Only our soprano was silent. When she performed on the stage, she sang with passion and great artistry. Now she did not so much as open her mouth, but sat there demurely. The sunlight danced on the windowpane. Her profile, set off by this backdrop, was beautiful. Perhaps she didn't want to spoil the picture.

"Will we have time to climb Mount Hua?" the archaeologist Hu eagerly asked.

"The train will stop only for a few minutes," Ma Li answered.

"What a pity." Hu sank back disappointed.

"Perhaps we can climb up there on our way back," suggested Liao, gazing at the height wreathed with clouds.

An impish smile spread over Chu Hua's face. "So you too want to climb Mount Hua? 'Mount Hua in the midst of clouds and rain.' " To anyone who recognized the classical erotic association of mountains, clouds, and rain from folklore and literature, it was a daring remark.

Liao immediately blushed in response; luckily Dai Shi, never much of a scholar, missed the reference entirely. Ma Li, however, looked over at me, her eyebrows raised in sudden astonishment. I caught the soprano looking me straight in the eye, unblinking but with a hint of a knowing smile on her lips. Hu was too taken up by the scenery to notice anything else.

As Ma Li held up her cup to drink, she motioned with her little finger, pointing to the corridor. A moment later we were standing together outside the compartment.

"Shall I warn Chu Hua not to make a fool of herself?" She was clearly worried. Her big, black eyes were solemn. "You know how old-fashioned the peasants are. If Chu Hua talks and acts like she is talking and acting now, they'll think it's nothing less than free love and the end of the family. If even two of us misbehave, they'll suspect all of us. It would be a disaster."

"But we aren't in the village yet. Why not let them enjoy each other's company while they can? Don't be such a moralist."

"Don't you be too permissive," she retorted, unconvinced.

As I turned to re-enter the compartment, everyone was still crowded around the windows. But now the train had passed Mount Hua, and Wang Sha, who had come in while Ma Li and I were out in the corridor, was the center of their clamor.

"All right, all right," he was saying, "when we reach Xian you can spend a whole day visiting historical sights."

Mount Hua was forgotten. Now the talk was all about Xian, the Changan of the great dynasties of Han and Tang; China's Athens, Rome, and Constantinople rolled into one.

Arriving in Xian, we were like any other group of tourists in this ancient capital. We wanted to see everything: the Bell Tower, the White Crane Pagoda where the Buddhist scriptures were translated, the famous Tang dynasty reliefs of horses. Remembering our schoolday poetry lessons, we all wanted to see the Wei-yang Palace of the Han emperor with its

> *Rafters and ridgepoles of magnolia wood,*
> *Carved apricot wood for beams and pillars, and*
> *Golden clasps holding securing rings*
>   *on doors studded with jade.*

But most of all we wanted to see the E-fang Palace of Qin Shi Huang, the first emperor of the Qin dynasty, who had unified the warring petty feudal states into the first great empire of China. We were constantly told, "The peasants are waiting for you," but we gladly sacrificed sleep, rest, and food to satisfy our curiosity and look two thousand years into the past.

Leaving the gateway through the city wall, we bumped and clattered over farm roads in an antiquated bus until finally it came to a stop on the edge of some suburban farm fields, and our guide, a thin, bespectacled young man from the Archaeological Institute, solemnly intoned, "This is the E-fang Palace." We craned our necks out of the windows, looking for the palace. What we saw was a flat space with some haphazardly scattered mounds of muddy earth and old tiles, surrounded by a few trees, brambles, and fields. We were a bit cast down, but our guide could see a great deal more than we. He pointed out to us where once the famous audience halls and pavilion stood, gracing the earth with their splendid courtyards and gardens and sparkling streams. He described them all with enthusiasm and imagination as if all that splendor and magnificence were actually there before us, with towering columns of cedar and vermilion lacquer, marble pediments and golden ornaments tinkling at the corners of upturned eaves.

In the afternoon, we made our last excursion. We went to bathe in the Hua-qing hot springs where the famous beauty Yang Gui-fei, favorite of the Tang Emperor Ming Huang, had come to bathe twelve hundred years before. The once luxurious bathing rooms were now not much better than the bathhouses in any second-rate county town, but the water was still as delightful as in the days of the imperial favorite. Bubbling hot out of the ground, it filled the room with steam, and we were all flushed with the heat. Our eyes sparkled. In the half-light and vaporous clouds, pretty girls seemed prettier than ever. I was in a room with the soprano and Chu Hua. Eyes smiling, Chu Hua positioned herself in front of a long mirror, wiped the steam off it, and did a slow series of ballet movements, back straight, arms rounded and upraised, slender legs stretched forward and back, toes pointed, and then a graceful arabesque.

She darted me a glance through the mirror. Childishly she drew her neck down between her shoulders and put out her small pink tongue.

The soprano was reclining on a wicker couch covered with bright towels. Suddenly I heard Chu Hua say to her, "I am in love." Chu Hua's eyes opened wide as if surprised by her own words. "I am in love with someone," she repeated, standing motionless before the soprano as if her whole life hung on the outcome of this conversation. But the soprano did not seem to hear her. Unhurriedly she took a small pot of cold cream from the army duffle bag she carried.

"What did you say?" She carefully massaged her neck and throat with the cold cream. "You are in love?"

"But I don't know whether he loves me or not," Chu Hua pouted.

"Ah! Unconsummated love." The soprano paused in her movements, gazing at Chu Hua with a sentimental look in her eyes. The next moment, she sighed softly and a look of sadness veiled her face. With the stage thus set, she spoke to both Chu Hua and me in a subdued, earnest voice with great sincerity and relish about her own romance. "I was just sixteen when I fell in love with a man who lived on the same block as I did. We used to pass each other almost every day. He wore a French beret and looked very handsome in it. One day we began to say 'Hi' to each other, and soon we had made a date for dinner.

"I was in a fever of expectation as I waited for him in

the restaurant. I felt a sudden premonition of happiness. Then in he came, the same man, yet totally different. He wasn't wearing his beret."

Chu Hua, on tenterhooks, asked, "Did you confess your love for him?"

"To that total stranger? Of course not. I was in love with the man in the French beret."

"But it was the same man," I cried.

"Yes and no," said the soprano, and she went on lamenting her lost love.

We had been carried along with her story. She spoke expressively. Chu Hua could not get a word in edgeways about herself. When the soprano finished her story, she paused and then gave us some advice.

"Real love is always tragic. Read the great love stories. They are all great tragedies. Right? But who wants to fall in love in an ordinary way?" She looked from Chu Hua to me, obviously including me as one of three special people, with special sensibilities. Love, she continued lecturing, was a wonder that came in many forms. A fancy sometimes, a phantom; sometimes a splendid reality. We should not be rash. We should wait for that special person and be satisfied with no one else.

I learned later that she had recounted her story to many people. She herself never tired of it, and neither did her listeners, old or new like myself, because each time she told it there were new details and aspects never revealed before. Her lover was part real, part an amalgam of past loves, part fantasy—her ideal. Merging past and present loves into one, she invested that new creation with a life of its own. If some cynic asked her, "Which love are you talking about?" she would answer artlessly, even with tears in her eyes, "I was only in love once: my most cherished first love."

Hearing her talk gave Chu Hua time to cool off. But the warmth, the mists of steam, the associations of the place were heady. Perhaps as we emerged from the grotto it wasn't just we who felt like the beloved imperial beauty.

5 ★

Cold Welcome in Longxiang

Early the next morning the shrill voice of Dai Shi brought us back to reality and the task at hand. She strode down the corridor of the Xian Guest House, banging on doors and shouting, "Meeting! Meeting in the ballroom! Ten o'clock sharp!"

Xian was crowded with hundreds of cadres, work teams gathered from Peking, Tianjin, and other northern cities. Of the southern cities, only cosmopolitan Shanghai could send å large number of cadres who for some reason or other could speak Mandarin, the northern Chinese dialect. The Guest House, the tourist hotel once operated by the Guomindang government's travel agency, where we were staying four and five to a room, had the only hall in the city large enough to hold us all. We packed it wall to wall, and the old, worn clothes we wore especially for our coming stay in the villages seemed to mock the fancy chandeliers and the plush red velvet curtains still adorning the windows. From Xian we would disperse to the villages of the Northwest. This would be the final meeting before we left.

The speaker was a veteran Party member, full of years and experience. He had helped with land reform during the recent civil war, and at first we listened intently, expecting revelations. But he was too pedantic and humorless, and he droned on and on. I knew that I should listen and, like all the other cadres, I diligently noted down in my notebook everything he said. Whenever he paused all one could hear was the scratching of pens on paper.

"It is now more than a year since the Liberation. Things are in better shape. In the places where you are going, landlords' rents and rates of interest should have been lowered. That is the law. The peasants should have formed their Poor Peasants' Associations and their own militia. These will be the backbones of the land reform campaign. As it gets going, the middle-income peasants will side with them. You must try to get the rich peasants to remain neutral at the very least.

"Generally speaking, a bare three to five percent of the population in these areas are feudal landlords, but they hold sixty percent or more of the land. Expropriate all their land, tools, and draft animals, but," he paused and significantly repeated, "but not their needed houses and personal property. When a new local government is elected it will distribute land, tools, and beasts to those who need them. But you must see to it that the landlords and their families also get a share large enough to support themselves on."

We had heard most of this before, and I began to nod. He must have been an army propagandist once. When the troops marched, he was there by the roadside, beating his drum and shouting slogans so that, tired as they were, they would not fall asleep on their marching feet.

Just as I was beginning to doze off, he suddenly raised his voice: "What you are doing is something unprecedented in China and the world. Three hundred million peasants, one-sixth of the world's population, must liberate themselves from thirty centuries of feudal landlord domination. Smashing the landlords' economic power means smashing their political power. Only that can make secure the power of the people."

As I recall it, perhaps it would have been better if we had paid more heed to his words: "Put frivolous thoughts behind you. Concentrate all your thoughts on the work at hand."

• • •

We left Xian the next day at daybreak. It was a short journey by train due west to Baoji, where at that time the line ended. There a convoy of open trucks was waiting by the side of the unfinished railroad, and soon we were roaring along the ancient caravan trail to the Northwest, first to Lanzhou, the capital of Gansu Province, and then on again across the bed of the Yellow River, almost dry in the autumn drought.

We entered the panhandle of Gansu, the long neck of upland valley leading to the Plateau of Central Asia. This is where the Great Wall ends, fifteen hundred miles from where it starts on the Gulf of Liaodong. Then we drove across the northern spurs of the Big Snow Mountains, whose peaks, solitary and grand, thrust into the autumn clouds.

Soon the road was climbing the steep flanks of a mountain. Looking down I saw a river raging through a gorge with a sheer precipice on either side. I had never seen such landscapes except in picture books. I tightened my hold on the side of the swaying truck. I was glad to be with Ma Li and clowning Cheng. It reassured me to know that Wang Sha was in the last of the convoy of trucks bringing up the rear. Sometimes, as we zigzagged up the mountain road, I could look down and see the last truck directly below us, two hundred feet down, laboring up the steep rise. Wang Sha sat in a back corner, covered with yellow dust.

Our ancient truck, a resurrected wreck made of cannibalized parts, wheezed and creaked along the road. Once near the top of a narrow pass, where the wheels of countless carts had worn deep dust-filled ruts in the track, it groaned to a stop. The driver tried to coax it back to life, then at his urgent command we all sprang to the ground and put our shoulders to its wheels, pushing and dragging, getting it moving slowly inch by inch up the hill, until, with a sudden spurt, it made the summit.

As we went further west our convoy grew smaller,

groups of trucks branching off to the north and south to carry the work teams to their destinations.

The wind howled down a gorge. I remembered words from a classical poem:

> *The wind called up columns of sand and stones,*
> *They madly whirled as if they danced on wings.*

Now I saw this with my own eyes. Thick yellow dust dimmed the light of the sun. We had been issued surgical gauze masks, and although I wore one over my mouth and nose and kept my lips shut as tightly as I could, the fine sand still seeped through and I felt grit in my mouth. A Tang dynasty poem called this a "barren, barbarous land never reached by the Spring breeze." I could well believe it.

As dusk descended quickly in the gorge, making further progress dangerous, we stopped for the night at a small inn near the head of a pass. Inn is perhaps too fancy a word for a couple of hovels tucked in a cleft of the cliff where they were partly sheltered from the wind. They had no beds or separate rooms or any conveniences. Just two bare rooms with half their space taken up by low kangs.

Here at least for foreign and southern readers who sleep on beds, and never saw kangs, I think I should explain that the kang in a northern house does not only serve as a bed. At night when you spread your bedding on it, it is your bed. During the daytime when you have rolled up your bedding and stacked it on one side, the kang can be used as a place to work, eat, and receive visitors on. A large kang can take up half the space in a room. It is actually a raised room within a room, a split-level room, the inner, raised one with a flue beneath it where a fire can be lit for warmth. Here, in the northern villages, when guests come visiting, you invite them to sit by the low-legged table set on the kang: "Come onto the kang. You don't have to take your shoes off. It's quite all right for you to keep them on." But, of course, polite guests will certainly remove their shoes before getting on the kang or they will sit with their feet dangling over its side.

In these two hovels there were only the kangs for beds. The men left these for us twenty-five girls. They brought in bundles of hay which they had found outside and spread this on the dirt floor to make extra beds for themselves.

It was decided that we should start next morning at first light and press on to the plateau which was our destination. Exhausted by the day's journey, we hurriedly ate what food we had ready with us and then threw ourselves down, dressed just as we were and huddled together for warmth, to sleep.

My drowsy eyes wandered around our inn. A little light came in through the cracks in the door, which was close to falling off its hinges, and through the single window, which was hardly more than a hole in the wall roughly latticed with slivers of wood and white paper. But those same cracks in the doorway and around the window let in drafts of cold air. An oil lamp in the wall niche burned smokily. In its dim, flickering light, I stared in mounting alarm at the beams overhead, black and furry with soot and grime. Ugly black bugs and spiders crawled jerkily across them.

"There's worse to come." Ma Li lay beside me, pressing her mouth against my shoulder.

"Umgh."

"Do you hear that wolf howling?"

"Umgh." I did not want to say anything stupidly comforting that might only increase her misgivings.

"The latrines are all outside. If we go out in the middle of the night, will the wolves attack us?" Chu Hua asked anxiously.

"We'll go together." Reassuring, but what good I would be in case of an attack by wolves I hadn't the faintest idea. I was afraid even of a cat.

"I'll go with you," Ma Li added. She knew my weakness.

"I hope we'll be assigned to the same village," Chu Hua sighed.

"I doubt if the three of us will work together. But you two might try," Ma Li said with the magnanimity of one who felt stronger and superior.

I looked around again at our inn. The earthen walls were

pitted with ugly dents where large pieces of loess and straw plaster had fallen off.

The innkeeper was of a piece with the hovels he looked after. His face was a dense web of wrinkles. Although he said he was still in middle age, he looked like a hoary veteran of seventy. His perpetual squint against the wind-borne Gobi sand, the blinding summer sunshine, the bitter winter cold had etched fine lines around his eyes. His habit of silence had formed deep-set lines around his mouth. His clothes were so patched with different shades of cotton that there was no way of telling the original color of his suit. Never had I seen such poverty, not even in the slums of Shanghai where at least the poor could rifle through the garbage bins of the rich.

We had traveled for a whole day over this ancient land. The further west we had come, the more poverty-stricken, worn-out, and dilapidated was the countryside. We were on the Old Silk Road where once rich caravans passed laden with silks and brocades, jades and other finery. Imperial couriers in princely trappings had coursed through here at breakneck speed bringing the emperors news from the Western Regions. Surely they never slept in such squalor.

At first, we had marveled at the strangeness of the landscape. It was a plain riven by deep gullies so that the dirt road either meandered wildly to avoid the slits in the earth or plunged zigzag down and up the sides of the ravines that couldn't be avoided. The earth had been ravaged and made desolate. I knew from my history books that these eroded lands were once pastures and forested plateaus. Then the pastures had been ploughed up to grow crops and the forests had been cleared for farmland. The natural rhythm of nature had been disturbed. The animals had disappeared and so had their dung. War had devastated the farms. Marauding warlord armies had chopped down the remaining trees for firewood. Without vegetation to hinder them, the rains and run-off rivulets of centuries had eaten into the fields and carried them away. The green clothing of the earth had been filched and the naked earth was dying of cold.

I sighed disconsolately.

Ma Li and I were separated at the county town which would be the center of our work teams' activities. We learned that since there were not enough women cadres, only one could be sent to each township group of villages and hamlets. By this time the leaders, headed by Wang Sha, had a pretty fair idea of the work teams' rank and file, so it was not too difficult to decide the makeup of the small groups of work teams. I was quite inexperienced in mass work so they teamed me up with Malvolio Cheng, a veteran; Wang Sha himself would be the third member of our small team. As a senior cadre, he would have a great deal of work to do supervising several teams and helping with overall guidance at the county center; in fact, he would stay for another day or so of talks with the county leadership to plan the first steps of work in the area, but Cheng and I were told to prepare to leave for our work post immediately.

Next morning the work teams dispersed in groups of three or four to their several destinations in the surrounding villages. Cheng and I piled our baggage onto an ox cart and arranged our bedding so that we had something to sit on. Like everything else in this region, it was a decrepit wreck, a travesty of a cart. No single piece of wood on it was straight or flat. Its cartwright had evidently lacked tools and proper timber and hacked it out with an adze. It jolted along the rough track that served for a road. The wheels squeaked maddeningly for lack of grease, and the cart's shape changed alarmingly as it negotiated the ruts and potholes. I was worried that it might disintegrate at any moment and was thankful that the bullock in the shafts was plodding along even slower than a man could walk. I sat next to our taciturn driver and dozed as we swayed. Every now and then I roused myself to look at the slowly passing landscape. Sometimes I got off impatiently to walk ahead, but that simply meant a long, tedious wait for them to catch up with me or added anxiety that I might have taken the wrong road.

Malvolio Cheng was as cheerful as I was at the start. But after the first hour or two he too fell silent, lulled by the monotonous swaying of the cart and the bleak landscape around us. Finally the only sound was the creaking of the cart. We passed few people on the road.

Towards noon we approached a district market town where we stopped to rest and feed the ox. This was smaller than the county center we had left but larger, I supposed, than the township of Longxiang we were making for. Near a river crossing, it was a walled town with most of its wall intact, fifteen feet high, made of hand-hewn stones surrounded by a now empty moat. Crossing a low, humpbacked bridge, we entered it through a narrow gateway. Weathered wooden gates bound and studded with rusty iron lay back in niches in the wall. I noticed that the hinges were black with grease. It was evident that they had only recently become museum pieces. Beyond them, the tunnel of the gateway opened onto a narrow cobble-stoned street between rickety, low houses. They were so close together that long poles spanned the space between the windowsills of opposite houses and washing fluttered above the heads of pedestrians. Open drains flanked the roadway. There was limitless land outside the town walls, but over the decades, banditry and freebooters had driven more and more people to seek safety in the crowded space within the stout medieval walls. From there they sallied out each day to the surrounding farm fields. I had seen just such a street scene in a Song dynasty painting. It had not changed for a thousand years.

A few open-fronted shops were doing business. A mosaic of color spilled out from the opulent dry-goods shop: bolts of blue and white cotton, colors of life and death; enamel washbasins with gaudy old designs of simpering, rosy-cheeked beauties or flowers and birds; gay ribbons and socks dyed with red and emerald green stripes; cheap mirrors and colorful, shiny Thermos bottles, a fantastic luxury that most peasants could only gape at. Further down in front of a food shop were a few large vats of dark, unappetizing-looking pickles, dried herbs, and salted meat encrusted with brine and dust. In an ironmonger's shop covered with a grey film of iron filings a tinsmith was cutting up old kerosene cans to make crude kettles and pans. The bare shelves of other shops gave no clue to what they sold. The owners or apprentices lolling over the counters followed us with lackluster eyes. They were like Rip Van Winkles wakened by the noise of our approaching cart, sleepy and annoyed rather than curious at the disturbance we made. We smelled the sharp odor of vinegar, the barnyard stench of latrines, and the fragrance of incense sticks.

Slow as it was, our cart crossed the town in a few minutes and emerged through the opposite gateway into the open countryside. Ancient, crumbling, feudal, the half-awake town still dominated the parched land around it. When I looked back I thought how much the battlemented walls looked like stage props now, and yet two thousand years ago generals of the Han dynasty had fought great wars here against the Huns and driven them westward to crush the Roman Empire. Then this became a western borderland of China. The emperors used to send exiles here, criminals or dissidents, rebellious scholars. Desperate characters, outlaws and free spirits, used to make their way here seeking safety in anonymity in the wild and harsh Northwest where one did not ask possibly embarrassing questions of a newcomer.

As I looked at the desolation around me, I knew how far I was in time as well as space from the always green southland and Shanghai, that Paradise of Adventurers now purging itself of its past and boldly proclaiming itself a new modern city. Here in the Gansu countryside, everything—land, sky, cottages, even the people in the distance—was yellow-grey in the fading autumn light, dun-colored, cold. I could not see a single green leaf or blade of grass. And yet there was change here too. We trundled over a new bridge built of stone. It was then that I noticed that the town wall on this side had been pulled down and its stones brought here to build the bridge.

Twilight began to fall. We passed even fewer people on

the road. Soon our ox cart was the only thing moving on
this wide, dead plateau stretching emptily into the distance, a speck in the yellow valleys of Gansu. Something
damp and cold fell on my hand. I started, surprised, and
then realized that it was Cheng, our clown, holding my
hand. I drew my hand back slowly, slowly enough to let
him understand that I had no wish to hurt his feelings, but
not so slowly as to allow him to mistake it for shyness on
my part. I was sympathetic and yet had no intention of
obliging him when he needed a loved one in this loneliness. He turned his head away. I caught a glimpse of a
triangular scar on the back of his head. A blow? A wound
in battle? I wondered, and yet I never asked.

It was almost dark when, passing an empty pond and a
grove of now leafless trees, we finally reached Longxiang,
our destination. The village was nothing more than a sorry
collection of cottages built of rammed earth, loess soil
mixed with puddled clay and chopped straw, and roofed
with the same adobe. The roadway between the cottages
was deeply rutted and eroded by the rain-wash from their
roofs. A few houses, built of blue-grey bricks and roofed
with black tiles, had solid walls around them and arched
gateways leading to inner courtyards. Dim lights from
small kerosene lanterns lit a few of their windows. In the
peasants' homes, too poor for oil lights, they groped
around in the dusk. It was too dark for work, too early for
bed; immobile, obscure shadows, they stood or squatted at
their front doors. Tiny dots of flame in their pipes flickered
red in the twilight. A stray dog sniffed and licked at the
roots of a leafless tree. Some ragged children, still stuffing
their evening meal of porridge into their mouths, ran after
our cart.

Our cart stopped outside what seemed to be an abandoned shop. A roughly painted sign beside the door indicated that it was the office of the Longxiang Provisional
Township Government and Communist Party Group.
"Group" meant there were not even the five Party members needed to form a committee. Two peasant cadres hurried out to greet us.

"Welcome! Welcome!"

It was good to hear their obvious pleasure at our arrival. They bustled around and helped us take our baggage from the cart. We introduced ourselves. Their names were Shen and Tu.

Something was wrong with Shen's eyes. When he spoke to me, one eye looked at me and the other squinted at something else. But he seemed quite jolly all the same. Tu, after a perfunctory greeting, looked on soberly while Shen did the honors. Tu was tall and strongly built, clearly well able to take care of himself. His jacket was unbuttoned even in this chilly evening, revealing swelling muscles under his vest. The lines of his face were set, hard, and immobile. I didn't like him.

Shen's first greeting had been cheerful, but when he looked beyond us, saw no one else, and realized that there were only the two of us, he showed some surprise with a touch of disappointment. "Just you . . . !" he let slip. But to tell the truth, if I had been in his place I wouldn't have been much impressed by this work team either. So I hastened to reassure him: "Comrade Wang Sha, the head of our work team, will come later."

After our long journey, this subdued reception was a real letdown. The newsreels had shown peasants meeting work teams on the road with clashing cymbals and drums. In other places there was less fanfare, but I had never heard of any cadres getting such a cold greeting as this one. Our village, as I quickly tried to rationalize, was abysmally poor and remote and off the beaten track. Shen and Tu did make some effort as our hosts. They poured hot water into a battered enamel basin so that we could at least wash up, and they gave us a simple meal of a strange dish they called pian-er gruel. Then Tu took my heavy bag and escorted me to my home while Shen guided Malvolio Cheng in the opposite direction.

Tu led me to a cottage on the outer fringe of the hamlet. It had three doors and was inside a walled enclosure, but the wall offered small protection; it merely indicated the limits of the compound. Opposite was a courtyard with another cottage in it. As I shone my flashlight to see where I was going, from the corner of my eye I glimpsed a female figure in a red jacket disappearing around the opposite corner.

A single family, Tu told me, inhabited two rooms of the cottage which would now be my home. I was given the empty end room. I felt the coldness of the welcome even more. My neighbors must have heard us approaching, but their doors remained tightly closed. No one even put his head out to take a look.

My quarters turned out to be an outer room empty except for a shaky table with three sound legs and a broken fourth. Beyond was a smaller, inner room—tiny, windowless, with no door in its doorway, containing the kang. Tu gave me an oil-blackened earthenware lamp with a smoky wick and abruptly said good night. When he had gone I looked around my new home. I found that the latch on the door was broken. My unease increased. I had heard many times already that landlords had murdered land reform work team cadres. Had I played into their hands? I didn't even know where Cheng was. I felt a cold shudder pass through me. Trying to put these thoughts aside, I dusted off my clothes, threw myself fully dressed on the kang, and covered myself with my quilt.

Time went by, but despite my fatigue I could not sleep. In a corner near the kang a spiderweb glittered in the moonlight. I inadvertently touched it with my elbow. It quivered and a villainous-looking spider dashed out of hiding. Trying to sense its prey, it stopped short on the swaying web. It circled around menacingly and then once again retreated into its hiding place.

I heard a rustling sound at the latticed window. I thought it might be a rat gnawing at something on the windowsill. I threw my slipper at the square of light. I missed it, but a tomcat poised outside gave a screech of alarm and fled. My neighbor to the right thought that the cat was attacking her chicks. I heard her unlatch her door, mutter a curse, and reset the old millstone that secured the door of the chicken coop.

I got up, wetted my finger, and pressed it through the paper which covered the window. I could see through the small hole I had made. A light flickered in the gloom opposite and then went out. Someone had lighted a match. Who could be up and about at this late hour? I grew even more apprehensive as I kept my vigil. From the shadows of the doorway in the cottage opposite a man and woman emerged for a moment into a fleeting gleam of moonlight. The woman was the one I had seen earlier in the red jacket. Now she was buttoning it up. She inclined her head in my direction as she whispered to the man. When he turned to follow her gaze I saw it was Tu. My heart skipped a beat and then fluttered like a mad thing as Tu made what seemed a stealthy step towards my room. Then he stopped short and gaped. The woman withdrew into the house.

I did not know what to make of this charade. It certainly boded no good. For a long time I kept watch at the window, but all remained quiet. Finally, drained by fear and weariness, I dragged the three-legged table against the door, threw myself down on the kang again, and slept the sleep of utter exhaustion.

The next morning, breakfastless except for a piece of stale steamed bread I had saved from the day before, I went early to the township office. I wanted to move out of that courtyard, but I thought I should discuss the matter first with Wang Sha when he arrived. The office was empty. Shen and Tu had not yet come in.

Longxiang still had no telephone, or even a single bicycle. The only way to contact the county town twenty miles away was by ox cart or on foot. Anxious to talk to someone, I decided to find Malvolio Cheng, and knocked on doors till I finally found a soft-spoken old farmer who agreed to lead me to the cottage where Cheng was staying.

I found him sitting cross-legged on his kang smoking a small-bowled peasant pipe with a long stem and a tiny bag of tobacco hung on it. With his half-closed eyes staring at the pipe bowl while he listened to me, he was already the very picture of an old peasant, a new and interesting role for him. Peasant men did not look at women. When they talked to a woman, they looked at something straight ahead as if they were talking to some other man in the same room.

I told him of my experience the night before, leaving out the fact that I had seen Tu and the woman in red. I mentioned only that I had seen someone moving near the courtyard opposite.

"Cheng, are you listening?"

"Yes."

"What shall I do, then?"

"Well, I think . . . I don't think . . ." He even mumbled like an old peasant talking to a strange woman. I could hardly hear what he said.

"Cheng, please don't act awkward," I cried, exasperated.

"Well then," he spoke in his normal voice. "You don't want Shen and Tu to know that you are already scared out of your wits even before we start our work, and yet you want to shift your quarters?"

"That's about it."

With a sudden twinkle in his eyes, he waved his arms like a dancer. "You learned to do the peasant *yangge* dance and sing peasant folk songs before you came here. Why don't you go out and dance and sing? That's the way to make friends in the village. Then you can move to your new friend's home."

"You want me to put on some kind of monkey show on the street to entertain the villagers? How about coming with me? I'll dance and you can hold out your hat to collect the coins."

"I'm serious. You girls were asked to learn dancing and singing, because that's the sure way to win the peasants' hearts. They like it."

I stalked out of the cottage and slammed the door shut in half-mock anger. But outside in the bright autumn sunshine I thought over what he had said. I could think of no better plan; why not give his a try? As I wandered rather aimlessly around the village, Cheng's crazy idea came back to mind and, my courage aroused, I began to weave romantic fantasies of carrying out the land reform all on my own. But when a mongrel dog approached me, growl-

ing angrily, my heart sank into my boots. I have a phobia
about dogs, but to bolster my courage I picked up a stick
and put on a bold front. Fortunately the dog took fright
first. This little comedy attracted several children and,
curious, they began to follow me around.

With a burst of confidence, I decided to give singing a
chance and, coaxing them into line, began with a simple
children's song composed for the land reform by some Peking musicians. One boy, about eleven years old, took to
the idea with gusto. He sang at the top of his voice, rolling
his eyes and swaying his head comically in time with the
beat. We attracted a crowd of more children, and even a
few adults. This further inspired me to introduce myself to
them formally. With the children's chorus ranged in front
of me, I addressed my words over their heads to the knot
of older folk gathered behind them.

"Fellow villagers," I began. We had been told to identify
ourselves immediately with the peasants. "We have come
to help you carry out the land reform. You toil on the land,
day and night, all the year around, and yet you are dressed
in rags and you are hungry. Why?"

I thought these words would act like a spell and inflame
their souls. I thought I would hear them give answering
shouts to my slogans: "Long live the land reform!" "Down
with the feudal landowners!" But after listening soberly
enough while I spoke, some drifted away as if embarrassed. Others laughed as though I had been a street per-
former doing tricks or a patent medicine seller making his
pitch. They had enjoyed it. It wasn't every day that you
could see a young girl making a speech, but when the
show was over they sauntered off to gossip about it to
their neighbors.

I found myself alone with the children, alone except for
an attractive and robust young girl about my own age who
stood on a slope of parched grass about ten steps away.
We caught each other's eyes. She looked away shyly, lifting her eyes to the sky and then lowering them to gaze
fixedly at the ground below her.

I went over to her. "What is your name?"

"Xiu-ying," she replied in a barely audible voice.

"Xiu-ying, did you understand what I was talking about?"

She was too shy to say anything, but gave me a friendly smile.

"My name is Ling-ling." To liven up our chat, I added, "Actually my real given name is Ling-long. Do you know what Ling-long means?"

She made no reply but waited for me to continue.

"It means 'lively and pleasant.' But when I was small, it was easier for me to remember my name as Ling-ling. Do you know what your name means?"

She shook her head again.

"It means that you are a pretty, intelligent, and brave girl."

"I wish my mother could hear you say that."

"She will. Why don't we go to tell her?"

We found her mother at home. A heavyset woman, like many northerners, kind and hospitable, she was bustling about her household chores. The father, a similarly thick-set northerner, was a gruff-voiced patriarch, very much the head of the family. Her younger brother was the very image of his father, but pint-sized. I wondered from whom Xiu-ying had inherited her good looks.

Xiu-ying was unusual among the girls of the township in several ways. First, she could read and write. She had had three years of schooling, and she showed me her tattered old textbooks and exercise books and even a world atlas. Her education had come about by one of those strange quirks of fortune: An enlightened local administrator, an old scholar, came to the village filled with lofty ideas of rebuilding the nation through education, and he had a feminist wife who had bobbed her hair and taken a minor part in the 1924–1927 revolution. Xiu-ying had attracted their attention and had been recruited for the school they had briefly run before being removed by the Guomindang government for "radical activity." Xiu-ying had kept alive the glimmer of enlightenment she had received, and it flared to life again immediately when she got news of the arrival of our work team. She would never have dared present herself to Shen or Tu or Malvolio Cheng, but a girl was different. We had much to tell and learn from each other.

Her brother peered inquisitively around her shoulder and put his head over the textbook she was showing me, vainly trying to elucidate the large characters. I could not see the pages. Xiu-ying slapped his shaven head. He cried "ouch," compressed his lips, and pulled away. Their mother apologized for her daughter.

"Although we are poor people, we have spoiled her. Xiu-ying is still childish. She often squabbles with her little brother."

"When we start a reading class, please let Xiu-ying come," I begged.

"She is a girl. What is the good of her studying?" the mother said, stroking the boy's head.

"Aren't I a girl too?"

"But you have a lucky face. She is fated to suffer."

Learning from my experience that morning I did not press the point. There was no shaking her belief that women were not as good as men and they had better know that their proper place was in the kitchen. Over two thousand years of Confucian teaching had molded her mind: "The sovereign guides the subject, the father guides the son, and the husband guides the wife," even if experience and common sense had shown her many ways of guiding her husband.

That evening, Xiu-ying helped me carry my bags to her house. She cleared a place for me to sleep beside her in a room barely larger than the kang. As soon as my head touched the pillow I fell asleep and, secure, slept like a log till morning.

6

The Women

At that final meeting in Xian we had been told to take two days to get settled in. "Get to know your way around. Even if it's only groping in the dark." I was really happy to be with Xiu-ying and her family and share her kang; she in turn was delighted to show me around. That was the easy part of settling in. Some other things were not so easy to get used to.

We cadres did not cook for ourselves but ate with the poor peasants. Going from house to house in rotation, we ate two meals a day in the homes of peasants introduced to us by Shen and Tu. To live, eat, and work with them was the way we pledged our loyalty, service, and friendship to them; fine ideas, but my first meal with a poor peasant was close to disaster.

Malvolio Cheng and I sat cross-legged in the center of the kang in the home of one of the poorer peasants. Our hostess, apologetic and dying of consumption, lay propped up in a corner beside us. The light filtering in through the small paper-covered window suffused her face, sad-eyed and listless. Our host took his bowl of gruel to sit beside the stove. He did not eat it; he threw it down his throat. Then he licked the bowl all over.

"You see, one's tongue can do the same job as a washing machine," Malvolio Cheng said, trying to cheer me up.

I looked down into my bowl. This was my second encounter with pian-er gruel, our daily fare as long as we lived in Longxiang. I never did find out what it was made of. Sometimes it had a bit of flour in it and sometimes corn with generous additions of husk. An unappetizing greyish-yellow color, thick as paste and spiced with rough-ground salt and dried peppers, it was as gritty as sand and rasped my tongue. I took a mouthful.

It crossed my mind that they probably only owned three bowls, so our hostess could not eat with us. Either Cheng or I was using the dying woman's bowl. A wave of nausea rose from the pit of my stomach. I put down my bowl.

"Go on eating." Cheng's voice was stern.

"It's too hot." My throat indeed was burning. I swallowed hard to get rid of the pain.

"Go—on—eating." His voice was now terribly insistent.

I took my bowl up again and felt no better for noticing a roach twitching its feelers before burrowing itself in a crack of our low table. Finally my manners prevailed. My aunt had taught me that if I saw something go wrong at table, such as someone dropping coffee on my dress, I should pretend not to notice it. Clenching my teeth tightly, I finished everything in the bowl.

"Thank you for a very good meal." Having licked his bowl and wiped his mouth with his sleeve, Cheng bowed to our hosts.

"Thank you very much." I followed his example, dutifully performing the whole ritual.

No sooner had we left the house than I felt that I was going to throw up all the food that I had managed to hold down up to then. My stomach was churning. I gave a terrified start and turned to run. I collided with an old tree and vomited on and on as if I would empty out everything that was inside me.

"Don't make such a noise!" Cheng admonished quietly. "They may hear you inside. Don't forget that they are feeding us free as their contribution to the land reform work."

"I can't help it." I felt weak and sat on a handy broken wall. I clenched my hands together, braced them between my knees, and tried to hold my aching sides with my elbows.

"Yes you can," Cheng snapped. I looked startled. The sharp tone was so unlike him. "Just remember that your expensive life style was supported by the labor and want of the millions like our hosts."

"Don't give me that stuff," I moaned.

"You had better get used to it. It's the only dish you'll get and you'd better learn to like it." He refused to feel sorry for me. We parted at the crossroads without another word.

And so I began to wander around the township "groping in the dark." A few minutes' walk in any direction always brought me out to the surrounding earthen wall and moat and the fields beyond, dotted with groups of cottages or isolated, more solid-looking houses of brick with tiled roofs, surrounded with brick walls, quite evidently the homes of better-off peasants or landlords. There were no hedges or walls in the fields, and with the autumn harvest in, there was no way that I could see of telling where one farm ended and another began. Foot-high stone markers didn't offer much help. Stubbled fields and barrens spread as far as the eye could reach, broken only by low hills or ravines. Bare mountains ringed the horizon.

Returning to the township center I stopped here and there to chat with women I met. Here again my aunt's training in making conversation with guests came in handy.

"Isn't he a cute baby?" "Are you making a jacket for your husband?" I had soon learned the peasant's usual morning greeting: "Have you eaten?"

Hoping to take a shortcut in my "groping," on my second day in Longxiang I went to chat with the village cadre Shen. His office was just an ordinary peasant's room, but a bit larger than most. There were quite a number of empty houses and rooms in the village—many peasants had left during the last famine and never returned—and the provisional government had simply requisitioned one of these, a former shop on the main road, for its office. Shen had knocked two rooms into one to form a single large room.

On one side of it was a large kang; in the opposite corner was a dusty, broken cabinet, and in the middle a long trestle table with a few wooden benches around it. A poster on the wall showed how to build better latrines, while a chart with pictures showed how to develop a compost heap in six steps. Hanging from a nail in the wall by a string tied around its spine was the "library"—a copy of the *Farmers' Calendar*. Shen was affable and readily answered all my questions.

"Is this the Longxiang Party headquarters too?" I asked, and he nodded.

"And how many Party members are there?"

"Just me. I joined the Party right after the area was liberated a year ago. Tu is still a candidate member. But I'm sure many more men will join in the coming land reform campaign."

"And you have a Poor Peasants' Association already formed?"

"Right here," he grinned.

"And the headquarters of the Peasant Militia?"

"Here too." The grin was wider.

"And the Chairman of the Peasants' Association?"

"He is in Lanzhou with his eldest son's family."

"When will he come back?"

"Who knows? The old man likes to nag. Last year he quarreled with his second son and he left home. Just like that," Shen said. I marveled at his serenity, but continued to "grope."

"Old Shen," I said in a confidential tone. "Do you really have a Poor Peasants' Association?"

"Of course." He went to the cabinet and took out a sheaf of papers. "Here you are: the complete list of members," he proudly declared.

I thumbed through the sheets carefully. "How come most of the members are either men over sixty or boys under ten? Where are the able-bodied men and women?" I felt the darkness thickening.

"Well, when we asked them to put their names down, they suspected that we wanted to press-gang them or something like that, and yet they didn't want to be left behind if we really intended to hand out land. So they sent their old fathers and uncles to register in the Poor Peasants' Association. They reasoned that if it was a trick, there would be no use taking in old men over sixty. If we really meant business, they could always argue that the old man represented the whole family. Some families hadn't got any old men left, so they put down their small sons' names."

"How can a small boy represent the whole family?"

"Oh it happens all the time. My son's name is Spring Boy. Our villagers call me Spring Boy's Pa and my wife Spring Boy's Ma, and—"

"But where is the man in charge of the militia?" I was determined to sort the situation out properly.

"He went off somewhere to peddle goods during the last spring hunger."

"Old Shen," I brushed aside the lists, "these are meaningless pieces of paper, filled with meaningless words!"

"But that's what reports are—words, right?" It was his turn to be mystified.

"What reports?"

"Aren't you going to write a report about our work here?"

I burst into helpless giggles. "Old Shen, if I ever write about this place, I will certainly give you a good write-up. You deserve it."

He beamed at me. "I try to be a good cadre. I hope by now the villagers can see how different I am from the old village head, Landlord Chi. He was a favorite of the Guomindang. Landlord Chi got rich quick when he took over that post—he was a good gambler, and whenever he wanted money, he forced the peasants to gamble with him. When they played with him, they were only allowed to lose, you know. But since I took on this job, I became poorer. I don't get paid for it, and my three children and my wife and I live off what we can grow on our own few *mu*. If I could help my wife work on it, we might eke out some sort of living. But you see how busy I am. Do I get any thanks? No, none at all. I get criticized and criticized. You know, whoever is the housekeeper gets the blame. A

whole crowd even came here to criticize me openly—it
made me so mad! They shouted at me and I shouted back,
'You foul-mouthed bastards, throw your dirty words at the
feudal landlords if you dare. Did you ever dare? No, you
cowards!' My wife wanted me to quit. I told her to shut up.
'Woman,' I said, 'you cannot quit the Revolution.' "

Intrigued by what he had said, I asked, "What makes
you so determined to hang on to this job?"

"Because I am poor," he replied simply. "From the beginning my wife didn't like it. 'You fool, haven't you got
yourself into enough trouble by being meddlesome?' she
whined. I told her, 'Woman, I was born that way and I
cannot help it.' " He waved his hand in a "who the hell
cares?" gesture.

"Old Shen, thank you for your help. I hope we can talk
again soon."

"No problem. Anytime. I tell everybody that he can drop
by and have a chat anytime and they do." Shen did not
seem to realize that some people might be trying to exploit
his warmheartedness. He was pleased with his popularity.

Wang Sha arrived on the third day. We had a meeting
with Shen and Tu and it was agreed that we should start
making a systematic round of all the peasant households
and ask them to join our meetings. We hoped that there
they would tell about their lives in the past. It was, as
Wang Sha put it, a means of "raising their level of consciousness." "Speak bitterness meetings," as they were
called, would help them to understand how things really
had been in the old days, to realize that their lives were
not blindly ordained by fate, that the poor peasants had a
community of interest, having suffered similar disasters
and misery in the past—and that far from owing anything
to the feudal landlords, it was the feudal landlords who
owed them a debt of suffering beyond all reckoning.

Wang Sha and Malvolio Cheng, Shen, and Tu rallied the
men; the women and children were left to me. Xiu-ying
and her mother were of invaluable help in this task.
Through them I met quite a few women in the village, and

for several days I visited them in their homes and talked with them.

Talking with Xiu-ying's family first, I thought my job would be a simple one: They had their differences, but it was a close-knit, happy, outgoing family. The mother was living again through her daughter, whom she loved. The father, though grudging, was trying to restrain himself from interfering.

But they were exceptions. Most women I met would only speak guardedly about their lives; as to doing something about changing their lives, they believed that was useless. Their suffering had little to do with landlord exploitation. Everything was predestined, all their hardships and subjection. The landlords or whoever were simply the instruments of fate. Once when I urged a middle-aged woman to speak further, she gave a heavy sigh, pressed her hands to her breast, and murmured, "The bitterness is here. I can't get it out." They refused to accept me as a living example of a girl who had "come out of the kitchen." I came from Shanghai—another planet to them—where the natural laws were different; besides, I had what they considered "a lucky face." For these reasons they tolerated my often "strange" behavior like mixing with men almost as if I were a man myself.

Only two women refused to talk to me at all.

First there was the virgin widow, a short, big-boned woman with over-broad shoulders. Twenty years previously, when she was only fourteen, her betrothed died suddenly on the very eve of their wedding. But the compact had been made, the marriage presents had been given, and she was married anyway. A small wooden tablet with his name inscribed on it "stood in" for the groom. But the death was taken as a sign that Heaven's curse had fallen on her. Barbarous old village custom regarded her as being responsible for the death of this man whom she never even laid eyes on and she was semi-ostracized by the village. The silence of the grave had surrounded her for twenty years, and she had almost lost her capacity for communicating with others. I could not get a word out of her.

The other one was the wife of the farm laborer Sun Zu-guang.

If I had played my aunt's garden hose long enough on the Suns' hovel it would have dissolved back into the yellow loess earth it was made of. Nothing would have remained except for a few rafters, a door and window frame, a couple of rickety stools, a table, an iron pot, and some chipped crockery. Sun was at home when I went to visit his wife. It was a bright day, and their door was open to let in warmth and light. I stopped with one foot on the doorsill, waiting for them to invite me in. But Sun shot a sidelong glance at his wife, and she scurried to hide herself behind the stove in the room. I just caught a glimpse of her: two emaciated arms folded over an enormous belly and a pair of short, stick-like legs. I tried to exchange a few pleasantries with him, but he stubbornly stared into space in front of him, lips compressed, not saying a word. I sat myself down on the doorsill. He did not budge. I began to give a lengthy explanation of my visit. I spoke loudly and slowly, so that every word would be clear to them both. Several times Sun's wife, consumed with curiosity, took a peek at me and I saw her tousled hair, scanty and brownish because of malnutrition, appearing above the top of the stove, but each time Sun growled like some watchdog, and immediately his wife's head disappeared. I had been told that Sun's mother, a widow, had run away with a stranger when Sun was only six or seven years old, and he had been left an orphan. Ever since he had sulked in a perpetual state of obstinate sullenness, never trusting any woman or any "intruder" again. He shut his wife off from the outside world. I hated to see his glowering face grow mean, the forehead strained and protruding, the chin jutting out, the mouth curling into a cruel snarl as he turned in the direction of the hapless woman who was his wife.

Fearful that he would take his anger out on her after I was gone, I hastened to say good-bye and left them. My lack of success with them bruised my self-esteem, but I comforted myself with the thought that Wang Sha and

Cheng had not succeeded either in getting on friendly terms with Sun.

Back in Xiu-ying's little room I took out my diary and confided my frustration to its pages.

"Are you writing about us?" Xiu-ying asked, sitting down on the kang and pointing at my diary notebook on the short-legged table between us.

Her question took me by surprise. Flustered, I closed the diary and stammered no, then added more truthfully, "Well, not really."

"That looks like our house and yard." She pointed to the paper lying beside my diary. It was a rough sketch I had made to use in our next study class. "Even the wooden loom is the same as ours."

"It's the house of a peasant family in the Han dynasty, two thousand years ago."

"So long ago?"

"Even before that time, it seems, the peasants lived practically the same way they do today."

"Did that mother tell her daughter the same thing Mother tells me?"

"What's that?"

"When a girl lives at home, she must obey her father. When she is married, she must obey her husband. And when her husband dies, she must obey her son."

"Exactly the same," I said emphatically and with obvious disapproval in my voice.

"If a good teaching has lasted for two thousand years, why do you want to change it?" Xiu-ying's father interposed from the next room. He looked at us through the open door, his eyebrows raised, dubious and puzzled.

"It's not a good saying. People believe it because it has been drilled into their minds."

I tried to speak quietly and reasonably, but I felt a rising impatience and I could not keep it out of my voice.

"Nobody can drill wrong ideas into my mind. Let me tell you: You say I can get the land without paying for it and I don't believe it."

His honest, broad face grew red and his stubbornly pursed lips quivered. "I always tell my children not to take anything they haven't worked for. I don't want them to be led astray."

Xiu-ying's mother stopped spinning and looked imploringly from her daughter to her husband, and then to me. "Are you going to your study class this morning?" she asked hurriedly.

"It's early yet," I replied stiffly.

"Let's take a walk," interrupted Xiu-ying. There was a conciliatory note in her voice. And she added in a whisper, "Don't take him too seriously."

Goodness knows there was plenty that needed to be done in the village as well as in the fields, but when winter set in, the peasants seemed to abandon work. Low on food supplies and energy, they passed the cold months in near hibernation. So when Xiu-ying and I announced we would start a class to study "women's questions" we met unexpected enthusiasm from the restless village women. When we came to the class on the first day, several women already sat on the ground on the open space in front of Tu's house, chattering while they waited for the class to begin.

Some had come to learn, others to watch the new "show" and, while watching, do their morning toilet. Water was a precious item in Longxiang, which had only one pond and a scattering of half-dry wells. A person in Longxiang was only assured of getting three baths in his whole life: one on the day he was born; one on the day he got married; and one on the day he died. So instead of washing their children's faces and brushing their teeth with precious water, they cleaned their families by catching the lice which plagued everyone in the village, big and small, rich and poor.

Some young mothers suckled their babies as they talked. As modest young girls and matrons before their first baby was born, they had buttoned their blouses up to the neck. Now they opened their jackets and exposed even their bare breasts and bellies. A toddler in split pants squatted down and made water. With great interest and concentration she watched it flow in a little rivulet through the dust. Then she thrust her fingers into the mud and patted it against her cheek like rouge. A sheep languidly relieved itself of a few droppings; Tu's wife hastened to sweep them up with a dustpan and throw them into her compost pit.

About a dozen women had now gathered in a rough circle on the ground. When I took my seat among them, they all looked expectantly at me. It was clear that only I had some idea of what we were there for, but even I could only put general questions.

"How many of you have worked in the landlords' households? Please raise your hands." I started to count. "Did they pay you as much as they did the men?"

Only a sharp-chinned woman sat still without even lifting her little finger.

"What about you?" I asked her.

"She doesn't want you to know that bungler Landlord Wu paid her a lot more," a masculine-looking woman interposed. As she spoke, she twisted her neck and head in an odd way. "He hired her to cook for his farmhands during the harvest. Sister Ling-ling, you know, the harvest was a big occasion for us here and Landlord Wu was generous. He wanted to give his men some special dish. But this woman here, she took the money and bought cheap food. You should have seen her soup! It was nothing more than water, a few drops of oil, and some rotten vegetables that the stirring ladle brought to the top when Landlord Wu came to look at it. And her pancake! It was so coarse that it stuck in their throats. They couldn't swallow it and they couldn't throw it up."

"So you can't keep your big gap closed! Then speak again!" the sharp-chinned woman screamed, and turned to me: "She worked for Landlord Chi. See if she's honest and tells you the truth about him!"

"Why not?" The other woman tossed her head angrily, but I noticed that she quickly lowered her head again, pretending that some dust had blown into her eyes as she shot a quick glance in the direction of the main road. "Landlord Chi didn't pay me on time, so I went off to work for Landlord Bai."

"Any more?" I asked.

"What's more?" She squinted at me with an arch chuckle. "Maybe you want to know how Landlord Bai treated me. Not too bad. But he was stingy, never gave me a cent more than he had to."

"You mean he never miscalculated?" Tu's wife interjected.

"Oh, he did miscalculate now and then by giving me a cent less."

"That's the way they are!" and they laughed and chuckled.

"Now, be serious. We're not at a tea party—" Before I finished speaking, there was a sudden hubbub among the group of children playing nearby. They shouted furiously at each other. I recognized Xiu-ying's brother and A-rong, the boy I had taught to sing on my first day there, but it was difficult to see who was doing what to whom. A-rong was shrieking out the accusations that he had heard us make against the landlords. "Thieves!" he shouted. "Bad eggs . . . feudal landlords!" He blurted out bits and pieces of ideas he only half understood.

"He needs a good beating." Tu's wife threw a small stone at him. "Get away from here, all of you. Don't shit on my doorstep!"

Tu's wife was a tiny little woman. She had a perpetually alert look in her darting eyes as though she were scared that she would get beaten at any moment. Now and then she cupped her hand behind her left ear and bent forward to catch what you were saying. It was said that once Tu had slapped her so hard that she had become partially deaf.

The other women paid no attention to her complaints. A few merely lifted their heads to gaze indifferently at the brawling children. Shouting vengeful threats, the boys scattered in different directions as she advanced on them wielding the long-handled dustpan.

"I'll tell old Tu to give you a good beating," A-rong shouted defiantly over his shoulder and made an ugly face.

"You little son of a bitch! I'll settle you," and she moved a few steps after him.

"Can I join you?" asked someone in a high-pitched, na-
sal voice. Her face struck me as familiar. I knew I had seen
it before, but couldn't remember where and when.

"I am a poor peasant woman, but you didn't come to
visit me," the newcomer complained in a coquettish way,
pouting.

"Didn't I?" I studied her intently. She didn't look like the
other peasants. Her eyebrows and the short hairs around
her forehead were meticulously plucked, accentuating the
blackness of her once fine eyes. But the powder and rouge
heavily applied to her skin could not hide the wrinkles,
distended pores, and blackheads.

"I have been robbed of everything," she declaimed dramatically.

"Are you saying that you have been exploited?" Xiu-
ying liked to use her new vocabulary and made every effort to memorize the words and phrases she was learning.

"Exploited?" The newcomer wrinkled her nose, trying to
puzzle out what Xiu-ying meant.

"Robbed . . . made use of by others." Xiu-ying assumed
a superior sardonic air. I was puzzled by this change in her
attitude.

"Do they rob you or do you rob them?" asked Tu's wife
sharply as she returned from chasing away the children.

The other women giggled and nudged each other.

The strange woman leaped to her feet and yelled, "All
right. So I am unclean, but none of you is clean. You all
wait and see and one fine day I'll blow the whole thing
up."

Tu's wife quickly averted her eyes from us and turned
around. The newcomer lowered her head like a snarling
cat and spat out a curse as she hurried away. Her gesture
had jogged my memory. She was the woman in the red
jacket I had seen with Tu on the night of my arrival in
Longxiang.

As soon as she was out of earshot, Tu's wife came back
to us and muttered vindictively, "That 'Broken Shoe'!"

That explained their hostility: A "broken shoe" was
ready to fit any man's foot, big or small. I wondered if Tu's

wife knew that her husband was visiting the Broken Shoe at night.

"She is forced into it," said a woman with a flat, freckled face. She stated this as a fact rather than with sympathy and stressed the word "it" with a meaningful drawl.

"There are other widows in this village. They may re-marry—sometimes that's fate—but they don't sleep around," said another woman, looking up from her task of cleaning her little daughter's head.

"Da Niang's husband died when she was not much older than Broken Shoe. But she has remained virtuous." Tu's wife spoke with a vehemence which stirred my curiosity even more. I remembered someone—Cheng, I suppose— telling me that she herself had been married before she met Tu, but she obviously chose to ignore this fact now.

"Who is Da Niang?" I asked Xiu-ying.

"She's the old widow who lives in that cottage you stayed in before you moved to our house. A-rong is her younger son," Xiu-ying whispered in my ear.

I remembered: Da Niang was the woman who had kept her door closed against me the night I arrived in Long-xiang. And she and Tu's wife were friends.

"A-rong is making trouble again." Tu's wife spat in the direction where the older children were running together again with bloodcurdling cries.

All of a sudden there was a confused, scuffling knot of boys, shouting and yelling. Another band of children rushed around the side of a cottage and showers of stones fell on the scuffling group. A battle was raging. Some chil-dren cried as the rocks found their targets. They were from all the homes in the village, children of landlords and rich peasants as well as poor peasants and laborers. Xiu-ying's brother was among them.

One child was knocked off balance and fell as he ran. Two other boys pounced on him and mercilessly began to pummel him. The beaten child screamed. It was A-rong. He was down on his belly and tried desperately to raise his back, straining to throw off his tormentors. I bent my arm over my head to shield it from the blows as I ran into the crowd of children and bent over A-rong. I wanted to cover his escape, but he crawled out from under my arm, and darting at a boy twice his size, butted him with his head.

"You sons of bad eggs! You rotten feudal landlords!" he screamed, beside himself with rage and hurt.

A stone hit him in the chest, and he doubled over with his hand squeezed to his breast. For a moment they all stopped fighting and circled around A-rong, watching expectantly and stamping their feet with excitement. Then, with a movement as swift as lightning, he snatched up a stone and aimed it wildly at the children around him.

As he did so, another stone hit his forehead. Blood trickled down over his eyebrows, around the corner of his eyes, and over his cheek, forming bright red lines on his face. My heart ached at the sight. I grasped him by the shoulders. "Go home," I ordered him sharply.

His shirt collar was in tatters and it came off in my hand as he wriggled free. He seized the chance to rush at his enemies again. I tried to hold him from behind but only got a grip on his trousers. There was a rent and half of his bottom was left showing. The children burst out laughing and clapped delightedly. The more helpless and humiliated he looked, the more hilarious they became. Friends and enemies, they screamed with laughter. Doubled up with glee, they rolled on the ground. As suddenly as it had begun, the tension broke. Then, feeling a little guilty, they slipped away to find other games to play.

Slowly, all by himself, A-rong got to his feet in a daze. Shaking with fear and anger, he turned to me, stretching out his skinny arms. His clothes suddenly seemed to dangle on his thin body. His eyes, filled with confused tears, seemed to be saying to me, "But I was only doing what you taught me to do. Wasn't I right?"

7 ★

Meeting

Wang Sha and Malvolio Cheng were having as difficult a
time as I was. The men were no more open-minded than
their wives and even more cautious. Alone with Wang Sha
or Cheng, however, some would reveal what they knew
about the situation in the township, and in this way, with
Shen and Tu's help and Xiu-ying's confidences to me, we
gradually began to build up a picture of Longxiang.

No one knew for certain, but it appeared that three or
four families owned a little less than half of the arable land
thereabouts and with this hold on land had dominated the
place. Among this handful of landlords the most powerful
was a man named Chi, and though he kept a low profile
these days, he was clearly still their leader.

Under this landlord domination, the landless hired
hands were the worst off. They were at the beck and call
of the landlords and the few peasants rich enough to hire
them. To get enough land to make a living on, the landless
and landpoor peasants had to rent land from the landlords,
and they paid dearly for it—usually half or more of the
harvest—and all of them were over their heads in debt to
them as well. The middle peasants, as we had heard before
we came, were subsisting on their own land, but precari-
ously. There was little leeway for error or bad luck in their
farming. There is an old peasant saying: "Snatch the harvest from the dragon's maw." In peasant folklore the

dragon is a symbol of rain and here in North and North-west China the rain appears sometimes with startling suddenness during or right after the summer harvest. In just a few hours the weather turns cold; a chill wind blows, the dragon's breath; black clouds fill the sky; and the rain comes down in torrents. If the harvest isn't stacked but lies out in the fields or on the threshing floor, a farmer can be ruined in a day. Such a ravening storm the previous year had forced several farmers into debt despite the fact that the new government had prohibited usury.

Now it was all so clear to me. The only way to give the peasants a fresh start was to break the grip of the likes of Chi by taking away their power over land.

"Let's go ahead and do it," I proclaimed boldly when we met to go over our first week's work.

"We can't do it for the peasants. Only they can find out how much land the landlords have and who owns what," Wang Sha pointed out.

"The landlords can't make the land disappear," I rejoined aggressively. I wanted to hold his attention with my cleverness.

"Yes they can," he replied mysteriously.

"They don't look like magicians to me. They all hang their heads and walk around like ghosts. I can't tell one face from another, because I've hardly seen them."

"You had better believe me when I tell you that the landlords can make not only their land disappear but a lot more too. They have probably already bribed or black-mailed some of the peasants to join their conspiracies. Those peasants will claim land that actually belongs to the landlords and hide other property for them as well. They'll wait for us to leave, and then all that will go right back to the landlords." He spoke with a slightly condescending touch of authority, but it sounded provocative to me.

"Then Cheng and I will have to work something out," I said decidedly, to show our independence. There was more truth in my assertion than I realized then; Wang Sha in fact had very little time left from his many duties to lead the work in Longxiang personally. He was in charge of twenty work teams scattered around the county. He checked over their activities and kept contact between them in the intervals between the periodic meetings of their delegates. While he was away, we in Longxiang were responsible for day-to-day work. At the moment, this was to get the more active farmers together and in such numbers that they would feel strong and sure of themselves. But Longxiang was cautious.

With few exceptions, everyone was waiting to see which way the wind was going to blow. One of the young farm laborers put it succinctly: "What if I stick my neck out and things don't go as you say they will? I'll be left out on a limb." And he pulled his worn jacket from his back where Landlord Chi's cudgel had left a long, red weal.

As time went by, though, the peasants grew to like Cheng. They liked his unassuming ways, his clowning, and his good humor. They appreciated his sober good sense, increasingly took him as one of their own, and often stopped in just to chat with him.

Some youngsters were already solidly with us. There was Xiu-ying, of course, and two young men as well. Little Tian was a strapping youngster with a swarthy face. He was helping Shen reorganize the Poor Peasants' Association. Little Gao, with his two large ears always flapping out of his hat, was getting fresh recruits to train for the Peasants' Militia. When they heard that the Poor Peasants' Association ought to accept most of the middle peasants, Little Gao brought along his cousin Gao, a man in his fifties and the village sage, while Little Tian recommended his great-uncle, Old Tian, to Malvolio Cheng.

Old Tian, a middle peasant in his seventies and an unofficial village elder, became a frequent visitor. Although he could not read, he was thoroughly versed in the folktales. His political and social beliefs came from his understanding of tradition and folklore, and the other villagers had great respect for his erudition and opinions. His crony Gao, who could read, was regarded as an intellectual in the village. His clothes were always carefully patched, his chin and head clean-shaven.

"In my lifetime I have seen quite a few dynasties change. They rose and they fell," said Old Tian, stroking

the wispy thread of beard on his chin. To him all the rulers
of modern China were still emperors.

"So there was no difference between them?" asked Malvolio Cheng, comprehending both the words and the dis-
passionate tone in which they were spoken.

"No. They all sent their inspector-generals to Longxiang. The landlords entertained them with banquets and
gave them presents. After that, they said they were satisfied with what they saw, and they left. Nothing changed."

"But this time we come to be your friends, not the landlords'," I interposed. "We are your guests, not the landlords'." I was annoyed that they completely ignored me in
their conversation and seemed to take it for granted that
young women should be seen—if at all—but not heard.

"Once in my native place . . . um . . . erh . . ." Gao paused
and thought for a while, unhurried. "It was more than
twenty years ago that there came some imperial inspector-
generals. They talked like you do and they dressed like
you too." He pointed the stem of his pipe at Malvolio
Cheng's cadre-style jacket to emphasize the point. He was
answering my question through Cheng. "They came to
talk to us. They seemed to be nice people. But the landlords came back with their militia, and that wasn't all. An
army came from Changan with shiny new arms—an all-
conquering host, like the Emperor's army of old. Your
guys with rusty old guns were no match for them. They
had to clear out. We found ourselves in deep water. Everyone who had accepted land was called a rebel. The landlords settled accounts and killed us like flies. I was lucky. I
have long legs and could run faster than they. In fact,
that's how I came to settle here."

"I well understand your misgivings. In more than
twenty years I have worked with the peasants in many
places." To bring me into the conversation Cheng turned
to me and added, "That was during the civil war period.
Every time we moved into a new area and took it from the
warlords and the Guomindang, we tried to help the peasants get back their old lands. But as soon as the Guomindang army reoccupied a place they undid what we had
done and gave the land back to the landlords. For a time it

was a seesaw struggle, and in some places it was a terrible time for the peasants."

Taking Malvolio Cheng's cue I added, "But this time the landlords and their gangs are finished for good. And what's left of that 'heavenly host' has run away to Taiwan along with Chiang Kai-shek."

They did not deign to answer my assertion and there was a moment's pause. Later I learned that they had never even heard of Chiang Kai-shek anyway. They only knew about the local Guomindang military governor whose name was Ma.

"Now we have come from Changan," remarked Cheng, slowly withdrawing his pipe from his mouth. It was shrewdly said. There was an immediate but hardly perceptible change in their attitude. Old Tian stroked his beard, while his crony Gao hunched his shoulders so that his neck disappeared into the collar of his jacket. But they did not so much as exchange glances. Changan was the capital of the great Tang dynasty; it had rivaled Rome at the peak of its glory. To these men Changan was the symbol of governmental power. Their imagination could picture no city greater or more powerful than Changan. Nanking or Peking meant little to them. Who came from Changan must have solid backing. They were the people to be reckoned with.

"Have you seen the old palace?" Old Tian threw his companion a significant look. He had put a question to test our worth. How it was answered would establish or discredit our credentials.

Cheng more than rose to the occasion. He moved from the kang to the center of the room. With eloquence and gestures in the style of the traditional storytellers he described the palace. Outshining even our very imaginative Xian guide, his words and actions unfolded before us the full splendor of that edifice: the marble terrace and vermilion halls, the emperor and his generals and ministers, courtiers and palace beauties promenading in their gorgeous costumes. He changed his expression, voice, movements, and gestures as he changed his roles, conjuring up an enchanting picture of the ancient capital. He ended by connecting this ancient glory to the center of the new provincial government. The two elders were so fascinated by his narrative that when Chen turned to me for corroboration and asked, "Isn't that so?" they looked straight at me for the first time since I had entered the little room. I nodded my head.

"Did you see the Hua-qing hot spring?" asked Old Tian. This was another important question. "When Yang Gui-fei went there in the middle of the night she saw fairies bathing in it."

"No," corrected Gao, the younger man, "Yang Gui-fei bathed in it first and then became a fairy."

"Both are believable," admitted the older one, a little put out.

"She bathed in it," said Cheng, nodding in my direction.

"Yes, I did," I exclaimed joyfully.

They stared at me with new interest. It was obvious that my status had risen in their eyes. It was as though they expected to see multicolored clouds appear any moment beneath my feet to carry me away. They hastened to say good-bye. They could hardly wait to spread the absorbing news they had received.

"Please come to our meeting tomorrow. We'll be reading the new land reform law to you." Cheng bowed to them and they returned his bow.

The meeting room was a large empty hall to the right of the township office. It had once been used by the local magistrates to try cases. It could hold up to thirty people, and we did not expect more than that number to attend. There would be members of the reorganized Poor Peasants' Association, some members of the new Peasants' Militia, and members of my study class for women. The middle peasants in general still kept their own counsel, though many of them were almost as poor as the poor peasants, but we expected that this time some of them would attend the meeting. We hoped that after hearing the land reform law read out and discussed in public they would spread the good word among their families and friends.

It was still early. The bell we hung outside the hall on a branch of a locust tree was still reverberating from its last toll, but as I approached the door of the hall I already heard a hum of conversation. Glancing around the crowd inside, I spotted Xiu-ying's father squatting by himself in a corner, staring hard into the top of his pipe. He had not wanted to come, I knew, but at my urging Xiu-ying had literally dragged him there. His reputation as an honest, hardworking farmer would be a major asset to the meeting.

Xiu-ying's mother was there too, sitting with a few other women apart from the men. Her little son lolled beside her with his head resting lazily on her knees. Old Tian the village elder and Gao the village sage were there, just as we had hoped, with a group of their middle peasant friends. Most had never yet attended our meetings and they carried much weight in the village. The young activists, most from poor peasant households or landless laborers, and the regulars of my study class were in full force. They squatted around the low table that supported the kerosene lantern, or leaned against the walls, the young men on one side, the girls on the other.

It was all too clear that the older men, like Xiu-ying's father, were uncomfortable there; they were unsmiling, even sullen. Despite the chatter of the young folk, the atmosphere in the room was strained. The women were not their usual gossipy selves. They knew that they were the cause of the constraint. It disconcerted them and the older men to have men and women discussing serious matters in public as if they were all equals. It broke all traditions. And more than that, I knew quite well that most of them were still apprehensive. Before they jumped on our bandwagon, they wanted to be sure that they would not be left stranded somewhere along the road, as they had been left stranded before.

The room was already stuffy. The lantern light showed a mist of smoke and body heat forming and reforming above the heads of those who sat cross-legged or squatted on the earthen floor. There was a strong and rancid odor of sweat, dirt, and tobacco smoke.

I took a seat on the floor but then edged back to rest my shoulders against the wall. My neighbor made a space for me and then twitched her shoulders in an effort to ease the itch between her shoulder blades. A louse was biting her. I smiled at her understandingly and then inwardly braced myself. In the heat of the room my lice—my newest affliction in Longxiang—would surely come crawling out of the seams of my clothes and make a meal of me too.

Someone—by the looks of the hand that held the door, a woman—stood outside. She opened the door, peeked in, and then closed the door again timidly, but it flew open abruptly when the Broken Shoe brushed her aside and sailed into the crowded room. When she took a seat with the other women, they all squeezed together not so much to make room for her as to put a distance between her and them. The Broken Shoe had handled this sort of situation before. She made herself comfortable and paid no attention to them.

Cheng opened the meeting by reading out the land reform law as we had promised, explaining some of the more difficult passages as he went along. When he had finished there was a short pause as neighbors in increasingly audible whispers asked each other questions and made comments on those portions that had caught their attention. Wang Sha and the Xian Party leader had drilled it into us until Cheng and I knew it almost by heart, but for most of the peasants it was too much to take in all at once.

After an animated discussion, the group around Gao the village sage fell silent. Gao cleared his throat and, when Cheng turned to him, said with typical circumlocution, "Some people didn't quite catch that part about the rich peasants."

Turning back the pages of the pamphlet before him, Cheng answered readily, "I'll read it again. Here's what it says: 'Protect the property of rich peasants including the land they till themselves or rent out. However, under certain special circumstances, part of the land or all of the land rented out may be confiscated if the authority higher than the provincial government gives its approval.' "

"What are those 'special circumstances'?" Gao pressed the point.

"For example, if a rich peasant has committed crimes."

"Only then will he lose land?"

"That's the law." Cheng gave it a moment's thought. "Otherwise rich peasants can keep everything they own."

After another buzz of conversation, Gao spoke again in a tone of great gravity: "But I have heard that in some places rich peasants are being attacked along with the landlords. Is that so?"

Cheng gave me a quick, sidelong glance which said, "Don't speak unless you're sure of what you are saying," and then answered Gao's query.

"Ordinary rich peasants should not be troubled," he said. "Perhaps in the case you have heard about they were mistaken for landlords. They leased out some land or they lent out money at high interest. Sometimes there is not a very clear-cut line between such a rich peasant and a landlord. And sometimes hotheaded people act before they investigate and they do what should not be done."

"Is there always a clear-cut line between rich peasants and middle peasants?" interjected the Broken Shoe mischievously, as the other women gazed at her with astonishment at her boldness in a conclave of men. Yet we all knew she was saying out loud what everyone else had in their heads.

Old Tian immediately took up the cue despite its source. "In our village, we have all sorts of peasants: poor peasants with just a bit of land, tenant farmers, landless farm laborers, middle income peasants, rich peasants, and a few landlords. When the land reform starts and the landlords lose their land, rich peasants will naturally get worried. It might be their turn next. If rich peasants are attacked, we middle peasants, of course, will fret."

"Ordinary middle peasants will surely have nothing to worry about if an ordinary rich peasant hasn't," said Cheng emphatically. "I am not saying no mistakes will ever be made, but there will be less danger of such mistakes being made if we all work together well and know exactly who is who. That's what we are here for tonight. We want to know your views. What we are going to do is not an easy thing." Cheng spread out his arms as if to embrace them all, even the Broken Shoe, in brotherhood.

"What does the law say about taking land away from rich peasants?" asked Gao the village sage, ignoring Cheng's invitation to join the brotherhood. He did not want to talk directly about middle peasants.

"The law says that a rich peasant can keep as much of his land as he tills himself. If he has surplus land that he rents out like a landlord, then that land may be put in the pool to be shared out among the landless or landpoor peasants," said Cheng, thumbing through the book in front of him even though he knew the answer by heart. Then he added, "But no other property of a rich peasant will be touched."

"But after the land share-out some of us middle peasants will still have more land than most other peasants. Will that land be taken from us?"

"No, oh no," exclaimed Cheng and I simultaneously. And Cheng added, "I'll read that part out." As he fumbled for the right page in his book, he leaned over to me and whispered, "Now you see why Shen and Tu have kept out of this. We're being tested, and we mustn't flunk."

He found the page he wanted and read out loud: " 'If there is still a difference between the holdings of the middle peasants and those of the former poor peasants and farm laborers, this is permissible as long as it is not great.' That's clear, isn't it? And 'activists among the middle peasants must also be drawn into the committees of peasant associations carrying out the land reform.' You see the difference? The landlords and rich peasants cannot join the association, but middle peasants can. You will be helping to run things."

Old Gao took out his own copy of the land reform law from his pocket (we had passed several out among the villagers during the last few days) and compared its cover with the one held up by Cheng. Satisfied that they were identical, he started to read the page silently. His index finger moved deliberately from character to character. When once he paused and scrutinized the page even more closely, Cheng motioned to the peasant activist Little Gao standing near Old Gao to go to his help. The young man nodded and, squatting near Old Gao, gave him the sound of the character he was stumbling over.

"Sure, sure!" exclaimed Old Gao querulously. "Unite. Yes, it says 'firmly unite with the middle peasants.' My eyes are not what they used to be. When the light is poor and the print is small, I can't see the characters clearly."

"Take my glasses." Cheng took off his spectacles and handed them to Gao. "How's that?"

Gao, with Cheng's spectacles hanging loosely on his nose, slowly and ponderously read out the passage in question.

When he had finished, Cheng looked all round the room and then asked, "Isn't that fair enough?"

Once again the room hummed with the murmurs of a dozen discussions. In a momentary pause I caught the voice of the Broken Shoe. She smirked at her neighbor: "Talk is talk. Who's to say they won't kick us around after they've got what they want?"

"What do they want?" her neighbor asked doubtfully.

The Broken Shoe did not answer but got to her feet and strolled over to where Gao was reading to his cronies from his book. She stepped on a woman's foot as she threaded her way through the crowd.

"Who do you think you are, stepping on people's feet!" came a quick response. "It's like a carpet, eh? Soft and warm."

"I didn't see your foot."

"That's just it. You don't care where you step."

"Or where you sit either." The Broken Shoe thrust her face forward pugnaciously. Did she want to start a fight and disrupt the meeting?

"You stinking cunt!"

"No more stinking than yours," and with that the Broken Shoe lunged out at her opponent. Cursing, they began to pull each other's hair until the other women separated them.

Xiu-ying tried to persuade the Broken Shoe to leave. But she would have none of it. She yelled, "I'm not leaving! I am a poor peasant woman. No matter how much you hate me I'm still a poor peasant woman."

Her eyes wild and her hair disheveled, the Broken Shoe plumped herself down on the floor again. She made it clear that the only way to get her to leave would be to throw her out bodily.

"Why are you trying to disrupt the meeting?" Xiu-ying turned fiercely on her.

The Broken Shoe drew back at the suddenness of this direct accusation. She frowned at Xiu-ying. "Why are you picking on me? I say things that you don't like to hear. But they have all said things about you behind your back!"

"Our tongues are not as long as yours, though," jeered a voice.

"So now it's my tongue you don't like? Why don't you cut it off?" The Broken Shoe raised her voice again, blustering as she dodged Xiu-ying's question. On her knees, she snatched a pair of small scissors that Cheng had used to cut the burned-out wick of the kerosene lantern and had put on the table. Holding the scissors to the corner of her mouth with one hand, with the other she mimicked the act of excruciatingly forcing open her mouth and extracting her tongue.

No one said a word.

The performance had fallen flat. Abashed, she put down the scissors and muttered sheepishly: "You don't want me here. All right, I'll go. No hard feelings." There was a pause. No one answered her.

When she spoke again, her voice was unsteady. "I'll get my share of land, eh, won't I?"

Xiu-ying looked to me for a lead and when she saw me shrug my shoulders, answered ambiguously, "It depends."

"What!" The Broken Shoe jerked her head back astonished. Her voice came low when we had expected a new strident outburst. "Why?"

"You have your landlord pals to help you!" came a voice from the back of the room. The speaker had deliberately disguised his voice so that the Broken Shoe could not recognize it.

"To help me?" She lowered her face and wiped her eyes and cheeks with her hands. I doubted if there were any tears there. But when she lifted her head, her expression had changed. She was no longer the defiant tigress. She needed to overcome their stony faces, to win them over to her side.

"You all know that I was sold as a slave girl into a landlord's house. I worked like a beast of burden, and I was treated worse than one. At least oxen and donkeys had their fodder and a warm stable; I was cold and hungry, hot and overworked. Then I was raped. They said it was I who raped him. His wife sold me off to a poor peasant. That was how I got here. My husband died and left me nothing. Who ever helped me? I never knew my father or my mother." She gagged on the words and could not go on. The trembling hands she moved to her breast had broken fingernails and calloused palms. She beat her breast three times as if trying to beat down the bitter memories that were surging up and would choke her. "The cook-woman in that landlord's house was the only one who had a kind word for me. I felt for her as for a mother. She told me that I should try to settle down with some man, however poor, who had a bit of land. 'With land you cannot starve. Raise a family,' she said."

That one word "land" resounded around the room.

"You see what I have here?" Broken Shoe pressed her finger against the tarnished copper hairpin that still held up some of her bedraggled hair. A white gauze thread was twisted round it. "She wore a thread like this for a neighbor who had died, dead broke and without a husband or children to remember her. The white light from the thread would help her soul grope its way to the Underworld King. That way she would not be doomed to wander forever in the dark and cold. Now I wear this thread for her. If I die now who will put on a thread for me? Land. I must have land of my own. Then I will have a home and family. Now I am afraid. Afraid to live and afraid to die."

Her voice trailed off as she looked around at the roomful of hazy faces. When she saw the phalanx of men, she glared and bridled up again: "You spit at me and call me names. You think you're better than I am? How many of you have sisters here? None, eh? Where are they? They were sold off to pay your family debts. They were killed or exchanged for your food? How do you know they're not living as I am? And you call yourselves men, you stuck up—"

Her eyes flashed with bitterness, but her shoulders sagged. She walked in silence to the door, and her steps were shaky as she passed out into the night. No one moved or spoke for a moment, long enough for us to hear a sob outside the door. I felt it as a terrible rebuke to me. I had treated the Broken Shoe just as we had always treated "her kind." I had never considered what it meant for her to have been poor and exploited and oppressed.

Xiu-ying's mother broke the silence. Pointing to Little Tian she said, "His mother was sold to a very bad place in a far-off town. A very bad place. He was only four years old then. He held on to his mother's leg and wouldn't let her go. They had to pry his fingers loose one by one."

"What are we waiting for? Let's go ahead and take back our land and be done with it," a young voice cried impetuously. No other voice echoed it right away, but the meeting had found a new momentum. The room buzzed with a dozen conversations and arguments. The Broken Shoe had begun by disturbing the meeting but she had ended by spurring on her listeners to push ahead more vigorously with the work of reform.

When order was finally restored, Cheng read the next section. All went smoothly until he came to the passage that said the landlords and their families should get a share of the land and tools so that they could make a living. At first, several young peasants immediately raised a clamor. Cheng explained that honest work would make a new man out of even a feudal landlord. "You know, many, many years ago our earliest ancestors were monkeys. Work transformed them into men."

"Monkeys? No!" The old men looked at each other in

bewilderment as if trying to see if there were really any resemblance to a monkey in their neighbor.

"Yes," continued Cheng, "they used their forelimbs, worked very hard, and gradually their paws became hands. If work could turn a monkey into a man, surely it can transform a landlord into an honest toiler."

"Our ancestors were not monkeys," Old Tian said assertively, voicing the conventional wisdom. "They were like us, tilling the land—farmers, good farmers." He reinforced his argument with the evidence of the classics. "Three thousand years ago, King Zhou met a wise man at a fish pond and asked him how to rule the kingdom. The wise man replied, 'Teach people to know their places. Since most of them are farmers, tilling the land, they must never desert it.' "

"That's true," responded Cheng, "but I am talking about times long before three thousand years ago."

"No matter," said Old Tian with an air of finality. "Men have always tilled the soil."

"Old Tian is right," Xiu-ying's father nodded his head in agreement. "The spirits of our ancestors are always with us. Is it proper for us to call them monkeys? Cheng, you assure me again and again that the revolution will make us happy. But how can we be happy if we insult our ancestors and they curse us?"

"But Papa, why do you sometimes call me a 'son of a monkey'?" Xiu-ying's little brother queried.

"Quiet!" bellowed his father. "When your father is talking, you keep quiet. Never talk back to your elders."

Xiu-ying murmured reflectively but loud enough for others to hear, "Twice a year at Qing Ming and the Spring Festival we have saved and denied ourselves to buy spirit money and incense to burn at the graves of our ancestors. We knelt and prayed before their tablets. But we got poorer and poorer. Now we are depending on ourselves and we will get back the land we lost."

"How dare you contradict your father?" The old man glowered at her. But what else he said was drowned out in the new wave of excited talk that swept through the room.

"The landlords forced us to work so hard that we were turned back into monkeys," a young activist cried.

"Well, anyway, we mustn't be too hard on the land-lords," said Old Tian. "Otherwise we will turn them into monkeys, troublemakers. A restless demon possesses people with idle hands. People must have land to work on. If they don't work and support themselves, who will feed them? Live and let live."

So our discussion started with Malvolio Cheng's smattering of Marxism and ended with peasant pragmatism.

8 ★

The First Sacrifice

Our work went better after that night's discussion. We began to hold weekly meetings in the office, and more and more peasants attended. The constraint that was so obvious in the early meetings disappeared, and bit by bit they exposed the skulduggery of the landlords, the tricks that were used to make more money and seize more land. We learned much about how the landlord system worked. It seemed that a peasant could not just go out and rent land. He had to have guarantors of his "good character"; he had to give "gifts" to the landlord—a few chickens, a lamb; and he had to put down a guarantee deposit. If he didn't have money, a father even had to sign over one of his children as an indentured servant for a fixed number of years; during that time he could make no claim on the landlord even if the child was worked to death. He had to pay over fifty percent or more of the harvest as rent, even if, as in some famine years, the total crop was not big enough to feed himself and his family. As harvest time approached, suspicious landlords made sure that they received the right amount of rent by going out to the fields and estimating the size of a tenant's crop before it was cut. Landlord Chi took the lead in seeing to it that these barbarous old customs were observed.

Some middle peasants spoke out because they wanted to claim the advantages that superior suffering bestowed.

They viewed the meetings as a place where combatants jostled for their future status in the new society. They wanted to rival the poor peasants in the extent of their sufferings even if they had to exaggerate their woes. We understood what motivated them, but still we welcomed their support. The important thing was that much which had been left unsaid before was now out in the open. Deeply buried memories were the talk of the village. Trees, cottages, stones told stories where before there had been silence.

Encouraged by the way the peasants were rallying behind the work team, Wang Sha, Malvolio Cheng, and I gathered in the township office one afternoon to discuss what our next step should be. Wang Sha passed on the county leadership's instructions to open a study class for our young activists, a mixed class for both girls and boys. Cheng and I would devote some time each day to teaching them reading and writing, and giving some of them a grounding in elementary math and geometry. They would then be responsible for taking a census of the households, keeping accounts, and measuring the fields to be confiscated for later redistribution. If they lacked these tools and abilities, the only other literates here—the landlord and rich peasant families—could still pull their old tricks on them. Of course, we could still enlist the aid of the middle peasant families, but it was too much to expect that such peasants as Old Gao could suddenly change their laissez-faire attitudes and become not only capable administrators but revolutionaries. By educating and training the poor peasants and the young ones in particular, we were preparing the ground for an all-around advance in the villages in which all would share, but some of the older generation shortsightedly viewed our efforts as simply a way of pulling the middle peasants down one rung in the social scale.

Wang Sha had been discussing all this with Cheng and me when Xiu-ying burst in. She leaned against the door-frame, panting and hardly able to speak. Wang Sha stopped in mid-sentence. I jumped off the kang and held her arm as she caught her breath. "What's the matter?"

"He's been beaten to death!" she cried, a look of terror in her eyes.

"Who?"

"A-rong, Da Niang's young son—you remember? You taught him to sing the first day you came."

Yes, I remembered the comical way he had swayed his head as he sang

"Who killed him?" Cheng asked.

We were astounded to hear her reply, "His brother."

"How could that be?"

"Tu's wife likes to wag her tongue too much," Xiu-ying blurted out and her face clouded over. It hardly seemed an answer to my query.

"What has Tu's wife got to do with it? Aren't Da Niang and Tu's wife friends?" I asked.

Wang Sha took her arm and led her gently to the kang. "Sit down and tell us what happened."

There was a moment's pause while she calmed herself. Then she told us that Tu's wife had told old Da Niang about the fight between A-rong and the landlords' children. Da Niang, who had already suffered a great deal from the local landlords and was terrified of crossing them any further, wanted to punish her son both to silence him and to try to appease the landlords' wrath. Her elder son, a great lout of a youth and known as the village idiot, had carried out her order to beat the boy. He had accidentally hit him on some fatal spot, and A-rong died instantly. Now the mother was wailing beside the body.

"Xiu-ying, go home now," I said. "I'll go to Da Niang and stay with her until you can come and relieve me. All right?" She agreed to this and left.

I turned to Wang Sha and queried him silently with a gesture.

"You two go and visit Da Niang. After I finish up work here, I'll join you." He thought for a moment and then added, "Or you join me here."

As on a screen before my eyes I saw A-rong's comical

little face raised in song; then it was blotted out in blood. It was only at that moment that a full realization of what had happened came home to me.

Da Niang sat inside the door of her cottage—in the compound where I had spent my first night in the township—a distraught look on her face. As soon as she saw me, she threw up her arms and her cries rent the air:

"I may be poor, but I'm not crazy. I don't believe in getting anything without paying for it. I'm fifty years old now and going downhill, but I've managed to survive. Why should I worry now? But my son is dead!"

Strange disjointed cries. She burst into tears, beating her breast. She slapped her own face, punishing herself. I tried to comfort her, as did the other women gathered in the cottage. Then all of a sudden she stopped crying and became very quiet. She leaned forward, listening, straining her ears. To our surprise she darted out into the courtyard. She was no longer the mother distraught with sorrow.

"You son of a bitch, how dare you drink from my pail?" she yelped and let out a string of curses against a mongrel that had wandered into the yard. She returned carrying two pails of water. After she set them down, she angrily hit her elder son with the flat carrying pole. "You lazybones, why did you leave the pails outside? Oh, you'll be the ruin of me!"

She was so frail that the blow hardly jolted him as it glanced off his shoulder. He just looked up, staring at her from where he sat by the wall. Tu's wife gingerly took the pole from Da Niang's hand.

Da Niang resumed her seat with a thump. She settled her feet comfortably apart and immediately began wailing again about her misfortunes.

The child's body lay on the kang in the inner room. His face was blue and swollen. Vomited blood had congealed at the corner of his mouth. I had never seen death before and I trembled with fright, but under the gaze of so many pairs of curious eyes I was determined not to show my fear. I bit my lip to prevent myself from crying out. I placed the white sheet I had brought with me in Da Niang's lap.

"Da Niang, let him take this with him."

Da Niang wiped off her tears and narrowed her one good eye—the other was opaque and blind—to look at my gift. She felt the sheet lovingly and murmured, "What good cotton. Wrapped in this, he'll be luckier than his father. His father died in the depths of winter, but still he had nothing to wear but his summer clothes. I dream that he shivers with cold in the underworld."

The women neighbors came over to feel these burial clothes, chattering all the while. They took my gift to the window and held it up to the light to scrutinize every seam. Though it was worn, it was fine, machine-stitched Swatow linen, from my aunt's linen closet. They had never seen anything like it.

Da Niang folded the sheet. Her elder son, who had not uttered a single word, now came up wanting to touch the sheet too. But I angrily pushed his hands away and said sharply, "It's none of your business."

Da Niang shot a glance at him. He stepped back, perplexed, and stood still. His long, flat face was immobile, but his disproportionately long arms with their thick veins were twitching spasmodically at his sides. I knew the boy was not responsible for what he had done, but emotion got the better of me. Cheng, who had also come to offer condolences to Da Niang, succeeded in irritating me still further with his whispered admonishment, "Be considerate. He didn't know what he was doing."

Instructed by an old and experienced neighbor, we began to prepare the little corpse for burial. First, we fetched water to wash the child's face and body, though Da Niang nagged us not to waste precious water. Then we clothed him neatly and placed the little body wrapped in the sheet on two boards set on trestles in the front room. While we hastened to complete these dismal rites, the idiot son sneaked away. The other women soon departed, leaving Cheng and me to keep Da Niang company.

She was tired. She had suffered a terrible loss. Who

would look after her now in her old age? Her cheeks, the skin stretched tight over her high cheekbones, shone red as if with fever. We insisted that she go into the inner room to rest on the kang while we kept vigil beside the corpse.

Night had fallen. Only the dim light of the oil lamp remained. I felt that the place was haunted by the wronged ghost of the boy. I shuddered at Da Niang's intermittent whimpering. My teeth chattered uncontrollably. Cheng was mumbling to himself while he paced the room.

A rat was gnawing at something in a corner. I've always particularly hated rats, with their nauseating smell. Oddly, now I felt friendly towards this one. At least its presence meant life, and it lessened my fear.

There was a knock on the door, and at my answer it opened softly. Xiu-ying stood in the stream of bright moonlight which flooded in.

"You can go home now, Elder Sister," she said quietly. "I will keep Da Niang company."

Returning to Wang Sha's room, Cheng and I found him seated before a pile of papers which he had been reading. He pushed them aside. "Do you know exactly how it happened?" he asked. "Is what we heard the full story?" He looked grave.

"I don't know," Cheng replied. "It was no time to discuss the matter with Da Niang."

I felt that I ought to tell them about that midnight meeting of Tu and the Broken Shoe, and I did. "It was Tu's wife who egged Da Niang on to punish the boy. Are all these things somehow connected? Perhaps Da Niang has been hoodwinked by them," I suggested.

"How could Tu choose this moment to get mixed up with such a woman?" Cheng wondered. "It'll ruin his career." He cautiously glanced around. "You can't make accusations like that in an offhand way. I'm sure more than a few solid family men around here have played around with the Broken Shoe. No one will take her word for it; you have to catch them in the act. And then—well, I've seen villagers tie two guilty parties together with ropes and expose them publicly. It would be disastrous for all of us."

"Cheng is right," interjected Wang Sha, no doubt wishing to skim over the appalling picture Cheng had called up. "It's a touchy question and we mustn't act rashly. Tu is a peasant activist and one of the first in the village. If we wrongly accused him it would be a first-class scandal."

Wang Sha paused to take a sip of water. He rested the bowl for a moment on his knee and then got up to place it on the low table by the wall. He stood there for a moment nervously shifting his feet. "Now, let's see what we can do about all this." He talked not so much to us as to himself.

I wished that I could do something to help him, to lessen his worries. I had been considering one idea and now said, "I think I'll move back to stay with Da Niang. Maybe having a friend in the house will be of help. And if I can get her to talk about the past, it will influence every other woman in the township. Da Niang is one of the poorest of them all, the one who has suffered most from the landlords, yet she is the most stubborn in refusing to say a word against them or even come to our meetings." Surely that offer would impress Wang Sha!

Wang Sha looked at me as if sizing me up. He frowned.

"If you move back there it could be dangerous," he said. "Those landlords, well, there's no telling what a vengeful man will do."

Malvolio Cheng furiously knocked the ashes out of his pipe by striking it on the leg of the narrow bench on which he sat.

The sharp noise jogged my conscience. Suddenly I realized what I was really thinking about. Da Niang had lost her son, that bright boy, and was being driven out of her mind by sorrow. And I was snatching this time to think of impressing Wang Sha. I was using her sorrow and bereavement to gain my own ends, and yet at the same time I knew I truly wanted to help her.

"We must find out what's at the bottom of this murder," I cried. "Somehow I feel responsible for that poor boy's death."

Night Shadows

I moved back into Da Niang's ramshackle cottage, and this time, although she didn't give me a joyous welcome, she did at least come to the door to greet me, and eventually her good nature got the better of her. She helped me sweep and dust the neglected room next to hers and cover the kang with a mat woven of split millet stalks. We moved the rickety table nearer the paper-covered window, set up my wash basin on a stand of bricks, and placed my last piece of furniture, a small, square stool, in front of the table ready for work.

This time Da Niang and I began to spend time with each other. In the morning, before I went off to work, I helped her with the household chores, sweeping the yard and fetching water from a nearby well. In the evening after I came home she sewed beside the small oil light in her room and I read and wrote. She was an unpredictable companion. Sometimes she was silent and self-absorbed, at others irascible and sharp-tongued. If someone did her a mischief, either real or imagined, she could curse them for hours, muttering to herself or aloud to their faces equally without restraint.

We seemed to become quite friendly, but as soon as I tried to get her to talk about her past and the hurt she had suffered at the hands of the landlords she became tongue-tied. After exchanging a few evasive words on the subject, she would turn about abruptly and go out into the yard to do her "chores." What these were it was hard to say. She was too poor to own even a single sheep or pig. Her one chicken spent the whole day fruitlessly clucking and scratching in the empty yard. It was only too obvious that Da Niang was determined to evade my questions, and that made me more anxious than ever to get her story.

One day when she beat her usual retreat I followed her out. I looked around the courtyard and beyond the broken wall without seeing a sign of her. She had vanished.

"Da Niang," I called.

Her wizened face popped out above the dried millet stalks piled on top of the chicken coop. She looked like a gnome. Her sunburnt, yellow skin was wrinkled like a dried orange. Deep brown blotches left by illness or malnutrition disfigured it. Her shifting, hooded eye showed her misgivings. "Now I have to get some water from the well," she said, and went off with the buckets. I was knocking my head against a stone wall of evasiveness. I was sorry to pester her, but she held the key to her own liberation and I needed that key for her sake as well as my own.

That night I lay on the kang racking my brains for an answer to the riddle of Da Niang's silence. Certainly poverty, ignorance, and fear played a part, but the more I thought things over, the more perturbed I grew. If Da Niang weren't somehow linked to the silence and apathy that still shackled half the township, why did she keep such a distance between us in spite of our friendship? Was she deliberately playing a double game—in with the landlords as well as the work team? It was an open secret that her idiot son sometimes slyly visited landlords and drank with them. Who knew what dark impulse might sway his sick mind? The death of Da Niang's younger son looked like an accident, but it could have been planned as a lesson to anyone who shouted accusations against the landlords. Soon I began to wonder if by staying with Da Niang I had unwittingly played into the hands of our enemies.

The light of my oil lamp flickered. It was just a snippet of wick burning on the lip of a saucer. Peasants had used lamps just like it in China's countryside for five thousand years. As it danced, it seemed more fragile than ever. Fantastic shadows moved across the wall. I had not slept soundly one single night since coming back to Da Niang's cottage. I was half-conscious and apprehensive all the time. I felt my body floating up and down endlessly. I never dared sleep and lose consciousness completely.

I was a stranger here and everyone seemed strange to me, at times even Xiu-ying. In a fit of despondency, I wished that I had never volunteered so rashly for this bleak Northwest. Everything here was so totally different, even down to the guttural sounds of the northern dialect. I would at least have felt more at ease speaking our Shanghai dialect closer to home. These thoughts made my brick kang seem all the harder and colder. I was also constantly afraid that one of the landlords' hangers-on would break into my room—to steal, to rape, to murder. No one expected all the landlords to take their losses quietly.

When I walked in the township now I would occasionally pass men dressed in sober black jacket and trousers. They would go by silently, eyes to the ground to avoid being snubbed. They were either landlords or their agents. The peasants turned their eyes away from them, now condemned to live in limbo. Particularly in front of a land reform team worker, greeting the wrong person in public, no matter how long they had known him, meant taking the wrong side. The township was dividing into hostile camps.

I thought I heard footsteps outside my door. I strained my ears. Nothing. My imagination was playing tricks on me. My senses keyed up, I did not know how long it was that I dozed and worried. I heard light steps again approaching my door. This time it was not my imagination. When they stopped at the door, my heart sank. My scalp tingled and I could feel my hair rising in terror. Now he was testing the door. He paused. He was trying to find out how to open it. I listened intently. His hand was on the door, shaking it. I could follow his every movement. My heart jumped into my throat. It stuck there, preventing me from uttering a cry. Slowly, so as not to disturb the intruder, I moved aside the quilt. I took my flashlight from under my pillow and grasped the stick I had placed at the head of the kang. This was the moment I had been dreading.

The door was flung open violently and an immense black shadow moved into the room. I lost all self-control. I screeched like a stuck pig and covered myself with the quilt, clutching it to me as if it were armor. I heard feet padding around the room. I awaited annihilation. Then silence. Nothing happened. Hours seemed to slip by. Nothing had happened. My left leg, doubled up under me, was numb. I stretched it out, slowly, quietly, tentatively lest he should see that someone was there huddled under the quilt.

Again I heard footsteps. Was he waiting outside the door? I had only half unbent my leg. Now I dared not move it further.

"Did you have a nightmare?" said Da Niang's voice. It sounded unutterably comforting there in the dead of night.

"Da Niang," I breathed, "someone broke into my room." I slowly emerged from my quilt fortress.

She chuckled. "It was just a dog."

What a mess I had made of things! And what a coward I had shown myself to be. Fortunately only Da Niang could see me now; but if the joke got around the village, it would mean a complete loss of face. If I had been scared to death by a dog, what about a landlord? Who would believe then that I would stand up to them?

"Da Niang, please sit down here." I moved and made room for her on the kang. "Da Niang . . ." I began, abashed. Da Niang sat down. I held her arm. "Da Niang, please don't tell anyone about tonight." My voice trailed away into the darkness.

"I won't. That I won't," she whispered back. She shook her head and spread her hands palm out and fingers outstretched in opposite directions, to stress that the incident was over and that she would never break her word. Sharing this secret drew us closer together. In that moment she could see me as just an ordinary teenager despite my cadre's uniform; it opened a flood of words and feelings in her.

Suddenly she began chattering away with me as she would with any village girl.

"You city people are really strange. Aren't your parents worried about you in this faraway place? If we marry a daughter into a family ten miles away, it's as if she was at the other end of the world."

"My parents died a long time ago."

"Oh, then that's why you could decide things for yourself. Poor girl, you have no one to guide you." She clicked her tongue sympathetically. "Dear child"—it was the mother in her that spoke—"listen to me. You had better go home. This place can be hell."

"How could I run away before I even have a chance to look around?"

Seeing me twisting around uneasily, she asked, "Lice?" As I nodded uncomfortably, she said, "Bite it." She pushed my hand holding the louse I had caught towards my mouth. "Take your revenge on them and they don't dare come back to bother you."

"Oh, no!" I exclaimed, appalled.

"Let me bite it for you." Apparently it did not matter who wreaked vengeance on the lice, so long as it was done.

"Oh, no. I can't put you to so much trouble," I said, remembering my manners, and I did as the peasants did. I crushed the louse with the back of my nail on the edge of the kang and brushed the remains with distaste onto the floor. What a Shanghai young lady I was now!

"If you stay with us much longer and drink our water, your blood will turn bitter. Now it is still sweet and the lice like to drink it." Genuinely concerned, she shared with me her peasant wisdom.

How could I suspect her? She was not unkind or devious by nature; but like some gnarled tree on a windswept mountainside her body and soul had been twisted by the harshness of her environment. I began to like her, but the mystery of her attitude to the landlords remained between us.

"Da Niang, if I hadn't moved here to stay with you, we might never have got to be friends." I put my hands behind my head, lying back on my pillow. "Perhaps I ought to stay with some other family next. How about the young widow?"

"No, Heaven forbid! That house is haunted by the ghost of her husband." Da Niang was really disturbed by my proposal. She darted a stealthy glance at the darkness outside the window. She edged closer to me and spoke almost in a whisper. "The widow is so haunted that he has become a living ghost."

"What is a living ghost?"

"Every night he comes to her kang."

"Da Niang, surely you don't believe that?"

"I have never seen him myself, but some people say that they have heard her talking and singing to him in the middle of the night." Then, deciding she'd said enough for one evening, she pulled up the quilt and tucked it under my chin. She trimmed the wick of the sputtering oil lamp so that I would have no trouble lighting it in the morning, frugally blew it out, and left me to return to her own room.

The day had not yet broken when I woke again. A cold twilight filled the room. Half awake, my thoughts wandered idly. My vest was damp and sticky from perspiration and dirt, and I remembered the louse. I had not bathed once since coming to the village. There was no bathhouse and no one remembered when there had ever been one; there wasn't even a tub in any of the peasants' houses, for, of course, water was too precious to waste on such an activity—so I had had to make do with a sponge bath every now and then. I thought how nice it would be to soak myself in a real bathtub like the one in my aunt's house in Shanghai—hot and cold running water and an overhead shower, white enamel gleaming, blue tiles glistening with steamy drops, chrome taps sparkling; or, better yet, swimming in a pool; or, better still, in the sea. I saw in front of me an emerald green sea, shot through with blue-green currents; an ultramarine sky with fleecy clouds, rust-colored cliffs crowned with green. Square-sailed junks against a background of white skyscrapers piled one above another up the mountainside, far away on the other side of the strait. And the lazy waves lapping the golden sand, calling me in.

I must have dozed off again. I was in my uncle's house in Hong Kong. I had drunk tea on its porch, watching the sunset play on the sea. I had walked down to the beach and dived into the reflection of the high-sailing clouds, swimming away from land, letting the water caress my cheeks and lull my body. And then suddenly I was in trouble. Something was pulling me down. The water closed over me. My lungs ached, gasping for breath. I flailed my arms and kicked my feet frantically in an effort to keep my mouth above water, to get a gulp of air.

I woke up again with a start, my heart pounding. My eyes stung and I seemed to be enveloped in a heavy fog. My throat was parched. Suddenly I sat up, alarmed. The "fog" was smoke, and it swirled around my tiny bedroom. Had someone set fire to the house? I jumped off the kang. Coughing and groping, not feeling the cold earth of the floor, I stumbled into the outer room. Here the smoke was even thicker and it billowed out through the front door, which was ajar. I caught sight of a vague figure in the corner by the brick and mud stove and I was just about to scream when I heard Da Niang's voice ask, "Is there too much smoke?"

The room was swimming in smoke. But she had spoken quietly, excusing herself as if it were nothing—a small cooking mishap. I felt the cold on the soles of my feet and hurried back onto the kang to put on my clothes. Da Niang followed me carrying a basket of what looked like mud cakes.

"The weather has turned cold and I wanted to heat your room up a bit before you got up." She fumbled in her basket and took out a few pieces of mud cake which she put beside the flue of the kang. "When it gets really cold, you can use more of these. It's just dung, chopped hay, and a bit of coal dust, but it burns. Put a few twigs and some stalks in first as kindling. Trouble is it stinks when it burns, and it smokes something awful, but what's to be done? We have no wood to burn here."

"Da Niang, it's good of you to think of me," I thanked her.

She wandered into the outer room in that vague way she sometimes had, mumbling to herself, and I was left alone. I took a clean vest from under my pillow and changed into it in the warmth of my quilt. Then I got up and hurriedly washed and dressed myself while I still felt warm. I opened the battered front door and the cold air of the half-dawn brought me fully awake. The sky was leaden grey and so was the expanse of plain beyond Da Niang's broken wall. The horizon was lost in the morning mist and the little courtyard seemed like an island in a grey void. My head throbbed painfully after my troubled night, and I thought I would walk the ache away, but my limbs felt heavy. I breathed hard even though I had walked only a short distance. I sat down to rest on a rock jutting into the narrow footpath in the field. Dew from the weeds had beaded my shoes and the ends of my trousers.

It was quite dark. Gusts of wind blowing across the empty fields around me chilled to the bone. My whole body was numb and aching with cold. Many peasants started their day at this hour and would soon be getting up. I could join them. And then I was struck by a thought even colder than the morning wind: Why did I not admit at least to myself that I was not one of them? I didn't belong here. It was completely alien to me. I could just do what was normally expected of one in this job. Why strain to do more? I was making myself sick. If nothing else, this cold would kill me. It had never been as cold as this in Shanghai. "Oh, Mother!" It was the first time in my life I had called out to my dead mother. I felt lost like a child in the wilderness.

I heard footsteps in the mist, and my first instinct was to turn and run; fighting that impulse, I froze in my tracks.

A figure carrying a mattock on its shoulder emerged out of the darkness. It was the virgin widow. Accustomed to her solitary existence, she either did not notice or ignored me. She entered the unkempt field near me and began to break up the clods of earth. Her mattock's blade was broken and blunt. The handle was too short. Soon she was breathing hard from this back-breaking toil. As she paused to rest and straighten her back I greeted her and offered to lend a hand.

She turned her face to me. As I looked into it, at the wide-set eyes drained of all expression, my heart contracted.

She gave me her mattock and then walked away, still without a word. She disappeared into the darkness, but soon returned with another broken mattock in her hand. We worked together in silence. The earth was dry and frozen hard as stone. Layers of some whitish substance ran through it. I knew enough country lore by then to recognize that this was poor alkaline soil and that no matter how much she toiled on it with her broken tools it would never yield enough to feed her and her parents-in-law disabled by age and illness.

I wondered what she was going to plant. But then I thought that it would make very little difference unless there was a radical change all around. Since coming to Longxiang I had never seen a peasant eat meat or fish, fresh vegetables, or rice or flour. Yet how they toiled with their broken hoes on this grudging soil! Year after year the virgin widow had slaved drearily on her little plot of land with never a hope of release. With tears of rage in my eyes, I felt like crying out loud to the whole world about this exhausted, barren land and its owner. Then a spasm gripped my empty stomach. I was famished, my head dizzy, my hands trembling. I swallowed my anger.

"Soon you will have more and better land," I said, comforting her as well as reassuring myself. "About nine *mu*—four times what you have now."

She did not appear to hear me.

"Doesn't that make you happy?" I persisted.

"Even if we get more land I can't till it all by myself."

"What will you do then?"

"We will sell it," she said matter-of-factly.

"Sell it?" I exclaimed, aghast. "But then when you have used that money up, you will be as badly off as you are today."

She paused in her work and gave me a long, hard stare. "No tools, no plow, no water, no work hands—no nothing. We are too poor to till nine *mu*."

Her words were like a slap in the face. All this effort and struggle for the land reform and then she would turn around and sell the land and after a few months be back where she was now. I was going to remonstrate with her but I stopped with my first words. Suffering, want, and ridicule had utterly crushed her spirit.

She went back to hacking away at the earth with her blunt mattock, and I joined her, working silently while I collected my thoughts. Her last words had been a complaint, but also a query and a challenge. She wanted an answer to the bitter questions in her heart, and I wanted to be sure that I gave her the right answer, if I could.

Mutual aid, cooperatives, mechanization, electricity, modernization—we had discussed all this in our study classes back in Shanghai. Although the details of these plans were still not clear to me, because I knew next to nothing about farming, I accepted them on trust. It had seemed to me then that the peasants' problems would be easily solved once they got land of their own and had the will to prosper. Once you had your own plot, what was so hard about raising a good crop on it? I had had no conception of the magnitude of the problems the peasants faced. No wonder the young widow could think only of traditional ways of solving her problems: If you had land and were driven to extremities, you sold it and staved off the final catastrophe for yet another few months. The inadequacy of my answers was clear. There was no way short of a miracle for a poverty-stricken widow with two ailing parents to prosper.

The day was really breaking now. The sky grew brighter. The bluish-grey mist which shrouded the fields rose and was scattered by the rays of the sun. Soon it cleared completely. The houses, cottages, and hovels of the village, the open fields and distant mountains were revealed under the deep blue sky. In the brightness of the cold North China winter's day things looked better; even the harsh features of the widow were mellowed. Her figure was still slim except for her slightly thickened hips. Her still-firm breasts bobbed up and down rhythmically in time with the movements of her arms swinging her heavy mattock. The sleeve beneath her armpit was torn. The thick black hair gleamed wet with perspiration. Despite her sorrows and hardships her feet stood firm on the earth. "Some day I will advise her to find a good man and sleep in the warmth of his arms instead of clinging to a piece of cold wood every night," I said to myself and made a mental note of my resolve. "I'll tell her, 'Don't listen to that nonsense about being burned eternally in Hell if you enjoy life and break these stupid old traditions. Free yourself of vain anxieties about the next life and enjoy this one, the only one you are sure of.' "

Aloud I told her, "You are strong and capable. You can till a few *mu* and others will help you till the rest. You will get tools to till the land and seed to sow. Soon the peasants will have tractors to do the heavy work. Even a young girl can drive a tractor and plow thirty *mu* a day."

"Thirty *mu* a day?" the virgin widow repeated in evident doubt. No man in Longxiang could do that, not even the strongest. "But what is a tractor? I suppose that needs an ox to pull it?"

The sun had risen well over the horizon.

"I must go and boil water for Father and Mother."

I gave the mattock back to her. "I'll come again. Why don't you come to one of our meetings and hear about the land reform?"

She paused and thought for a moment or two, and then turned away without a word.

Criticism and Self-Criticism

By early winter, Wang Sha, Cheng, and I had talked with nearly every poor peasant of the township and with many others besides. Most of them were part-time farmers like the blacksmith and carpenter, two peddlers, the local herb doctor, and the "vet" who had no diploma but knew more about animals and their ailments than anyone else around. A core of activists had gathered around us, and when it was made generally known that all landless and landpoor peasants and middle peasants could join and vote at meetings of the Poor Peasants' Association, we soon had enough members to establish—or rather re-establish—it as the real headquarters of the land reform. From what we heard, all the work teams had made similar progress, and the county leadership and Wang Sha thought the time ripe for us to get together to sum up our experiences and plan our next moves. A conference of all the work teams was called at the county center, twenty miles from Longxiang.

I looked forward to a chance for a good talk with Ma Li. So much had happened since we'd seen each other. I was eager to share my thoughts with her and compare notes. It was not a matter of personal hopes and expectations, successes and difficulties only, but of the "big picture" too. Had anyone found the right key to unlock the secrets of the villages?

I also had to admit that after a month in tiny Longxiang

with its six hundred people even the dilapidated county town seemed appealing. I studied the conference schedule to see if I would have enough free time to do some shopping, to eat at least one well-cooked meal in a restaurant, and perhaps see a local opera. By the looks of it, it seemed that if everything went as planned I could do all that I wished.

Wang Sha went ahead of us to prepare for the conference. Malvolio Cheng and I set out together the next day at dawn. It was a fine day in early winter. The morning air was cold and fresh. The sun rose in a cloudless sky and gilded the mountains on our western horizon. I was not walking; I was dancing along the road. Cheng whistled joyfully. We took a shortcut through a grove of pine trees on a sandy knoll.

"Wait a minute, I've got some sand in my slipper," I called out. I supported myself with one hand on a towering pine. With the other I took off my slipper, but I lost my balance. As I tried to steady myself, the slipper fell out of my hand and rolled a few feet down the slope.

"Hold on," cried Cheng. "I'll get it for you."

He leaned down to pick up the slipper. I saw a vein beat fast at the side of his muscular neck. I snatched up a handful of pine needles and dropped them down his collar. Cheng gave a start and twisted his neck to shake off the prickly needles. He frowned at me in a super-villainous way, and I chuckled. We went on our way in high good humor.

The courtyard of the county office was crowded with work team cadres when we arrived. A musician was playing an accordion and Liao was entertaining the crowd with some sort of Russian or Hungarian folk dance. One moment he was circling the courtyard with his arms outspread, then he was squatting down on his heels, his arms crossed calmly on his chest, throwing out first one leg and then the other. Next he would leap high in the air, clicking his heels together first on one side and then on the other. Finally he whirled in the air and spun like a cartwheel while the accordionist's fingers fluttered with lightning speed over the keys. When he stopped, he stood perfectly balanced on his two feet, arms spread wide as if it had all been effortless. It was a marvelous performance. When we applauded him a smile lit up his face. Then I saw him cast a shy, sidelong glance at the pretty dancer Chu Hua who had so attracted me at Yang Gui-fei's hot spring. A blush spread over her face, and I smiled too in sympathy with them. Liao was not much to look at in his dusty cadre's uniform, but when he danced, his whole being radiated vitality.

Ma Li greeted me warmly, as I did her, and we could not get the words out fast enough to tell our tales.

"I've heard that when we go back to our villages we're going to start searching landlords' houses!" she whispered to me.

"Who told you that?"

"Don't be inquisitive." She turned around with a short laugh and walked backwards, saying, "They'll tell us in the conference. We aren't supposed to know about it yet."

By mid-afternoon all seventy of us were gathered together in the largest hall at the county office, which for lack of suitable accommodation was temporarily located in part of an ancient Confucian temple. Everyone, it seemed, wanted to talk at once. Everyone had "unique" experiences, everyone had triumphs, and all had problems. But there was no doubt of the enthusiasm that animated everyone. From the reports given during the two days of the conference we learned that the work teams had indeed more or less kept pace with each other, though no two townships were alike. In some the peasants had moved ahead a bit faster than most, while in others it had taken a bit longer to get going. But no two townships posed exactly the same problems. In a couple of places where there were sizable congregations of Moslems there had been greater resistance to freeing the women and giving them equal rights. In two others, due to the covert influence of the landlords, the work teams had not managed even to organize effective Poor Peasants' Associations and everything hung fire. The county leadership arranged to reinforce these lagging teams with more experienced cadres. Cheng gave the report of our Longxiang work team and it appeared that we had done only about as well as the average, which was still better than we had thought.

When all the reports were in, it was clear that in most townships, including Longxiang, the landlords, seemingly quiescent at the start, were now moving on the sly to counter the arrival of the work teams. "Bamboo tele-graphs"—swift-flying village gossip—carried news and rumors from village to village. Events were moving to a confrontation. And just as Ma Li had predicted, it was de-cided that we should keep the initiative in the work teams' hands by confronting the landlords directly by a search of their homes. The aim would be to unearth incriminating evidence of sabotage of the land reform. On this note we prepared to return to our villages.

I looked at my watch as we were dismissed. A few hours remained before our departure, and a general hubbub broke out as we began discussing how to enjoy them shop-ping and sightseeing in the town. The chairman had diffi-culty making himself heard, but by banging on his table he finally regained our attention. Wang Sha announced that the deputy county Party secretary wished to chat with a couple of dozen of us, all working in villages lying close to each other, while a few other teams would meet sepa-rately to discuss matters that concerned them only. A bit mystified, we reluctantly saw our friends move off to en-joy themselves in the town.

I was delayed a few moments and entered the office to find the deputy secretary—the same one who'd given us that boring lecture on propriety in Xian—seated on the kang, one leg folded under him, the other dangling to the floor. But his uneasiness showed through his exaggerated-ly relaxed air. He was smoking one cigarette after another and the butts littered the floor around him.

"Welcome, welcome," he said cordially. "Please sit down. Have a cup of tea." Then he corrected himself with a laugh when he recalled that there was no tea. It would have been a luxury here, with so many people to be served. "Have a cup of hot water," he offered instead, and without waiting for an answer he rose, opened the Thermos bottle on the office table, and filled several bowls for us.

We thanked him and passed the bowls around. This broke the tension for a moment, but we wondered why he wanted to talk with us.

He cleared his throat. "I want to thank you for your work in the land reform. Yes. I thank you personally and also on behalf of the county leadership for your public spirit in coming so far to help us. You are doing fine. Yes. Doing fine."

His cigarette was burning to the end. He took a last frugal puff, holding the short stub carefully at the very tip between two fingers. After the hesitant pause he continued:

"Before you came, we wondered whether you city people could adjust to life here or not. Writers, artists, actors, dancers, we thought, are rather special people, unused to hardship, especially those from a big city like Shanghai. But all of you are working hard and have accomplished a lot." He paused again and then, remembering that he was not supposed to be giving a lecture but just having a chat, said, "I'm afraid I'm boring you again." His face, bronzed by years of work in the countryside, in the fields and the mountains, suddenly showed embarrassment.

"I hope we haven't disappointed you." Wang Sha's laugh was a little strained.

"Oh, no. I'm sure not." Then he turned to Wang Sha as our representative. "I think that's all I want to say now. Just, 'Thank you.' You will excuse me now, I hope. I have a few words to say to some of the other work teams."

He seemed very anxious to leave us in Wang Sha's charge. Something had gone wrong, and our group must have gone more wrong than the others, otherwise Wang Sha would not be devoting all his time to us this afternoon. A buzz of conversation broke out as soon as he closed the door but ceased immediately as Wang Sha began hesitantly to speak:

"You have heard what the deputy secretary said. We are working hard, and doing fine. But as our host, he did not think it polite to tell us where we had gone wrong; he left it to me. Let me put it this way: We can work harder and better and we must avoid making mistakes."

"What precisely do you want to tell us? We won't feel hurt. If we've done anything wrong, I'm sure we all want to know what it is." It was Ma Li speaking. She glanced around at us as if asking if everyone agreed with her.

"I'm sorry to take up more of your time. I know you want to go out and enjoy yourselves during the small amount of free time that you have. You deserve it. But what we're going to speak about now is most important for future work. There is going to be a direct confrontation with the landlords and we must be well prepared for that. We must have strict discipline. We must act as if we were real soldiers, because this is a real battle. There is real fighting going on in Korea. American planes are dropping Guomindang leaflets calling on the landlords and the people to oppose the land reform and reporting that the cadres and peasants are committing all sorts of atrocities as they take the land from the landlords. Arms are being smuggled in to the reactionaries and our army is having to guard the coast across from Taiwan.

"We here are far away from these events, but you can see for yourselves that we are all part of the same battle.

"Unfortunately, some comrades have forgotten the discipline that we have been told about again and again both in Shanghai and in Xian. We can't allow that to pass easily. Today three people will criticize themselves. Who will speak first?"

There was a moment's silence. We had had quite a few of these criticism and self-criticism sessions back in Shanghai. Every two or three weeks those who worked in the same department got together to hold one. It was a cross between a family council, a group therapy session, and a Roman Catholic confessional. One could bring up any topic: work, marriage, love affairs, sins committed in fact or in one's head, anything under the sun. There were all sorts of ways of communicating one's thoughts, the consciousness of one's transgressions, anxieties, and criticisms of others. This was not something new to us, but this was the first time we had been called to such a meeting here in Gansu. We wondered who had been "undisciplined" and how seriously. Where? When?

Someone coughed discreetly either to distract attention or to cover up his confusion. It was the amateur archaeologist Hu.

"Shall I speak first?" he asked Wang Sha, half rising to his feet.

"Go ahead, please. But there's no need to stand up."

"Well, as you all know . . . " He lowered his eyes and searched for something on the floor of the office before looking up and proclaiming, "Well, I am always very proud of our ancient culture."

"What has that got to do with your mistakes?" a voice interjected querulously.

"Well, one afternoon I picked up a piece of pottery near the courtyard I live in. I inspected the pattern on it. It could be Tang pottery or even earlier, a piece from the Han dynasty."

The amateur archaeologist began to describe his find with growing relish. His eyes and eyebrows danced. His fingers traced patterns in the air.

"To the point. Let's hear about your mistake."

The young man who had interrupted before spoke again, but this time he stood up impatiently, legs wide apart, hands on hips. He was an actor who usually played the role of a young factory worker or a dashing guerrilla fighter. With a heavy dose of sarcasm in his voice, he added, "If you would be kind enough to cut a long story short, we might still have time enough to take a look around the town."

"I am coming to the point. Well, I thought that if I could identify it, I could send it to the Palace Museum in Peking. It might lead to some important discovery."

"Are you praising yourself or criticizing yourself?" another voice asked.

"I am not praising myself. I am presenting the facts. Now you have interrupted me. I've forgotten where I was." And he scratched his head perplexedly.

"You were in the Palace Museum," someone said helpfully.

"Ah, yes. I thought I could send it to the Palace Museum if I could identify it. But how was I going to do that, I asked myself. The farmer whose cottage I share is a poor peasant. Yes, there I take a firm class stand: I live with a poor peasant, and I'm glad of it." Realizing that he was boasting again, he stopped short. "Anyway, my host told me that there was a landlord nearby who had a very good library. He suggested that I might find a suitable reference book there."

"So you went to visit him and became his friend." To hurry him up Ma Li finished the sentence for him. "Did he throw a dinner party for you?"

"No. We only drank tea."

"Tea?" exclaimed Dai Shi, as quick to fire as ever. "You call it tea! Who drinks tea here? It was blood. He sucked blood from the peasants and you sucked with him." She still could not resist the opportunity to show off her super-revolutionary spirit.

"Excuse me. I don't want to defend him, but a sip of tea does not make him a bloodsucker," interjected the soprano with mild reproof.

"There is no need to exaggerate. But that was a deplorable mistake to make," said Ma Li sternly. "Here we are trying to deflate the arrogance of the landlords and you go out of your way to boost their prestige. Many peasants are still hanging back, waiting to see how we will handle the landlords, and this is the way you handle them. No wonder some of the peasants are still afraid to speak out against the landlords!"

We all chimed in at this and gave him such a tongue-lashing that he hung his head with remorse and finally promised never again to forget his class stand.

Now, who were the other two culprits? They must have made worse mistakes. The worst culprit always speaks last at a criticism meeting. I looked over at Wang Sha. He was gazing out of the window at the clouds scudding by.

Without any introduction, the pretty dancer Chu Hua cried, "I said, 'No, no, no,' but he said it was all right." Her voice quavered to a stop. She was on the verge of tears.

It did not take much guessing to know that the "he" was the agile folk dancer Liao who sat next to her. He sat with his long legs stretched out in a half-reclining posture, his arms crossed defiantly over his chest. He tried to put on a devil-may-care expression but it lacked conviction.

"Why did you seduce her?" Ma Li upbraided him indignantly.

"Now come," protested one of our young actors. He was good at acting proletarian parts. "Now it's you exaggerating. It was mutual seduction, that's clear."

"No, we didn't seduce each other." The folk dancer Liao mumbled something else that was unintelligible. We did not understand what he was trying to say. He was probably glad that his speech puzzled us; it gave him time to reconsider. "We were talking about work."

"Work!" exploded Dai Shi.

"We cannot blame you for being engrossed in your work," the amateur archaeologist Hu smiled benevolently. His ordeal now happily over, he could use his experience to point out loopholes in other people's stories.

The folk dancer felt he had to explain himself. "While we were talking, we were walking through the woods," the young lover went on, ignoring the archaeologist's remark.

"In the woods?" the soprano exclaimed involuntarily. She raised her hand to her mouth to stifle a cry of surprise, or maybe sympathy.

"May I ask what is the difference between forgetting yourself in the woods or in the house? A mistake is a mistake," said Ma Li irritably.

"In the woods, one can become intoxicated with the beauty of nature. They might have forgotten themselves completely, thrown away all discretion, forgotten all precautions. You are a dancer. If you became pregnant what would you do?" the soprano spoke gently to Chu Hua.

The gasp of fright in the dancer's throat strangled another bout of sobs.

"But we plan to get married as soon as we get back to Shanghai," Liao asserted in defense.

But Dai Shi was unmoved.

"I think it's disgusting the way they've behaved! Send them back to Shanghai immediately," she demanded.

"Oh, no! That's too much of a disgrace!" cried several voices, mine included. We deplored the young couple's lack of discipline, but we were also repelled by Dai Shi's lack of understanding, her self-righteous arrogance. We made it clear that we would resist any such harsh treatment of the two lovers.

"Do the peasants know about this?" Cheng asked.

"No, it's not yet public knowledge," answered Wang Sha.

"Then why don't we keep it quiet, 'in the family,' as it were."

"No," retorted Ma Li. She turned to Liao and addressed him directly with great severity. "You know the peasants abhor the idea of young people falling in love and choosing their own marriage partners. To their minds, free choice in love is the same as adultery. If they find out what you've done they'll distrust all of us. Then how can we go on working as before?"

The dancer hung his head. All his earlier bravado had disappeared.

Ma Li stood up. Now we knew that she would certainly give us a long harangue, full of moral admonitions and sententious remarks. The young actor, who could himself make such speeches admirably on the stage, helplessly rolled his eyes at the ceiling. The soprano adjusted herself more comfortably in her armchair, the only one in the room, and shielded her eyes with her hand. She would doze away the coming session. Those like me who had not yet spoken now felt obliged to prepare speeches that would match Ma Li's. I regretted that I had not spoken earlier.

But my reluctance to criticize hardly surprised me. I knew only too well that I could have made the same mistake myself if circumstances had conspired against me. Now I would have to pretend by implication that my own thoughts and conduct were wholly above reproach. The thought crossed my mind: Should I make a self-criticism instead of criticizing them? Waves of anxiety and indecision rose in me.

I remembered one afternoon in Longxiang when I had gone to Wang Sha's room. He wasn't there. I went in and touched the places on his mattress burnt by his careless cigarettes and roughly patched over. I trembled with longing for him. I stood by his kang. I felt his kisses and embraces. An idea took shape in my mind: Only once, just once, let passion sweep me off my feet. Let them punish me afterwards, I wouldn't care. The confession was on the tip of my tongue. I swallowed hard, trying to swallow it back down my throat. No, I couldn't bring myself to bare my soul in public, especially in front of Dai Shi. She would screw up her face in scorn of me. No, I would not give her the satisfaction of humiliating me. But then, perhaps in criticizing them I would be criticizing and exhorting myself, giving myself strength to resist a similar temptation.

I felt Ma Li's eyes were on my face, questioning my silence. When I looked back at her and caught her eye, a shadow had come over her face. I had to say something.

"At the beginning of this session, when Comrade Wang Sha was talking, I recalled a scene in my childhood." I halted and made an effort to fight down the memory of that other scene that would have exposed the impropriety of my conduct. I spoke falteringly. "I was a little girl then, a first-grader on her first day of school—" I stopped again. My thoughts were still in a turmoil, so that I hardly knew what I was going to say next. Even if only Wang Sha and Ma Li had some idea of what I was really thinking, I knew I must go on rambling until I could articulate thoughts more relevant to the present situation. So I began again. "I stood at the school gate, watching my aunt getting back into her car. The car moved off and I felt as if my world was coming to an end. 'Ling-ling, let's take a look at our garden,' a quiet voice addressed me. I turned around. Here stood my first teacher, an American nun. While walking around the garden, she said to me that some day I might forget many things about the school, but I would remember the beautiful garden. She was wrong. I remember many things I learned there. I still can quote Patrick Henry's words, 'Give me liberty or give me death.' I still can quote Lincoln's speech about 'government of, by, and for the people' and the American Civil War to liberate the black slaves. I still observe our school's motto, 'To serve,' to serve the poor as Jesus Christ had done. Those words inspired me. This is one of the reasons why I'm here. Maybe you're wondering why I'm telling you all this?"

The hint of drama in my tone implied that I was about to confess something important. I felt Dai Shi's eyes fixed on my face. I calmed myself by telling myself that it was always safer to confess a past mistake than a current sin. "You see, because I was raised in American missionary schools and heard these things, I trusted the Americans too much. I never believed that the Americans could do to China what they are doing now: to thwart our revolution to liberate the peasants from slavery and try to tell us what government we should have. I can see now that everything is linked together. We really are in one big battle, and everything that interferes with our fighting that battle successfully must be severely criticized."

I paused to steal a glance at Wang Sha. From the way he gazed out the window I knew that he was paying careful attention to all that was being said. Reassured, I spoke out even more vehemently.

"As for Chu Hua and Liao, I think they deserve severe punishment. What they have done was indeed thoughtless because it has happened at this particular moment, in this particular place. Individual happiness has to be sacrificed to the demands of the revolution. We all of us are living under the same voluntary constraint. Each one's failure to live up to our undertakings weakens us all."

When I had finished my speech, Chu Hua shot me a flabbergasted "You too, Brutus" look. I felt uneasy about myself; I didn't like myself for what I had done. I had used the same strategy that every participant in a criticism meeting was familiar with: Focus the attack on others in order to escape it yourself.

"What shall we do about this affair?" Wang Sha asked. I wondered if anyone besides myself noticed that he spoke with a touch of sad helplessness. For a moment he looked with compassion on these two erring lovers. Then he collected himself and said in a firmer voice, "You two cannot go on working in the same village."

"Send them back to Shanghai. They are no better than traitors," Dai Shi persisted stubbornly.

"Keep them together and see that they behave in the future," said another voice.

"Oh, God, what a punishment," Malvolio Cheng muttered under his breath. He was sitting just behind me. Aloud, he said, "I suggest that one of them be transferred to another village."

"I second that motion," I added quickly, trying to make amends for my harshness of a few minutes before.

"Why don't you exchange your place with her?" Dai Shi asked me in an insinuating voice.

Wang Sha's lowered eyelids blinked almost imperceptibly. He darted a glance out of the corner of his eye in my direction, but not at me.

"I don't mind exchanging places with her," said Ma Li in a more conciliatory mood.

This was a reasonable solution and the whole group accepted it. But in the meantime I realized that while I might have voted for a good solution to their problem, I was now facing a new problem of my own.

At this meeting we had been learning to run affairs, to dispense justice in a fair way, but I was worried by the way in which even-handed consideration of a problem had been mixed with flagrant self-serving, and by myself as much as any.

11

The Search

It was an unusually mild winter night. Moonlight softened every line of house and tree. Stars twinkled in the dark-blue sky. The air was scented by the breath of still-distant spring. On such a night at another time I would have lain down on my bed, content to gaze peacefully through the window at the heavens. But tonight I was too troubled to go to bed and sleep. Tomorrow we would start searching the landlords' houses. Wang Sha, Malvolio Cheng, Shen, Tu, and I had discussed and planned everything—or so we thought—but, as my aunt used to say, I'm a "worrywart." This head-on confrontation could lead to violence, and while I had no fear of a verbal battle I knew my ninety-five pounds stood no chance in a real fight. I had heard that the peasants could get so aroused that they threw discipline to the winds. I knew that the landlords could get so desperate that they resorted to murder. I doubted if we could control events completely, but I put my hopes in Shen and Tu and Cheng. Any mishap would be our responsibility. We had plenty to worry about all right.

I had come to rely more and more on Malvolio Cheng. For all his eccentricities, I found that, when needed, he was a mine of information and level headed, too. Twenty years of activism put him that many years ahead of me in experience and judgment. That evening I asked him, "Cheng, tell me truly. Do you think the landlords in Long-xiang are hiding arms?"

"They're guilty until they prove they're innocent, if you get what I mean." He was frowning with concentration as he considered how best to explain this to me. Finally he said, "Look at it this way. The landlords' houses are fortresses, real fortresses, spiritual strongholds. We have to break into those forts. Right now, I can bet that some landlord is drinking wine with some peasants, perhaps with a few of our own people. The antique furniture, the old paintings on the walls, family heirlooms, shelves of books, solid walls of brick . . . all these things create a feeling of stability, of something unchanging and imperishable."

Cheng spoke with an unaccustomed seriousness that gave depth to his voice. He knew what he was talking about. He came from a landlord family himself; I knew little more about it than that. But while I had seen the world from a high-rise apartment building or a villa in the middle of modern and almost wholly bourgeois Shanghai, Cheng had lived in and grown up in that old world of village feudalism. Intellectually he shared the progressive beliefs of our time, but at the same time he seemed unable to shake off a lingering memory of life in his landlord father's home. Bits of this conflict had come out in conversation as we got to know each other better during our time in Longxiang, and now I posed a direct question about it.

"Cheng, are you talking about things you've felt yourself?"

He started, surprised at the bluntness of the question. Then he looked at me frankly, full in the face, for a long while.

"Yes. But I long ago rejected that life." His face and voice showed that he had no regrets on that score. He shrugged his shoulders and continued:

"After a few cups of wine the slightly tipsy guests will be feeling cozy and safe inside the impregnable fortress. With a confidential air their host will show them the deeds to his land embossed with imposing vermilion seals. He will tell them that to his certain knowledge Chiang Kai-shek is by no means finished, that he has gathered a huge army on Taiwan and one fine day will be coming back. Other peasants, not favored to enter these halls, finer than any they have ever seen in their lives, will believe that these fortresses are protected by the spirits of the land-lords' ancestors and the gods who have always served the rich.

"Those myths must be destroyed. The only way is for the peasants to invade those fortresses and see for them-selves that they are not impregnable, that there is nothing sacred about them." From that we went on to review the details of our next day's activities, reading through our notes from the recent conference and racking our brains to uncover possible flaws in our plans.

Finally Cheng yawned and stood up to stretch his arms and back. "Let's call it a day. No matter how we plan and calculate, something will always crop up to take us by sur-prise."

Next morning at daybreak we found an encouraging number of activists, including Xiu-ying, gathered in the courtyard of the office. But we waited in vain for Shen and Tu. Finally a ragged urchin rushed up with a message that they would both be late because they had been called to another village on "urgent business." At this late moment we could not delay or postpone action. Left to ourselves, Cheng and I gathered the group around us and gave them some last encouraging words of exhortation. We told them to observe the discipline and laws of the laboring people; incriminating evidence or ill-gotten gains found in the search were to be turned in to two older peasants who would record it all in a notebook. At this point nothing else should be removed from the landlord's home.

As we moved off, a busily chattering group of more than a dozen, I was surprised to see several old women with their children edge their way into our ranks. A few other men and women straggled along behind us, far enough away so that they could still turn back but near enough to see what was going on or even join in the action. Most of the villagers went about their business as usual or timidly looked out of their doorways.

Our first target was the nearest landlord, a man named Bai. His house, surrounded by a stout brick wall with a single gate, stood a little apart from the cluster of build-ings, farm houses, and hovels that made up the central village of the township area. We marched without order and without ceremony straight across the stubbled fields that made up his estate. In the lead was Little Tian, one of our young activists, carrying a small red flag on a pole.

We had sent ahead no word of our coming, but when we reached the gate of Bai's walled compound, he already stood there waiting to receive us like guests. He was dressed in a worn but warm padded gown with a small black skullcap on his head. His black trousers were caught up at the ankles with black bands. On his feet were white socks and black cotton slippers with thick white soles. He had everything ready that we demanded: land deeds, account books, contracts, receipts for sales and loans. He said he had decided to cooperate and do everything according to the law, and so it seemed, but the smile on his sallow face was forced, and his eye pouches were baggy from lack of sleep. He led us politely inside the courtyard murmuring, "Please, please."

As soon as we stepped into the courtyard, the hubbub died down and the villagers became very quiet. They craned their necks looking around, inspecting everything, touching nothing. These decorated courtyards and rooms, which seemed almost dowdy to me, filled them with awe. Many had seen such opulence before when they worked in the landlords' households, but then they had been only servants. Here for the first time in their lives they were being treated like honored guests by the "master" himself. It threw them off balance, as it was intended to, and they followed him sheepishly. It was like a lugubrious housewarming. Nothing was going according to plan. Something had to be done to rouse our docile troops.

Cheng motioned me aside. With a jerk of his head he directed my eyes along a dark corridor out of the main courtyard.

"I'm going to break the kitchen door. You get hold of the biggest pot you can find and smash it on the ground."

"What for?" I was bewildered.

"That means we challenge him by destroying his honor. It's the peasants' custom in the South. We break his rice bowl. If he doesn't accept the challenge, then in their eyes he will have lost face. Maybe it won't work here, but it's worth a try!"

Cheng rolled up his sleeves and picked up a cleaver in the kitchen. In a corner, I found a big iron cauldron that was used to cook food for at least fifteen people. I dragged it over to Cheng who was dismantling the door.

"I can't even hold it up, how can I throw it down?" I asked, my face already bathed in sweat from the effort I had made.

"I'll help you."

"No, you have the door to attend to. It will be more effective if we can smash both the door and the pot at the same time," I said.

"That's right." But even Xiu-ying and I together could not lift the pot. So we decided to switch roles, even though according to Cheng's ideas this seemed to spoil the aesthetics of the operation.

While Cheng dragged the heavy pot out to the center of the courtyard, Xiu-ying and I took a leaf of the kitchen door and carried it along behind him. Some of the peasants stood in a ring, watching expectantly but not helping us. The three of us struggled to lift up the pot but when we let it drop on the flagstones it refused to break—a dull thud and that was all. After recovering our breath we tried to lift it higher. We failed again, but this time the flagstone cracked. Suddenly I had a brainstorm.

"Cheng, you take the cleaver and smash the door. I'll take a hammer and I'll beat the pot like a cymbal."

"Good idea." At least we could do something with the pot!

Hearing the noise, the rest of the peasants ran out of the rooms into the courtyard, not believing what they saw. These cadres were certainly full of surprises! The landlord's face turned deathly white. We clearly had spoiled his strategy. He was trembling uncontrollably. Even his head shook. It was a miserable, pitiful sight.

"Search!" shouted Cheng, theatrically pointing at the master bedroom.

But the peasants now showed a will of their own. To our consternation, the activists, followed by their supporters, who had unexpectedly increased in number, scattered in different directions like the Furies unleashed. Cheng and I were left standing in the courtyard while chaos reigned. We heard the sharp crack of objects breaking, the splintering of wood, sounds of dragging heavy objects. There were cries of anger, triumph, surprise, and rage. Two children, their pockets bulging with small loot, scuttled out of a room and shot like arrows across the courtyard and out the gate before we could stop them. Their mothers looked pleased, then affected surprise.

One of the old peasant tally men had the presence of mind to close the compound gate and stand guard over it. Now no one could get in or out.

I shouted to Cheng above the hubbub, "We came here to get criminal evidence, but this is a total mess!"

"We can't interfere now," he returned. "We wanted the masses to move and now they have! We can't stop them now. Anyway, I'm sure the landlords know what we're after, and you can be sure they're already one step ahead of us and our search."

"But the peasants are carrying out whatever they fancy—and some are stealing to boot!"

"The owners have surely hidden away anything that's really valuable. We can't let the peasants go away empty-handed, but we do have to stop them from wholesale stealing."

"What are we going to do with all this?" And I pointed at the store of clothes, furs, quilts, and all sorts of chests and bric-a-brac that was piling up in the courtyard. It looked like a junk sale.

"Don't worry. We'll let Landlord Bai keep what he really needs and divide the remainder among the needy peasants later."

"But . . ."

"It's legal in a revolution," Cheng cried. He did not wait for me to finish my question but hastened to reassure me as he and the two tally men pulled and tugged things to bring some sort of order to the mounting pile of goods.

The landlord's family, women and children, were driven out of their rooms into the courtyard. His mother, bent with age, sat on the verandah step. Closing her eyes to the chaos around her, she pressed her forehead against the knob of the walking stick she held in her powerless, wrinkled hands. Meanwhile, the peasants continued to bring out whatever they found of value and piled these things in mounds under the direction of the two tally men. Every time a peasant threw something new onto the pile—an antique vase, a jacket—the eyes of the landlord family followed the object. But what use was it to keep count? After a while they simply hung their heads and ceased to pay any attention. They seemed crushed by their ordeal and fearful of the future.

I saw Cheng throw a glance at them. I knew what he was thinking as surely as if he had spoken: merited retribution.

Four peasants carried out a carved mahogany bed from the old woman's room. On this bed she had spent her first night with her bridegroom. On this bed she had conceived her children. She struggled to stand up. The younger women helped her. She pushed them aside impatiently. She tottered forward a step or two on her tiny bound feet and spoke with offended dignity to Cheng.

"We are a decent family. I brought up my children properly and I treat my servants kindly. Look at my white hairs. You cannot do this to me!"

She threw back her head and seemed to choke. Never before in her life had she been treated with anything but deference. She swayed on her feet, on the verge of fainting.

Her son rushed to her side and begged her to keep silent. She shook her head. Wiping away the tears with the back of her hand, she sat down again. She had made her protest. She also knew it was in vain.

Her son knelt down in front of her and said in a plaintive voice, "Mother, it is your son's fault. Your son is a worthless creature. He is not able to carry out his filial duty." He hung his head. His words were stifled by spasmodic sobs.

The women and children standing behind the old lady knelt down and let out a tremulous, prolonged wail.

"Stop, you fools!" Cheng pounded on the broken door, his lips and jowls moving as if chewing something he didn't like. "There is no death around here. This is justice. What the hell are you starting a funeral chant for?" He hastened away into the next courtyard, presumably to see what the other peasants were doing.

After the search we marched through the village carrying the broken door. The great pot and the rest of the things we had confiscated followed us piled on a couple of ox carts. The effect on the peasants was electric. The whole village was galvanized into action. A crowd of peasants, the "moderates" who had held back, waiting, now fell in behind us.

Children clapped and shouted gleefully, whether they understood or not. In the middle of the village, where the crowd was thickest, several young men took the broken door and the pot and held them as high as they could for everyone to see. We had made a wooden archway over the gateway of our new headquarters and had sent Xiu-ying with a group ahead of us to decorate it with evergreens and red flags. As we marched through this arch of triumph I felt intoxicated like any soldier in the flush of victory, but I felt a sharp twinge of conscience when I remembered the shattered home we had just left.

When the hubbub had died down and the crowd had dispersed for the midday meal, Cheng and I had a moment to ourselves and I confided my doubts to him.

"That Landlord Bai doesn't seem to be such a bad fellow," I said with a query in my voice.

"He went in for usury and other ways of fleecing the peasants, but on a small scale. No big deal. You can call him an 'ordinary landlord.' But unfortunately he's gotten caught in the wheel of history."

Malvolio Cheng paused as if considering something and then continued. "My father was a benign and liberal-minded landlord, the sort of man who liked to read modern books and studied how to improve the lot of the peasants. He sent me to a modern school, because he thought that modern knowledge would reinvigorate the country, but he himself never went further than raising the wages of his farm hands. He was afraid to do more than that. He didn't want to antagonize his friends, the other landlords."

"What happened to him?"

"Fortunately for him, he has been dead a long time."

"If he had not died?"

"The same thing that happened to Bai would have happened to him."

"If your father were still alive, what would you do?" I looked into his face to see if he really meant what he said.

"You are too inquisitive." He raised his right hand as if he were going to smack me, and then threw up both of his hands, resigned to my impertinence.

All through the county the peasant activists and work teams were breaking down the landlords' kitchen doors and smashing their pots. From what we heard, the great majority of the dispossessed peasants had joined forces with us. They say that in a civil war, five percent of the people support this side, five percent support that side, and the rest of them take the side of the winner. Our offensive against the landlords made it clear who were the winners. There were sporadic acts of violence, particularly when a landlord resisted the searchers. We heard that Dai Shi, working in a mountain village, led a militia unit like a woman general into a fight in which people had had their noses broken and a landlord's house had gone up in flames.

I got overtired and my nerves were on edge, and I felt increasingly depressed. In my eyes, with my memory of Shanghai wealth, these wretched landlords had just managed to make a mere pittance in these godforsaken villages, and now they were paying a heavy price for it. The faces of Bai and his innocent family haunted me that night as I tossed sleepless on the kang.

12

Two Confrontations

Tu was in charge during the searches the next afternoon. At the last house, taking a bullying tone from the start, yelling insults, he spattered ink over the landlord's clothes, tied his hands behind his back, and hung a cardboard sign around his neck that read, "Counterrevolutionary Landlord Xia." But Xia was hardly a big landlord; he was more like a rich peasant who rented out some of his land. But thus humiliated, he was paraded around the little hamlet near his house. When I heard of this I was furious, but, taking my cue from Malvolio Cheng, I said nothing.

Xia had not been on the list of landlords to be searched, and the reason for the unscheduled search was bizarre. Xiu-ying told me that as Tu's search party was passing Xia's house on their way to Chi, the biggest local landlord and their final target, a dog inside Xia's courtyard barked. "A warning to its master?" Tu asked no one in particular. And so they broke in on Xia.

I was even more outraged when Tu gave his excuse for abandoning the search of Chi's house, which our plans had clearly included. "Chi's house was far away and it was getting dark," he said. But it had not been too late when he had started out but then had dragged out the search at Xia's.

"But it's our responsibility too. It was all very well to give responsibility to Tu, but why on earth did we leave him entirely on his own?" I said.

"It's a touchy situation," said Cheng. "He said he knew how to handle things. After that, if we had insisted on going along with him, he would have felt we didn't trust him."

"Maybe we should have started on Chi first."

"But we needed to build up momentum."

When Cheng and I reached Xia's house after the incident to see things for ourselves, we found him dazed and shocked, utterly mortified at his humiliation before the entire hamlet. He was sitting disconsolate on the step outside his cottage. It was a shambles. He and his wife had kept a tidy home. The walls were well repaired, the paper on the latticed windows fresh and whole, the courtyard swept clean. Now clothes and knick knacks were strewn around on the floor amid overturned furniture. Books lay scattered in a large inside room. I picked up one—the *Romance of the Three Kingdoms*, a popular classic novel, part folklore, part history. There were pamphlets and charts showing new methods of farming, composting, close planting, and irrigation. A torn page of an account book was covered with neatly written characters and figures. Xia had started out life as a middle peasant. Thirty years of hard work had enabled him to realize at least in part the ancient dream of every Chinese countryman: a farm, land, and a house of his own. And now in one afternoon all his hopes had been dashed.

For the moment there was nothing that Malvolio Cheng and I could do about what had happened, but we did at least speak to Xia consolingly and say that a full investigation of the matter would be undertaken and, if necessary, restitution made for any losses.

"Why didn't we at least rebuke Tu for bullying Xia?" I asked Malvolio Cheng as soon as we were out of earshot.

"Because it would not do to have an open clash with him on such a controversial issue in front of the peasants."

"But you know as well as I that Tu's action was unnecessary. No court has yet indicted Xia as a counterrevolutionary. And he's certainly not a feudal landlord—he's just a hardworking peasant who's managed to become well off. But by attacking him in this way, Tu is forcing other rich peasants to make common cause with the landlords when it's to our advantage to keep them neutral."

"You're tired," he said. "Tomorrow I have to go and meet Wang Sha for a conference in the county town. Take a day off. I mean, you can do some paperwork in the office or just go to your study class."

"Every time you try to dodge my questions, you say I'm tired. I am not tired. I know why we didn't interfere: because allowances are always being made for people like Tu. They are given the green light to do anything in the name of the revolution." Cheng never wanted to "rock the boat," and I couldn't contain myself any longer.

I spent a poor night. Tu was only too clearly demonstrating his "firm revolutionary stand" at the expense of a harmless landowner while postponing a clash with a landlord tyrant whom most suspected of being the ringleader of the reactionaries in Longxiang. Landlord Chi had been given a whole extra day's warning to prepare for the search which he knew was coming.

Next morning my head ached as if from a hangover but I dragged myself to my study class. It was more crowded than ever before.

Everyone wanted to talk about the recent events. Most agreed that Landlord Bai was not such a bad egg himself, but several confirmed that the older Bai, his father, had been a high-handed scoundrel who had used every base method to grab land which Bai now owned. Several families were bankrupt and broken because of him.

"Why haven't we gone to search Landlord Chi's house?" asked Little Tian, the young peasant with a hoarse voice. His tattered old cap was pressed down over his eyebrows so that it was difficult to see his eyes.

"Because he can still scare us out of our wits, especially Shen and Tu," rejoined a voice from the back row in a tone that set going a ripple of laughter.

"Who's afraid? Speak for yourself." Xiu-ying tossed her head to emphasize the bravery of women.

"Then let's go now. Ling-ling can lead us."

"Why not?"

"What the hell!"

I hesitated and played with the end of my short braid. In their eagerness, they were pushing me where even I didn't want to go yet. It wouldn't be easy to control them once they got going, especially if I alone led them to search Chi's house. This I had already learned. I considered calling in Shen, but he would insist on consulting Tu and that I didn't want.

"Let's plan this out first," I said, playing for time.

"What's there to plan? We've made searches before," cried a tousle-haired youngster.

This was the first time they themselves had taken the initiative in such bold action. If I held them back now it would be difficult to arouse their enthusiasm again on a later occasion. It was like riding a tiger or a green dragon in full flight: To go ahead was less hazardous than getting off.

"All right, let's go," I said finally with more resolution than I really felt. I gathered up my notebook and pencil and made for the door.

Walking fast and outwardly determined, I kept hoping that someone would come and head off this expedition. But no one appeared to intervene. Only a few peasants looked at our marching column, but without much curiosity. The sight was no longer unusual in the township. If they had known where we were going, I doubted that they would have crowded after us. Very few people wanted to antagonize Landlord Chi.

After less than half a mile, I suggested that we take a rest and we all sat down by the roadside. I sat a little apart from them. I had a premonition that I would be killed and at this thought I felt a wave of cold rise from my feet and envelop my body. My knees trembled. My aunt had warned me that I might end up this way. "Ling-ling," she had said just before she left, "I know you don't want even to listen to what I say now, but I must tell you that you will suffer for your willfulness. You are taking an irrevocably fatal step that will lead you to another and another."

Death, I thought, was certainly irrevocable.

"What a waste of your life," Aunt had said, shaking her head. "No, Auntie, I haven't wasted my life. I've tried to make something out of it. I wanted it to shine once, just once, like a moth I once saw trying to reach the flame of a storm lamp. It dashed against the glass globe and fell to the table stunned. Bruised, it skidded across the glass, wings trembling and shedding a light yellow powder. It was so weakened that it fell to the table before it could complete another lunge, but the insect would not stop moving towards the light. Finally, I removed the glass globe to let it fulfill its wish. It stretched out its wings and made its last desperate dash to the flame. It caught fire. The light shot up, flickered, and died."

I would write this message to my aunt.

The young activists were looking in my direction. Let them think I was working out plans for the search.

Again my aunt's voice: "Ling-ling, you are trying to justify yourself and your own stupidity. Your life did not shine, not even for a moment. You died in complete obscurity."

"Auntie, it is not my fault that I failed. We can dream, but the possibility of really shining depends on so many conditions. We are limited by our talents, our physical and mental strength and stamina, the play of fortune, and a thousand other factors. In the end you can only do your best." That sounded right.

I took out my notebook and pencil. The young activists gazed at me with respect. They were even more convinced of my devotion to the work at hand.

How would I look lying on a board like Da Niang's younger son? Wang Sha would be among the mourners who would pay their last respects to my corpse. It would not be a pretty sight. My eyes fell on my shoes. And my socks! My lifeless, waxlike toes would stick out of the holes in those socks. Would that be how I'd look?

I glanced up from my notebook. Some travelers appeared at a distance. Our villagers? This might be my last chance to get more people to join us—or to pass a message back to the village to send us reinforcements. I shouted and ran towards them, ignoring the activists' calls. Before I had caught their attention, the travelers had disappeared around a turn in the path.

I stopped, panting. I should have waited. Wang Sha and Malvolio Cheng would be back tomorrow. We could search then. If I went after these travelers now, I could gain time. I didn't want to die. I made a few tentative steps forward.

"Come on, we know where it is. Don't worry, we won't take you to the wrong place." Xiu-ying and the others caught up with me. And so we went on, until Landlord Chi's house came into view.

"Let me walk in front," I said.

They looked silently at each other.

"Then you take this stick," a rosy-cheeked girl said to me, offering a pinewood cudgel.

"Landlord Chi has spread it around that if anyone makes trouble for him, he'll do him in," said Little Gao, the young man with the unruly head of hair, an uncertain expression coming over his face. "A stab in the back and when the dagger comes out it is red with blood, so to speak." He used the phrases of the classical horror stories.

"I can't take this stick," I said a bit huskily. My throat was dry. My tongue felt heavy. "I won't let them have the satisfaction of being able to accuse me of brandishing a weapon at them."

"Suppose they start first?"

"We can't fire the first shot or strike the first blow. That's against instructions." I lost my voice completely, but Xiu-ying came to my rescue.

"Come here," she ordered two tall, muscular men, members of the new Peasants' Militia being trained by Shen and Little Gao. "You stand on each side of her and if you see anyone about to attack her, you hit them first. Don't spare them."

When we stood before Landlord Chi's gateway my heart was thumping. We had allowed Chi's reputation to frighten us, just as that young activist had said, but now we all put on a bold front. One of my bodyguards used his cudgel to thump on the door and the peremptory knocking evidently threw the household into confusion. We could hear women calling to each other and whispering. Someone finally opened the door when I announced that we were the representatives of the Poor Peasants' Association of Longxiang. We pushed our way in.

Only Chi's wife, two concubines, his aunt, and his children were at home. Our array of strength seemed excessive, and my fear subsided. I decided to adopt the strategy of the "short attack." We would finish the search as quickly as possible before Chi returned or had time to take countermeasures.

This was our fourth search in three days, and this time the search party was experienced and disciplined, no longer distracted by a crowd of unruly villagers. Businesslike and without theatrics, we went through Chi's rooms systematically and made a full inventory.

We found nothing particularly incriminating in the house. The account books, all started recently, were straightforward lists of rents paid, debts owed, purchases, and sales. This did not surprise us. Only the most thorough of searches now yielded any secret hoards of grain, real valuables, or evidence of wrongdoing. We all realized now how important it would have been to have searched Chi's house first and taken this biggest landlord by surprise. But psychologically we had not been prepared to take on Chi at that time. And now the search of his house seemed like an anticlimax.

We were just preparing to leave when Chi himself entered the courtyard. He took in the situation at a glance. His eyes burned with venom. He fixed his gaze on me as if he wanted to remember my face forever. "One day, one day," I could almost hear him think, "I'll take my revenge on you." He was fat, his nose was flat and discolored from drinking. I knew he was ill-humored and crafty but the sight of him did not scare me. I only felt repulsed. But we knew he was tough. It was said that once he had lost all the money he had in his pocket, but he did not want to leave the gambling table. He staked his little finger, cut it off when he lost, then borrowed money and won back all that he had lost and more.

For a moment there was a palpable tension in the air. But seeing the odds were heavily against him Chi held his rage in check. We presented him with the inventory we had made, room by room, and told him that he would be held responsible if anything was hidden or destroyed before it was decided what should be done with it. With a shrug, he quickly went over it and signed it. On that note we left.

Out of sight and earshot of his house, the disciplined silence of our group broke down. Everyone wanted to talk at once. The things they had seen! Landlord Chi's house was richer and larger than any other in the township. A two-story building—the only one in Longxiang—with a heavy tiled roof, interlocking courtyards shaded with trees, and a private well, it seemed to the youngsters to be the last word in comfort and luxury. On this point I kept my own counsel. Chi's heavy old teak furniture was lasting, solid stuff, but it would never have gotten into even a third-rate Shanghai furniture shop. Feudal landlordism had reduced the whole country to such a state of destitution that even its main social props were impoverished.

But the search party was excited, chattering on about the chests of warm quilts and fur-lined clothes, the good food in Chi's cellar, his livestock, farm tools, and land. It was rumored that Chi had a store of silver dollars, grain, and other valuables squirreled away, but where these were no one knew but Chi. We had seen no trace of them. But apart from this we now knew what he did have, at least aboveground, and most important, we had tackled the biggest of the Longxiang landlords head-on in his own domain. Our young people were elated and ready for anything as we dispersed.

Even before we returned to Longxiang the whole village knew about our exploit. Da Niang welcomed me at the front gate and brushed the dust off my clothes.

"Good girl," she exclaimed admiringly. "You are bold."

"Da Niang, you . . ." I thought it was a good opportunity to try again to break through her silence, but she interrupted me.

"I know. You young people even tackled Master Chi."

"But the chain that binds you has not yet been smashed."

She gave a quick glance over her shoulder. She leaned

her head on one side and looked up to the heavens as if to see where the chain was.

"Da Niang, that chain still holds you back. You simply won't listen to me!" I pretended to be angry with her.

"My dear child, how can you say that? How can you think I'm taking the landlords' side?" She winked at me slyly. "Da Niang cares for you. I'll prove it. I will cook a good meal for you. This afternoon you eat with me."

She sat on a small stool and fed dried grass and twigs into the stove. After looking for matches, she started the fire and the smoke from the stove made her eye smart. She used a corner of her tattered old jacket to wipe away the tears.

"Da Niang, let me light the fire."

"I'm all right."

"But wasn't it smoke that blinded your eye?"

"Oh, no, it wasn't only that. I bore ten children. Today only this idiot is alive. And their father died too. We were poor people. When we fell sick, we couldn't even afford noodle soup to drink, much less medicine. Our old master didn't care. Poor people's lives were cheap. I cried. Every day I cried. That was what blinded my eye. This one went blind. And the other one is blurred. I can't see clearly with it. Well, it's better this way. Since I got blind, that eye doesn't hurt anymore."

Her crooked smile revealed the gaps in her brown, jagged teeth. For the first time I noticed her thin grey hair, so sparse it hardly covered her scalp and scarcely made a bun at the back of her head. Her words echoed in my mind: "It's better this way. It doesn't hurt anymore." In my mind I saw her, frail and light as a dried twig that a summer breeze might blow away, tottering along the road all by herself, shoulders bent, resigned to suffering. I wanted to say some words of comfort but my chin was shaking as if with a fever. If I said a word, I knew the tears would gush out.

"What's the matter with you?" She paused with her hand on a bundle of twigs half-thrust into the mouth of the stove.

"Da Niang, how you have suffered!"

She raised her head quickly. There was puzzlement and surprise in her face. Her life had seemed so spent, so worthless to her. For the first time someone felt for her. She lowered her head slowly and slowly let the dried twigs fall from her fingers.

The kindling in the stove had burnt out and the embers cast a red glow on her face. The water stayed cold on the stove.

"I felt happy when I knew you had searched old Chi's house," she blurted out to my surprise.

This was the moment I had been waiting for.

"Da Niang, tell me about your past," I coaxed her.

She hesitated. She was apparently of two minds about it.

"As I think back, I cannot say that old Chi was too bad, to us at least. If he had not hired us, we might have become beggers. There were too many poor people. They were all hardworking, but even more unfortunate than we were. No one hired them. They were forced to leave their homes and go begging, and who knows where they are today." Da Niang, who could curse like a real shrew, now looked resigned.

"Da Niang, what do you think of Tu's wife?"

"Don't talk about her. Tu is her second husband. A decent woman would never agree to marry more than once." Da Niang was very proud of her own virtue as a chaste widow. Self-righteously, she continued: "About fourteen years ago she fled from her own village with her baby daughter. There was a famine there. She came to beg in our village. Tu had just become a widower. He was dirt poor then with no chance of getting a virgin bride. He sheltered her and they lived together as man and wife. He often beat her. The daughter could not stand it and ran away some time ago. No one knows where she is."

"She never came back?"

"No." The word came out of her after an almost imperceptible pause, as though she had remembered something.

She changed the subject: "You must be hungry. I'll start the fire again."

13 ★ ⋮

In a Grove of Trees

When I look back now, I understand some but not all of our mistakes. We had been told to seize only such things as enabled the landlords to exploit the poor peasants and which the peasants urgently needed—such as land and implements—but we had taken away personal belongings and so created needless animosity. And we had timed our searches badly. Only simultaneous surprise searches could have prevented the landlords from hiding property and arms.

The land reform laws and regulations might be written down in a very cool and rational manner, but once the reform actually got going all sorts of unpredictable forces were released. Touching as it did on every aspect of their lives, more and more people were deeply stirred. Each person touched was an emotional as well as an intellectual being. And while their intellectual side both calculated and miscalculated, their emotional side often reacted in the most unpredictable ways. There was an unexpected strain of anarchism and violence in the villages that should have been expected and guarded against, and later on this was to have evil consequences.

Nevertheless, after the searches had demonstrated the firm resolution of our young activists there was no doubt that the peasants had greater confidence that the actual distribution of land could be carried out. Xiu-ying, Little

Tian, and Little Gao had put into action what before had been only theory. Now, even as we faced harder and harder decisions, they were ready to take on greater responsibilities instead of always waiting until someone from above told them what to do.

By this time we had a fair idea of how much land would be confiscated from the landlords and how many peasants needed land. It worked out to about three *mu* or half an acre each for the landless and landpoor peasants and everyone else eligible to receive a share of land, which included the landlords themselves and their families. From that figure we determined that if each member of a family already owned four to six *mu*, they were designated middle peasants. Rich peasants were those who owned about twelve to eighteen *mu* apiece.

According to that standard, Xia actually fell between the categories of more affluent middle and rich peasants. His family of four owned about forty-five *mu*, but his children were little more than toddlers, so, shorthanded for the moment, he rented out quite a portion of his land. This fact had made him look like a landlord. The strict letter of the law said that that portion of his land could be confiscated, but any law has its ambiguities. It was up to us to find a solution to this problem.

Talking over such matters with Wang Sha one afternoon, I sat with him on the old millstone that served as a public bench on the outskirts of the township center. "We're playing God now," I sighed. "If we register Xia as a small landlord, that will put a label on his children that will hurt them in the future."

Wang Sha said, "We have made one mistake about Xia already, it seems. We mustn't make another."

"That's for sure." At least I could now carry on a conversation with Wang Sha without blushing at every word.

We began to wander along a path trodden crookedly across the fields. We talked as we strolled, weighing the pros and cons of Xia's case and other village problems. We had nearly reached the foot of Green Dragon Mountain before we realized how far we had walked. Actually this was no mountain but just a low hill, the only oasis of green in the midst of the dry loess plain. Its pine trees probably guarded some ancient tomb, and it was green even in winter. The peasants said that spring came here earliest, guided on its way by the dragon that gave the township its name: Longxiang in Chinese means the Dragon's Township.

We followed the zigzag footpath between the trees. The only sounds were our own soft footfalls cushioned by the twigs and pine needles and the scratch-scratch of small animals that could only be heard if one held one's breath. Sacred legends had protected this place from ravagers. Some trees were so tall and straight that they seemed pillars supporting the sky. Others, overshadowed and weak, arched towards each other and intertwined their branches as if for mutual support. I felt that we had entered another world, a world far away from land reform, Longxiang, mundane tasks. It was a world of dreams, and of a beauty that was always there for the taking.

Wang Sha and I were totally alone. It was rare now for this to happen, and as I grew conscious of his presence I felt a sudden anxiety and then a strange perturbation of spirit.

"Let's sit down for a while," I said. I caught a glimpse of alert apprehension in his eyes when they looked at me from under his bushy eyebrows, but, ironically, for once my intentions were entirely innocent. I simply needed time to collect myself.

We sat in silence apart from each other. Little by little I regained my composure as I compelled myself to recall what we had all vowed to do after that conference: avoid all scandal involving "men and women relations."

After a while I managed to force myself to turn to another subject.

"Do you know what I'm thinking about now? I'm keeping a diary. I want to write about the land reform as I am seeing it and experiencing it."

Wang Sha shot a quizzical glance at me, but he seemed relieved to talk about something specific and "objective."

"Diaries can sometimes be dangerous things to leave lying around," he warned. "You've told me several times that you want to be a writer. That's fine. But you will need to know much more about the peasants before you can write about them. Be patient." He paused. "And there's another thing: You imagine that after the land reform everything will go smoothly and writers will have much greater opportunities to write and publish. You're seeing things with your own young eyes. When I was your age, it was no use telling me anything I didn't want to hear."

After another pause, he added, "Do you know how long I've tried to do what you're trying to do now? It's more than twenty years since I first went to work in the countryside. Yes, more than twenty years ago. It's strange, I didn't realize how long ago that was."

He laughed to himself at some escapade or mishap that he recalled, then, serious again, he resumed his lecture. Both of us still felt ill at ease; our eyes rarely met. He, because he was lecturing me, and I because I didn't want to be lectured, but couldn't say so, for his lecturing was oblique.

"I remember the first time I went out. It was with Cheng and many others. We were all youngsters then like you, just thinking of beginning our careers—would-be scientists, artists, writers. I think I had some talent as a writer, and if I had devoted more time to writing, perhaps I might have done something worthwhile in that line. It was up to us to decide what to do.

"Many of us came from fairly well-to-do families. We had some freedom of choice. We could have left the Communist areas; we could have avoided going to the villages to work with the peasants. But we were living in a guerrilla area. We knew that the peasants were starving and had to have land. Their first need was for food, not plays or poetry. I chose to make revolution because for me there was really no alternative. I realized that what might be good for the vast majority of the people might not be so good at the moment for individuals like myself. I thought the land revolution would be successful, the peasants would quickly prosper, and so would the whole country and then literature and art. I put off writing, for the moment, but that moment dragged on and on. More than twenty years have gone by since then and I still haven't done much writing. The peasants have made some headway, but you see yourself how far they still have to go. It may take another twenty years before they achieve some measure of prosperity. Or fifty years. Or more." He gave a mock rueful smile. "I'll be gone then."

"So will I." As I said this, I suddenly felt let down.

We lapsed into a long silence. He was moody, and my spirits plunged as the meaning of his words sank in. Both of us were debating with ourselves. Conflicting ideas and emotions jostled together and kept us silent. Several times I saw him looking hard at me, as though counting my freckles. Then suddenly he would grow conscious of his stare and abruptly turn away.

"I don't write much now myself," he said again, "but I still keep churning out reports about the difficulties writers face, and especially about the meddling and ineptitude of bureaucrats and political busybodies who think that they know everything, including how to write plays, novels, music, and poetry. I send these reports to various conferences and committees and then they travel back to me. We stumble along. I'm in the middle of the cross fire: On one side are the dissident writers—some of them gifted, some of them not too wise either; and on the other, these know-it-all dogmatists. I can land myself in a hell of a mess. One day I'll have stepped on too many toes, and that will be it. 'You've let off enough steam. It's time to shut you up.' "

For the first time I saw him unsure of himself, insecure. "Sometimes I've felt as if I were on a treadmill exerting a lot of energy but going nowhere." This was not the familiar Wang Sha talking.

I was slowly scribbling on the ground with a twig. The characters in the dust overlapped and as I scribbled faster became less and less legible. Just a jumble, like the chaos of thoughts in my head. Every one of us—peasants, work teams, and landlords alike—was caught in the wheel of history. Immense forces beyond our control were moving us forward, but at the same time molding and remolding all our hopes regardless of who and what we were. This thought thrust like a dagger into my chest. A blind and stubborn determination to hit back welled up within me. I pressed the twig so hard that it broke.

I had missed some of Wang Sha's words. ". . . I can guess, now and then, you think about going back to your aunt and uncle. That's natural. But if you uproot yourself and leave China, your own land, you will find it even harder to grow as an artist and a writer. You told me before that your family wanted you to go to the United States. It's true, there are immigrant writers and artists from Europe, and some of them have managed to integrate themselves into that kind of life. But Chinese culture is too different from the American for you to bridge that easily. You'll be like a fish out of water." He halted, casting a questioning glance at me. "Don't delude yourself. There's censorship everywhere. In different forms, wherever you go, you'll run into it."

"Have you finished?" I asked. I was more than ready to move on to something less painfully personal. "Let's do something practical while we're here. Look at all this good firewood lying around. Let's make a bundle and carry it home for Da Niang."

I wandered about picking up dry twigs. My mind, however, kept coming back to thoughts of Wang Sha. I understood that he was trying to give me a word of warning, to alert me to the hard facts of life. They were exactly the same hard facts that had scared several generations of women back into the refuge of marriages of convenience. They were scaring me now.

When I was a younger girl, I used to eavesdrop behind the door of my aunt's small upstairs parlor, listening to her friends confiding to her about their love affairs. Some had been to middle school and college and in the twenties and thirties had taken part in the various revolutionary movements that had swept the country. For more than a hundred years, ever since the Opium War with the British, China had been a nation in continuous upheaval. Women too had been caught up in the turmoil. Some had breasted the waves like bold and agile swimmers. Women like Ding Ling, the novelist, and many others both famous and obscure. In their young days these women had left home seeking a more fulfilling life; some had found the struggle too hard. Disillusioned, they had returned home and got married as their parents had wished. But their lives of luxurious monotony drove them crazy. These were the ones who confided in my aunt. Some went into a second adolescence and had girlish crushes on men; through them they felt that they could bring more meaningful encounters into their lives. Each time love promised a new realm of feeling, a new world. But these had all been little worlds in which nothing much could ever really happen—a new house, a dress, friends—things not so new after all.

I think it was from them that I first heard about books such as *Anna Karenina* and *Madame Bovary*. Wondering why these books had such an emotional impact on them, I took them down from my aunt's bookshelf and devoured them. They were intoxicating, and I yearned to act out the same grand passions in real life. For a time this had been an obsession: The pages of fiction became my real world.

But in the past year I had moved into a very different world, one filled with living women of creative achievement, and women of the slums. Here in Longxiang I had gone even further into a whole new environment. The sufferings of Anna and Madame Bovary seemed like luxuries in which only ladies of leisure could indulge.

"Have you picked enough?" Wang Sha came up with a small bundle of twigs under his arm.

"Yes, but not as much as you." My tone was natural and tranquil. The flood of feeling that had nearly made me lose my head had receded. I wanted to be off before anything else should happen.

"Shall we go back?" I said abruptly as I gazed at the thin, glimmering stream below us. Tears misted over my eyes. I could not quite comprehend what was going on in my heart, though my mind seemed clear and it was saying over and over again, "Beware, beware."

Back in my room, I could see my problems in a more objective way.

The paths of Wang Sha and myself had crossed at a crucial moment in our lives. For me it was a starting point of an adventure that by turns exhilarated and appalled me. For him it was just another turn in a road he had long traveled. He knew that although he could choose, the choice was already made; there was no turning back for him. He fought for creative freedom in a "legitimate" way as a leading cadre of the Party. In his committees and conferences he argued, debated, and haggled for it. Eventually, however, even though it fell short of what he wanted or thought necessary, he would obey the decision of the majority of the Party members or those who spoke for them. To win this sort of seesaw battle took time. It was no overstatement when he said it might take another fifty years before it was possible for writers and artists to get where they would like to go. It was not in my nature to sit, pray, and wait patiently. So I couldn't fit into Wang Sha's picture and he certainly couldn't fit into mine.

I could still decide to end this adventure and probably be welcomed back by my aunt like a Prodigal Daughter. But were there really only two options open to me: To press ahead and be engulfed by the revolution or to turn tail and resume my old life? I didn't want either. Could I find a way to walk the knife edge between these two fates? I had always believed that if one concentrated hard enough to solve a problem, one would probably come up with an answer, and I lay down on the kang to think.

I pulled the quilt up to my chin and closed my eyes tight. My thoughts trailed away. Instead of a solution, I found myself sobbing. I cried until I entered that hazy, dreamy realm between sleeping and waking. Outlines were blurred in a world of grey.

I don't know how long I lay there before I dozed off, nor how long I had slept when I heard footsteps. A man, immense and threatening, was coming up the steps slowly and ponderously, his left hand sliding up the handrail. His face was shadowed by his cap. He wore a belted tunic and heavy boots. He was conducting a search. I called to my aunt but no sound came from my throat, and the man came relentlessly on. He moved to my desk and put his hand out to take my diary. I overcame my paralysis enough to leap out of bed and snatch the diary and run.

The footsteps chased me. "Ling-ling," I told myself, "run for your life!" Out of breath, I came to the alley where Ma Li had once lived in those tiny partitioned spaces. Partitions inside partitions. I could hide in this labyrinth. But the footsteps kept coming nearer. There was no escape. I screamed, but my voice sounded like a whimper.

I sat up in the dark, still trembling with fear from the nightmare. These people who were chasing me were the same people who had been chasing Ma Li. I could not care less what they called themselves: Guomindang or Communist, rightist or leftist, counterrevolutionary or revolutionary. They were the same people.

I eyed my diary among the few books stacked in the lower corner of the kang. I pushed aside the quilt and bent forward to pick up the diary. But at that moment I felt too weary and listless even to lift it, and I leaned back against the wall. I recalled Wang Sha's words: "Diaries can sometimes be dangerous things to leave lying around." In mine I had written down as frankly and vividly as I could my perceptions of Longxiang and the people I had met there.

How would all this look when read out at an interrogation? I had heard that in the turbulence of the so-called rectification campaigns such as the Yanan Purge, even thrown-away papers of no importance had been found and sometimes caused serious trouble, attacks in open meetings, secret torture, and even death. Some people developed special talents in reading between totally innocuous lines and deciphering nonexistent codes showing that the owner of such papers was involved in "subversive activities." If I dropped that diary and lost it, if Dai Shi should get so much as a glimpse of it, that would be more than enough to undo me. Compared to mine, Chu Hua's sin would look like a childish prank. I decided to burn the diary.

My feet touched the cold earthen floor and, shivering, I felt around for my slippers. With an effort I got up from the kang and took the match box from my table. I lit a match and started to burn the diary page by page. On one page I caught a glimpse of some lines that I particularly liked. I tried to snatch it back, but it had already caught fire. I slapped the flame with my hand and my fingers got burned.

Tightly hugging the remaining empty pages of my diary I threw myself back onto the kang. I was sure that I was not the only secret writer. If we refused to bow in submission to tyrants, small or big, some of us would outlast them.

I lit the small oil lamp on the table and began to write about my nightmare, jotting down every single detail.

14 ★

Electioneering

It was time to elect a new government in Longxiang. Since the old Guomindang officials had fled late in the previous year, Shen and Tu had in effect been the local provisional government. They received orders from the county government in Yuzhong. But the presence of the work teams and the land reform movement were changing all that. In all the villages and townships, including Longxiang, a growing number of militant peasants were beginning to want to take affairs into their own hands. Responding to the new situation, the county leadership had sent word that every township should elect a local council that could throw its authority behind the land reform and carry it through. Every work team had been told to cultivate good candidates and get out the vote.

Like all the other instructions we had been getting from the county this was easier said than done. We wanted a government that represented all the peasants, but the work teams had sometimes been too successful when they encouraged the middle peasants to become more active. I had heard of elections in which the middle peasants, despite being a minority, had carried off most of the seats. The power of this group should not have been underestimated: They had not gotten where they were by accident. They had to be skilled and toughly egotistical to survive and prosper in conditions where most others had sunk into abject poverty. Usually, they were astute enough not to exclude the poor peasant candidates entirely, but they did their best to get their own candidates in.

We in Longxiang tried to prepare for the election by fostering some very good candidates: veteran farmers like old Gao, the village sage; adults in their prime like Shen; and a few forceful, capable younger people. We felt it very important to have at least one woman cadre in the government, and we were hopeful—indeed, confident—that Xiu-ying would be elected. But even with such a strong slate, Wang Sha, Cheng, and I knew that we would have to do all we could to help elect our young poor peasant activists and have a good turnout at the election.

One morning two weeks before the election I went to visit Xiu-ying. She wasn't home, and her mother told me that she'd gone out on an early-morning errand but would soon be back. There was a pile of dry stalks in a corner of the courtyard and I lay down on them, snug in my padded coat and trousers, and waited for her. The winter sun played warmly on my face but was too bright for my eyes, so I turned over to lie face down. The scent of the stalks was pleasant and I closed my eyes to enjoy the quiet and the calm.

"Ling-ling is here," I heard Xiu-ying's mother call out from the cottage.

"Where?" came Xiu-ying's voice.

"Right under your nose."

"She's gone to sleep."

"No, I'm awake." I rolled over and lay on my back. I smiled up at her. "Where have you been?" As I asked this I got up and followed her into the house.

"I was chatting with Shen and Tu. They're worried that they are going to lose their authority when the new cadres are elected."

"Rubbish. There'll be much more work to do after the land reform. They couldn't possibly do it all by themselves."

"Shen said he doesn't care how the voting goes. He was bragging that he would go to Xian to visit relatives and

that they will get him a job in a factory there. He says that
city life is much more interesting."

"He's just talking. Of course he cares if he's elected or
not." I looked right at her. "What do you really think of
Shen?"

"He's a bit lazy and he doesn't like to take on big responsibilities. But he'll win. He has many friends in the
Poor Peasants' Association. Everyone knows now that
that's where the power will be when the land share-out
takes place. So he sits there all the time and lets people get
used to him sitting there. They will vote him in, most of
them, because his face is familiar. Why choose someone
you don't know?"

"Xiu-ying, you are exaggerating," I chided her.

She laughed. "Not much."

Xiu-ying was a delightful chatterbox. The activities of
the land reform had brought out her real capabilities and
opened up a world of new possibilities. Every day I discovered some new facet of her character as she asked questions tirelessly, thirsting for knowledge. She wanted to
know how my watch worked, how a bank operated, how
women lived in the cities. One day we were talking about
marriage. In Longxiang, a new bride immediately puts up
her hair. Xiu-ying asked me, "Do girls keep their long
braids after they are married in the city?"

"Some do, some don't."

"Uh." She thought this over while she reached into the
stove and pulled out a roasted ear of corn, which she
handed to me.

"Here, eat this," she said.

"No, you eat it."

"Let's share it." And she broke it in two.

My hand was reaching out for the half, but her hand
holding it suddenly pointed at the door leading to the bedroom, from which were coming some muffled sounds and
then some angry shouting.

"Listen. Father is beating Mother again."

"What's the matter?" I had come to love this family, and
I was genuinely concerned.

"Nothing." She shrugged as if there really were nothing

unusual going on, no reason to get upset. "My father is good-tempered and will only give her a taste of his fist."

Indeed, Xiu-ying's mother soon emerged from the room, unhurriedly, smoothing down her disheveled hair with her hands. She asked kindly, "How do you like the corn, Young Sister?" and passed on out into the courtyard. She picked a dock leaf, spat on it, and put it on her red swollen cheek. Then she sat down on a millstone, some old clothes on her lap ready for patching and her arms resting idly. Looking quite serene, she sat for a while basking in the morning sunshine. We watched her as we munched on the ears of corn, enjoying the kernels' sweet burned taste.

"Mother told me that men all beat their wives," remarked Xiu-ying. "There are no exceptions. I'll be lucky if I marry a man as kind as Father." But even as she said this, her face clouded.

The older woman bent over her sewing, using her worn teeth to break a thread. The leaf fell from her face. As she picked it up, she glanced at me out of the corner of her eye. She squirmed in her seat like a child as if to say, "Aren't I shameless? An old woman acting as awkward as a child who has been spanked."

"Do men in the cities beat their wives?" asked Xiu-ying.

I didn't know how to explain to her, so that she could understand, that I grew up in one circle in one city at one specific time; it wasn't that easy to generalize about a vast city like Shanghai. I said, "I've never seen it happen among my friends. But I do know one wife who beats her husband."

She stared at me, speechless, for a while, and then throwing away the finished cob, reached for its stalk. She chewed at this, peeling the shiny skin away with her strong, white teeth.

"See how I do it? You try!" She suddenly broke into a peal of laughter. Her eyes lit up and she gazed beyond the cottage walls.

"It's a—what is that word that means very, very happy? I can't remember." She was vexed at herself. "What a poor memory."

"What word? Oh, don't bother with that now." I changed the subject. "Now we've got the election to think about."

She looked down her nose pensively. After a while she exclaimed, pointing her finger upward at nothing in particular, "Oh, I remember: 'blissful.'" She laughed and flushed with joy. She carefully intoned every word: "You—live—a—blissful—life."

"It's too soon to be thinking about a blissful life. There's too much to be done right now." I brushed aside her further questions, laughing. "We must get going. It's our job to get everyone to vote," I reminded her.

We walked up the main street between two rows of cottages. Villagers gathered there exchanged the latest news. As she passed, Xiu-ying called out greetings to her friends and neighbors as she usually did, but there was a subtle difference in her manner. The election was evidently very much on her mind. She was no longer greeting just neighbors but constituents. With a mixed sense of amusement and disquiet, I watched her move through groups of people, engaging them in animated conversation like a seasoned campaigner.

When we finally reached the crossroads at the end of the lane, we parted, she to visit a group of women who had not yet registered to vote, I turning right along the path that led to the cottage of Old Tian with the wispy goat's beard, Malvolio Cheng's friend. He was sweeping his courtyard, and a layer of dust covered his naked feet like brown suede slippers. He greeted me cheerfully. By now his old attitude to me had completely changed. I was no longer just a woman or a girl, but a "cadre," one of the new neuter gender that the revolution had created.

"Come and have a drink of water with Old Gao and me," he offered.

I was pleased with this cordial invitation and stepped through the gate. His crony sat on the stone steps which led into the house. By no means accidentally, Old Tian's voice rose higher, warning Gao that I was coming into the courtyard. They apparently had been discussing something they didn't wish me to hear.

"Good morning," I answered Old Tian. "You start the day early."

"You started even earlier. I saw you with Xiu-ying." And he shook his head disparagingly. "She was showing off again, huh?"

"Grandfather Tian, why do you say that? She isn't in show business."

"Well, she might be, the way she carries on. She doesn't walk any more. She dances."

I smiled because it was partly true. Xiu-ying walked with a confident spring in her step, not like the village girls of old, always prepared to take second place.

"She's working very hard because it's getting near election time."

"Election?" There was a shrewd twinkle in Tian's eye. His attention roused, he rested his chin on his hands cupped over the end of the handle of his "broom," a whisk of twigs tied to a pole. A small smile creased his face.

I could read his every thought. When you come down to it, he was thinking, the local rulers have always been appointed by the higher-ups. From time immemorial, it had always been so. Before, the higher-ups were landlords like Chi and the old Bai. Now there might be different people, but the election would still be staged to cover the deals behind the scenes. He was grinning from ear to ear as if to say, "You can't fool me. I know the rules of the game." The old fox.

"Grandfather Tian," I said politely, "I hope you'll join one of the voters' small group meetings to name and discuss the candidates. The small groups will recommend fifteen candidates and put them up for general consideration by the voters." Then I added with a smile which I hoped would be meaningful enough to drive the point home: "Do you know what the young people are saying? They bet that you won't take part in the election. But I said you will."

"I don't go in for a lot of talking." Tian's voice showed that he couldn't be caught so easily. "But I am plain-spoken. I say what I mean."

I saw that I had touched a raw spot. His face grew red and the veins in his temples stood out. He threw down the broom, took one step away, paused, took another step, and then halted. He thought for a moment, then with a stride as agile as a youth's he marched into the cottage. He picked up the piece of board that served as his dustpan and began furiously sweeping chicken droppings onto it.

"Please don't be angry about what they say. They are young and full of pranks," I apologized.

"Have you heard that old saying, 'Don't trust the judgment of a man with a beardless chin'?" he said to me sharply.

"Well . . . um . . . I told them that there were different kinds of old people. Some grow senile, but others become braver and wiser with age."

"What did they say to that?"

"They laughed, I'm sorry to say."

"Let's see who has the last laugh." He swept up the dung so vigorously that it overshot his dustpan.

"It's interesting that you're telling him about the election," said Gao. "I was just urging him to come to our discussion meeting. He knows so much about everything and everybody around here. His words carry weight."

Gao was campaigning for himself, that was clear, and his chances were good. But he had enough skeletons clanking in his closet to worry him. One story going the rounds about him concerned the notorious death of a goat. Several years ago he had rented a goat to mate with his ewe. He had paid a fee for a single mating, but when he brought the goat back to its owner he practically had to carry it through the gate into the goat shed. At that time the owner just thought that Gao was being extra careful with the animal. But the goat died soon after, and suspicions crept in. A rumor went around that the poor animal died of exhaustion. Gao, of course, denied any responsibility. And now interest in the matter had revived.

Gao himself now brought up the subject. "About the goat, you know . . . I don't like to talk about myself."

"That's right," interjected Tian. "It wasn't his fault. If he made a mistake, it's because he's bighearted. When he had

the goat in his pen, some poor guys brought their ewes
along to be mated. They begged him with tears in their
eyes. He didn't have the heart to refuse. Is he to be pun-
ished for helping poor peasants? Why make such a fuss
about that goat? One goat died. Five goats were born. Isn't
that a good thing? Why make a fuss about that goat? I
know." Old Tian waved a crooked finger to press the point
home. "Jealousy! Yes, jealousy. Old Gao has a few more
mu of land so they think he's not as good as a poor peasant. Poor is not always good. Do you know why some people here in this village are poor? Not virtue. Just
laziness—"

"Grandfather Tian," interposed Gao. "Just a few of
them are lazy, not many." Gao needed the votes of conservatives like Tian, but he had no wish to antagonize the
poor peasants.

"I had to work for my few *mu* of land. I was poor once.
Very poor. Let me tell you something. This happened only
about seven years ago. I didn't even have a hen to hatch
my chicks. My only hen died. Why, I don't know." He
paused dramatically, his face clearly signifying suspicion
of foul play.

"Why should that hen die suddenly without cause?"
Tian stroked his wispy beard to emphasize his point.

"Yes, it was strange, now I look back on it," continued
Gao. "It died just before it was time to sit and hatch those
eggs. I had a cock too then. My neighbor had a hen but no
cock. You know my neighbor?" He mentioned a name.

I did; he was a poor peasant candidate.

Gao continued: "I lent him my cock. With no cock
around there would be no chicks for him from the eggs his
hen laid. In return, he agreed to let his hen hatch my
chicks. But he forgot until I asked him point blank—"

"He forgot? How could that be? He has a good memory," exclaimed Tian indignantly. "He never forgets even
a pinch of salt that he lends to others and he must get it
back even if he has to hound them to death."

"Um . . . Well, that is what he told me. I'm a simple
fellow. I took him at his word. I only asked that his hen
should hatch four eggs for me. I drew red circles on my

eggs so they wouldn't be confused with his. Well, to cut a long story short, his chicks came out of their shells one day earlier than mine. If he had taken his chicks and put them out of sight of the hen for a day or two, my chicks would have hatched out all right. But no. He let his chicks go chirping around. Can you blame the hen for wanting to look after her own brood? She left my four eggs in the coop. I could even hear one or two of them moving, almost ready to break their shells. My wife wept, worried to distraction that the chicks still in their shells would stifle to death if they couldn't come out soon enough. She put them in her bosom and covered them with my winter jacket. It was late spring and already warm."

"The summer came early that year. It was really hot," added Tian.

"Yes, you are right. It was hot and my wife sweated under that jacket. Only two chicks survived. Was that fair? Why did no one criticize him for acting in that way? Just because he is a poor peasant?"

"Why didn't you speak out about all this at the time?" I asked.

"He's too generous and openhearted for his own good," answered Tian with a gesture of his arms deploring these traits in his friend.

Gao, seemingly unable to bear such praise, turned his eyes away with a look of long-suffering resignation.

"We really need good people on our township council," urged Tian. "Old Gao has real merit. Not only honest, but a fine farmer too. Look here." He squatted down and plucked a weed up out of the ground to demonstrate for me. "Everybody knows how to plant, but very few know how to plant to get the best yield possible. See how I place the roots and bury them, packing the earth around them and leaving a basin round it to collect the moisture. And there's much more to it than that. Not everybody knows these secrets. Old Gao does."

Clearly I was not the first recipient of Gao's and Tian's explanations. They were campaigning like veteran politicians.

After I left Tian and Gao, I stopped over at the township

office. I was curious to know if Shen was really campaigning as Xiu-ying had described, so I sat down on the wide stone step in front of the building. With my back leaning against the wall and the door half open I could hear most of what was said inside. If anyone accused me of eavesdropping I could say that I was just enjoying the warmth of the noonday sun.

"A year ago I took the lead in coming down here to set up the township office." Shen's voice was clear. "But do you know what some of those young people are saying? 'Shen is doing nothing.' Why last night I was so busy I hardly had time to sleep. Sometimes I don't even go home but sleep right here on the kang."

"Some of those young people are so busy they've set everything in a whirl. You are levelheaded. We will vote for you so as to balance them out." It was an old man's voice speaking.

Several voices now spoke at the same time. They seemed to be considering a plan to get Shen to help them back another candidate. Then the conversation wandered off in a new direction: Would Shen take on the job of supervising the division of the surplus property of the landlords, the things confiscated in the searches of their houses? Someone sighed that his whole family had used the same quilt for twenty years. Another grumbled that he had no money left to buy even two cakes of soap and two towels to complete his daughter's dowry.

Suddenly they dropped their voices as if they had gone into secret session. As I moved nearer to the door, an old woman's voice interjected crossly, "Shen isn't listening. He's dozed off."

"He said he hadn't slept last night. So he's tired." The old man spoke again. "People always doze off when you go to ask them for a favor. Even the Buddha is no exception. Look at him in the temple at the county town. His eyes are just slits. He can hardly keep his eyelids open. But you know he hasn't missed a word you've said."

Shattered Jade

The first time I saw Xiao Yu, Little Jade, Landlord Wu's daughter, I was passing the half-open gate of her house and caught sight of her in the courtyard. Seated on a low stool, with her head bent over her embroidery, she looked like a beauty in an ancient Chinese painting come to life. I was struck by the loveliness of her face, the sheen of her black hair pulled tightly at the nape of her neck into a single, long braid, a pink bow fluttering like a butterfly on the side of her head.

I saw her again when we went to search her father's house. She stood motionless beside her mother, paler and thinner now, in a bulky dark blue jacket and trousers that accentuated her fragility. When the peasants shouted and pushed her parents around, they took care not to touch her. Her quiet dignity fenced her off and commanded their respect and compassion. But for how long, I wondered. Her distant beauty was a provocation.

My forebodings were justified. A week before the election she was raped in the middle of the night. As soon as we learned of this, early the next morning, Wang Sha sent me to investigate.

Landlord Wu's house was a wreck of its old self even before our search. After Wu's father died, five years before, the family fortunes rapidly declined. The courtyard was unkempt. A broken moon gate draped with dead ivy was partly visible through the washing hung on a long bamboo pole supported on one side by a forked tree and on the other by a nail driven into one of the columns of the verandah fronting their main building. As I turned into the gate of the courtyard I glimpsed Da Niang's idiot son lumbering along in a grove of trees on the opposite side of the road. I stopped and glared at him, and, discomfited, he skulked away.

No one was in the courtyard and the door of the main house was ajar. I knocked and called. Landlord Wu, holding the broken frame of his spectacles in one hand, peered out at me as he opened the door wider. He was a thin stick of a man with a sickly paleness to his face like that of an opium addict. His wife, a big, dumpy woman with bound feet, scrambled on to the kang as if trying to hide something behind her. Seeing it was only a girl, Landlord Wu let me in. I went to the kang.

"It's just me," I said reassuringly. "That idiot has gone."

Little Jade lay inert, her arms lifeless at her sides. It seemed to me that she had lost the will to live; to die in that dark room would end at once the shame and terror that she would have to face in the bright light of day outside.

"Our home is no longer what it was," her mother mumbled. "Our daughter is no longer what she was. She has lost virtue. Even the idiot knows that." She rocked her body back and forth and pressed the back of her hand against her mouth to prevent herself from crying out.

"Now tell me from the beginning," I said.

"Three men broke in last night. We could not see who they were. They hit us. I fainted, but he didn't." She nodded with her head towards her husband. "He could have done something to save our daughter. But he is not a man. He is spineless. He has never been able to take care of us. Everybody steals from him. We have lost money, land, and now our only child. He is a landlord because his grandfather and father passed their land down to him. He never robbed anyone, but he has been robbed right and left. What have we done to deserve this?"

Landlord Wu stood listening shamefacedly, too crushed to defend himself.

I asked him why he hadn't run out and shouted for help. He took a long breath. The tip of his nose turned red and he blinked his watery eyes.

"Who would help us? Besides, I was afraid to do anything to provoke them. They might have killed us."

"They might just as well have killed us and her too," interjected his wife. "If they had killed her she would at least have saved her reputation."

"What could she do? How could she have put up a fight against three strong men?" I retorted.

"No matter. Now people will say that she asked for it. The gossip will kill her."

"Do you have any idea who those men were?" I asked them.

A vacant look came into Landlord Wu's eyes. He murmured, "No. I don't really know."

"You don't really know, but at least you have some idea?" Suppressing my exasperation, I spoke quietly and tried to encourage them not to be afraid to accuse the criminals.

Landlord Wu stood irresolute, rubbing his arms and body, twisting his head around in an agony of fright and confusion. He looked from me to his wife. She took the hint; sometimes a woman might dare what a man would not.

"Who do you suspect?" I asked again. "You may not know for sure, but you must suspect someone. Whoever did it certainly knew your house—did you recognize a voice? Is it someone you know?"

Landlord Wu's wife murmured ambiguously, "They could be any young men . . ." and then hastened to add, "perhaps from another village."

"Young men?" I echoed. I tensed up: This is what I was afraid of—that some young, poor peasants, excited by their newly acquired power, might have raped the girl. Wu might believe that this was part of their new privilege, just as a landlord had had the right to buy a poor peasant girl like a slave, even to rent her from a desperate husband, or simply to take her by force. Why shouldn't these privileges work the other way, now that the rest of society was turned upside down?

I knew then that I had to reassure the two parents doubly if I expected them to confide in me.

"You must understand," I spoke calmly, emphasizing every word. "They have attacked a girl. That is against the law. Committing such a crime, especially now, is against the land reform."

I waited for this to sink in, then asked, "Why did you say that they might have come from another village? How could they know your house if that were so?"

I sensed a little less constraint in Wu's voice when he answered, "I used to hire farm hands from other villages."

"Could you recognize any of them? Do you remember their names?"

"I didn't see them clearly in the dim light. I was too confused. Anyway, those men only came to work for me for a few days during the harvest. But I might know them if I saw or heard them again." He gazed blankly at me. And then his head drooped again in despair.

The mother was talking partly to herself, partly to me. "It's all my fault. When she was a child, a fortune-teller prophesied that her good fortune would not last long. He advised me to send her to a nunnery. I didn't want to believe him. She was a happy child. She laughed and giggled a lot . . . and so pretty." Tenderly with the tips of her fingers she brushed her child's disheveled hair back behind her ears. "Why did Fate pick on her? She is still a child—only fourteen years old."

As she held her face in her hand, her eyes looked larger than life because of the dark circles that ringed them.

"Can you get a doctor to treat her?" It was the first hopeful sign from the mother.

"Yes."

"Thank you. She mustn't die." The mother wavered between hope and fear. "We don't know what's happened inside her. Perhaps she is pregnant already? If she dies now, that may be the best thing for her." If the girl lived and gave birth to a child, according to village tradition she would be left alone in a sheep pen or beside a latrine when it was time to deliver. She would be in labor without a soul to help her. If she knew the meaning of shame, after the baby was born she would kill both the child and herself. Only that grim ritual would atone for the sin of being a woman.

I had heard of a similar case around this area some years before, but the girl who had been raped had refused to take her own life. The whole clan had then taken her to the ancestral temple and put her alive into a coffin. Her father had been assigned the task of nailing her in, while her mother listened to her shrieking for mercy. It seemed to me a grisly and unforgivable act, but, as they saw it, it was their duty to preserve the stability of society, to carry out justice.

"Will they come to drag her to her death?" The mother's face was suffused with terror.

"No."

"Even after you people have left?"

There was a moment of uncertainty. Then I repeated, "No."

"It wouldn't have happened if we had sent her to our relatives in Xian just one day earlier, before you came to search. It was I who delayed her departure. I was beginning to pack her things, but my heart ached when I thought of her going there like a poor relation, asking for shelter in a strange place. So I decided to make her a few new things to take with her. We delayed one day, just one day." Landlord Wu's wife drummed her temples with both fists in a fit of remorse. "I sent her to hell myself. But how could I tell that this would happen? I should have sewed faster. But I sewed as fast as I could. Late into the night. My daughter only had time to try one new jacket on. Heavens, you should have seen how her face glowed! Then all her new clothes were taken away with other things after the search."

"You mean to say that if the search had been one day later your daughter would have been spared this fate?" I could hardly get out the question.

"No. I said that if we had sent her away one day earlier

she would have been safe in Xian. How can I dare complain whether you did something earlier or later?"

I stood up. As they stared, puzzled, I looked around me and then walked around the room, pretending to search for some clue, some trace of the criminals. All the time, I was beset by the thought that I had been an unwitting participant in this crime. All this might never have happened if the search had been delayed. At the meeting at which we had discussed Landlord Wu's case, Malvolio Cheng had proposed postponing the search so as to give Shen and Tu no excuse for not taking part in it. I had disagreed, and finally Tu had in fact been forced to lead the search himself. The timing of the search had been my doing. Wasn't I at least partly to blame for this crime then? My arrogant ego cringed and asked forgiveness, but I dared not say anything aloud.

When Wang Sha, Cheng, and I met that afternoon to pool what we had learned and discuss the situation, it appeared ever more likely that Little Jade's attackers were indeed men from outside the township but who knew the township well. This made it more difficult for us in Longxiang to investigate the case further. We reported it to the county authorities, but they were inundated already with all kinds of complaints and investigations, and the misfortunes of a landlord family had a low priority. It was all we could do to get the county's one half-trained modern doctor to treat Wu's daughter.

We were disturbed to find that the innocent girl was becoming a pawn in a political battle. The conservative older villagers accused the young people of getting out of hand, while the young activists accused the conservatives and landlord reactionaries of being in league to frame them. It was only too clear that public opinion was swinging against the young candidates in the election. The plight of the victim was forgotten.

The conservatives pressed their advantage. They broadened their attack to include the whole idea of women's emancipation. The real cause of the crime, they argued, was the way girls and women were now flaunting themselves in public. The unbridled behavior of young people in general was leading to the breakdown of social order. It was time to call a halt.

Inspired by the talk around him, Da Niang's idiot son now began to make a public spectacle of himself. After he had exposed himself in the middle of the township lane, women and girls fled whenever they saw him approach. The excitement he caused only encouraged him further. He took to lying in ambush and suddenly appearing before approaching women with his trousers down. Da Niang tried tying up his pants with a complicated system of strings and knots, but this led to other problems. At length the uproar subsided and with it his interest in the game.

These events left me anxious and on edge. I took every convenient excuse to tag along with Wang Sha or Malvolio Cheng, so as not to be left by myself at any time.

16 ★

By a Grave, in a Wineshop

In the dark I wandered down an endless village street gazing at rows of dimly lit windows. I was shut out in the cold
and no one would open his door to me. I peered in one
window; inside, beside a stove, sat Cheng dressed as Malvolio. Dai Shi, that little shrew in cadre's uniform, sat opposite him, knitting. She raised her eyes from her knitting
needles to give him a wifely smile. So he had married Dai
Shi! But how could he have forgotten me so easily? I tried
to break through the window, but as I beat on it with my
hands I woke with a start.

I could not bear to be alone. Lying sleepless, the same
thoughts constantly gnawed at my mind. I could have had
marriage, a home, and, perhaps, love. How could I have
given all that up so lightly—just to pursue an ideal which
might never materialize?

Only the pressure of work kept me from brooding fu-
tilely and endlessly. Luckily for my peace of mind, with
the election almost upon us, every waking moment was
occupied. One of my tasks was to bring out the women's
vote. I was especially concerned about the virgin widow
and the wife of that drunken misanthrope Sun. While most
of the other women had at least promised to come and
vote, these two still showed no sign of rousing themselves
from their apathy. I determined to approach them once
again.

I got up, put on my padded cotton jacket and trousers, and pulled my cap down to cover my ears before I stepped out into the winter morning. I reached the field where I had first met the virgin widow, but no one was there. A cold wind stirred the dust between the still-unbroken clods and the stubble of the last scanty harvest. It moved the mist that darkened the early dawn. I moved along the narrow footpath by the field. All was quiet, but in the silence I sensed rather than heard a disturbing, muffled whisper of sound. I stopped to listen beside a pool of stagnant, algae-covered water, the last remaining moisture in the pond until the snow fell. Something, glimmering coldly, was reflected on the water. I looked up to find a square of thin white paper hung on a twig. It was a piece of sacrificial spirit money usually placed on a grave for the use of the departed one. Some naughty child had picked it up and hung it on the tree.

My eyes moved from it to a recently dead toad near the tree. Its intestines still oozed blood. Its legs spread-eagled, its eyes popped out glowering at me. Someone had evidently taken its heart. Placed in a small box beneath one's pillow, this was a talisman which could exorcise demons. The outdriven demons would take refuge in the dead toad.

Again I heard those muffled whisperings, and peering into the mist, I saw the virgin widow not far away kneeling in the dust beside a grave mound. She was wrapping something in a piece of cloth and then she stuffed it into the pocket of her jacket. She uttered a deep, stifled sob and threw back her head in a gesture of total despair. Hearing her cries sent a thrust of pain from the pit of my stomach up to my heart.

In the classical stories and folktales, I had read about lovelorn women being possessed by demons. I remembered Da Niang's story about the widow talking to her dead husband in the middle of the night. Perhaps it was not her husband but some other man who entered her dream and seduced her. She dreaded that he was a demon disguised as a man. Waking, she felt guilty and came to ask for her husband's forgiveness.

She bent forward, and her long uncombed hair cascaded over her face as her hands rhythmically stroked the sparse weeds on the grave. She was begging him to take her along with him. Why should she cling to a life which was empty of everything?

I hesitated to intrude on her sorrow, but I could not leave her in such a state. I approached her slowly. She heard my footsteps and raised her head.

"Please don't go." I put my hands on her shoulders. "I want to talk to you."

"About what?" she asked dully.

"A lot. About you and about myself."

We sat opposite each other on each side of the grave, motionless and silent. She looked at me closely. I wondered if my face showed that I, too, had cried out in the dark.

"Are you—are you the same—as I?" She paused and waited for my answer.

"You mean—was I given to a man by my family and he passed away like—" I looked down at the grave. "It was not quite the same, but something like that."

Her interest was kindled.

"We sinners." It was her soul speaking. Her face darkened and then cleared, becoming younger and comelier. A struggle was going on within her: her duty to mortify the flesh, as she had been taught was the right thing to do, and the urgent, instinctive will to live and love.

"The man was my parents' friend," I began. I was not inventing this story. There had been a bachelor, a friend of the family. One day when my aunt asked him why he did not get married, he dodged the question by turning to me and saying that he was waiting for me to grow up and be his bride. My uncle said that he would not object to having him as a son-in-law. It was only half a joke.

"Did he give you any presents?"

"Yes, he gave me many presents, at the New Year, on my birthday—"

"Birthday?" she asked.

"The day I was born. It was a happy day for me, so he gave me nice presents. You must have a birthday too."

"Before my mother had me, she had a miscarriage. It was a son. They believed that I had squeezed that boy out before his time, so they cursed the day I was born."

"What nonsense!" I added decidedly. "A birthday is a day of happiness."

She merely looked askance at that.

"Your family accepted his presents. You are his," she said, returning to the previous subject.

"No, I am not. Some day I will get married."

"Won't he haunt you?"

"No. Do you believe me?"

"You people have changed so many things—I don't know what to believe anymore." She puckered her brows, bewildered but also relieved to have my assurance.

"Much more will change. Soon you will all choose people to look after village affairs. Look at Xiu-ying—"

"She is always trying to attract attention," the widow interrupted with more envy than censure, combing her hair with her fingers.

"Let me do your hair."

"Oh, no. My hair is dirty. Your hands are clean—" She took my hands in hers. "Fair and smooth."

I withdrew my hands and hid them behind my back, speaking in a more lighthearted way. "You're making fun of me. My aunt never allowed me even to wash my handkerchief, but she was still sorry that my hands weren't as pretty as she wished. When I was a child, I used to hide my hands like this, like now."

"If only she saw my hands—" said the widow. She lowered her face as she did up her hair into a bun at the nape of her neck. But I could discern a hint of a smile flitting across the corners of her mouth.

Encouraged by her more friendly spirit, I told her, "My aunt once asked me to knit a sweater for that man. You know, as a present. He was rich, and there was nothing I could buy him that he needed. So my aunt said that if I knitted a sweater for him, he could wear it at home and think of me. The trouble was that I couldn't knit. I still can't! Anyway, whenever he came to call on us, I took up my knitting, doing a row or two. I did it this way, look, this way," and I went through the motions, "so he could not see my hands. Then I put it down."

"How did you finish it?"

"I didn't. One of our servants finished it. She was good at knitting."

"Why didn't you ask her to teach you?" She was growing more intrigued.

"I had no time. I was busy playing with friends my own age. We were all about thirteen or fourteen then."

"So all the time he thought you were knitting for him you actually were laughing at him." She stood up, sighing.

"I suppose he never found that out. If he knew, he would surely haunt me."

"That's true," she said pensively.

We were walking towards her cottage.

"But you are—" She grasped my elbow, looking at my face with her eyes suddenly becoming bright with affection. "You are laughing at me too."

I pressed my lips with my hands, laughing silently. We chatted on until it was time for me to go on my other errands. I had to visit Xiu-ying to tell her more about the election and then go on to visit Sun's wife.

As I left the widow and looked back to give her a farewell wave, I saw her throwing something away. I guessed that it was the heart of the dead toad. At least some new ideas were buzzing in her head.

I picked Xiu-ying up at her home and together we made our way across the field paths to the isolated cottage where Sun lived with his wife. By this time the winter sun, a large pale orb, had dispersed the morning mist.

For several days Xiu-ying had been quiet and subdued. The rape of Landlord Wu's daughter and its aftermath had not been without its effect on her too.

"Xiu-ying, didn't you go to see Sun's wife just a few days ago? Tell me how she's been doing."

"So-so."

"Is she going to give birth to her baby soon?"

"I guess so."

"Then she won't be able to get to the election."

"It won't make any difference to me. Sun will not let her vote for me." Xiu-ying was still moping.

"We'll see. If she even gets to the election that alone will be something."

Sun's wife was about twenty years old. She had been married to Sun when she was thirteen. She had given birth to three babies and now she was carrying her fourth, yet the couple had no children: All three babies had been girls. As soon as they were born, Sun had taken them away from his wife and left them in the brushwood on a mountainside. There they had died of hunger and cold, not knowing they had lived.

Old ideas die hard. Girls were still considered "useless baggage." You raised them and just when they could be useful around the house they were married off and went to serve some other family. For a poor family hardly able to keep body and soul together a girl baby sometimes seemed an intolerable burden. According to local superstition, if the first three babies were girls, the fourth must be a girl too. However Sun wouldn't dare dispose of this new baby like the others because the work team in the village would surely hear about it. Yet he didn't want another baby girl and he hoped that it would die. As the time of birth neared, he spent more and more time in the wine-shop, wasting his money on drink, leaving his wife unattended and hoping that the baby would perish at birth.

We entered the bare cottage to find Sun's wife huddled on the floor in a corner. Sun seemed to have absorbed every evil superstition about girls. He would not let her lie on the kang—the bridal bed—and pollute it. To give birth to an unwanted baby girl was something dirty and fraught with evil portent, so we found her at that moment abandoned on the floor, not daring, even in his absence, to drag herself onto the kang. Her eyes were dilated and terribly bright. She was in the grip of a fever and near delirious. She opened her dry, blackened lips and cursed her husband. I had never in my life heard such dirty, obscene words as came out of her mouth. Normally she was a kind, patient soul, but the pain she suffered shattered all restraint and vented all the bitterness pent up in her heart. She was a woman possessed. She had torn her blouse from back to front and exposed her woeful, undernourished breasts. Her nails had left bloody marks in the hollow between her shoulder blades. Suddenly she was silent and lay motionless as if all energy had been drained out of her. Her eyelids closed over her blank stare.

Xiu-ying and I lifted the stricken woman onto the kang. I dipped a rag in the cold water from a jet in the kitchen and applied it to her forehead to bring the fever down, but then I paused because her brow, dripping with sweat, turned deathly cold. I held my breath. Was she dying? My God! Why had I never been told about such things? That fancy education at St. Ursula's had never taught me what to do in face of these elemental facts of life.

To my horror, she writhed with pain again, her face livid. She repeated the same curses as if they were a litany to the rite of this abnormal birth. I wanted to run away, but I knew that was impossible so I sent Xiu-ying off to get help. I stared at this tortured mother-to-be until her image was imprinted indelibly on my mind. I have hated to remember it; but I do not want to forget it either, for I felt that she was bearing the sufferings of us all. I could have been writhing in a dark corner of that hovel on a patch of rags on the floor with some monster kicking inside me. I was in a cold sweat.

Xiu-ying persuaded the old woman next door to overcome her fear of Sun and help his wife. Now she tottered in and began to feel the stricken woman's belly.

"The baby's feet will come out first," the old neighbor gasped. She barely finished her sentence. "That's bad. I can't handle that."

"Go and get a midwife," I said in a hoarse voice.

"Who will pay her?"

We were not allowed either to lend or borrow money from the peasants. We wished to give no grounds for rumors that we bought over peasants or were bribed by them.

"Sun will," I answered peremptorily. I turned to Xiuying. "You go to my room and fetch the first-aid box, the one with the red cross on it, and bring it back here. I will go and hunt for Sun."

"All right," she answered dully.

"Let's go then."

But as we turned to take our separate paths, she stopped and faltered out in a low voice, "I don't know anything about—erh—" She twirled her tongue to skip the word "childbirth." According to local tradition it might bring shame on her if she, an unmarried girl, mentioned the fact of childbirth. Childbirth was associated with sex and sex was associated with shame, especially for an unmarried girl. Tradition was weighing Xiu-ying down, it seemed.

"Why don't you let me go to look for Sun?" she asked.

"That could be even worse," I cried. "Who knows where you might find him?" If things were hard for me, they were doubly so for her. "I know some narrow-minded people are criticizing you for not behaving as a young girl should."

"Not just *some* people are saying bad things about me. There are many, especially after the—you know—after Landlord Wu's daughter—" she stammered on in a gloomy voice. "I think I've already lost quite a lot of po—po—"

"Potential votes," I helped her finish the sentence. "But do you think it is right to bow to their pressure?"

I was not sure of the answer to my own question. She was a candidate now and near to being elected. Should she reflect the opinions of her constituents? Was that compromising? Or should she defy them? What was practical common sense? In this case, what was common sense and what was selling out one's principles for votes? If she compromised now, what guarantee was there that she wouldn't make peace with the conservatives once she was installed in a place of power?

"Didn't you say we must win the election?" she asked.

"Yes, I did," I replied a little sheepishly.

"I'll tell my mother to come here and bring the first-aid kit."

By this time I knew more about Sun, and I was sure I would find him with his cronies in the wineshop. As I hur-

ried on my way I brooded on how to deal with him. I felt
so angry I could hardly speak. I would grip him by the
collar and drag him to his wife, shouting, "You can't get
away with murder!"

I must have looked like an avenging virago as I went
into the market center. Dealers at their stalls looking out
for customers didn't even try to attract my attention as I
raged past. Several peddlers were clustered on the roadway in front of the wineshop. In my haste, I almost
knocked over a tray filled with needles and thread. Right
next to the wineshop a man with a charlatan's face was
selling an ointment. His jacket open, his chest bare, his
belly bulging over his tight-drawn belt, he was demonstrating the efficacy of his "medicine." Keeping up a
stream of patter, he took a stone from the square of cotton
cloth on which he displayed his wares, and struck himself
in the chest. Immediately the skin at that spot turned blue
and seemed to swell. With a flourish he then applied a dab
of his ointment to the wound, which began to lose its dis-
coloration. To show how effective the cure was, he jumped
up and down like a child, waving his arms. He was a special kind of cheat—"a sharp beggar"—well known in
cities but still a rarity out here in the Northwest. These
men used cheap tricks and scare tactics to shock credu-
lous onlookers into wasting a few coppers to buy worthless concoctions. Another mountebank's tray had an even
stranger assortment of goods on display—teeth, both real
and false. The latter were made of a deathly looking white
porcelain. Their owner styled himself a "dentist." He
grinned ingratiatingly and constantly, baring his own array of dirty, decayed dentures. They said he was a body
snatcher and dug up corpses in the middle of the night to
steal their teeth. A blind man sat against the wall of the
wineshop itself. He was singing, accompanying himself on
the *hu-chin* violin. His two blind eyes had the texture and
color of the stomach of a dead fish. They looked all the
more disgusting because there was dirt in their corners.
He blinked now and then at the sky as he sang a song
about the violent death of an adulteress, and the *hu-chin*
whined away. Another man, poorly but rather neatly

dressed, held a small teapot at his shoulder, and as the
blind man finished his song, he put the spout of the teapot
to his lips and fed him in an intimate way.

The wineshop was the center of town gossip and it
hummed with chatter. Behind the brown-stained wooden
counter its portly owner sat on a high-backed chair higher
than the stools around the rickety tables. His half-closed
eyes almost buried in the fat of his face, he reminded me
of an obese frog sitting on a lotus leaf. On the wall were
faded strips of red and green paper, pasted up at random.
They exhorted us to "pay in cash. Friends and relatives no
exception" and promised "Honest salesmanship to everyone, children and the elderly included." With an eye to
pleasing the new society, the proprietor had even pasted
up a slip: "Long live the People's Government!" Scratched
on the wall beside it were graffiti, erotic drawings, and
pornographic doggerel.

The only waitress was none other than the Broken Shoe.
She had taken this new job to show she was now a re-
formed woman. She walked in what she evidently imagined was a fetching style, wagging her bottom as she wove
her way with a mincing step between the tables.

As I looked about for Sun in this dimly lit den, I felt as if
I had fallen into a cesspool. It turned my stomach. Next to
the counter, nearest the proprietor, sat a local "capitalist."
He owned a tiny photo shop equipped with a large and
impressive box camera and two painted backdrops, one
showing the famed West Lake at Hangzhou and the other
a Model T Ford in front of the Forbidden City in Peking.
He was held in high esteem by frequenters of the wineshop. They thought him farsighted. As long as six years
ago, he had sold most of his land and invested his money
in various commercial enterprises including this photo
shop. It was a shrewd move. Under the laws of the new
government, a man, whether a former landlord or not,
whose income mainly came from an industrial or commercial enterprise, was rated a "national capitalist" and as
such, if he obeyed the laws, was considered to be a member of the national democratic united front and one of the
"people." This new capitalist had memorized the text of

the land reform and carefully read all the proclamations of the new government. He never missed an opportunity to tell people, "I am a citizen with full civil rights. Do you see our national flag with the five stars in its upper left-hand corner? One of those stars symbolizes us patriotic national capitalists. Our representatives stood on Tian An Men on the national birthday with all the leaders of the country."

Because of his forethought, he was indeed a certified "national capitalist," a positive contributor to China's economic and social advance, while his old crony Chi was labeled a reactionary feudal landlord, an obstacle in the way of historic advance at a time when the prime target of the revolution was feudalism and its main prop, feudal landlordism.

There were several other drinkers with blurry, bloodshot eyes. But finally I spotted Sun slumped over a table in the farthest corner of the room. He seemed to be dozing, nodding his head over his tiny wine cup and pitcher of spirits.

"Sun!" I called sharply.

He started and looked up at me, glassy-eyed, as if having some difficulty bringing me into focus. I was amazed to see such pain and misery in his eyes. Suddenly moved, I could not upbraid him.

"Sun, let us go. Your wife is going to give birth to your baby," I said in a low tone. Every eye in the den was fixed on us.

He sighed heavily, his face drawn and contorted. "I spent all I had to buy that woman. I sold my goat. Yes, I sold my goat. I looked after that goat as if it were my own mother. But what did I get? A useless creature. She cannot give me a son."

The Broken Shoe had casually strolled over to hear what we were saying. Before I had a chance to reply, she advised in a knowing tone, picking her teeth the whole time, "Make her keep on trying. She is young. She is fertile. After another ten babies there must be a son for you."

"I don't think there will ever be a son. You know, that part of her body has no hair."

Sun must have been utterly distracted with grief to reveal such a secret. I gasped.

"Good Heavens!" The Broken Shoe raised her meticulously plucked eyebrows in astonishment and delivered her verdict: "It's clear that she was born under an evil star. Nothing can be done about it."

I pulled at Sun's sleeve to get him to leave, but he ignored me. By this time several men around us had gotten into the conversation.

"If you want to know whether a woman can make a son or not before you marry her, you must listen to her shitting. If the sound is resonant, her womb is fertile," a drunkard put in. He spoke matter-of-factly, entirely without lasciviousness. The cigarette between his lips bobbed up and down as he spoke, punctuating his words of wisdom. "Isn't that so?" He turned to the photographer deferentially.

Women were the photographer's favorite subject. He believed he was a lady-killer and he acted the role. He inhaled and puffed out smoke in a debonair way, waiting to join the discussion.

"Not only that. You also have to see how her hips sway," the photographer responded in the same businesslike manner.

"Your wife has come to us with complaints against you," I interrupted him loudly so as to make sure that he understood what I implied: His position was not as secure as he thought it was. "Wives who have been wronged can bring their husbands to court and obtain a divorce if they wish. In that case it will be her right to share half of the family's joint property. If brutal treatment is proved against the husband, he may be sent to jail."

At first the photographer had scowled, but then he switched tactics and was all smiles. He knew I was speaking the truth. He half rose from his stool as if bowing to me. "Yes, yes. I'll gladly accept any criticism. Which of us doesn't make a mistake sometimes. We should be glad to be told about them. Still, I should point out that I'm a law-abiding citizen, a citizen with full civil rights. I bought my

concubine before the new Republic was established. I
didn't do anything against the law."

Sun seemed to be oblivious of our arguing. He wailed
on, following his own train of thought. "I am a man without a son. What will become of me when I get old? Who
will look after me? I am honest, decent, and hardworking.
Why does Heaven punish me so?" he whimpered.

"Sun, we have said that every pregnant woman should
come to register her unborn child, because it too will get
its share of land in the land reform. Why didn't you come
to our meetings?"

"She is carrying a girl. How can I be so shameless as to
ask a portion of land for her?" A teardrop collected at the
corner of each eye and slowly trickled down his cheeks.

"Sun, talk sense. You have no one to blame but yourself.
You won't join the literacy class. You cannot read, so you
don't know what is in the land reform law. But we keep on
inviting you and your wife to our meetings. We can explain it to you item by item. You don't want to come. You
won't let your wife come or even talk to us. So now you're
making a fool of yourself."

I had more than Sun as an interested audience.

"The land reform policy states plainly that girls have
equal rights with boys. Every girl will get her own portion
of land—and listen carefully—in her own name. Your
baby is being born at this very moment. I don't know if it
is a boy or a girl, but whatever it is, it and its mother will
be given the best land in the village. Since you are in the
same family, naturally your portion of land will be in the
same area and as good as theirs. But remember this, you
will share their honor, not they, yours."

"Are you sure?" The Broken Shoe surveyed me with a
swift, flashing glance.

"Yes."

She wrinkled her nose, trying to puzzle out whether she
should believe that I spoke with authority.

"There is Old Cheng. He probably knows more about
the whole arrangement. Why don't you go ask him?" The
photographer now spoke to Sun in the assertive tone of a
sophisticated man giving himself face. By his stress on the

"him," he insinuated that my woman's words did not carry too much weight. Then, to placate me, he turned to me and spoke in an obsequious, barely audible voice: "Sun is feudal-minded and he prefers to deal with a man. I know that Old Cheng must agree with you. I'll tell Sun to go to Old Cheng to let him find out himself that a woman's word is as good as a man's."

Another drunkard was not aware of the photographer's secret truce with me. Rising to his feet he addressed the whole room in an offensively rude manner: "Please allow me to walk out. The air in here has become a little sour," he sniggered.

Sun's bigotry had been reinforced by their goading; that and a few drinks on an empty stomach had befuddled his brains more than usual.

"What a world," he wailed. "Women are rising against men; servants against masters; children against parents; sons against their ancestors. The temples of the ancestors are used indecently," he blabbered on, sniveling and banging his forehead against the table.

"They are used for people to study and work in," I protested.

"Pah, I don't buy that kind of garbage. When men and women mix together like that—" He spat on the ground. "It dirties my mouth to say it. Worst of all, now monks and nuns want to get paired up!"

"Those monks and nuns were put in the monasteries when they were children. They didn't know what they were doing. Now they want to be happy like other men and women."

"They were happy until you people came and put ideas into their heads. You have turned things upside down. The Heavens will be angry. We'll see blood flow yet. We'll come to grief. Oh, what misery!"

I was astounded by Sun's besotted rage. I looked hard at his drunken, tear-streaked face and felt a twinge inside. What was I rushing into? If the political climate changed, wouldn't he and his kind gladly hand me over to his masters?

The wineshop keeper could see that I was thinking over

Sun's wild words and he looked around uncomfortably. It was not wise to make an enemy of a land reform work team cadre at such a time and rave about shedding blood to boot. Although he had been told to do so, he had not yet removed from his wall the half-legible, half-torn strip of paper left over from the old warlord days. It said, "Don't talk politics!"

"Sun, don't talk nonsense," he remonstrated in an affectedly reproachful tone. "These comrades are really kind to come here and help us."

"If they really want to be kind they should leave us in peace." Sun stopped short. He was not so drunk that he couldn't see the wineshop keeper's upraised hand and the warning in his eyes. The photographer had even half risen to his feet and leaned towards the hapless Sun.

I couldn't stand their presence any longer.

I turned away swiftly and stormed out of that cesspool. The photographer raised his wine cup in my direction, motioning Sun to follow me out. The habitués of the wineshop compared notes in hushed voices. The "frog" behind the counter busied himself with his bottles and wine cups and grumbled to himself. Just as we got beyond earshot I could hear him shouting at the Broken Shoe.

17 ★

The Election

The day before the voting, Xiu-ying's mother was as busy as anyone working for her daughter's election. But while most of the Longxiang peasants shrewdly suspected that influence and money were still the best allies of a candidate, Xiu-ying's mother had her own ideas. She was certain that only a good, full meal would give her daughter the courage and stamina she needed to carry the day.

"Only a man with a full stomach can make himself heard," was the way she put it. The peasants of Longxiang ate two meals a day. The election would be held at noon after the first meal. The logic was obvious.

Xiu-ying's mother had raised a hen and, no matter how sparse the meal, always shared her bowl of millet gruel with it. In return, it occasionally laid an egg, though without good feed this was usually no bigger than a dove's. Most of the eggs were sold; a very few were kept for a special dish on important occasions such as the Spring Festival at the Lunar New Year. Now she decided to kill the hen to make a special meal for her daughter. Her husband vehemently disapproved of this sacrifice, but tyrant though he was, he knew the limits of his power.

"A girl going to be an official! The world is turned upside down," he grumbled.

Xiu-ying's mother had once thought as he did, but now she said to me, "It breaks my heart to think that Xiu-ying might be doomed as I am. She's as good as anyone. Perhaps this really is a way out."

Her face was a study in split-second metamorphoses: A pathetic look passed from it to be succeeded by the gloom of despair, and then all dissolved in a look of hope and happiness. This first attempt by her to defeat fate, however naive, elated me and made me more eager than ever to see Xiu-ying elected.

It was not for financial reasons only that Xiu-ying's father wanted to keep the hen. I believe he was a bit awed as well as astonished at the thought of his daughter becoming an official. In all his experience, in all history as he knew it, no woman had ever become an official. He was appalled by the idea and grasped at anything that might prevent it from becoming reality. To keep the hen alive might do the trick. Like his wife, he believed a man who had enough to eat could not fail, and perhaps the same held true for women.

But the mother this time seemed to pay no attention to his objections as she set about the task of sacrificing the scrawny bird. Perhaps she was wavering in the face of her husband's objections or perhaps she just loved the hen too well. Her hand went weak as she brought the chopper down on its neck; its neck was broken, but its head was not severed. The intractable bird squawked and fluttered from her nerveless hands. It flapped its wings and flew all over the room, spilling feathers and throwing us all into a panic. Xiu-ying's mother rushed to close the door and then dashed back to protect the food with her apron from the falling feathers and the rising dust. I seized a carrying pole and chased the luckless hen in circles. The old man quite forgot his faked nonchalance and thrashed around, adding to the general confusion. Finally, with Xiu-ying and her brother's help we caught the hen. The mother, setting her teeth, resolutely wrung the chicken's neck. The election had to be won.

For the past week, Xiu-ying had grown too nervous to sleep. Blue circles appeared around her eyes. Now, as she chopped the vegetables you could see her lips moving wordlessly, reciting her acceptance speech.

"Let me say it once again." She pressed the paper into my hand. "Word for word, now."

She had learned it by heart already, and if she had been more relaxed she could have spoken it perfectly. But she faltered and stuttered and sometimes stopped short in mid-sentence.

"Why do I always get stuck at the same sentence?" Her face clouded over. She bit her lips to choke down her tears.

"Xiu-ying, where is my new scarf?" her mother called from her room.

"I don't know," Xiu-ying replied crossly. She was engrossed in her task, puckering her brow, sucking her thumb in concentration.

"You spoiled brat," her mother nagged. After a while, she raised her voice in triumph. "I've found it!"

"So what? Why yell?" Xiu-ying was annoyed to have her thoughts interrupted. Her mother chattered on.

"I bought it after your brother was born. Was it a year later or at the end of the same year? I've got it all mixed up now. Anyway it was about seven or eight years ago." She came in holding up the grey scarf for us all to see. "I only used it a few times. It still looks new. Xiu-ying, it's yours now."

Xiu-ying stopped her worrying for the moment and was delighted.

"But the color is too subdued for a festival," I said doubtfully. "Let's dye it."

"Dye it red," suggested Xiu-ying. So she did think there would be a reason for celebration!

When she gave the money to her brother to buy the dye, she looked up at the sky. "It may rain tomorrow. The sky is reddish with small clouds." She was worried again and stamped her feet. "The election is in the open air. The rain will keep people away and mess everything up."

"It's hard to tell whether it will rain or not," I said truthfully, scrutinizing the sky.

Every now and again, in mid-sentence, Xiu-ying put her head out the door to study the portents of the sky.

• • •

I stayed with Xiu-ying that night. As we prepared to sleep, she begged, "Just before I fall asleep, read my speech into my ear. Then I'll be able to learn it in my dreams."

"Will that work?"

"Why, yes!" She had already put one leg in the folded quilt, but leaped up again, dashed to the door, and took one final look at the sky. "The stars are twinkling. It looks like a fine day tomorrow!"

"Xiu-ying, do you really believe you can learn your speech in your dreams?"

"Of course." There was no hint of doubt in her voice. "Once when my brother was hungry and we didn't have anything in the house to eat, my mother whispered in his ear just before he fell asleep. She described his favorite dish, so he dreamed about it and wasn't hungry."

"What is his favorite dish?" I asked.

"Pian-er gruel with green onions."

"Pian-er gruel?" I could hardly believe my ears.

Xiu-ying nestled her face to mine as though she had some secret to break to me. "Tomorrow we will have onions in the pian-er gruel. Mother exchanged an egg for them. And the pian-er will be made of flour, only flour. Now you can start reading."

I read to her so solicitously that it must have sunk deep into her consciousness, so deep that it left no trace.

It was already late, but Xiu-ying's mother was still puttering around preparing the election feast. Her father sat dozing, rhythmically heaving deep grunts.

"Why will we eat chicken this New Year's Day?" Xiu-ying's brother asked him.

"What New Year's Day? The New Year Festival was over a long time ago," he roared.

"Who will eat the chicken then?"

The answer was a resounding slap. Then silence.

In the middle of the night, Xiu-ying shook me and asked, "Is it day yet?"

"No." I pointed my flashlight at my watch. "It's still a few hours away. Try and get some sleep."

"Do you think I'll get elected?" Her bright eyes shone through the darkness and were fixed intently on my face.

"I do."

"Do you think my acceptance speech will be a success?"

"I do."

"I'm not sure. So many eyes will be staring at me. My heart will beat so hard." She raised up her smiling face as she imagined the scene. She looked younger, childlike, in the dim moonlight filtering through the window. She saw herself on the platform, speaking like a cadre. The people were listening attentively.

"If you don't get enough sleep, you will be too tired to do a good job," I admonished her.

"I'll be scared to death even before I open my mouth," she wailed.

"Right now, we must go to sleep." My words fell on deaf ears.

She pushed her pillow aside, then cried in dismay, "I can't find my speech." She snatched up her jacket lying folded on the edge of the kang. She turned every pocket inside out.

"Here it is under my pillow," I said in a deliberately unhurried manner.

"You hid it! You're so wicked. This is how I'll handle you!" And she tickled my ribs. We scuffled and rolled over, giggling. Her father gave a warning cough, dry and hoarse. I pressed my lips with my finger, shaking my head at her. She nodded in agreement. We lay down. She put her hands under her head as a pillow.

She was quiet for a while. I hoped she had dozed off, but she soon continued thinking aloud.

"You know, sometimes I wish I could be elected, but sometimes I don't want to be. Even now, though I'm only an activist, the other women want me to do what they themselves would like to do if only they dared. When I become a cadre they will ask even more of me! Can I live up to their expectations?"

She paused again. I was drifting off to sleep. Suddenly she sat bolt upright. "Can I?"

"Let's discuss that tomorrow," I murmured drowsily.

"Tomorrow—tomorrow, can I speak as well as you cadres do?" She covered her face with her hands, looking timidly through her fingers at me.

"Xiu-ying, I'm not any different or more intelligent than you; I've just had a bit more experience." The irony of my words escaped her. "Actually soon you'll be speaking just like the rest of us. But not unless you go to sleep now!" And with that, no more was said.

In the morning, Xiu-ying was the first to get up; she looked as if she'd gotten no sleep at all. She didn't even mention her speech, but she silently helped her mother do the housework. Sometimes she stopped in the middle of a movement, blankly staring forward.

"Silly girl, why are you in a daze?" As if her mother didn't know the cause!

Xiu-ying looked to the left and right.

"What are you looking for?" inquired her mother, puzzled.

With her head inclined to her shoulder, frowning as if lost in thought, Xiu-ying said, "The sun is high now." Then she turned away abruptly and went into her room.

I found her there a few minutes later sprawled on her stomach on the kang, her cheeks supported by her hands, her speech propped up in front of her eyes.

At mealtime, Xiu-ying's mother told her, "Go sit with your father!"

Instead Xiu-ying edged towards the kang but didn't get onto it. She stood there fidgeting, avoiding her father's eye. In a well-ordered home only men could sit at table to be waited upon.

When all the dishes were on the table, she joined us but ate mechanically whatever her mother put into her bowl. She drank the pian-er gruel without noticing what it was. Only when she saw the chicken thigh, supposedly the best part of the bird, placed before her did she start in surprise.

"I want a thigh," her small brother cried, stretching out his hand. He had always shared the chicken thighs with his father. They, the men, were the only ones in the family so privileged.

His mother pinched his ear. He squealed.

"Take this one," the old man interceded, passing the chicken leg in his bowl to his son.

"Father, take this," Xiu-ying said, proffering the leg from her bowl with her chopsticks.

"Do you think your father will snatch food from out of your mouth?" the old man asked in a gruff voice.

We all watched Xiu-ying as she ate the precious chicken leg. She swallowed it without tasting it. But no matter, it would work its magic anyway.

Just as we were about to leave, she sat down flushed as though she were going to faint.

"You go ahead," she told her parents and brother.

I sat beside her and took her hands in mine.

"Have they gone far enough?" she asked.

"Yes, they are well down the road."

We walked down the village road, hand in hand. Her hand felt damp in mine. I could feel the turmoil in her heart.

The election was to be held in the large walled courtyard where, from time immemorial, theatrical performances had been given in the open air. By common consent and convenience this had become the center of the new political life of the village. Apart from the open fields, it was the only place in which all the people could gather together. It was already crowded when we arrived. People sat on stools or benches they had brought with them or cross-legged on the ground. A few hunkered down in circles, chatting. Some stood with their backs leaning against the wall. Men smoked their pipes, argued about the candidates, or talked farming. Women gossiped, sewed, stitched cloth soles, plaited cushions of straw, and kept the children in order. Now and then someone burst out laughing, shouted to a neighbor at the top of his voice, or a child screamed and hollered. As the crowd grew so did the hubbub. The villagers took this as a gala occasion and behaved as unconstrainedly as they would have done at a performance of an opera.

From time to time we glanced at the stage to see if there were any sign of the proceedings starting. The platform was covered by a pavilion roof with up-curving eaves supported on two columns and the back wall; today it was gay with red bunting, branches of evergreen, and fresh slogans. Down each column, whitewashed characters on red cotton spelled out "Down with feudalism!" and "Long live the land reform!" The banner over the top of the stage read "Long live the People's Government!" In the middle, at the back of the stage, hung a large picture of Mao Zedong. Fifteen stools were placed along the front of the stage. Behind them were fifteen large eating bowls on a trestle table.

Nothing ever started on time in Longxiang. Only the landlords had clocks; only the cadres had watches. Everyone else told the time by the sun or the stars. As time went by, children got tired of sitting still and began to play hide-and-seek, running through the crowd. Some fought. Their mothers dragged them away by the ears. Attracted by the brightly colored paper, children set to tearing off the yard-long slogans which we had spent days composing and writing and pasting on the walls. This was too much for me and I too began to shout and run after them, adding to the ever-growing noise and confusion.

When they caught sight of Xiu-ying standing in a corner near the stage, several young women shot her curious glances and whispered their comments. Xiu-ying pretended not to notice.

"Here comes the bride," a band of children cried, pointing at Xiu-ying's red head scarf, clapping their hands and stamping their feet with mischievous joy. The smallest toddlers shrilly took up the cry, not knowing what it meant but thoroughly enjoying the racket. Xiu-ying blushed and made a start to run away. I grabbed her arm and led her to another part of the compound. But the little rascals nudged each other and followed us. They stood right under Xiu-ying's nose, making faces and stretching their arms and legs sideways and backwards like little clowns. Xiu-ying's brother, a brash seven-year-old, took it upon himself to drive them away. He stood beside his sister, puffed up with pride, his eyes glaring and roving around belligerently to catch would-be troublemakers.

I had done my part by leading in the only woman candidate. Malvolio Cheng had to lead in the men candidates who had gathered at the township office, but they were late. The sun mounted high in the sky and began to dip. It was well past midday. A few women grew impatient, rose to their feet, and dusted off their trousers.

"My hen will soon lay her egg. If I don't put it away in time, it'll be stolen either by the rats or the kids," someone proclaimed. "I'd better go home."

"I should go home too," said another."The wall of our courtyard collapsed more than a year ago. There's a gap there big enough for a cart to drive through. Every day that lousy son of mine promises to repair it, but he still hasn't started on it. When it comes to helping other people, he always has time. When I ask him to do something for me, he's always too busy to do it. I must see to it that that goat next door doesn't get into our yard." A middle-aged woman rose to her feet and began to walk away.

"The sun is so bright," said another woman, shielding her eyes with her hand as she looked up pointedly at the sky. "I have to take a look at those turnip tops drying on the roof. I'm making pickles, dried turnip top pickles. If they get too dry, they'll be leathery. My kids eat them like locusts. Poor kids. I hope one day I'll have enough money so I don't have to sell the turnips and can keep them for my children."

Some really did have work to attend to, but we knew others just had no intention of voting; they came to the election just to show their good will. Voting meant choosing, taking sides, something they had no wish to do. Xiuying as a candidate could do nothing about this, but I and other girl activists busied ourselves trying to persuade the waverers to stay.

"The election will soon begin. Nobody move!" Tu had scrambled onto the stage and was now shouting like a bandit at a holdup. However, most turned a deaf ear both to him and to us. They walked their own way leisurely towards the gate. The more people noticed their departure, they thought, the better.

Fortunately the fourteen men candidates, including Shen, now arrived in a crowd. Shepherded by Cheng, they took their seats on the stage, facing the voters. Some looked self-conscious; some assumed an unconvincing air of nonchalance. I led Xiu-ying to the central stool. Sitting there with her flushed cheeks and her red head scarf she certainly caught one's eye.

A leading district cadre took the stage. He had a small, round face, and looked more like a child wearing false whiskers than an overworked adult who had not shaved for days. He was known as a good conversationalist and could talk with a city man or a farmer. With his aplomb and happy nature he had no difficulty making instant friends. He had become a popular character in the hamlets of the district, which was why our work team had asked him to help us at the election.

"Comrades!" He coughed in order to clear his throat and attract attention. Then he repeated with more solemnity, "Comrades!"

"Who is Comrades?" An old woman, perplexed and a little deaf, spoke loudly and querulously.

"You are," the old man beside her answered knowingly.

"My name is not Comrades," said she.

"We are all comrades now."

This needed thinking over. The old woman lapsed into befuddled silence.

" . . . Here sit fifteen candidates for our People's Council. We all know them." The district cadre named them, pointing each one out in turn. "We will elect seven of them to represent us. They must do a good job for us. At this time, when we are carrying out the land reform, this is a very special and important occasion. The future is in your hands now. Walk up here on the stage behind the candidates. You will be given seven beans. Put your beans in the bowls of the candidates you wish to elect. Every bean counts as one vote."

There was a surge to the steps up to the platform.

"How come I have only seven beans?" said a woman who was breast-feeding her baby. She turned to the child tagging along at her side. "Did you eat some? Open your mouth. Let me see."

"They gave me only seven beans." The woman next in line wet her thumb and forefinger with her tongue and rubbed together the ends of a broken cotton thread. She joined it and went on sewing the sole of a cloth slipper. "But there are fifteen bowls. What shall I do?"

"You need to choose only seven of them."

"Good Heavens! What will the eight of them say just because I prefer the other seven? Oh, no!"

"But the candidates can't see what we're doing. They don't have eyes in the back of their heads."

"But they have eyes in the queue."

As this thought was expressed several lovers of peace slipped away. How many times had the activists explained these points about voting? But despite all our efforts, many of the peasants simply refused to understand.

"This is our first election," the young district cadre exhorted them. "Cast your votes carefully. Today no landlords dare order us around any more. We make decisions of our own free will."

Some of the peasants were there because they had heard there would be some sort of theatrical performance and they wanted to see the "sights." They knew that some members of the work teams could perform. But they had never been to any of our meetings and were quite mystified by the speeches and strange goings on. The suspicion grew into a certainty that the land reform team was trying to lure them into something complicated, shady, and mutinous. What could illiterate peasants do without well-educated, brainy masters to supervise? And a young girl too among them! And all this rigmarole about beans and bowls. They wanted no part of it. "Stay and vote! The voting is just going to start!" the activists shouted. Some of them began to push people into line but this only created more confusion. The waverers sidled to the gate and disappeared despite all efforts to get them to stay and vote. Thinking to ease the misgivings of part of the crowd, the young people stepped aside to let the old people of the village mount the voting platform first.

The first in line was Old Tian with the wispy goat's beard. He was dressed in the traditional style with no concession to modern fashion. Baggy black trousers, bare brown feet like roots thrust into enormous, ungainly cloth slippers, long jacket belted at the waist with a sash of white homespun into which he had thrust his pipe, and a fresh-washed towel which turbaned his grizzled head. He was determined to show the youngsters and his wavering neighbors how men did things in the new society. But in a flurry of excitement he threw all his seven beans into the first bowl he came to, which happened to be that of his crony Gao, the village sage.

"One bean for one bowl!" the district cadre shouted for him and for the others.

The old man gaped. Someone took six beans out of the first bowl and returned them to him. He put the remaining six beans into the next six bowls. Then he turned to face the others on the platform, slapped his thighs, and threw his empty hand out as if to say, "Sorry, I have no more beans left. It's not my fault if I can't elect all the candidates!"

To speed up the voting, the district cadre got two lines of voters to form right and left of the stage and drop their beans in the bowls as they passed along the two sides of the table behind the candidates' backs. But it became clear that all the voters were following the first old man's example and were not choosing candidates but simply putting their beans in the first seven bowls they came to. To get a bean or two in at least some of their friends' bowls, some people started switching sides if their favorite candidates sat on the other side of the platform, without breaking the basic pattern of putting their beans in the bowls in order as they came to them. This meant that they voted for some candidates they liked and some they did not particularly favor. But at least they made some choice.

To my dismay I saw that Xiu-ying, sitting in the middle seat, was getting no votes. No matter which end they began on, the voters had run out of beans before they reached her.

Just as I was wondering what to do, a young peasant in our reading class moved up to vote. The contrast between him and the previous voters was sharp. This young man was tall. His newly shaven head shone. He was relaxed and with a certain swagger as if to say, "I can do it." Smiling, he strode straight to Xiu-ying's bowl and dropped a bean in it so that it tinkled. It was the breakthrough. Several people who were carefully watching the voting clapped and shouted, "Bravo!" Encouraged, Xiu-ying's mother led a few of her friends to vote for her daughter. Two of them stealthily put two or three beans in Xiu-ying's bowl. When they were caught, they giggled merrily. Xiu-ying sat strained in her seat not knowing what was going on, aware only that her fate was being settled there behind her back.

Several other young men and women followed the tall voter's example. Even a few older people began to follow suit, voting more in accordance with their real wishes. But a number of people still hung back, their beans clenched in their fists. Something had to be done. The quick-witted young district cadre had the answer. He halted the proceedings and advised all voters to protect the secrecy of their ballot by putting their hands into every bowl in turn but only releasing beans in the bowls of their chosen candidates. In this way no one would know how they had voted. One of the first to vote in this new way was the virgin widow, whom I escorted to the platform. Now the voting proceeded with a swing.

When the bean ballots were counted, Xiu-ying; Shen; Tu; Gao, the village sage; Little Tian, the future deputy chairman of the Poor Peasants' Association; Little Gao, the young militia leader; and the village well-digger Wong Ching-lun were declared elected. We had registered three hundred and twenty voters who were over eighteen years of age and eligible to vote. One hundred and ninety-two votes had been cast.

One by one the seven newly elected cadres gave their short acceptance speeches. Shen spoke first. A veteran cadre, well known to everyone and trusted despite a certain proclivity for "playing politics," he said all that was appropriate to the occasion. After the other five, finally it was Xiu-ying's turn as the youngest cadre. She came to the center of the platform, where stage fright transfixed her. I motioned to her little brother, who like the other children, sat on the front of the stage as he would at a theatrical performance, swinging his legs. He scrambled up and nudged her. Startled, she opened her eyes wide, childishly bewildered to see before her a sea of faces, a blur of heads and eyes.

"Speech!" someone shouted half jokingly. "Don't be shy!"

Others cried, "Come on, say something. Pour on the sauce!"

She opened her mouth and rubbed her hands together like a singer.

"Quiet!" a stentorian voice tried to shout down the chatter of the crowd.

Xiu-ying turned pale. She moved her lips but no sound came forth. Then her lips stopped moving. All of a sudden someone began to clap, an embarrassed, isolated clap. Then a few more joined in. Scattered, it sounded weak. Then more and more joined in until it burst into a thunder of applause and cheers.

Xiu-ying came down from the stage and threw herself into my arms.

"Did I forget and leave anything out in my speech?" She held her breath waiting for my answer.

"No. You said everything. It was a wonderful speech." I was overwhelmed by emotion, throwing my arms around her shoulders, weeping and laughing at the same time.

18 ★

Three Deaths

The last time I saw Xia was in the township office when he came at our insistence to a meeting to settle his precise status—rich peasant or landlord. He was a changed man since Tu had led the ill-advised raid on his farm. He was edgy, sullen, and morose. I noticed a touch of grey in his hair. I knew we had not handled his case as well as we might have. Tu had been primarily responsible, but none of us could evade our share of responsibility. I wanted to do what I could to make up for that.

"Don't think we are just picking on you," I told him in a friendly tone. "Several other people are being called to such meetings. Some of them are barbers, peddlers, part-time craftsmen, part-time farmers. They want land, but no one is sure whether they're entitled to a share or not. Some are well-to-do peasants like yourself but have problems to settle. Please don't take this as a personal affront. It's one of many things we have to talk about and settle in the land reform."

He was not listening to me. He simply feared the next blow to fall and did not know what direction it would come from.

"We have discussed your case. We have determined that you are a rich peasant, not a landlord. We will confiscate all the land belonging to a landlord. But you only have to give up part of the land that you are renting out to others—only part, not all. I have been told to ask you which part of that land you want to give away."

I tried to assuage his fears, but it did no good. He wouldn't respond. He seemed, in fact, to grow more nervous, as if I were only putting him off guard so we could deal him a fresh blow.

In the flickering light, our shadows grew tall then shortened suddenly. I felt an irritation rising, and waited until I had regained my calm before I turned to face him.

"Xia, we have done you a wrong and we want to make up for it," I said, trying to meet him more than halfway. "If you don't want to give away the land you rent to others, then choose some other patch. That piece west of the pond is poor—would you prefer to give that up?"

His body began to sway slightly from side to side, as it became more and more difficult to suppress the tension mounting inside him.

"That piece of land was passed down to me by my grandfather. He refused to sell it even when he was very ill and had no money to get a doctor. He said, 'Keep the land and let me die.'" Xia's voice was thick with emotion. "And he died."

I was about to shrug, but the doomed look on his face stopped me. "Xia, you don't have to give an answer right now. Go home and think things over." I stood up and, making an attempt to end our conversation on a light note, added brightly, "Come around when you have made up your mind."

He didn't come back. Three days later he committed suicide by hanging himself. He had always been known as a plodder rather than a man of action, but he showed unexpected determination when ending his own life. When found, his right hand was still grasping the clothes rack nailed to the wall. If he had changed his mind, even at the last moment, he could have swung his foot back to the stool placed against the wall and saved himself. In that last fleeting instant, he had put his hand on the rack. He wanted to go back to his wife and children. But then his humiliation and despair became too great to overcome.

Wang Sha was deeply troubled, but I was shocked to

find that it was not Xia's death itself that troubled him; it was rather the effect of that death on others. "It's bad," he exclaimed. "We must stop such things from happening or they will panic people and rouse them against us. Landlord Bai's old mother has already made one suicide attempt. Thank goodness it failed. We mustn't have another."

He had hardly got the words out when Malvolio Cheng rushed in with fresh and disturbing news.

"The young activists are moving Xia's family out of their comfortable house as a warning to others not to follow Xia's example."

"The man is dead. Can't we leave his children alone?" I cried in protest.

"We mustn't let the landlords and rich peasants think they can browbeat us into making concessions by turning themselves into martyrs. We mustn't overreact, but Xia must still be held responsible for what he has done." Wang Sha spoke with a harshness that I hadn't known was in him. As Wang Sha, the official, saw it, committing suicide was an unforgivable sin, an indictment against the new society. I was repulsed by his seeming callousness. "You must have seen many such tragic cases in the last twenty years and now you've gotten used to them," I said.

"I've gotten used to making a decision when I have to," he replied impatiently. He looked me over coldly: "If you think I'm hardhearted, tell me what you'd do if you were in my position."

I tightened my lips.

"We mustn't waste time. We must at least see to it that Xia's family is not put into too dilapidated a hut. And make sure that the young activists don't needlessly harass other landlords and especially rich peasants if they behave themselves."

But we were too late. The young activists had already moved the mother and children into an almost roofless hovel. We decided not to say anything more about this for the moment, and after a few days we would suggest that Xia's family be moved into a better home. But two days later the invalid widow died of nervous shock. We allowed an old woman who had helped the Xias keep house to stay with the two orphans. I was told to keep an eye on her and the hut they now lived in, so that nothing more unpleasant would happen. We didn't want anyone to use the occasion of the funeral as a sort of demonstration.

The hut was in a neglected corner of the village. Three sides of it were crumbling. The fourth side had already partly collapsed and was patched with a rough screen of twigs, stalks, and mud. A tangle of shrubs and weeds had overgrown the small courtyard.

As I approached it, the winter wind whirled clouds of snow around it, and the forlorn hut seemed to shiver with the cold and loneliness. I entered the single dark room.

"Your Mama made these two dresses herself for you before she died," the old woman was saying to the little girl as she fished out two tiny dresses from a bundle.

"Give them to me," the small girl cried happily as she snatched at them. "I want them both."

"Poor children. They'll be marked forever as the off-spring of a bad rich peasant. They won't stand a chance." It was the wife of Sun, who had gotten a daughter instead of a son. She had been friendly with Xia's wife, who had given her small presents of food and old clothing. "They must have committed some terrible crime in their previous lives and so merciful Heaven is punishing them now," she added philosophically.

Her face turned blank when she saw me enter the hut. She offered no explanation for why she was there, nor did I seek one. After a few moments she quietly disappeared.

"Don't fight with your baby brother. Now you have only him with you in this world," admonished the old woman.

"My Mama can give me many, many more baby brothers," the small girl went on merrily.

I didn't need to see any more. I walked away swiftly, but her laughter still rang in my ears.

"Ling-ling, you cannot show personal sympathy or regret over this matter. You have to think, speak, and act as one of a team, not as an individual," I nagged myself, but my nose smarted and tears welled up in my eyes. I viciously kicked a stone out of my way.

I threw up my head in an effort to regain my composure

and in looking up I caught sight of Sun's wife half hidden by the bushes ahead of me. I turned to take another path, but she cut across the corner to intercept me. She came up running and slightly out of breath.

"Wait a minute."

At that moment I simply did not feel up to another tussle with her problems. After the birth of the baby, another girl, her husband had hardly improved his attitude to her or to the work team. He had had to find money to pay for the midwife, was now deeper in debt, and had another female mouth to feed. He wandered around with a perpetually hurt expression on his face as if he had been cheated.

His wife caught her breath. "Are you angry with us?" she asked timidly.

"Not angry," I replied, "only disappointed. After all we've tried to do for you, you and your husband haven't raised a finger to help us with the land reform work."

"I want to do something now, for the Xia orphans. Their mother was always very kind to me. It's the least I can do to help the children. Can you help me?"

"I don't see how I can."

"You can."

She spoke with unexpected finality. I peered hard into her face, seeking some clue to her meaning. Her brownish hair, eyebrows, and eyelashes seemed lighter in the sunlight and gave her face a strange cast. Xia's wife might have told her that I was the last cadre to talk with Xia before he died, that I had precipitated his suicide. I looked at her warily. At the slightest insinuation I was ready to repulse her. But she said only, "You're so kind."

Again her words took me by complete surprise. Perhaps she thought she had already gone too far in her subtle game of blackmail. Maybe she could help me now. I tried to sound her out on what part she might think I had played in Xia's suicide. "Did Xia's wife notice anything odd about him the night he died?" I asked.

"She dreamed that he called out to her. She sort of woke up but then brushed the whole thing away as a dream. When she learned of his death the next morning she remembered that dream and then realized that perhaps in reality she had heard him call out." Tears came to her eyes. "Those poor children," she exclaimed. "How can that old woman look after them? She can barely totter on her own feet."

"How can you help them?" The words slipped out before I could stop them. I cursed myself silently for showing too much interest in the matter. Perhaps it would confirm her suspicion that I had a guilty conscience. Also, it was not too polite, showing I doubted whether she, who could hardly look after herself, could take on an extra responsibility.

"I have heard that Xia's children will be allowed to move back to their own house."

"They will take up only one room in the house."

"There are greedy people." She frowned. "They say they have big families and should have that house."

"It's a nice, solid house. But it can house only a small family besides the orphans and the old woman."

"My family is small, just the three of us. The midwife told me that I would have no more children. I don't want to leave my little girl all alone in the world when Sun and I pass on, and one of Xia's children is a boy. I would like the three children to grow up together as one family."

"So you are interested in that house too," I said, not without some irony.

The gossips of the village were already speculating about who would finally get the neat house that Xia had so painstakingly improved. I pointed to the group of peasants who could be seen completing the survey of the landholdings. "You will have to discuss it with them."

The distant earth, damp with the melted snow, looked rich and almost black. The peasants in their black jackets and trousers blended in easily.

"I also heard that Xia's orphans will get back part of their father's land. It's good land." She spoke in a quiet voice, looking not at me but at the fields before us and the activity going on there. "Sun and I will plant wheat on it for them. After the harvest I will make pian-er gruel of white flour and they will carry it to offer at the graves of their parents."

"You really wish to adopt the two orphans?" All sarcasm in my voice was gone.

"Yes."

"Will Sun agree? That means one more girl in the family."

"We'll have a son, and the four of us will have four times as much land as Sun has now." There was a flash of the same, sudden fierceness in her eyes that she had revealed during her childbirth. "He had better agree."

Then the two children would no longer be orphans of a stubborn rich peasant but adopted children of a poor peasant family. I breathed a sigh of relief, my guilt subsiding.

"You will plant more wheat. The whole of the plain will be a splendid sea of golden wheat!"

"I don't care how it looks. It will feel good here." And Sun's wife patted her flat stomach and smiled. "Will you put in a good word for me?"

"I hope that everything will end well," I answered her in a roundabout way.

We parted and walked in opposite directions. She went to join the peasants in the field. I walked straight to Wang Sha's office. Before I made the proposal in Mrs. Sun's favor, I wanted to know what he thought about it.

Wang Sha was seated at the table, tapping with his pencil on the boards, deep in thought.

Without lifting his eyes to look at me, he said, "Cheng and I are going to Ma Li's village."

"Oh, good. Can you pass a message on to Liao for me?" At that he looked up, but immediately dropped his head again.

"Tell him, when he has time, to come here and see the boys dancing and correct their movements. When the work here is done, they and the girls are going to put on their first concert as part of the celebrations." With a giggle, I added, "Tell him that Chu Hua will be here to supervise the girls. Then he'll be sure to come."

Wang Sha didn't even smile. He heaved a sigh, opened a matchbox, and started building up something with the matches.

"I've just had a brainstorm," I went on. "They can compose a dance drama for the children to perform." Still getting no response from him, I continued undaunted. "I can add my bit to it—you know, not the dance, but the story line."

The matches fell apart and, as if his mind wasn't aware of what his hands were doing, he patiently put them together again.

I rattled on. "I want to pick your brains before I talk to Liao and Chu Hua. It may be only a little thing, but why not try out some new ideas in dancing? Why not . . ."

Looking blankly across his pagoda of matches at me, Wang Sha knocked one match out and the whole stick structure collapsed.

"Now, look at what you've done!" I exclaimed.

"Ling-ling," he finally got out, "Liao has been murdered."

"What?" My arms dropped to my sides. I said in a hushed voice, "No, I can't believe it."

"Did you hear me?" And he repeated his words.

I was appalled. "So finally they've really hit back at us."

"Cheng and I are going to his village to help the cadres and activists there investigate. You must stay here and keep things going until we return."

"How long will you be away?"

"A day or two."

"Let me go with you. I don't want to be left alone here. What's happening to this place? Hatred, hatred everywhere. Where will it end?"

Wang Sha ignored my agonized questions. "While we prepare to go, you write out a short report asking permission for Ma Li to be transferred here. She must leave that place as soon as possible. The county leadership can send some other cadre there. Send the report by messenger to the county town." He turned away hastily.

"Take me with you," I cried again.

He stopped for a moment at the door. But he left the office without looking back. His head was bowed so low that his chin rested on his chest.

19 ★ ∴

Vacillation

By twilight the next day neither Wang Sha nor Cheng had returned. I paced uneasily up and down the narrow space of the township office, which was now our headquarters. I could neither sit nor stand still. I felt as if the ground beneath me might open at any moment and swallow me up. Liao—naive, agile, loving Liao—dead! I kept looking through the door and down the road in the hope that Wang Sha would suddenly appear and allay my fears and worries.

At the end of the village road not far from the office was a dried-up pond. Along its eastern bank a footpath ran obliquely up and down a mound. Returning to the village of an evening after work, the peasants, shouldering their mattocks, took this shortcut. When they reached the top of the slope, for a moment they were outlined against the sky. As they continued down on the near side to enter the road, their legs, bodies, and heads gradually disappeared into the shadow, so that for a time the mattocks were seen as though moving by themselves. Anyone entering the village from this side would normally take this footpath. To be sure of meeting Wang Sha or Cheng at the earliest possible moment, I walked to the top of the mound and scanned the path beyond. It was empty. I waited, undecided.

At the turn of the path into the cart track, the figure of a

man in cadre's uniform suddenly appeared in the dusk.
Wishing, hoping that it was Wang Sha, I ran forward. The
figure stopped. I recognized Cheng. Wary because of the
recent bloody events, he looked around, ready to put up a
fight.

"It's me," I cried out. "It's Ling-ling."

"You gave me a fright," said Cheng.

"Where is Wang Sha?"

"He went to the district center to consult with the deputy Party secretary of the county."

"Did you see Liao? His body? Did you bury him?"

Cheng blinked his eyes and shook his head in an embarrassed way as if he wished I wouldn't continue.

"Did you see him?" I persisted.

He opened his mouth as if to reply, but he only put out
his tongue and licked his dry upper lip. He locked his
mouth shut, his lower lip curled over his upper like a child
about to cry.

"What on earth is the matter?"

"Don't ask me." He threw his arms out. "His head—
was—as—his head had been twisted round, as if some-
body wanted to wrench it off. It was horrible." He told me
that Wang Sha would not soon return. He was himself
directing the investigation of Liao's murder.

Cheng's distraught look stopped my further questions.
We spoke no more about the murder as we walked back to
the village. As he left me he took an envelope out of his
pocket.

"I met the mailman on the way and he gave me this
letter for you. It's from Hong Kong, sent on to you by
someone in Shanghai. It's got your aunt's name on it, but
the return address is the old Shanghai one."

The letter was full of Hong Kong gossip and the difficulties of furnishing the new house to her satisfaction. She
ended, "Look after yourself. Eat well and keep yourself
warm. Don't get your feet wet. And keep out of trouble."

I returned home exhausted after a full day's work in the
fields and the neighboring hamlets. Seeing how tired I

was, Da Niang told me to lie down and take a rest. She would watch out for Wang Sha, she said, and would call me as soon as she saw him.

I lay on the kang with my back propped against my pillow and a folded quilt. Looking out through the doors into a corner of the courtyard, I could see Da Niang's son squatted there against the wall, his head lowered between his knees. Da Niang had trained him to do certain things. If a neighbor's hen made the mistake of trespassing on Da Niang's terrain, he would throw stones at its tail. It was believed that if a hen's bottom were hurt, it would stop laying eggs. But his twisted mind had composed variations on this theme. When a goat strayed into the yard, he cut off its tail and enjoyed the bloodletting. If there was no war on between Da Niang and these trespassers, he would pounce on a mouse and beat it to death with a stick. It was a horrible sight. I was afraid that one day he might try his gimmick out on people, and I never felt safe when he was around. Fortunately he was seldom home. Even at night he would loaf around, and he would fall asleep wherever he happened to be.

I wondered why he loitered in the yard now. He raised his head. His eyes were dull, and saliva trickled out of the corner of his mouth. His two big hands clenched and unclenched as if strangling something.

Later I was writing at my rickety table when my pencil snapped and I couldn't find my pencil sharpener.

"Da Niang," I called. "Can you lend me a small knife? I want to sharpen my pencil."

"Yes, but it's blunt."

"Let me see." I took the knife from her hand. "It won't do much good."

"What are you writing?"

"I'm copying an urgent report. It says that investigations in other areas have turned up many cases of sabotage." I paused for a moment and looked at her. "Here in Longxiang we know that there must be similar trickery going on behind our backs, but it baffles us that we haven't discovered a single instance of the most common kind of such trickery—fake land deeds."

"What is a fake land deed?" she asked innocently.

"Haven't you ever heard about them?"

"No."

"Well, it's like this. In order to cover up their real holdings, some landlords have hurriedly deeded land to poor peasants. They 'give' a few *mu* of choice land to an accomplice who, when the land registration starts, will declare this to be his property." The pencil point broke again. "Drat. And just when I'm in a hurry too."

"And later, the landlords will take back the land? Will they?" She seemed seriously concerned. "That's our trouble, the poor people's trouble. We are so easily deceived!"

"The landlords are not stupid. They won't take back the land. Later on, when the land reform is over, they hope to get a large part of the harvest from this land. They will let the peasant they have duped keep just a bit more of the harvest than the former tenant had been entitled to keep."

She frowned and brooded for a minute. "If that peasant refused to go along with the landlord, he could get his own land in the land reform and then he needn't share his harvest with any landlord."

"But he got hooked up with the landlord before the work team arrived and he doesn't believe he will be pardoned if he confesses. All in all he trusts his old master more than he does us." I finished the sentence for her.

"He is stupid. However, I think you're right. Stupid people are always stubborn." She pursed her lips in an indignant sneer.

"What shall I do with this pencil? We want to turn in this report as soon as possible and get the county leadership to send someone to strengthen our work team. Actually, I already know who will come. She is a really smart girl."

"Smarter than you?"

"Smarter and tougher. She'll leave no stone unturned, until she finds out everything."

She gave me a slow, ambiguous glance and asked, "Have you got another pencil?"

"Yes."

"You go on copying with that one. I'll sharpen the knife

first and then sharpen this pencil for you. I can sharpen the pencils by turns. Will that help you to finish copying the report more quickly?" She was delighted with her solution and gave me a heartening smile. I went on writing.

Some time later I jumped to my feet when I heard Da Niang talking to someone. But it was Xiu-ying, her hair in disarray, her face tearful and drawn. Her hands nervously fingered the hem of her jacket.

"I'm in terrible trouble. I want your advice," she cried.

I already had more worries than I could cope with. How could I attend to all this at once?

"I came in late last night after the meeting. Now Father is furious. Ling-ling, he is arranging to marry me off! He says that he can't control me, so he wants my future husband to beat me, tame me, and make me bear children. After that, he says, I will behave as a decent girl should."

The murder had reactivated all that was feudal and backward in the village. A number of peasants, terrorized, were beating a retreat. Xiu-ying's father felt the ill wind blowing and was borne along by it.

"Xiu-ying, it depends entirely on you, yourself. The new marriage law states that you and only you have the right to decide whom you will marry. If you give in, your father can say that you agree with his arrangements. But once you say no, it's against the law to marry you off against your will. Make that clear to your father."

"I could never accuse my own father of wrongdoing," she cried in distress. Her eyes filled with tears. "Father gave me my life. He worked and sweated like a slave to rear me. I am grateful to him. To accuse him in public. . . . No. I could never do that."

"Xiu-ying, I don't know what's at the back of your father's mind. You'll have to puzzle that out yourself. What does your mother say?"

"Mother wants to consult relatives and friends. She'll find out whether the young man is a decent sort or not. Mother says now that I'm a cadre with some education I can make a better marriage, even though I have no dowry."

"Xiu-ying, use your own judgment."

"Mother says that I have only one pair of eyes and that I won't be able to see through sham. They've got many pairs of eyes, so they can rightly size up any young man at a glance."

"That could be true," I said feebly.

She turned her face to me, looking for advice, for reassurance, for support. But what advice could I give her? Should I tell her truly that this was only the beginning of her troubles? The more she strove for her ideal, the more problems she would have.

Xiu-ying took a deep breath and then blurted out, "Mother has already consulted our relatives and friends. The young man's family owns a shop in the county town. He's had a few years of education and is going to find a job in Xian where his eldest brother is working in a factory. Several families have sent go-betweens to make inquiries, but his family has turned them all down. They want a daughter-in-law who has had some modern education."

I uttered an annoyed exclamation. Was it Xiu-ying's father or mother who was planning to cash in on her new career? A new, unfamiliar silence came between us.

"I've met him." Her voice was almost inaudible. "No, not alone. His uncle and aunt and my parents were present too." Her face burned red with embarrassment.

"So you're engaged!"

"No. I asked a few questions about the new ways of living. His answers were not as much to my liking as I had hoped. I told him he'd have to wait while I thought things over."

It was hard to tell if Xiu-ying was being very modern or if she was using feminine wiles and playing coy. She was making the most eligible bachelor in the village await her pleasure.

"He will be your stepping-stone to Xian," I commented flatly.

Xiu-ying took a hesitant step towards the door.

Though I made no move to stop her, she sensed that there was more to say. She squatted down by the door. Her arms held her knees and her chin rested against them.

She gazed at the toes of her own slippers, speechless and motionless.

"Xiu-ying, can you hold out until after the land has been shared out? You'll have more time then to handle your problem."

"Last night I came home late. It wasn't the first time. Father was afraid for me—" She didn't finish the sentence, but raised her eyes and looked at me appealingly. "He wants me to stay at home, and as long as necessary pretend that I am ill. But I don't want to leave you people in the lurch."

I gnawed on my thumbnail. I would go to the district town myself to seek out Wang Sha and get advice on our next move. This sally by Xiu-ying's father was no accident. Something weighty had to be done to restrain the gathering counterattack of the landlords and all who wanted the old ways preserved.

When Xiu-ying had gone, I told Da Niang, "I'm going to the district center."

She shook her head in disapproval. "You shouldn't run around so by yourself. My dear child, I'm like an ant in a deep, hot pot, knocking about right and left when you don't come home in time. It's too far—more than ten miles. Do you know, in all my life I have been there only twice."

"Da Niang, something is on your mind." I had caught more than she had meant to convey in her words. I spoke in a low voice to show that I would respect her confidence.

She looked at me with her one sound eye. It was directed to my face, but it was seeing something else. A moment later, she woke as if from a dream and asked softly and dreamily, "What did you say?"

"Do you trust us?" I asked her. "Do you trust us?"

"They are brutal. . ." she stuttered.

"Who are they?" I asked, leaning forward to catch her words.

"The landlords."

"Landlord Chi?"

"No, no. My old master is not too bad."

"Da Niang, from now on you have no old master." Why did she hasten to defend Chi?

"The worst of them are not in our village. But if you go to town you may run into them," she said urgently. "Don't go." She would say no more.

I ignored her warning; indeed, now I felt it was even more important that I contact Wang Sha as soon as possible.

Midway on the road I met Shen. He was coming from the district town office but hadn't seen Wang Sha or gotten any word from him. Strange. I grew more apprehensive. I told him about Xiu-ying's troubles and urged him to be vigilant.

"Who do you think is behind this change of feeling in the township?" I asked him.

For answer he raised his head and, just when I thought he was going to say something enlightening, gave a prodigious sneeze.

"Wrap yourself up warmly," he said. "The weather is treacherous."

It was late afternoon by the time I reached the outskirts of the district town. The street stalls had packed up for the day. Only a few shops were still doing business. Not much had changed openly since I had first seen it three months before. The only spot of bright color came from the new bookshop. A naked electric bulb shone a glaring light on its neat green-painted shelves packed tight with pamphlets, magazines, and books. It also threw its light across the entrance of the wineshop next door.

A man stepped out of the dimly lit wineshop. He opened a pack of cigarettes with a flourish, took one out, and lit it with a match, cupping his hands around it to shield it from the light breeze. The little finger was missing from his left hand. So that was why Da Niang was worried about me! Landlord Chi was here.

Chi was tough. If he wanted to use violence against me I was no match for him, but I had taken him on before and I put on a bold front. There was no alternative. Seeing me, he threw the still burning match in my direction. It fell near my feet and spluttered out. Without looking at him, pretending I had noticed nothing, I walked on slowly, as if taking my time.

Up the road, the only occupant of the district town office was a local county cadre. Wang Sha, he told me, was not in the town.

"He came here for a while and then hurried off. I think he went back to Ma Li's village."

The young cadre tried to dissuade me from traveling on further that evening. "By the time you get there, Wang Sha may have left already. He said something about visiting a few places."

"If I leave now, maybe I could catch him there."

"Hold on. I'll be back in a minute." He went to arrange for a peasant militiaman to accompany me at least part of the way beyond the border of the village. After that I would be on my own. We couldn't have every cadre in the countryside going around with a bodyguard.

I hurried to reach Ma Li's village before nightfall, but the sudden gulps of cold air into my lungs brought on a fit of painful coughing. The dun-colored late fall had passed into grey winter. The mornings and evenings were cold. Noontime temperatures went up but never caused a thaw. Dressed warmly for the morning cold, I sometimes grew overheated at midday without noticing it. In this way I had caught a cold in the last few days, but restless energy drove me on. The coughing grew worse. I had to sit down until it was over. But when I got up to walk again, I felt as if I had been drained of energy. After dragging on a bit, I was convulsed with coughing again and spat out bloody phlegm.

The moon, shining dimly through the clouds, gave just enough light to see my way by. I could see nothing clearly, but I sensed what was there. The scene of the murder went round and round in my head, transforming everything around me into something sinister and menacing. I heard the sound of weeping. A lonely ghost complaining? Or a landlord's bully trying to panic me before he made his attack? In that eerie light my fevered imagination told me that anything was possible.

The old wives say that a ghost always appears when you least expect it. When I was past the place where the sound of weeping came from, a face deathly white and streaked with blood suddenly appeared right before my eyes. The scream I suppressed hit my heart like a hammer. My knees went weak. I collapsed on the ground and for a few moments, although I was conscious, I didn't know what was going on around me.

Incongruously, out of this haze I heard a childish voice whimper, "I didn't do it." He was still crying in breathless gasps. "They painted my face!"

"Who are they?" I asked through my coughs.

"The other kids."

"Oh . . ." Another fit of coughing ended my unfinished sentence. Every cough now hurt me so much that I stuffed a handful of damp weeds into my mouth and chewed it to soothe my dry throat.

I gave the child a piece of paper from my notebook. He spat on it and used it to wipe his face so that at least he would look less like a ghost when he presented himself at home. It seemed that we were not far from the village. A few moments later I was in Ma Li's little cottage.

"Wang Sha is making the rounds of all the work team units. He will soon be back in Longxiang," Ma Li told me. "But you've caught cold. Let me boil some hot water." The kettle was soon rattling as steam billowed out of its spout and from under its lid.

The murder had deeply shocked Ma Li. She looked like a different person. She was listless now. She gazed at the kettle for quite a while and then with an effort roused herself to take it off the fire.

"Have you seen Chu Hua?"

"Yes." Her hand trembled. The water spilled on the table. With a slightly hysterical ring to her voice she cried,

"She should have refused to change places with me. If she had been here perhaps nothing would have happened. She could have guarded him from this. I can't help feeling that I'm to blame."

"Ma Li, don't work yourself up." I held her in my arms. I felt her body stiffen. She was driving herself into a fit of hysteria. "Please relax. Please stop shaking."

"I can't!" she cried through her chattering teeth. "I can't forgive myself. Cheng and the soprano suggested that since the peasants didn't know of it we should keep their love affair quiet, treat it as a family matter and not make a fuss about it. I should have agreed with them."

A lump was rising in my throat, but I had no tears to shed. I felt my chest constrict. There was a hate there, hard and relentless, for those who had taken that young lover's life.

I was shaken by another fit of coughing. Ma Li calmed herself enough to see that I needed as much care as she did. Her face grew red with the effort she made to get herself under control. She choked down her sobs.

"I must get back to Longxiang as soon as possible. If I'm not there, Wang Sha will be worried."

But Ma Li would not hear of my traveling further that night. She would get one of our peasant friends to escort me back to Longxiang the next day.

"Ma Li, to tell the truth, Wang Sha asked me not to leave the village while he and Cheng were gone. I ran away."

My confession didn't seem to surprise her, where before it would have exasperated her. "He'll understand," she merely said. "Now drink this hot water and try to go to sleep."

I got under the blanket first as Ma Li folded some clothes to make an extra pillow.

"Do you remember the last time we shared a bed?" Ma Li asked me in the dark. "Back in our school days."

"Yes, Matron forbade us to. 'No visiting after ten o'clock at night.' That was the rule. When Matron opened my room door she knew you were there. She asked, 'Ma Li, what are you doing there hiding under the bed?' " I mimicked Matron's voice.

"That night I came to tell you that I had decided to drop out of school and become an actress."

"Yes, I remember that." The image of a younger Ma Li rose before my closed eyes. I remembered the audience applauding her. Dressed as Juliet in a long white medieval gown with a circlet of gold web on her hair, she curtseyed to them, and her face, pale and ethereal under the glare of the spotlight, shone with happiness.

"We hoped we'd make a team. You would write a play for me. But why are we reminiscing like two old women?" She was piqued by her own question.

There was a long moment of silence and then Ma Li fell asleep. I listened to her soft and even breathing. She murmured something in her sleep. I pulled myself gently away from her arms. Half of her quilt hung over the side of the bed. One of her legs was uncovered. Her toe wiggled as it often did in her sleep, as I remembered from our school days.

I was feverish, and somewhere in my body I felt a pain. But I could not place it precisely. Gradually the pain gave way to a dull, aching sense of loss.

20

Riding a Tiger

Next day as I said good-bye, I asked Ma Li when she would come to Longxiang.

"I don't know." Judging from her voice and expression, I knew that she didn't want to make the move. She took pride in her stubbornness. That meant I too would have to stick it out on my own, and I wasn't too happy at the prospect.

A few days later, Liao's murderer was discovered and arrested. He turned out to be not a landlord or a rich peasant but a local troublemaker. He said he had killed Liao because he didn't like what we were doing to "overturn the natural order of things." It seemed that no mastermind was behind him, but we did find out that on that fatal night he had joined a drinking bout in a landlord's house. What they had talked about was anybody's guess. At the very least one could suppose that their grumbling had predisposed him to murder. And anyway, drunkards were drunkards. There had been wild talk, but was that plotting? None of them could remember exactly what they had talked about.

After the man had been tried in the county court and found guilty, the local authorities decided that he should be taken around to each township in turn to appear at mass meetings where the case was explained and the local people exhorted to maintain vigilance against their enemies. At each meeting, local landlord tyrants, guarded by militiamen, were put on the platform with him. The warning was explicit: Anyone who sabotaged the land reform was as bad as the landlords and would be severely dealt with.

Longxiang, smaller and poorer than most other townships, had only one landlord whom we could possibly put on the stage. This was Chi, and he was keeping a very low profile. We could gather no more information or evidence about him than we already had, and we felt frustrated. Finally, Little Gao, our new militia leader, devised a brilliant plan to smoke him out. He sent members of his militia to spy on him, and they played a lovely game of cops and robbers with him. Chi, harassed and suspicious and with nothing to do, wanted desperately to know what they were up to. On one occasion he followed them while they were following him.

One evening, Little Gao, agog with excitement, rapped at my door and after a cautious glance around to make certain that Da Niang wasn't within earshot, blurted out, "Our reconnaissance party has just told us that Chi is preparing an attack! He and his lackeys are in our headquarters and at this very moment are setting fire to it. Smoke is coming out of a window. Our people are surrounding the place on every side and we're going to catch them red-handed! Do you want to come with us?"

Almost not believing our good fortune, I hurried out with him to join a fighting detachment of militia gathered behind a cottage wall. Everybody carried some sort of weapon: sticks, mattocks, cudgels, carrying poles with knives tied to one end. Our group carried bags heavy with sand which trickled out through the sides—our fire extinguishers. Someone thrust an ax into my hand.

Little Gao inspected us with a critical eye. To raise our morale, he displayed great confidence and determination. When his eye lit on me, he looked at the ax in my hand and lifted his eyebrows inquiringly: "You are thin, all skin and bone. How can you wield an ax?" A good commander, he was concerned about his troops. He turned to give an order to his lieutenant: "Take that ax away and give her a stick instead."

He led us forward cautiously, crouched low as he crossed the intervening courtyard. He stopped at the door of the office. Smoke was oozing out of the crack at the bottom of the door.

Little Gao motioned forward the ones who carried the sand bags; we would defend them and overwhelm the enemy while they put out the fire. Little Gao suddenly leaped forward, breaking open the door with his shoulder. We rushed in brandishing our weapons. But the room was empty except for a little boy about six years old who was sitting on the floor. His parents had probably been busy and left him at home, and he had somehow wandered into the cottage room that housed the militia headquarters. He hadn't even been able to dress himself properly. His trousers hung below his belly. His jacket looked untidy because he had mismatched the buttons and the button holes. He had found a box of matches and was thoroughly enjoying himself burning bits of paper. When he saw us he gave us a toothless smile. Never having seen such an army before, he was quite unafraid.

While I did not relish Chi getting off scot-free, I was apprehensive that we might overplay our hunch about him with some hasty action. We simply couldn't believe that he wasn't guilty of some hidden crime or that there was no evidence to be found.

It was a busy time. Soon we would be entering the last stage of the land reform—marking out the land for each person who was entitled to get a share. Senior cadres like Wang Sha and Malvolio Cheng were shuttling back and forth between the villages helping them complete their work, and I had a grim foreboding that something might happen just when they were not around. I sensed that the different groups—the landlords and their hangers-on, the conservatives, and the impatient militants—were each groping their separate ways to forestall each other.

Da Niang tiptoed into my room during my noonday rest.

"I've heard that you people have caught Landlord Chi," she said. Her face revealed her fear.

I sat up on the kang as if I had been scalded. So they had struck even without telling me!

"Yes, we've finally caught him." I was improvising; I couldn't let on about my ignorance.

"Why?"

"We're looking into his case."

"What case?" she stuttered. She was not her usual quick-tongued self.

"I can't tell you now." I deliberately turned away from her.

"I understand." There was a tremor in her voice.

I dressed and walked out unhurriedly, but dashed off to our office as soon as I was out of Da Niang's sight.

I found Xiu-ying there, and I asked her in a low voice but point-blank, "Where is Chi?"

"We put him in the back room."

"Xiu-ying, I know you young cadres and activists can take care of your own village affairs and I'm glad that you can. Honestly I am. One of the reasons we came here is to pass on all we know to you, inside and outside the study classes. All we know." I paused for a few seconds to let my words sink in. "However, I might still be of use to you."

As I said this, several of the other young people came in. They beamed at me as if waiting for my compliments.

"Don't get us wrong! We didn't plot this behind your back," Xiu-ying cried, genuinely upset. She looked at the others for confirmation. "It all happened so quickly and suddenly that we didn't have time to consult you. Chi was prowling around the office. We ran into him and demanded an explanation from him. You know all the registrations, files, and documents are kept here. We don't know yet whether anything has been stolen or not. We were just going to examine that carton there when you came in."

A large cardboard box covered with a sheet of newspaper was set aside from a pile of similar cartons stacked against the wall. Xiu-ying gave a sign to a young peasant militiaman. He instantly put on a grave expression and approached the carton, stood awhile, arms akimbo, head thrust forward. A bit of overacting. He bent down and with a dramatic swoop of his hand lifted off the covering paper.

"Well?" I queried, skeptical but very willing to be convinced.

He replaced the paper cover on the carton, made a foolish, deprecating sound with his pursed lips, and stood back.

"While you go on examining things here, I'm going to ask Chi a few questions," I said.

"Okay."

A young peasant activist led me to the back room. He turned a key in the lock, pulled back the bolt, and opened the door. Chi lay huddled in a corner.

"Stand up!" the young peasant ordered in a gruff voice.

Chi looked up and hesitated for an instant. He stood up and nervously looked around. The young peasant twirled the chain with its ring of keys around and around on his finger. The whirling ring of metal reminded me of that ancient weapon used by Chinese warriors: two balls of iron joined by a chain which were twirled and then hurled with terrifying force against an enemy. I had read about it in some classical novels.

"Why were you sneaking around here?" I tried to sound impersonal and official.

"I wasn't sneaking around," he replied without lifting his eyes. The whirling of the keys speeded up threateningly.

"Are you complaining that we should not have detained you or that the activists are telling lies?" I pretended to be surprised, but I could hardly believe that he had been planning to raid our office in broad daylight.

"I was just passing this house. I wasn't near it. The main road goes by it, you know. I've walked along the road so many times that I don't notice this place anymore. That happens, you know. You must have had the same experience. Why did I arouse suspicion? Who knows? Everything is suspicious these days. Perhaps it was just my unlucky day. I should have looked at the calendar and stayed home. Anyway, I was stopped in the middle of the

road and these young . . . men . . . came up to me and
seized me by the collar. There was an argument which
ended up by my being locked in here."

"That's your story," I said.

"It's true."

"It's a lie!" The strong young peasant leaped forward,
grabbed Chi's wrist, and twisted his arm behind his back.
Chi screamed in rage and fright and pain. The young man
disdainfully loosened his grip and tossed Chi back into the
corner as if he were throwing away garbage.

"Hold on!" I thrust my arm forward to restrain him. But
then I looked at Chi. His face was contorted with rage and
hatred. If I let him out would he tamely accept these hu-
miliations without retaliating? Now he must really hate
me. He might not expect that he could prevent the land
reform from going through, but he might still be tempted
to enjoy a little vengeance at my expense. This was a critical moment. To waver might cost us dearly. Young Liao
had been murdered because he was good-natured and irresolute. He had gotten things moving and then couldn't
make up his mind what to do to keep the initiative in his
hands. When he appeared to be vulnerable, his enemies
had drunk courage into themselves and killed him. I didn't
want to repeat Liao's mistake.

"We'll come back later," I said, changing my mind.
"You'd better think again and make a clean breast of your
crimes."

Night fell early in the wintertime. When I returned, the
courtyard was in darkness. I had cautioned Xiu-ying and
the other young peasants to be on guard, but not even a
single militiaman was in sight. Had they moved Chi to
some other place? I looked at the window of the office. It
was dark. Not a sound was to be heard. Increasingly apprehensive, I began to imagine all sorts of explanations
when suddenly all hell broke loose. A sharp sound like a
clang of metal. A cat screeched and flew off the roof. Yells
of anger and of triumph. Imprecations. Pounding fists.
Scampering feet.

"We've got him!" a voice cried exultantly. Four young militiamen running up the road from various directions converged on the door of the office where a lantern, hastily lit, sent flickering shadows darting over the walls. They carried me inside with their rush. Several young activists were in the room. Two of them were still scuffling with someone. It was Tu! One had his neck locked in a savage grip, while the other was trying to get his arms tied behind his back. Tu's jacket was torn off and he was stripped to the waist.

"He has been nosing around here ever since he got back to town and heard about Landlord Chi. We began to wonder why. So we laid an ambush and caught him undoing the rope that tied Chi." Xiu-ying spoke fast in an excited voice.

Events were running away with me. Was I losing my head or were the young activists?

"Xiu-ying, send for Shen and Old Gao. We must get their opinion on all this."

Shen came promptly, Gao soon after. Newly elected to the township council, he had already become not only representative of the middle peasants but unofficial spokesman of all the go-slow moderates in the village who were doing their best to rein in the impetuous young activists. Both were alarmed at the unexpected turn of events, and they listened carefully to our explanation of what had happened.

"Is there any real evidence against Chi that we don't know of already?" Gao asked cautiously, his eyes still lowered over his pipe.

I looked at the neatly stacked cartons of documents covered with paper and replied a bit sheepishly, "Not really."

Xiu-ying had told me that nothing had been stolen.

Now Gao looked up. "I would say that Tu should first have discussed the matter of releasing Chi and not taken matters into his own hands. There was no need for such hurry."

"Tu is not a thoughtful man. He sometimes acts on the spur of the moment. Perhaps he thought he was doing the right thing. Maybe all he needs is a good scolding," Shen said with a heavy sigh. He had taken his cue from Old Gao.

Gao took over. "We country people do things differently from you city people. We tend to work in a sort of random way. The young activists also arrested Chi on the spur of the moment. They were also acting in good faith, thinking they were doing the right thing."

Gao deplored hasty action on both sides. We could not miss the hint. "So you think we should let both of them go?" I asked in a low voice.

"I didn't say so."

"Then what did you say?" I could not keep my impatience out of my voice. "You think that the young activists made a mistake. Then let's correct it. Let's not shilly-shally. What do you propose we should do?"

They both remained silent, looking at each other.

I warned myself, "Ling-ling, keep your temper. You've gone far enough." Struggling to calm myself, I got up and walked back and forth. I must have looked absurd there, pacing the kang in my socks.

Finally I said, "Landlord Chi was prowling around this place and the young people were right to protect the documents here and arrest him on the spot. There was no time to hold a meeting and consult anyone about it. But what Tu did was completely different. The young people were here all day. He could have come here at any time to consult with them. But he chose to act on his own, and he wasn't acting on the spur of the moment, but deliberately."

Old Gao did not comment on my last sentence. He asked me with some doubt, "Chi was prowling around this office?"

My silence answered yes.

"Well, I suppose it's all right to hold them, at least until Wang Sha returns and you can report to him." Shen stood up. He was so anxious to get out of the room that he stumbled over a carton of documents and practically fell out the door. Gao the sage followed him, shaking his head worriedly as he said good-bye.

Their departure left me with gloomy thoughts. Perhaps

it was some petty thing, some small present that Chi had given Tu to put him in his debt. I knew there had been a number of cases where peasants had gotten themselves entangled in landlord intrigues. In most instances, once these cases were sorted out, petty transgressions were ignored. If in other ways the peasant was a decent sort, as soon as he had made a clean breast of his wrongdoing he was considered to have been deceived by the landlord and was welcomed back into the revolutionary ranks. But what if Tu were innocent of any crime or wrongdoing? Untying Landlord Chi could have been simply an ill-considered act, an error of judgment.

I confided to Xiu-ying: "To tell the truth, I am worried that we may have made a serious mistake in detaining Chi and Tu."

Xiu-ying's silhouette against the windowpane was immobile, but I sensed her tense up. I thought I should reassure her.

"If we've made a mistake, I am the one who will be held mainly responsible. I won't try to shift that responsibility onto anyone else's shoulders."

I could already picture myself at a meeting being criticized and laughed at as a blunderer; then, thinking back on Tu's behavior—I had suspicions enough about Chi—I could not honestly exclude the possibility that there might be some clandestine relationship between the two, so I added, "And yet it may not be a mistake. Then we will be making a worse mistake if we let him go. I will be blamed still more if they stir up trouble later on. If we let them go now that will give them a chance to cover up their tracks."

"What shall we do then?"

"What shall we do?" I shook my head. "I don't know." Then a sudden thought struck me: "If I can get her to talk . . ."

"Who?" In the dim light Xiu-ying's eyes shone with intense interest.

I had kept my promise to Wang Sha not to mention that midnight meeting between Tu and the Broken Shoe to any villager, but Xiu-ying was no longer "any villager," but a cadre now. And I'd been told not to divulge it even to

Shen, a senior village cadre. If I told Xiu-ying, I'd be accused of breaking the work team's discipline. Yet time was running out. I poured the whole story out to her.

"I can't tell this to the villagers. To them I'm 'an outside cadre.' If I wrongly accuse Tu, I would be—that mistake would be too much for me to get away with."

"If you can't, then I can. If there is nothing really serious involved, then it will be dismissed as village gossip," said Xiu-ying. "I am one of the villagers." The corners of her eyes narrowed. This gave a certain sharpness to her expression. The childish naiveté I had seen before was gone.

"Xiu-ying, are you sure it will be all right? When this story about Tu gets out it may be like opening the floodgates of a dam. We must be careful. I'm going to talk to the Broken Shoe and we'll see what she says. You will be in charge here."

I thought I should make the situation even clearer to her. We couldn't afford any more mistakes.

"You and I are in the same boat. If we work well together we stand a good chance of pulling through this crisis. You know we didn't handle Xia's case very well. If we mishandle this case too, it will be difficult to restore the villagers' trust in us. I don't only mean you and me. I mean all of us who want to see more radical changes in Longxiang. All in all, what I really mean to say is that we must not permit any more horseplay."

"The young activists are clamoring to give Chi a real lesson. They say 'He's been beating and humiliating us for more than thirty years. Now it's our turn to give a bit back to him.'"

"Xiu-ying," I expostulated. "No more beating!" I made a gesture with my arms that I hoped expressed utter finality.

"All right," she grudgingly conceded.

21

Help from a Broken Shoe

I found the Broken Shoe at home. She did not seem perturbed by my sudden visit; as a matter of fact, she was almost friendly as she motioned me to a chair and then herself took a seat at the rough board that served as her dressing table. She bore me no malice. Affronts were a normal part of her life and were quickly forgotten.

Propping her elbows on the board, with one arm supporting her chin and gesturing with the other, she leaned towards me and asked, "What can a Broken Shoe do for you?"

I answered equally bluntly. "I saw you with Tu at midnight on the first day I came to Longxiang."

"You did?" Smeared with powder and rouge and with arched eyebrows drawn in black, her face looked like a mask animated only by her two lively eyes.

"You tried to egg him on to break into my room."

"On the contrary. I tried to persuade him not to. And he listened to me," she corrected me, unruffled.

"What did he intend to do?"

She giggled. "What do you think a man intends to do when he breaks into a woman's room in the middle of the night?"

"How did you stop him?"

"I warned him that you were a land reform work team cadre."

"Was that all?"

"Yes."

She wouldn't tell me any more than was necessary and even then covered her tracks by adding, as if it were an afterthought, "Perhaps that was just a joke on his part."

"That was a funny kind of joke for a Party member to make." She remained silent, and I tried another tack.

"If you were a friend of Tu's, why did you make such a spectacle of yourself at the meeting we held to discuss the land reform law?"

"Who said I was a friend of Tu's? And as for the meeting, I don't know that I made such a fool of myself."

The corners of her mouth lifted slightly as if she would burst out laughing. She knew she held a trump card in this game and she took a gambler's delight in playing it in her own good time. I lapsed into silence. Behind the mask of makeup, I saw a puffy face with sagging, tired muscles, tormented and vexed. A little sardonic, she was also appraising me. I had to say something.

"Why did you spread that rumor about attacking the rich peasants?"

"It happened in other villages. Everybody was whispering about it. I am just more straightforward and I say what's on my mind. I tell you things that others won't." Her steady, scornful stare said to me, "Everybody is sitting on the fence, why shouldn't I? If I play my cards well, you will yet have to thank me—me, the Broken Shoe."

"What else have you heard?" I asked.

"People in other villages are whispering about the death of that rich peasant Xia."

"Nobody killed him. He killed himself." But I felt uncomfortable as I said this.

"Yes, you might say that, or you might put it that he was killed by his own hand. I certainly understand why a person wants to take his own life. I tried a couple of times myself. Do you know how I felt at that moment? No, of course you don't. You've never been forced to consider taking that step." She said this with surprising feeling.

"Will you come with me to make a statement about Tu and sign it?"

"Whatever I know about Tu I've already told you."

"We need a written statement."

"I don't know how to write. How can I sign my name?"

"You can put your fingerprint to it."

It was snowing when we left the cottage. Whirled by a blustery wind, snowflakes merged earth and sky into a single void without paths or roads. The intense cold made breathing difficult. I covered my mouth and nose by wrapping my woolen scarf up to my eyes, but still I breathed hard. The Broken Shoe was stronger than I. She walked a little ahead of me, leading the way. I lowered my head against the wind and followed her footprints. About halfway to the township office, her pace slackened. Slushy mud, dragging at her slippers, made every step an effort. I was better off; the laced tops of my sneakers held them to my feet.

She suddenly stopped. I wiped the melting snowflakes off my face and eyelashes. The slush oozed up almost to the tops of her shoes, but she stood stock-still as if rooted to the spot. Not far ahead two figures chased and clawed at each other like two maniac children. While one figure took his stand, gesturing like a ringmaster in a circus, the other circled crazily around him, staggered, then fell. The ringmaster jumped up and down, flapping his arms.

"They look like the idiot and landlord Wu," I faltered.

"No," she whispered, her lips quivering.

The wind screeched and bit my face. I closed my eyes and protected my face with my hands. When I looked again the two figures were nowhere to be seen.

"They've vanished!"

The Broken Shoe explained: "They are wandering ghosts. We may not be able to see them now, but they may be following us. If you hear someone calling your name behind you, don't turn your head or look over your shoulder. If you do, you will blow out the little lanterns hanging on your ears."

"What?" I asked in perplexed anxiety.

"They are invisible, but those lanterns protect you from ghosts at night. Don't you know that? You don't? Good Heavens! Perhaps your lights have already been blown out. Did you hear someone calling you when you came to my place?" she asked earnestly, in a shaky voice. "You didn't? Thank God! All right, now you walk close behind me, so your two lanterns will shine on the ghosts and frighten them away."

"What about your invisible lanterns?"

"I don't have any," she replied in a barely audible voice. "I am the lowest of the low. I have nothing either in this world or the next." She bit her lip. "You will protect me from behind. I will walk in front of you and keep the wind off you. You are shivering? Hold on to me if you feel yourself falling."

And thus we entered the village, the Broken Shoe leading me as a shepherd leads a wandering sheep through the storm.

When Xiu-ying told the other activists next day about Tu's nocturnal doings, they were furious. Following my lead, others spoke out and soon there was more than enough evidence to show that Tu was far from being a model Party member, particularly when it came to women.

When the militia hauled Tu in, we faced him with the Broken Shoe's statement.

"Did you hope I would just disappear without a trace?" I shouted.

Tu's face turned ashen and his lips worked silently, but he blustered, "If you believe what the Broken Shoe tells you, you can round up half the men in the village. She has a story for every one of them."

The young activists no longer bothered to conceal their animosity. Tu had lorded it over them, and now they gave vent to their anger. "Tell the truth," they shouted at him. "Who else have you slept with? What were you plotting with Chi?"

While they were badgering him, Xiu-ying took me aside and whispered, "If we don't put more pressure on Tu and Chi, they won't budge. Words won't move them."

"I don't want them beaten." My nerves were stretched

to the limit, but I knew we dared go only so far to get a confession out of them.

"We won't beat them. But how about throwing a little cold water over Chi just as he used to do to his farm-hands?" the tousle-headed young militiaman urged.

"The weather is cold and it's still colder outside when the wind blows. I wouldn't shed a tear if he dropped dead somewhere else but I don't want him to get pneumonia and die in our hands." I surprised myself with these words; it was as if the spirit of brutality which I myself had condemned had entered my soul and was taking me over.

"If you don't want to douse him with water, then hang him up to a beam like he used to hang others. That way he won't get injured or die." The young militiaman would not relent.

I sat up straight as a judge and said, "Xiu-ying, you are my witness. I have tried to reason with Tu and Chi and persuade them to surrender to the law, but they are incorrigible," and I organized a full interrogation, first in Chi's "cell" and then in Tu's.

We took turns questioning the two prisoners until after midnight. We gave them no rest, no time to catch their breath, no chance to collude and synchronize their stories.

Tu was a man of few words. His answers were never more than a yes or a no, or simply silence. But Chi skillfully debated with us.

"How long have you known Tu?" I asked him.

"More than ten years. He was my farmhand."

"Was he a loyal one?"

"He was good at his job."

"Then how come you let him go to work with Shen?"

"He is a grownup, a mature man. I had and have no control over him."

"Who asked you whether you had or have any control over him?" I asked quickly.

"Nobody."

"Then you were answering your own question, the question asked by a guilty conscience: 'Do these land reform cadres know of my relations with Tu?' If you have nothing to hide, why do you defend yourself on a point that we didn't question you on?"

Chi refused to be baited. He said evenly, "Young lady, I know what you are trying to do. You are trying to force a confession out of me that it was I who instigated Tu to worm his way into the revolution and the Party. But that won't work."

"You son of a bitch. How can you accuse us so?" I sounded less and less like myself. I noticed with some satisfaction the effort he made to steady himself on his feet. He was weakening. But his stubborn defense, his continued efforts to picture himself as an ordinary landlord with ordinary sins enraged me. I moved towards him threateningly.

He recoiled. "Hold on, young lady!"

My arm, raised above my head, froze there.

"You dare resist?" A young activist hit him in the mouth. Chi staggered. His sallow face darkened.

"Take him away," I shouted.

Later I wondered at myself. It took this crisis to bring out traits within me that I didn't even know existed. I was exhausted and my head reeled. Intoxicated with the mingled babble of voices and stale air, I saw the table, the flickering light, the sweating faces of our prisoners, the ropes stretched tight across their chests and shoulders, all with a sort of heightened consciousness.

However, Chi and Tu had calculated correctly that, for all our bluster, we could come up with no real evidence that they had been working together. Even with the help of the Broken Shoe we had not made much headway in finding out the truth that would bring them to justice.

It was late, and since her home was nearer than Da Niang's, Xiu-ying took me with her. The storm had abated and the wind had dropped, leaving the night in a silence that seemed uncanny after the shouting and the tumult in the office. Our footfalls made no sound on the carpet of snow. Occasionally the tiny plop-plop of dripping water was punctuated by a slide of snow from a roof or tree.

Locked in our thoughts, we lay in silence on the kang. I was just dozing off when I heard a loud knock followed by urgent thumps on our door. Xiu-ying leapt up.

It didn't take too much effort to open a cottage door in Longxiang. To our astonishment Landlord Wu burst in. Someone had given him a push in the back and he stumbled in flailing his arms before he tumbled to the floor. Laughter cackled outside. Reeking of alcohol, Wu twisted around and, still seated on the floor, let out a string of abuse at the man outside. I saw it was the idiot. "What do you want?" I cried, utterly astonished.

Outside, the idiot stood gesticulating. I slammed the door in his face. The noise jolted Landlord Wu momentarily to his senses. But only for a moment. He looked confusedly from me to Xiu-ying and back and then cocked his head to one side as if recalling something. A hint of recognition appeared in his drunken, bleary eyes. For a moment he looked anxious and then again maudlin and stupid.

Xiu-ying's father's voice came muffled from the inner room: "What's happening?" and Xiu-ying calmed him with a "Nothing, Father!"

Landlord Wu slumped back to the ground and promptly fell asleep, snoring with his mouth open. I heard a noise like a cat clawing at the door. I thrust the door open and nearly knocked the idiot to the ground. Recovering his balance, he tugged at my sleeve, pointing at Landlord Wu and then at the darkness outside. He ambled to a tree that swayed its branches there and climbed into its forked cleft, squatting there like an owl and pointing now to the door.

Xiu-ying and I gazed in wonder at this performance for a while before we shook Wu from his stupor and drove the two intruders away. One of us would have to go to visit the Wus and find out what was behind this pantomime.

I lay on the warm kang with Xiu-ying beside me. In the

utter silence I half dreamed, half imagined a glimmer of light. A firefly's glimmer, shining for one instant. I was an invisible atom in that glimmer. If I disappeared, who would notice?

I heaved a deep sigh. Before I lost consciousness completely I felt as if a heavy load had been lifted from my chest.

"What have you been doing?" There was disbelief in Cheng's voice. "Did you see Chi's swollen feet? Did you see the sweat pouring off him in that cold cell?"

He had rushed into the office. Upset and perplexed, he nervously mopped his forehead, face, and neck with his handkerchief although there wasn't any sweat. He had caught me by surprise and I sat in silence.

Soon, his first sense of shock over, he considered the situation a little more calmly. "You must put a stop to this brutality." He spoke mildly enough, considering the provocation, but from the look he shot at me I could read the reproach in his eyes: "What you denounced others for doing you have done yourself—and overdone."

"You were disgusted with the way the feudal landlords dealt with people. They flouted their own laws. They ruled over their clans like tyrants. They could arrest, interrogate, and jail people, torture them, and even sentence them to death. They were the accusers, police, judges, and executioners all in one. And now you yourself are trying to do the same as they did!"

"I guess I've gotten into a situation where I can't help contradicting my belief that I should always be on my best behavior." I tried to give a short, cynical laugh.

"That's no excuse."

"Who's asking for it?" I asked defensively.

"I'll go tell them to untie Chi and Tu," Cheng said.

"You're the senior cadre. Your decision can overrule mine." I was beginning to feel that I didn't care what happened to Chi and Tu. I half hoped that Cheng would take over and clear up the mess. But then again I felt the urge to put up a last-ditch fight to save some of my self-esteem. As he turned to go, I shouted, "But don't release them!"

"I didn't say I was going to release them. Why did you shout at me?" The color was rising in his face.

"You came in and didn't ask anything. You jumped to conclusions and decided right away that I'm in the wrong."

"That isn't why you were rude. Maybe you don't think you have to listen to me, and perhaps you're right. I don't count for much, and I'm not very ambitious. Many of my old friends are now important people like Wang Sha." Cheng gave me a searching look.

"Sometimes a disagreeable thought flits across my mind: 'Cheng, what have you done with your life?' I always seem to fall behind everyone else. I fret and fume, but I don't get ahead. Oh, yes, I know what I should think. 'Comrade Cheng [he mimicked the voice of a lecturer], don't think about yourself. Put ambition behind you. Think only of service to the people and the revolution.'

"But sometimes what does one see happening? An eager beaver puts on a very revolutionary front, acts more left than the left, gets a gentle tap on the shoulder: 'Now, now. You are too left,' and then is promoted! I won't go in for that sort of thing." As he went, he threw his arms out in a mock dramatic gesture and declaimed, "To be left or not to be, that is the question."

He left me riled and irresolute. I was buoyed up again, however, when Xiu-ying came in to tell me what she had learned in a talk with the Wu family. As I had surmised, they did have a suspect in mind. They couldn't remember his name or which village he came from, only that he had borrowed money from Landlord Wu after he had gambled away all his earnings. They had no idea who his two partners in the rape had been. Only after they got news of Tu's arrest did they realize that not even a poor peasant or even a poor peasant cadre was immune from punishment for wrongdoing. Wu's wife had then nagged her cowardly husband to go and tell the work team all he knew about the crime and its possible perpetrators. Before he had gone halfway, however, he had lost his nerve and gone off to drink with the idiot.

"What has the idiot got to do with all this?" I asked.

"Wu's wife thinks that he hid himself somewhere in their courtyard that night and saw something."

"I think we're getting somewhere," I said with some satisfaction. I wanted desperately to track down the men who had ravished Little Jade. But at the same time I felt a bit guilty for calculating that if we caught these criminals it would to some extent offset what might well turn out to have been an appalling blunder—imprisoning Chi and Tu. But clearly Tu's exposure and downfall, whether right or wrong, was unlocking doors that up till now had been closed.

22 ★

Getting at the Truth

Wang Sha returned to Longxiang the next day at noon, and soon after called me to his room. When I went in, he did not turn around to greet me but just stared at the map of the county tacked to the wall. I waited for a while, but he still kept silent. Then I saw that he was actually looking intently not at the map but at a black, dirty spot on the wall beside it.

"You must release them today. First let Tu go, and then Chi. And you must do it yourself."

His face was set in rigid lines. I prickled at his first words until I realized he was speaking to me as frankly as he would to himself.

"All right," I agreed grudgingly. After all, his reputation as our leader was also riding on me and my gamble: How many of his friends had grown disillusioned, wavered and doubted, been disgraced and disappeared into obscurity? Wang Sha had gained both fame and position. If he went on striving, he would reach the peak of his literary and political careers. But I was in a different position. I was a very junior cadre, an unknown without social status or political prestige to lose. If I made a mistake, at worst it would lead to a reprimand: "A silly little bourgeois miss from Shanghai."

"I can't ask you to gamble on my suspicions. You have too much to lose if they should prove to be wrong," I said.

He was taken aback by my boldness and rudeness. He glowered at me as though he was ready to bring the roof down on my head. But again he held himself in check and changed his tone.

"Whatever I do, I am always in the wrong either in this one's or that one's view. But as you once put it, I've gotten used to that," he said without rancor. "You know, the county court won't sentence anyone on the basis of suspicion and hearsay."

He thought for a moment or two, and then continued in a different tone, one so peremptory that I was forced to understand that so far as we two were concerned the discussion was at an end. "I am only the leader of the work team, but I am in charge here. You'll have to do whatever is decided. Wait, one more thing. Keep this in mind: The meeting we'll hold is not being held for you to show off your detective talents."

The work team and activists were all called to a meeting set for the late afternoon. The whole affair would be thrashed out and a decision made on how to handle it. But I already knew what the outcome would be.

I hurried back to the outer office.

"Where is Xiu-ying?" I asked.

"She just left," someone answered.

I dashed out of the room. But I had forgotten to ask where she had gone. I dashed back. "Where did she go?"

"Probably home, but—"

"Thanks." Out I dashed again. They must have thought I was crazy.

No sooner had I started to run down the village lane than I saw her coming towards me. I was sure she had sensed she was needed.

"Xiu-ying!" I called joyfully. I stumbled over a stone and practically fell into her outstretched arms.

"Xiu-ying, let's go find someplace quiet. There's something important I have to consult you about."

The urgency in my voice alarmed her. She looked grave now.

"I've also got important news to tell you. Shall we go to my home?"

"No. There's no time to be polite to your parents or neighbors."

"Where shall we go then? Da Niang's?"

"No, no." I stopped in the middle of the road. "Xiu-ying, I can't wait. Every minute counts."

A few passers-by greeted us. We waved back and shouted the old greeting, "Have you eaten?"

"All right. We'll have to talk here."

"What's your news? Good or bad?" I asked her.

"It's good. A bit of luck."

"We'll need all we can get of that."

"Da Niang thinks she knows who the rapists might be, at least one of them." She stopped, wishing to see how I would react to this revelation. To her surprise, I frowned. Da Niang had let me down. Why hadn't she told me first?

Xiu-ying was downcast. She realized that I was discomfitted although I welcomed her news, so she hastened to add, "Da Niang didn't tell me. She told my mother. She says she didn't tell you because she never got an opportunity. You were hardly ever at home. I think she was afraid that we might ask her too many questions if she came to tell us directly and that it might put her in danger. The night the rape took place Da Niang saw the rapist and his two pals carrying packs and hurrying away from the village. She recognized him because she had been hired by Landlord Wu that year to cook for the temporary farmhands at harvest time."

"Does she know which village he came from?"

"Yes. It's not very far from here. It's called Xi Cun."

"We must report this immediately to Wang Sha. Perhaps it will get him to postpone the decision to release Tu and Chi this afternoon."

"But the rapist isn't from here. How does his case involve Chi and Tu?"

"I don't know yet. But what were they doing in Longxiang? What were they carrying away? If only Da Niang had told us this earlier we might have gotten a clue to other things. Damn her!" I stamped my foot furiously.

"Mother said that Da Niang was terribly shaky when she told her all this. She must have worried her head off during the last two weeks wondering what to do."

"What about my head? Did she think a tiny bit about what I've been going through? Anyway, Xiu-ying, will you go and tell all this to Wang Sha. You see, Landlord Wu only began to speak out after Tu was locked up. And Da Niang has only begun to speak out now that both Chi and Tu have been caught. That means her news must in some way concern them."

"Where are you going?"

"I'll tell you later." I had changed my mind. I didn't want anyone to know where I was going.

For some time I had thought of sounding out Tu's wife. She was weak and vulnerable—Tu browbeat her, taking advantage of the fact that he had "saved her life" and that of her daughter. I doubted that she knew much about Tu's outside activities, but I was sure I could get her to talk. Exploiting that vulnerability myself had seemed an unscrupulous thing to do, but I forced myself to put my doubts out of my mind. There was only a slim chance that I would gain much, and this was no time for scruples.

Before I knocked on her door, I stood for a moment, ears pricked up, listening. There was no one else inside; I didn't want anyone to witness what was to happen.

After a whole day and night of tense anxiety, Tu's wife looked pale and tired. Yet she pulled herself together when she saw me. Both of us were wary, but there were many advantages on my side. I was the attacker. I didn't shout at her but spoke in a friendly manner. I had to offer her some hope, some inducement to talk, or, failing that, frighten her into talking. As if in confidence, I told her, "If only I could tell you that everything is all right and your husband will soon come home—" I suddenly checked myself. She looked at me expectantly.

"But that wouldn't be true," I abruptly exclaimed. "The truth is, you're in serious trouble."

She looked at me wild-eyed. Her whole body was a question mark.

"You're in serious trouble. Your husband has confessed. Our militia is on its way to search your house."

She started as if stung. Her face turned deathly white, but this was no time for pity. Too much hung in the balance. I must beware of mercy!

"He has betrayed you, so it is pointless for you to try and get away from the facts. He will be treated leniently, because he has chosen the best way: to confess. But you—"

"It's him. I had nothing to do with it," she cried, trembling all over.

I shivered with nervous excitement. I was like a hunter on the trail, the quarry in my sights. I raised my voice in spite of myself: "Now you have betrayed him. The only thing that can save you is to make a clean breast of everything. Out with it!" I was partly playacting, but partly I was deadly serious. I gripped the table between us.

"Oh, good Heavens!" Her voice was so weak that she seemed to be at her last gasp.

Pressing on to break her completely, I said as solemnly as a judge, "It will be to your advantage if you confess. If you try to fight it out, you will be condemned."

"My own flesh and blood," she wailed. "Why are we born women? We have to accept our fate. How can you blame me? I am his property."

I did not understand what in the world she was talking about. I began shooting at random in the dark. Perhaps Tu was keeping hidden property for Landlord Chi. "Where did you hide it?"

She was silent except for her sobs, but she fixed her terrified eyes on a spot in a corner of the cottage.

"You buried it here?" I asked amazed.

She hugged her chest with quivering arms and her legs went limp. She was too weak even to hold herself on the stool. Her body slowly slipped down and she lay crumpled on the floor.

"Is that where the things are?" I demanded.

She turned and stared at me until the whites of her eyes showed. Then all of a sudden she screamed. She knew she had been trapped.

"Out with it, all of it, everything you have, the false deeds, everything!" I gasped out, not realizing until it was too late that I was overplaying my hand and exposing my bluff. The expression on her face was terrifying.

I don't know where she gathered the strength from, but she leapt up and lunged at me, murder in her eyes. Luckily she stumbled over one of the legs of the table. For an instant everything blurred before me. Then in wild desperation I snatched up a bottle and threw it in her face. It gave me time to rush out of the door into the daylight. She did not follow me.

What we dug out of the earthen floor of the cottage were the remains of a corpse. It was Tu's stepdaughter. When Tu's wife saw the men opening the grave, she fainted and laid her pitiful small figure on the kang. Her face was burning hot with fever. In her delirium, she talked incoherently. "Don't, don't," she gasped as if begging Fate to desist, to leave her alone, to heap no more suffering on her. Her spirit weakened and her muttering stopped. Her eyes were tight closed, shutting out the light of day and reality.

Leaving a neighbor to care for her, we went straight to Tu's cell. Wang Sha let Little Gao take the lead, as this was his responsibility as the militia commander in charge of the prisoner. Without introduction he told Tu, "We have found the corpse."

Tu gave a yelp and made a blind leap forward. He took us by surprise, crashed through the crowd of us and out the door. We chased after him. He raced madly up the village lane, the militiamen close behind him, and made for the open country.

Soon out of breath, I was left far behind. But Tu was also tired, and when he stumbled and fell, the younger men closed in on him. Ringed around like an animal at bay, he rose and stood, back bent and feet braced, arms spread as if he wanted to catch us all. Little Gao, creeping up from behind him, gripped his shoulders and pinned his arms. Tu made a frantic effort to free himself, then, under the weight of his assailants, collapsed in a heap on the ground.

It was not long before we had the whole tragic story out of him. Tu had raped the girl and, when she had gotten pregnant, afraid of the consequences, murdered her. Like a man pursued by devils, he suffered hallucinations. For several nights he screamed in terror. He saw the girl being stabbed, and when she disappeared her place was taken by a hundred girls with the same face. At her wits' end, his wife had turned to his old master, Landlord Chi, for help when Tu fell ill. Knowing what kind of a stepfather Tu must have been, Chi had literally smelled out the crime when he visited their cottage. He had confronted Tu with what he suspected and blackmailed him. Tu became his secret agent. But Landlord Chi was too cunning to use Tu openly. He bided his time, content merely to get information about the work team and its plans.

"What about the rape of Landlord Wu's daughter?" Little Gao asked.

"I had nothing to do with that," Tu replied thickly. "You ask Chi. He knows who did that."

Following up Tu's confession and the leads given us by Landlord Wu and Da Niang about the gambling fieldhand, it didn't take long to track down the gang that had ravaged Little Jade. To our disgust the ringleader was a newly elected cadre in the neighboring hamlet of Xi Cun, an old hanger-on of Landlord Chi's. The night of the rape, he and two of his pals had come to move some of Landlord Chi's things to hide in their homes. What better place to hide such things than in the home of a new cadre? Roused by the thought of Little Jade as they passed Landlord Wu's house, they had seized the opportunity to break in and rape her, hoping to throw the blame for this crime onto the young activists of Longxiang.

When Wang Sha and I discussed this news he was in a reflective mood. When I said, "But—" he forestalled my question.

"They didn't care whether Little Jade was the daughter

of a landlord or not. She is a pretty girl. Rapists are rapists. They were working for Landlord Chi, but they would
have worked for the devil himself. He's their kind of man."

As a precaution, Wang Sha, Malvolio Cheng, and I moved
to a large courtyard where several families of reliable activists lived. When Da Niang saw me off at her gate, she
looked downcast. She mumbled, "You're moving away because I didn't look after you well. Isn't that so? You are
right to complain about me, but please don't leave like this
with hard feelings in your heart about me. If my heart is
not with you, then who is it with?"

I wanted to part with Da Niang as friends, but I also felt
hurt because she hadn't been honest with me despite her
protestations to the contrary.

"I don't know who you are with," I said. "Only you can
answer that."

Spring Hunger

When Wang Sha told us that the county leadership had chosen the Spring Festival at the Lunar New Year as the date for the conclusion of the land reform, we all knew that this was most appropriate. There was no need to discuss the matter. But we would have to hurry to complete the division of the land and property confiscated from the landlords. This was no easy task. Livestock, tools, and grain, as well as land, had to be dealt with along with furniture, warm clothes, and food. The division had to be done in one sweep and everything evened out so that all the peasants were more or less satisfied. Those who received good land could not expect to get the best livestock; if someone got a warm coat, he could not expect to be privileged in the matter of housing as well.

What the peasants were most vitally interested in at the moment, however, was food. The spring hunger was upon us. When you knocked their storage jars, they sounded hollow; some were completely empty. Cheng and I learned that some poor peasants were already borrowing grain against what they would receive in the future. One old couple had even mortgaged their expected portion of land for a few bushels of grain. When we heard of this we proposed that the Poor Peasants' Association immediately do something about it.

We were all hungry. The pian-er gruel was thinner than ever. I had an empty feeling at the pit of my stomach. As long as I was busy doing something, anything, I forgot about it, but it was always there ready to force itself on my attention. I understood then why the peasants had been so lackadaisical in the wintertime. They had been hibernating, saving energy.

But when the time came to divide up the land and put in the new land markers, everyone who could walk came out to the fields.

It was a bright, clear day. The cold air was dry and the frozen earth was brittle. The empty bowls of ponds were cracked and peeling. Scraggly weeds gripped the soil like sparse hairs on a balding head. Gusts of dusty wind swept over the fields as if to gulp down the ragged throng. The group from the Poor Peasants' Association carrying surveying plans, measuring lines, and markers led the way and a great crowd followed them. Old men and women hobbled along; children hopped and skipped among them. Even the sick got off the kangs if they could and, bundled up against the cold, made their way to the place where the first markers were to be driven into the earth.

Something moved hesitantly in a clump of dry weeds. A pair of long ears wiggled over the tips of the thistles and then moved very fast. A small brown animal scurried across a bare patch.

"Rabbit!" a boy shouted with surprise and joy. Several men threw stones at it and, when these missed, snatched up clods of earth for another try. Our hungry eyes lit up. Visions of stewed rabbit meat made our mouths water. But in an instant the chase was over. The rabbit won—it was no ordinary rabbit that could survive in these hungry lands—and we all came back to earth.

The measurers worked steadily all through the morning. They went about their task dispassionately, or so it seemed, but the spectators watched with intense interest. There was not so much a look of joy on their faces as of disbelief held in suspense. Most could hardly believe that that great expanse of earth would really soon be theirs.

At the end of the day, Cheng and I went to eat our evening meal with our peasant host. I sighed. The pian-er gruel was little more than water, but it was a comfort to me—psychologically, at any rate. It was believed that if we filled our stomachs with water, the little food we ate afterwards would swell and make us feel as satisfied as if we had had a full meal.

I sighed again, this time in anticipation. When I got back to my room I would enjoy the second course of my dinner. Xiu-ying's mother had given me a pancake and I had saved a piece of this and some pickles. Delicious!

I closed my door and felt with my hand under the straw mattress, groping for my pancake. Strange, it wasn't there. Perhaps I had put it under the pillow. Since I had no cupboard or chest of drawers here, I kept some of my clean clothes and underwear under my pillow. I opened them out one by one and looked around the kang. No, nothing. I grew worried. I pushed the mattress aside and inspected each seam. Nothing. Was my memory failing me? I could have hidden it somewhere else, perhaps in the straw box that Xiu-ying's father had plaited for me. I pulled out the box. That pancake could easily have gotten mixed up with all the stuff I kept in it. But it was nowhere to be found.

Rats were running across the beams overhead, chattering. The rats—could they be the culprits? I thought back over my movements of the previous day. I had been in a hurry to leave, and when I stuffed the half pancake under the mattress it might have fallen under the trestle table next to the kang. Perhaps some of it was still there. I'd better rescue it right away, before the rats came back for it. The light was failing and my room was dark. It was even darker under the table. I was reluctant to light the lamp as I didn't want people to know I was home. I planned to enjoy this evening in solitude. All I could see under the table was a dim shape about the size of the pancake. I raked under the table with a twig. Only lumps of caked mud came out.

I spent a restless night, a long night with many dreams. One exquisite dish after another was set before me. I wolfed them all down, all my favorite dishes—stewed pork with a rich sauce, roasted Peking duck, steamed fish, a special kind from Yangzhou with sliced ham, mushrooms, and bamboo shoots, fried lobsters with fresh snow peas . . . I ate so much that I woke up with a salty, bitter taste in my mouth. My old pillow was lumpy. To spread the cotton inside more evenly I put my hand into the pillowcase. I felt something cold and sticky, and pulled it out. Wrapped in a handkerchief was my lost pancake. The yellow corn shone like gold in the room's darkness.

I wanted to enjoy every minute of it and broke off a small piece. I held it in my mouth, savoring it as long as I could. I summoned up my will power to keep from eating it all. I munched a bit more and put the rest back into the pillowcase. This time, to take better care of it and to hide it more securely, I folded it into some clothes. Now my pillow felt as soft as the ones stuffed with down at home. I rubbed my cheek on it, and rested easily.

The next day the work of marking out and dividing the land continued, and when I grew tired, I imagined taking out the other half of my pancake from my pillow and savoring it to the end. But, finally, fancy was no substitute for reality. And by the time the sun was high overhead, my knees had gone weak and my legs could no longer support my body. I had never been so hungry in all my life. Mercifully, Little Tian, the new deputy chairman of the Poor Peasants' Association, announced the lunch break.

The virgin widow and I walked with our backs to the icy wind and our hands tucked into our sleeves. When we came to a low bank that gave some cover from the wind we both slid down into its shelter. A few steps away stood two children about four years old. They were chewing on some dry-looking millet stalks. But they just gnawed on the ends. They didn't know how to use their teeth to peel away the hard outer skin and get at the juicy core beneath.

"Ling-ling, I'm hungry." The virgin widow's eyes were unhealthily bright. She stared at the stalks in the children's hands, devouring them with her eyes. "Do you know what I'm thinking about? I want to snatch those stalks out of their mouths. They are dried up, but they are better than nothing. They might help."

"No, don't!" I admonished her. But then I thought guiltily of my treasured hoard.

She took my hand and pressed it against her belly. "It hurts," she complained. Her head drooped. The wind caught the hair at the top of her head and blew it around her face.

The two children still stood there watching us and chewing on the ends of the stalks. The virgin widow motioned them to come over to her.

"You're not getting to the sweetest part. Come here. I'll show you," she said in a soft voice and, to my surprise, she managed a smile. Her sallow skin was the same color as the earth around us. When she smiled, her wrinkles deepened and looked like the cracks in the parched and hardened soil.

The children looked at each other and giggled. They shuffled a couple of steps nearer. The widow held out her hand. The ragged little boy, more venturesome than the little girl, came nearer to her and she fondled his tousled head. She took hold of the stalk.

"Let go. You don't know how to do it." And she pulled the stalk out of his grasp.

He looked robbed.

"There, now. Show him how to peel it and give it back to him," I advised. I was afraid that they would burst out crying.

She pushed my hand away and took another nibble, spitting out the hard skin and chewing on the soft pith. "See, this is the way." She took another nibble. Then she looked at the small boy's face. Suddenly ashamed, she handed me the stalk. I handed it to the boy. He snatched it and both of them ran away from us as fast as they could.

We heard voices raised and looked over the top of our wind shelter. It was Little Tian shouting to some stragglers.

"We'll start work again as soon as we've finished our meal," I heard him call. "You must come and check on our work."

"Let's go home," I said. But we hadn't gotten even half-way back before we had to sit down and rest again. At my feet I noticed a busy detachment of ants moving a small piece of turnip to their home. They were almost there when I picked up a long dried leaf to brush them off their booty. They panicked and scattered. I picked up the piece of turnip and wrapped it in my handkerchief.

The virgin widow was also looking desperately for anything edible amid the weeds. Careful not to drop my spoil, I walked slowly, scanning the ground. When I had first arrived in Longxiang I didn't know one grain from another, or so-called wild vegetables from bitter and inedible weeds. They all looked alike to me. But within these last few weeks, my senses sharpened by hunger, I had become an expert and a connoisseur. I could tell food from weeds at a glance. One wild vegetable with almost invisible hairs on its stalk was palatable but not digestible. Another had its own special bitter taste but was edible. Wild garlic shared only its name with the real thing.

We looked up hopefully at a locust tree. This flowered first of all trees and an appetizing meal could be made of its flowers and buds. But it was still too early for it to blossom. Then as my eye roved around, a tiny spot of red caught my attention. Something edible? Whatever it was, I dug it out, so tenderly that the twig I used didn't bruise it. It was a red pepper, half of it rotted away. Someone had dropped it. Perhaps he had dropped others. I dug around eagerly and found two more peppers, again only partly spoiled. This was my lucky day.

"I want to give all this to Da Niang," I told the virgin widow on a sudden impulse. "She can salt the peppers mixed with wild vegetables."

Da Niang thanked me profusely for my gift. She washed off the peppers and the piece of turnip and wild vegetables in a bowl of water. After cleaning the bits she put them one by one into a jar which contained a few wild vegetables pickled in brine. She stirred the wild vegetables and the pickles up to the top and pressed her new acquisitions to the bottom where there would be more salt.

"Thank you, my dear girl, thank you for thinking of me. I miss you since you moved away. I keep hoping you'll come back to my cottage."

"Da Niang, I nearly got killed by your good friend, Tu's wife. You know that, don't you?"

She stared at me as if she were only vaguely aware that I had said something important. It took a full minute before the meaning became clear to her. She exclaimed, "I won't let anyone hurt you. You don't understand me. And don't think too badly of Tu's wife. They say hell has eighteen circles, but for her it's bottomless. She's sinking deeper and deeper into it."

Da Niang spoke in a toneless voice. She too had walked the circles of hell, and she told me the story of Tu's wife as if it were her own.

Tu's wife had lost her first husband in the worst famine that anyone remembered in the Northwest. There was a drought and every single plant died. The leaves on the trees turned black and shriveled. The people ate dried bark. It was said that they ate dead bodies. Neighbors were afraid to look each other in the face. She watched her husband walk away with two other villagers to search for food, but they never came back. She waited for him all through the night. She sat there at the cottage door with her small daughter cradled in her arms.

She waited for four days but he didn't return. Finally, in desperation, when everything had been eaten up, she took the child and went off with all she could carry in a bundle on her back. She had no idea where she was going. She simply followed other people fleeing from the famine. In a town filled with refugees she got some food from a street kitchen set up by Buddhists. When the food there ran out, she took to the road again. She found herself by a railway station. The turmoil of the famine had affected the railway. There was no order at the station and people crowded onto the trains without tickets. Nothing could stop them. She too clambered onto a wagon with other refugees. They traveled all day, but when the train stopped, a crowd of hungry people forced their way on, shouting and angry. People around her whispered, "There will be bloodshed! Let's get off!" And before she knew what was happening, she found herself out on a road again, running along in the dark with a crowd of fleeing people. Somewhere to the side of her she could hear the muffled sounds of fighting. Then a rush of feet. Someone stumbled and almost fell. Cursing, he lit a match. Its flickering light showed the half-naked body of a woman spread-eagled on the ground. She didn't know if what she saw was real or a dream. She closed her eyes, but when she opened them again she saw the same scene and even worse. A burst of flames lit up the darkness. Through the opened doors of a cluster of cottages, men, women, and children rushed out in panic. Then suddenly the whole hamlet was ablaze and crackled and spurted sparks. She caught a glimpse of a man who looked like her husband. A firebrand crushed him. But some other part of her mind said that it was a bad dream. She wanted to rest, rest . . .

When she came to, it was still dark. She was covered with a torn cotton jacket and a woman sat beside her holding her child. The woman told her that she had been driven from her home by marauding soldiers. The best thing they could do was to get as far away from there as possible. Afraid to take the road, they made off over the open countryside. The undergrowth, sighing in the wind, could hide them.

Then suddenly the rain that the peasants had wanted so desperately began to fall. The whole earth turned to mud. A brutal wind flung the rain, in sheets, against her face. The mud held on to her feet—each step was an effort. She had lost all her companions. Through the wet darkness she thought she saw a dim light. Perhaps it was a station? She didn't know it but she had long ago left the railway far behind her. It was an encampment of a mule team caravan going northwest. Taking pity on her and her starving baby, they took her along with them, crossing the famine area as fast as possible and dropping her off in Longxiang.

At the end of her story, Da Niang added: "You know the rest."

Matter-of-factly she uncovered an earthenware pot and took out a piece of baked corn pancake. She fetched the small bottle of wild pickles and offered the pancake and pickles to me. "You're hungry," she said, "take them."

"No. I can't. You need them more. I am younger and stronger than you and I still have a bit of pancake left at home."

"You are younger and that means you need more food. This is your first famine. You aren't used to this kind of life. I just hope it won't be as bad as the last one. And I have some good news to tell you that I just heard. While you were all away in the fields a message was brought to Shen. It said that since the peasants were suffering in the spring hunger, some of the grain taken from the landlords should be distributed right away to those who needed it most. Shen told us we should thank Chairman Mao for that."

She looked contemplatively at a picture pasted on the wall beside the stove.

"But what have you done with the picture of the Kitchen God that was there?"

Noticing the surprise in my voice, she said, "I took it down and put up that picture of Chairman Mao. I thought you people had given Shen that idea."

"No. He must have gotten the message and the picture directly from the Party committee in the county town. But it's some politicians in Peking who came up with such an idea. They're much more important than any of us."

"You sound as if you don't like this."

"No. I don't like any superstitions, old or new. I think Chairman Mao owes thanks to you people for giving him a chance to see if he can do better than the old governments."

Da Niang looked at me with the amazement she usually reserved for what she considered our "strange remarks." Dismissing the matter of the Kitchen God, she came back to more practical affairs.

"I'll have some fresh grain soon, so you take this pancake now or I'll have to bring it to you this evening after you've finished your work."

I compromised by taking a piece of the pancake with some pickles wrapped in it and folding Da Niang's present into my handkerchief.

"Put it away carefully now. Hungry people know no shame," she said.

24 ⋆

Land to the Tiller

My neck was stiff and aching. I lifted my right hand to rearrange the pillow, but my hand felt numb. I licked it, but there was no feeling in it. Startled, I half opened my eyes, not knowing for sure whether I was awake or dreaming. Instinctively I looked for the door and the window. But no door faced me, nor was the small window there to my right. This wasn't my room. I struggled to raise myself, but my arm lying beneath my body had gone completely numb. I rubbed my hands together and massaged my arm to restore the circulation. I settled myself more comfortably and looked around in the morning twilight. Now I saw both the door and the window but they were on the side, behind my head. Then I remembered that this was my new room. I was no longer staying with either Da Niang or Xiu-ying. The hectic days of our land reform work were over.

Ma Li lay beside me and murmured something in her sleep. There was a slight frown on her forehead and the right corner of her mouth was pulled down in a wry grimace. She had arrived the previous evening to help us celebrate the climax of our work. This was the day when the actual distribution of land would take place and the new owners would receive title to their land. I had looked forward to this day with a sense of fulfillment. But an unalloyed sense of achievement would not be mine. I was already being nagged by the feeling that something more remained to be done. It was Ma Li with her bold ideas who once again confronted me with a new dilemma.

I was already in bed when she arrived. She pushed the door open with her back burdened with her bedding roll and for a moment I was nonplussed to see this strange, ungainly thing entering my room. Then she turned to face me cheerily. The tip of her nose and her cheeks were red with cold. She was in an exuberant mood and so eager to share her news with me that she sat down at the edge of the kang with the bedding roll still on her back.

"Let me help you unpack."

"Don't bother. Let me catch my breath first and then I'll take my time making myself comfortable."

As she undid the straps of her backpack she blurted out, "Have you heard that some of us may go to Qinghai?"

"Qinghai Province?" I cried, staring openmouthed. If Gansu was "beyond the Great Wall," then Qinghai was at the back of beyond.

"So you haven't heard? Well, it seems that, this autumn, land reform will be carried out in Qinghai. Some places there are much worse off than here. Mountain villages are snowed in for nearly half the year and I've heard that there are Tibetan villages where women slaves are still giving birth to babies to increase their masters' wealth. Since the situation there is so complicated, they want only volunteers who have already had some experience in land reform work. So I've volunteered to go. How about that?"

I didn't answer her immediately but crawled back into my warm quilt.

"Not many cadres are needed there. Early applications will be considered first." She paused. "This is a moment in history that will never be repeated. I don't want to miss any of it."

Later, as I looked down at her asleep beside me, I wondered if she were dreaming of Qinghai's snow-blocked valleys.

I crawled around her and off the kang. In the stillness of the early morning, every movement seemed to make a clatter. I did my best not to wake her up because I wanted to walk around the village and be alone with it to say good-bye.

I could not love it. Its bleakness and violence horrified me. Then I reminded myself that I had seen it only in the beginning and end of winter, neither in its autumn nor its real spring when green would cover the plain, the willows would shimmer with bronze and yellow-green buds, and the dark green of the firs and pines on Green Dragon Mountain would be shot with emerald. Would I love it any better then? But love it or not, I knew I would never forget it.

Three sides of the village were still surrounded by the eroded and broken earthen wall which had once surrounded it completely. I walked slowly from end to end along its narrow top where no one would cross my path. This suited my mood perfectly. When I reached the end of the wall on the opposite side I felt I had said good-bye. On this fourth side there was no trace of a wall or anything like a border line. They had hacked down the rampart to fill in the moat beyond it, and now the village was open on this side to the brown, flat immensity of a plain that stretched as far as one could see—without houses, trees, or even the grave mounds which usually dotted such a wasteland. Off towards the right in this direction we had gone to search Landlord Chi's house. Towards the left, the barrenness and monotony were broken by a stranded cloud, whiter than the sky, shimmering, rolling slowly in amorphous shapes like a writhing dragon escaping to the invisible horizon. Here it fused with the mist, which, like that in a classical painting by Mi Fei, did not stop at the horizon but floated far beyond it, too far for my imagination to follow.

I thought of Wang Sha. But I thought of him now with a strange detachment. During the months I had spent in Longxiang, and even before, my feeling for him had hardly for a single day at a time been one consistent sentiment. It had been like a melody played on a many-stringed instrument. First one string and then another had been plucked; then came cadences, delicious trills, sometimes subdued, sometimes tumultuous; and then resounding chords, un-

bearably exciting. But then the music had settled into a
quiet measure that was already almost a memory. A
theme and variations had been improvised by a mysteri-
ous hand. But the music had died away, unfinished, and
now I knew that it would remain unfinished.

The barely rising sun suffused the eastern sky with a
brighter light. The west, by contrast, seemed to dim until
the tip of a cloud or mist caught a glow of rosy light that
seemed to be focused on it exclusively. A mirage? Beyond
it I could see the Kunlun Mountains four hundred miles
away, the home of all the Chinese gods and goddesses
who had settled there long before Jove and Juno reached
Mount Olympus. Qinghai.

Now the whole sky was lit up. Day. The tops of the
mountains were sharp-etched against the light.

I was far from the center of the village, but I could already hear the early-morning excitement of an unusual
day.

I turned to make my way back when suddenly I thought
that I would go to see Tu's wife. She wouldn't come to the
land reform celebration; her sufferings had been too much.
After our confrontation and the subsequent trial and conviction of Tu, she had been confined to her bed with a high
fever. When that was cured she had gone completely deaf,
and now shè, like the virgin widow before, lived a life of
silence and alienation.

Thrusting my hands deep into my jacket pockets for
warmth, I walked with my head down looking at the path
in front of me.

Someone's basket brushed my elbow and the person
carrying it passed me and walked on ahead. Cotton slippers scuffed till they were grey; socks of blue and green
checks. I raised my eyes a little. The back of a dark grey
jacket with a large brown patch. Surely I recognized it as
belonging to Tu's wife? I looked into her basket. It was
empty. I followed her. When we reached her cottage, she
slipped the basket from her shoulder, put it on the ground,
and stared at it for a long moment. Then she carried it to
an empty corner where they used to pile their compost.

Here she tipped it over to add its emptiness to the emptiness already there. With a complacent smile, she stood for a while to admire her work. When she turned to me the smile was still on her face as if frozen into the fine wrinkles that had gathered on the bridge of her nose, at the corners of her eyes and mouth.

I followed her into the room. She didn't show any sign that she recognized me, or even that she was aware of my presence. I wanted to get through to her, wondering how to make her understand me. I stood still and didn't know what to do.

In a corner behind the door of the room was a little pile of potatoes. I picked up a cluster and shook the mud off them. Not a single one resembled the fine, fat potatoes I remembered from my aunt's kitchen. These shriveled spuds were her late autumn harvest, the last until the new year's summer harvest. Potatoes were rated "famine food." These would have to stave off the pangs of the spring hunger that tormented the peasants every year. And she would face it all by herself. I could not hold up my head. A tearless sob came from deep inside my breast.

She picked up a potato and scrutinized it as carefully as if it were a crystal ball telling her the future. She looked up at me over the top of the root with a look of utter sorrow.

I knew it was useless to reason with her in words. I took her hand in both of mine. I cupped it together with the potato. She did not seem to feel my touch. She had sunk too far into her own dark world.

When I got back to my room, Ma Li was already up and dressed for the festival.

"I thought you had gone ahead," she said.

"I was with Tu's wife," I said, dejected. "I wish I could do something for her."

I stopped as the door opened. Our soprano and our pretty dancer Chu Hua came in with Dai Shi.

This time our reunion was peaceful. In the flush of our success in the land reform, we were loath to find faults. We listened to each other's plans for the future with attentive tolerance. When Dai Shi said she was thinking of going back to Shanghai and writing a play about the land reform, I asked warmly about it. Only later did I think there was no need for her to invent excuses for not going to Qinghai. When Chu Hua admitted frankly that she could not bear the thought of going to a new, wild place like Qinghai, even stranger than here, Ma Li looked at her pinched face with compassionate understanding.

"I don't feel well," Chu Hua said. "I'm going to go back to Shanghai and ask for sick leave. I'll stay with my mother for a while."

"Then your mother must get you a husband and you will live happily ever after," Ma Li consoled her half jokingly, half in earnest.

"If you girls ever want to get married, it's better to marry young. Once you get used to living single it's difficult to adjust to married life," our soprano said. "Look at me. I'll give you one example. I like to eat my breakfast alone. That's when I feel most relaxed, and I need that moment if I'm to last through an exhausting day of rehearsals. A few years ago, I had a love-thirsty suitor. One morning he came to visit me just as I sat down to breakfast. I didn't want him to join me at the breakfast table. So he said that he would wait in the living room. But if I know someone is around, I simply cannot digest my breakfast properly. I asked him to take a stroll and come back in half an hour. Can you guess what he did? Try! I give you three guesses."

"I thought you had only one suitor when you were very young."

There was a touch of irony in Ma Li's voice.

"So you can't guess? Well, let me tell you. He never came back," the singer ended with a laugh.

"That's not funny," cried Chu Hua. "He was hurt."

"I can laugh about it now, but I felt very sad then. That's another reason why I came to do the land reform, to distract my attention from my worries and from love."

"So it happened only a few months ago, not a few years ago!" exclaimed Chu Hua innocently.

"We'll talk about that some other time. Now we must stop. The girls are coming. Listen," commanded Ma Li in a loud voice, her patience running out.

We could hear the crash of big drums calling the people

to the festival and their land. Four young activists, two to a team, were wielding drumsticks as big as cudgels, bringing them shatteringly down on the enormous red drums that the villagers brought out on grand occasions. The ra-ta-ta was punctuated by the clash of cymbals and the bursting of firecrackers. Little waist-drums chattered out the beat of the Yangko, the Northwest folk dance that, like the French Carmagnole, had become the dance of the revolution.

We danced the Yangko together down the village street. At first the girls were timid. Hesitantly they put their left foot forward and raised their arms high; their hands held the ends of bright scarves which were tied around their waists. They lowered their eyes because they didn't know where to look. But the steps of the Yangko come from the movements of working in the fields, and soon they were dancing with natural grace and feeling. They shed their shyness, which made them look solemn, and discovered their real, vital selves in the gay, bold rhythm of the dance. Their cheeks were rouged red. On their heads they wore bright red kerchiefs like Xiu-ying's on election day. A posse of boys before and behind them banged out the dance rhythm on waist-drums slung from their shoulders and decorated with red ribbons. They got me into the festive mood. By the time we reached the meeting place in the theater I had danced myself out of breath. Panting, I paused and stepped aside. In the crowd I saw Sun's wife waving at me with one hand while with the other she held her baby girl. Then she raised the baby's tiny arm and waved it to me too. Sun, her husband, still sullen, kept five steps away from them, far enough away to express his dissatisfaction with this topsy-turvy world, near enough to get some of the best land along with his family.

The stage was the center of attraction. The huge cauldron which we had confiscated from Landlord Bai was in the center, propped up on a low pedestal of bricks covered with red cloth. Behind it was a table neatly piled with sheets of white paper, the new land deeds giving title to the land allocated to the landless and landpoor peasants in equal shares. Off to one side was another table piled higgledy-piggledy with tattered pieces of paper—old land deeds belonging to the landlords, mortgage deeds, loan vouchers, account books. An ever-increasing crowd of villagers thronged about the stage.

I caught sight of the virgin widow hanging around diffidently at the back of the crowd. As they surged forward to get a better view of the proceedings she was jostled even further back, along with a stocky, middle-aged peasant, her neighbor. They seemed to have been thrown into each other's arms. I waved my hand to her. She nodded and threaded her way to me out of the crowd. As she neared me she felt her bare head and exclaimed, "My head scarf! I've lost it. I must go back and look for it." She turned and saw her neighbor holding up the scarf.

When she looked back at me, she saw that I was smiling, and to hide her confusion complained, "I get so flustered in a crowd."

"But he doesn't," I said meaningfully, and she blushed scarlet and cast down her eyes.

"We've known each other quite a while but we never dared to dream that my parents-in-law would give me permission to remarry," she murmured shyly.

"You don't have to ask for such permission now. Both of you are single and old enough to decide for yourselves. You just go to the township office and register as man and wife. That's all there is to it. That is what the new marriage law says, you know."

"That's what he told me," she said, but without the excitement that I would have expected in a new bride-to-be.

"I'm happy for you," I exclaimed.

"What is there to be happy about?" Her eyes filled with tears. It was traditional for a widow remarrying to express her apprehension about the future. A sense of propriety demanded that she show reluctance to change her state, even though deep down I knew she must have felt very differently.

We sat down with our backs to the wall, the warm, early spring sun playing on our faces.

"He's nothing much," she said deprecatingly. "If I weren't a widow, I wouldn't choose him. If he were more clever he wouldn't take me. You can't imagine how hard it is for a woman to live with an old, crippled couple and no able-bodied man around. The roof leaks, the wall crumbles. Who could I turn to for help? I tell my parents-in-law that I'm not going to remarry for my own pleasure and happiness. Besides, who knows whether he'll become a brute of a husband or not? An underdog must find an outlet for his unhappiness. He vents his anger on his wife. She's handy."

"You mustn't let him lord it over you," I admonished her.

"If he starts to beat me, to whom can I complain? It can't be my parents-in-law. They will sneer at me, 'You asked for it. Who told you to fool around with him in the first place?"

"You can always complain to the Women's Association," I advised her, and then with a sudden inspiration added, "You know what I can do? I will write you now and then asking you how you are getting on. If he knows that you have friends who care for you, he will think twice before he lays a hand on you."

"Will you?" Her face lit up.

At that moment I heard the soprano start to sing a long, thrilling note of joy.

"They're setting fire to the old land deeds and mortgages!" We scrambled to our feet and ran to join the crowd, shouting and cheering. Shen and Ma Li took great handfuls of the yellowed, time-stained documents and tossed them into the flames leaping from the cauldron. The peasants roared out their approval, and once again the drums crashed and the firecrackers crackled.

"Good, good!" yelled the crowd each time the flames leaped high to devour the papers heaped upon them.

Xiu-ying was busy sorting out the new land deeds, ready to distribute them. Gao the sage was there too. He turned to consult with a peasant whom at first I didn't recognize until I saw that it was Malvolio Cheng with a towel for a turban and a pipe tucked into his sash. I missed Wang Sha. He was at the big meeting in the county town. Fleetingly in the crowd around the platform I glimpsed the Broken Shoe looking intently and wonderingly at Xiu-ying. As I made my way to help Xiu-ying, I passed close by her and she tugged at my sleeve. Her eyebrows were still plucked and painted, but she had discarded the ridiculous rouge that she used to wear on her cheeks. She was in a high good humor.

"I've left that old scoundrel for good," she cried. "I'll get my own land today. Ah, how I've longed for this day! A pox on them all."

The surging crowd separated us. Everyone was trying to get as close to the platform as possible. I saw Da Niang picking her way through the press of people. She waved to me and I waved back. But she waved again with such urgency that I realized she had something to tell me.

"Da Niang, what is the matter?"

She did not reply. She took me to a quiet corner behind the wall of the theater. Her yellow jowls and the muscles in her face twitched.

"Da Niang," I repeated, "what is the matter?"

Hesitantly she raised the hem of her tattered jacket and with her old teeth unpicked the thread. From the opened hem she took out a tightly rolled piece of paper.

"My old master gave this deed to me not long before you came here." Her hands shook. The flimsy piece of paper fluttered like a leaf in the winter wind. She stared at it for a long moment with her single good eye. It was a meaningless statement "granting" her a few *mu* of land, actually less than she and her idiot son would receive in the land share-out that day.

"So he bribed you to keep quiet!"

She drew in her breath in a long sigh. She wanted to say something, but the words wouldn't come. Tears welled in her eyes. She bit her lip to stifle a sob. She blinked her eyes to hold back the tears that streamed from both her eyes. Then she spoke in a strangled voice. "He thought this would pay me for the ten lives that I have lost through him and his kind . . . my husband, my children. . . ."

The network of wrinkles on her face deepened. Bitter memories flooded back to mind. She gave a stifled cry, one she had wanted to utter for years. It was perhaps also a cry of fear relieved. She had been afraid that her old master Chi would expose her complicity and tell us about this false deed.

"Da Niang, do you think there are other peasants who still want to keep these fake deeds?"

"Yes, and not only fake deeds; they will be up to other tricks too." Her one eye, still wet, lit up with mischief. It was evidently irresistibly tempting to tease me, a meddlesome girl who went about bothering people.

I couldn't help being amused by her unblushing candor. I wouldn't let her spoil this day for me. I took her hand. Reassured, she tightened her fingers over mine.

"Da Niang, come. Come and get your land. It's time."